Hemingway's Storm

M.T. Harber

C000165507

Mainsail Breeze
Maryland

www.mainsailbreeze.com

Mainsail Breeze Edition, January 2012

Mainsail Breeze
ISBN: 978-0-9835898-2-2

www.mainsailbreeze.com

Cover art courtesy of

Florida Photographic Collection
State Archives of Florida
RA Gray Building
500 South Bronough Street
Tallahassee, Fl 32399-0250

Cover colorized by Paul Rose

revised Jan 24, 2016

A Sail/Dive novel

ABOUT M.T. HARBER

Michael T. Harber is a divemaster, computer programmer, artist, musician and writer of tall tales. He tends to live somewhere in the meniscus between daydream and reality.

Other Books by M.T. Harber

The Sweet Taste of the Bilge

The Eye of the Abyss

The Reverse of Babylon

Acknowledgments

This book is historical fiction. The heart of this novel contains real events which transpired in 1935. Therefore, I dedicate this story to all of those who participated in the long night of this tragedy. It includes those who survived the ordeal, only to live in the hell that followed.

The veterans who perished remind us that we as a society often work at forgetting our responsibility to those who risk their lives to protect ours. The loss of their lives and the neglect we bestowed upon our heroes is our humility.

I am awed by the force of nature that swept through the keys and am concerned that we are ignorant to the possibility of a return of such a violent onslaught.

I wrote this book both as entertainment and education. For those who may not see the lines between reality and fiction (as I tend to exist in the crack), I encourage you to explore this moment in time. At the end of the book I listed some of the sources which helped me build the framework for the tale.

I'd like to thank my family for allowing me freedom to daydream. To Jeanette – thanks for keeping me grounded in reality and helping me to surface when I wasn't.

Remember my forgotten man?
You put a rifle in his hand.
You send him far away.
You shouted "Hip hooray,"
But look at him today.

Remember my forgotten man
You had him cultivate the land
He walked behind a plow
The sweat fell from his brow
But look at him right now

And once he used to love me
I was happy then
He used to take care of me
Won't you bring him back again?

\-   *Al Dubin*

The soldier above all others prays for peace,
for it is the soldier
who must suffer and bear
the deepest wounds and scars of war.
-   Douglas MacArthur

The force of the water lifted him off of his feet and dashed him against the metal piping like a marionette jerked by its strings. He had little time to think before the momentary blackness of the violence was replaced by an agonizing thudding of his heart sending wave after wave of pain through his brain. The current swirled through the confined space wrapping around his legs with such fury that it threatened to pull him under. As the water rose he was unable to fight the natural forces and floated along with a few unrecognizable dead bodies that bumped into him as he tried to steady himself. Just then the lights went out and was cast in total blackness.

This was it. He was going to die.

From somewhere deep in the bowels of the submarine he heard the screams of his shipmates bellowing over the rush of the bone numbing cold water. There were pleas for help, cries of misery, and the unmistakable banshee wail of those seconds from death as their voice became a gurgle and then nothing.

As the water rose the current abated and Harry Burrows could feel his ears pop under the pressure as the sub sank to the bottom of the ocean. His breathing replaced the sound of the invading water. The deep brought an ever increasing chill as if readying him for his final demise. He was strong but there was nowhere to go — nothing to do. He couldn't claw his way out of the submarine. With the pitching, rolling and complete blackness, he wasn't sure where he was anymore.

He'd floated to the overhead, or deck or bulkhead — it didn't matter. Up was down or down was sideways. There was nowhere else for him to go. The small pocket of air was the bubble containing his final few breaths. He thought he'd voluntarily give up the ghost, dropping down under water, but he couldn't force himself to inhale the cold liquid. He resurfaced and began hyperventilating. He was witnessing his own death, slow and deliberate.

The AL-2 submarine groaned in its own final moments, as the pressure and water crushed and bent the vessel by some unseen, evil hand. Harry dove under, hoping to find a way out amidst the dangling cables, dead bodies and collapsed supports. He tangled himself in the floating debris. In the blackness it felt like a thousand snakes ensnaring him, pulling him ever deeper into the throws of death. He stopped trying to fight the unseen forces and just relaxed — resigning himself to death. But, the burning in his chest wouldn't die. Harry struggled back to that air bubble, but it was gone. He felt the cold wall as his body convulsed for a breath. His head screamed to inhale but his body refused to relinquish the last few seconds of life.

Yet as the muscles burned to bring final release Harry knew he was already dead.

Harry awoke, bolting upright from his sweat-soaked bed. His throat was sore, perhaps from his hypnopompic screaming or from hyperventilating and inhaling the dust that permeated every corner of his dilapidated Kansas farmhouse. As reality took control, he slowed his breathing now realizing he wasn't drowning. He took inventory of his surroundings as he rose through the haze of the recurring nightmare. The moon cast silver shadows throughout the bedroom with imperfect monochromatic light. Everything had a soft hazy glow about it. By the window, the small table was

9

the first sign reminding him that he wasn't on the sinking vessel of his nightmare. Nonetheless he still gulped the air as though it was some precious, and finite, commodity.

On the table lay the *Holy Bible* and copy of Zane Grey's *Riders of the Purple Sage*. The two books remained dusty and untouched. He'd tried reading after returning from the war. Reading was one of the gifts he'd gotten during his time away from his rural homeland, but now he'd lost any ambition to turn the leaf of a word-filled page. In fact, the slow spiral to the man he'd become bore little resemblance to his pre-war persona. Before the war he was just a farm boy with a knack for fixing motors. He dreamed of something more for his life than scraping by with nothing in his pocket. He was lured by the song "Over There";

> *Over there, over there, send the word,*
> *send the word, over there,*
> *That the Yanks are coming, the Yanks are*
> *coming,*

Harry wanted to be "over there" — wherever that was. He wanted to be away from his hard life on the farm.

> *Hoist the flag and let her fly, Yankee*
> *Doodle do or die*
> *Pack your little kit, show your grit, do your*
> *bit*

When he said he was going to enlist, his few friends deemed him a hero. His father disapproved, knowing that without Harry, things wouldn't get done on the farm.

Times were tough, and they'd had a few bad seasons. They'd struggled, but Harry was able to bring in additional income by working on the tractors in neighboring fields.

10

Some of the townspeople heard of Harry's gift as a mechanic and brought their Plymouth sedans, black and shiny, to his dusty barn. None in the Burrows family could afford such luxury as one of these fine autos, but word spread about Harry's ability to cure all mechanical ills. Harry had no idea he was charging only a quarter of the price charged by mechanics in the city. Some of the people took pity on the Burrows family, giving Harry a generous tip for his labor and offered instruction that he was to do something "special" with the money.

More often than not, he bought sugar or flour. So, when the war broke out amidst the cries of "Remember the Lusitania," Harry was caught up in the fervor of a fight for freedom he never really understood. The allure of "over there" was more about answering a call to the unknown possibility of something better rather than exist in the suffering lifestyle he'd always known.

He could barely read, and the reports over the radio spoke of places on a map that might as well have been a million miles away. But there was a pull in his heart to break beyond the borders of his home. The radio crackled the cry to join the ranks with his brothers. He tried to imagine the exotic places across the sea but he had no context for even what lay beyond his limited, farmland filled world. He'd never heard someone speak another language much less someone with a dialect unlike his own.

His world was Parsons, Kansas. As a child Harry's father would occasionally take them into the small town.

Harry's mom would stop by the large 'White's Furniture' store with its fancy decorated front window. Lace curtains edged the big picture window housing the latest chairs in green upholstery with hand turned wood spindles for the legs. She dreamed of owning a single room decked out with a table shiny enough to see her reflection. However, she never paused too long. She didn't want Harry's father to become upset. Forrester Burrows was a proud man and felt that only by hard work could one become honorable. His ranking of men was "hard worker" or "worthless" — there was no in-between.

In his father's eyes the city streets were lined with merchants who were cheats and criminals as far as he was concerned. But Forrester brought his family out on occasion to get a meal or some ice cream allowing them a few moments to pace the main street before returning to their life of hardship and struggle. Like his mother, Harry silently longed for those things in the storefront windows but he dare not utter a single word for fear of being beaten with the belt for his greedy and perditious ways. He never knew what perditious meant, but apparently his father did while not sparing the lashes.

When the opportunity came to leave for military service Harry didn't hesitate. Given Harry's lack of education, he should have been shuttled out as infantry destined for the French front line. But Harry's knack for motors took him from the hell of the trenches and put him in the confines of a state-of-the-art submarine. He'd never imagined such a contraption, but his instincts for all things mechanical quickly moved him among the maintenance engineers of the great submersible.

It wasn't easy for him to keep pace with his educated peers. He often had his ship mates read him the technical documents. For him, reading was a nearly impossible chore so his ship mates helped him sound out words and provided patient support. The captain never knew Harry's limitation and the tight crew made sure the captain never would.

After his training and deployment, he'd been given a week off and returned to the States. He wasted no time in tracking down the love of his life. Elizabeth was a dark-haired farm girl just down the long road. She exemplified the plain life but, like a flower bursting with color along a dusty road, Elizabeth glowed with a natural radiance that the hours of toil could not diminish. Harry, in his dashing uniform, asked for her hand in marriage. He still had no money to buy a ring. He fashioned the engagement ring from a washer exhumed from spare sub parts. He bore out and buffed the metal until it was smooth, resembling a jewelry store band of finest silver.

Harry and Elizabeth were married before he returned for his tour of duty. With his improving skills in reading, Harry was able to correspond with the love of his life. His bride was similarly challenged, so the letters were succinct and repetitious but conveyed the core of their love for each other.

Harry found solace in the few notes shared and looked forward to mail call. He gently rubbed the paper on which the words were scrawled and tried to imagine the hand that penned them.

There seemed to be an optimistic order to his life. Life on the submarine was structured and tolerable. It appeared that he'd adopted the planning and discipline of the military to his own life. Unlike his father, he would leave the military and receive a promised bonus which would set him apart from his father's world. Harry settled into the banality of wartime service and never saw the horror of the front line.

In a moment that all changed.

It was a routine patrol when Harry's captain spotted a periscope. It was close — very close. In an instant the tedium of submarine life was spun into a fury of orders. Harry heard the captain's cry as the torpedo launched from the German sub. They'd been spotted and were caught off guard. The crew, who had trained for such an emergency dive, now all scrambled forward to put as much weight as possible in the bow. Their doomed ship pointed its nose down as it made a mad scramble away from certain death. The proximity of the two subs was a mere few hundred yards. The fact that the Germans had gotten off the first shot spelled immediate death for the American crew members. As the men raced to the front of the submarine each held their breath and waited for the impact.

But it never came.

The explosion rocked the American sub as it pitched forward, but the AL-2 remained intact. Only later did the crew surmise that the German torpedo rudder stuck. In an odd twist of fate, the rogue torpedo was deployed and its bent rudder prevented it from making a bee line to its target. Instead, it circled in a wide arc spelling doom to the German sub that originally fired the weapon. All Americans on board the AL-2 that day were spared certain death by a small mechanical oversight.

Nonetheless, Harry felt that the torpedo shot that day was meant for him. He heard stories of the front lines. Those who died in the trenches were the real heroes. The German submarine housed men just like him. The reality of war lay deep in his conscious and spread through his thoughts like an unchecked weed.

Returning from duty, Harry felt guilt that he hadn't perished. The thought of actually surviving the Great War while his friends bravely gave their lives haunted him and slowly ate away at his soul.

The small parade which welcomed him and a few fellow soldiers back from Europe only helped to tear the fabric of his life asunder. He looked at his fellow soldiers, some with stumps for arms, others with scars where bullets tore through flesh. He returned as an outsider — untouched. The look in those men's eyes were far different from his own.

One by one, his life disintegrated. It was as if God had destined him for the life of Job. Unable to come to terms with his own survival, he drank. In his drunkenness, he failed to find the regularity required by farm life. The alcohol fueled his undirected rage and self destruction. On more than one occasion, he injured himself on farm equipment that was now broken and useless.

Harry was not the same person his bride knew when they kissed as he headed off to fight for the cause. Harry returned broken, embittered, and lost. Like so many of the veterans, Harry suffered from shell shock. For the first few weeks his wife waited patiently for him to get over the trauma of warfare like a child recovering from the flu. She couldn't understand the odd behavior that cropped up under what she considered normal circumstances. When he got in the truck, he sometimes started hyperventilating. He would roll out of the vehicle with his eyes wide like that of a fox caught unaware. While working on a car, she would come to the barn and find him beating a piece of metal while crying like a child.

She knew he hadn't endured the ordeal of trench warfare. Never before had humanity unleashed the chemical and artillery fury that killed thousands. Science had escalated death to an art. Elizabeth heard the horror stories of life in the trenches with widespread rats, mustard gas and the inhumanity of human carnage.

But Harry's world was different from those who saw their buddies killed near to them as the bullets and bombs flew in an unending barrage. Given his rather light duty, she couldn't reconcile why Harry hadn't returned the same farm boy she'd known from her youth. The violence, drinking and constant state of turmoil was too much for her. Her parents begged her to return before he became vicious. Some days he refused to go to bed in an effort to avoid the nightmares. Harry couldn't pull himself away from the possession of the invisible demons of war to love her. So one night while Harry was passed out from bad whiskey, she packed and returned to her parents.

With her absent, the farm seemed to die. The drought and wind of the great dust storms swept away the remnants of any good soil on over 100 million acres. Harry's farm was in the heart of this cropland turned desert. The government, which sent him away from farm life was now going to throw him off his own property. The loneliness and stress increased his self destructive tendencies. No one brought their cars by anymore for Harry to repair. Nothing grew because he wasn't in any state to plant.

And each night the same horrible routine replayed itself. One of a myriad of scenes of carnage filled nightmares played out in his mind with dreaded regularity.

He reached under the bed, grabbed the bottle of whiskey that had tipped on its side. There was a swig left. He drained the bottle and started to cry. His soft sobs echoed with muted resonance off of the wooden walls. Harry rubbed his neck as he sat up in bed and stared out the window. An opened pack of Chesterfields lay on the floor. He picked up the pack and lit one up. The smoke flowed through the air mixing with the floating particles reflected upon the moon beams. The red from the cigarette tip hung in stark contrast to the otherwise black and white world of this small bedroom.

The government had made promises to him, but hadn't kept them. He wanted his bonus, but it never materialized. He wanted to come home and find work, but the jobs had been taken. When he did work, the guilt and pain prevented any hope of normalcy. He became enraged. He became lethargic. Whiskey helped dull the pain, but it never totally removed the torment.

He knew he wasn't the only one possessed by the demons of war. While at the liquor store, he glanced at the news stand headlines. One particular article caught his attention. It was an article with the simple title "Bonus Army." Like Harry, his fellow veterans had also fallen on hard times. The politicians had offered a promise of a bonus — but it vaporized and reappeared in the seats of government like a carrot dangled in front of a horse. With nothing left, these aging, unemployed and bedraggled men set up a shantytown on the outskirts of Washington DC They protested their treatment and marched on the Capital. The hungry men, over ten thousand strong, assembled and started to march down Pennsylvania Avenue.

Chief of Staff, Douglas MacArthur watched the mob and chose to take action. While the mob left their tents and shacks to plead their cause, MacArthur ordered bayonet-fitted cavalry to take action. Half of the troops burned the tents and shacks while the others used mustard gas to disburse the rabble. As Harry read the newspaper, he wondered how many times his generation would have to fight the war that robbed him of his humanity. First, it was against the foreign army — now it was a fight against the injustice of his own people in his own land.

This action spelled defeat for Hoover and his administration. With Franklin Roosevelt now in power, there was a new sense of hope as he promised a "New Deal." The veterans were reassembling in DC, hoping that this President would come through and release the promised bonus and provide some financial relief. These aging men of the bonus army sought more than financial compensation. They were looking for wholeness. Harry empathized with these men. They were his people.

With nothing left, the farm being taken away and the love of his life abandoning him, Harry rose from bed and pulled on his trousers. In the wee hours of the morning, Harry padded his way downstairs to fix coffee. He'd not had enough whisky to create a permanent haze and the cold of the floor roused his senses. He resolved to join the new band of protestors fighting for their rights. He wasn't looking for a handout. Harry was starting his quest for that lost part of himself. He hoped that among his peers he would find a way to stop the conflict which raged in his head.

By dawn he'd loaded his flatbed Ford with a handful of tools and clothes. He grabbed what little money he had left and stuffed it into his dusty and wrinkled pants.

The black truck rumbled to life as the vast flat landscape and sky melded in colors of red, orange and yellow as the sun peeked over the horizon. The dust swirled as the truck headed east, abandoning a world of painful memories. Harry Burrows had hit bottom. He'd been alone long enough. Perhaps in DC there were answers. If not, at least he could share his pain with those who might understand.

He didn't look back.

*Why, it's the most exclusive residential district in
Florida. *Nobody* lives there.*

- *The Cocoanuts (Marx Bros.) - 1932*

Julius Stone hated when people were tardy. He
sat at "Pete's Pub" in the corner of the room at one
of the many small round tables whose maker
seemed to have deliberately constructed one leg
shorter than the other three. The seedy clientele
gave the well dressed Stone a dubious look as he
glanced around the establishment. These men were
hardened fishermen and traders. Many of them
transported cheap liquor from Cuba, marijuana
from Jamaica or opium from the great beyond. He'd
infiltrated a world where everyone knew each other
by some nickname. Rat Eye, Compass, and Cap all
darted looks before huddling close around their
beers. Stone sat erect and wondered if he should
hide his wallet somewhere other than his front
pocket. For a moment the lights flickered and the
place went dim. Stone looked around. No one else
flinched.

Though Stone would rather conduct business in a
government office, David Sholtz wanted to meet at
Pete's to avoid the public eye. Sholtz knew this
wasn't merely a visit from a White House official.
This was a shark planning a feeding frenzy. It was
Stone's administrative skills and bargaining savvy
which propelled him to a position of power in FDR's
Public Works Administration. Sholtz was the
governor of Florida and was in a bind. Key West was
flat broke and Stone claimed to have an answer.

A stench wafted from the streets of Key West
into the small bar. The garbage strike had entered
its second week and the city had no money to pay
its employees. It was a warm start to spring and the
putrid decay was quickly building up in the streets.
The descent of what was once a thriving paradise

wasn't instantaneous. First, the salvage companies disbanded. Next, the spongers headed for more lucrative waters. Finally, the cigar industry packed up and headed to Tampa. The only thing that Key West had going for it was the weather. And for Stone, that was quite enough for now.

Stone combed his thinning hair over the shinier spots on his head and rubbed his fingers over his waxed mustache. He looked down at the stack of papers he brought with him from Washington DC. Among them was a colorful picture of a palm tree lined beach with the slogan, "Help to All Who Help Themselves." Sailboats, ferries and canoes dotted the idyllic illustrated landscape. The background was dotted with whitewashed houses surrounded ornate iron fences. The drawing was a far cry from the dilapidated Key West that Stone just surveyed.

Sholtz entered tentatively squinting into the darkness, stopping at the door's entrance looking for Stone. Julius couldn't help but think how Sholtz's face looked like a pig sniffing the air as he waddled over to the table. Sholtz knew he was in trouble. He didn't have the upper hand to deal with Stone. Though this was the first time they met, Sholtz could smell Stone's political piracy more than the stench of this small town at the edge of the world. Sholtz preferred Jacksonville to this hellhole. Key West was loosely coupled and ready to tear itself apart. It had become a pirate town again and things weren't getting better. Sholtz needed money to pay the caretakers of the city, but knew anything doled out by Stone would come with strings attached. Washington was always like that.

Julius Stone stood and held out his hand. Sholtz had a weak handshake. Even in the heat of the tropics, Sholtz had somehow managed to keep his pudgy hand cold and clammy. They sat and, without a beat, Stone started in.

"You're in a helluva bind governor."

Stone's New England accent seemed at odds with this place.

Shultz squirmed and said,

"We've all seen better times. But things are getting better. You know 'Life is a bowl of cherries.'"

Sholtz laughed and tried to lighten the mood by half singing the lyrics to the popular tune. He stuck up one fat finger and started wagging it like the dancing floozies down the street. It did nothing to lighten the mood and Sholtz's Southern drawl made him seem uneducated and out of touch. He hadn't been to Washington in months. He didn't care to.

Sholtz's face was flushed from the heat and his discomfort at the circumstances. The big man continued, "You've come a long way from DC and I'm sure you're not down here just to see the sights. We need your help. FDR is gonna pull us through, right?"

Even Sholtz knew the small talk wasn't going to work.

"Let me put it this way. I want Key West."

Sholtz blinked. He wasn't sure if he heard Julius Stone properly. With a laugh, he asked, "Excuse me?"

"You heard me correctly. I want Key West, and you're going to give it to me."

Flustered, Sholtz started, "I'm not sure I'm in the position to..."

Stone interrupted. "I'm going to give you what you need to bring Key West out of receivership. You, I and the United States government are going to turn this place into a vacation paradise. I plan on investing my personal income in the foreclosed properties at a *significantly discounted* rate — do you understand me? This place will draw the best of the best - I promise."

Stone leaned back and waited for a response. This was his way to recover some of his wife's fortune that he'd lost in bad investments and the crash. With the remaining money, Stone was leveraging the "New Deal" in his favor to claim the city for himself.

21

Sholtz had thought the government was going to send Stone down here to negotiate a loan. He was ready to battle terms and interest rates. Stone had something completely different in mind.

Stone handed him the small poster with the slogan — "Help to All Who Help Themselves."

"We start here — with the people. They are going to do part of the work for us. I'm not looking to tear down the houses. That is part of the charm. But we're going to have to fund you, and for that — you need to hand the city over to me."

Stone pulled out a legal document that ran page after page.

"You need to formally declare Key West bankrupt. That way I can step in. FERA - the Federal Emergency Relief Administration is under my control. I can loan you the money and you can look the other way when I buy up a few city blocks."

"I'm not sure...." Sholtz began.

Again, Stone interrupted. "You don't need to be sure about anything. You just need to sign the document. Look — with a stroke of my pen I can bring this city to its height. I can make this place hum with cars and people. Or — with a stroke of my pen — I can take it out and make it worse than the trash heap it is right now. It is up to you. You smell that?"

Stone pointed toward the door.

"That shit you smell outside is Key West. if you don't do what I say that will stick to you..."

The overly enthusiastic Stone said these choice words a little too loud and a few gruff characters from a nearby table sneered at him. For a second, the hard political veneer disappeared out of real fear of those around him. He regained his composure as Sholtz finally caught up with Stone's intentions.

"I get it. You're going to turn this place into a tourist Mecca. We've got Hemingway, the light house, Fort Jefferson... and for the kids we got pirates — you know — skull and crossbones. So

22

what's gonna bring 'em here? Won't be the railroad. We have a helluva time when the storms roll in"

"You've got that right, *friend.*" Stone said the word *friend* as if it was an insult. "The train — Flagler's folly is belly up — just like this place. Nope, we're gonna build a highway. People are going to *drive* to Key West."

Sholtz snorted, thinking Stone was joking. He looked at Stone and realized this man was incapable of any humor. Stone, paused for the reality to sink in and offered up the details.

"Right now you've got two large stop gaps where cars have to be ferried from one place to the next. On a bad day, you have people waiting overnight at one of the rinkydink hotels in Matecumbe until the weather turns. Like the railroad, we're going to build bridges."

"I'm sorry," Sholtz said as he wiped the curtain of sweat that began dripping from his brow.

"Is the government planning on spending millions of dollars on a road? We're coming out of some of the worst economic times in our history. As I see it, FDR wouldn't look so good spending such a sum of money on a project like this."

Julius pointed at Sholtz. "That's the beauty of the plan. We're going to kill two birds with one stone. We got the bonus army — you know — those veterans in DC starting to raise another ruckus. We're bringing them down here to build the highway. In fact, we've already started setting up some of the camps."

"Are you serious?!" Sholtz sat back and folded his hands across his belly. The large man had sweated through his coat as darker patches formed under his arms. Sholtz couldn't comprehend such a move.

"That kind of work ain't fit for a nigger this time of year. You think we're going to get a bunch of old soldiers to do the work?"

"I've already talked with Roosevelt. He wants them out of DC and he doesn't plan on using a militia to do it. These men want work? Well, we've got work. They want a place and three square meals? Well, we'll put food on the table and pay them a dollar a day. They'll be a thousand miles from Washington and FDR will thank me for it."

"A dollar? They'll drink two dollar's worth before the day is done."

"That's their problem, not mine. We're giving them opportunity. If it means they have to spend the next year or two, hundreds of miles from Washington, then so much the better. And, once it's done, you and I will have hotels and restaurants crowded with the hoi polloi. This will be the Caribbean of the South — the playground of the rich. I tell you..."

Stone paused. He sat back and eyed Pete's pub. He lowered his voice.

"We'll get rid of places like this and get the finest chefs. Hell, we'll have ferries to Cuba and start buying up that island. Who knows where it will lead? But first, we have a couple of million dollars of renovations."

Stone sat back and folded his arms.

"You will, of course, help me buy the *Casa Marina Hotel*."

Sholtz couldn't believe what he'd just heard. Stone continued.

"I won't lift a finger unless I have my hand on that property. We can negotiate from there."

The Casa Marina Hotel was a vast structure built on thirteen acres which looked out along the sandy beach of the Atlantic. It was a grand structure with a ballroom fit for the royalty of American wealth. Stone knew the implications of owning this grand hotel. It had been built by the East Coast Railroad Company – the same railway Stone was going to bury with his new highway. Tennis courts, a private beach and a sculpted garden with rows of palm trees would become Stone's crowning mark for his burgeoning empire.

Stone knew that the Flagler railroad empire was teetering on disaster. The railroad was in receivership, and the properties the railroad mogul owned in St. Augustine were about to go on the chopping block. The Casa Marina Hotel was the playground of movie stars and oil tycoons. But the general state of the entire city had left the place vacant.

The important thing to Julius Stone was getting that clientele back to this little island. For that, he knew he needed a road.

Sholtz asked, "How many men are you planning on mobilizing? And where are they going to stay? Hotel Matecumbe? You gotta realize these folks don't take kindly to strangers. There is nothing out there for them. You're sending our veterans to purgatory. They'll be sitting on a little strip of land with water on both sides and nothing in between. I hope you stock up on whiskey, 'cause otherwise they'll go stir crazy."

"Leave that to me. I'm sure the locals will appreciate the business. These guys have been in the trenches in France. They'll manage."

Stone wasn't as concerned about living arrangements; he was looking to the dawn of a new age of tourism where families drove to the beaches. "*Governor* Sholtz," said Stone drawing out the man's as if he were spitting on the sidewalk, "the trouble of the matter is — these men are persons who have never readjusted themselves after the war. They got through the war all right, but peace was too much for them. I'm their answer to what has been plaguing them for some time now. I'm offering them a chance to reassemble as a disciplined force with a common goal. Hell, I'm offering prosperity and a future for these men."

Sholtz didn't quite see it that way. "You're sending these men to a labor camp. Do you have any idea what the Keys are like in the summer? If you don't roast in the sun, you are eaten alive by

25

mosquitoes. If the press gets wind of any of that, Roosevelt may regret casting them to this place."

Stone's face turned red. "Don't block me in any way, or I'll have you with a pick axe breaking up coral right beside those derelicts. You understand me? Sign this document and give me the power to make you a hero."

Stone slid the papers to Sholtz. He pulled out a pen and uncapped it. It rolled along the uneven table.

Sholtz took a long breath and glanced at the first page.

Stone broke the silence. "What? Are you going to read the whole damn thing? Sign the papers and you'll have the garbage off the streets before the weekend. Otherwise, I'll hand you a shovel so you can do it yourself."

Sholtz reluctantly signed the papers. Somewhere in the back of his mind, he knew this was going to backfire. Stone thanked him with all the insincerity his political rank provided and left.

Sholtz stayed and filled his head with an evening worth of rum. He staggered out into the street, hoping no one would recognize him. He'd ransomed Key West for his career. He never felt so much like a corrupt politician as he did right now and he just wanted to return to the hotel and take a bath.

It was only a matter of days before the story hit the newspapers. By signing over Key West as being in a state of emergency, the entire city could be handed to Stone. The Federal Emergency Relief Administration allotted two million dollars to be used at Stone's discretion to rebuild and revitalize the city. The dubious meeting had effectively set Stone as the dictator of Key West. It was only a matter of days before he started planting palm trees and remodeling the ailing Casa Marina Hotel.

To grunt and sweat under a weary life,
But that the dread of something after death—
The undiscover'd country, from whose bourn
No traveler returns— puzzles the will,
And makes us rather bear those ills we have
Then fly to others that we know not of?
-    *Shakespeare*

Harry Burrows parked outside Washington amidst rows of shanties. The veterans had reassembled on the outskirts of the nation's capital to protest the lack of bonus payment promised them. FDR had promised the payment but delayed the compensation. Though the president declared the depression officially over, these men still felt the hand of desperation on their shoulder and the hunger of poverty in their stomachs. For the aging soldiers, there was no work and no promise of work.

Harry was joining their ranks. He pulled up the old truck and parked it along one of the dirt roads that led to the land of Columbia – the goddess of America. He got out, surveying the landscape of people that lined the streets.

It seemed odd that in the heart of the nation's capital men in frayed jackets and weatherworn caps sat around a makeshift bivouac. And, within eyeshot along the Potomac River, the Capitol building gleamed pristine white against the slate gray sky.

Harry walked by row after row of men. Some had small campfires with tin coffee pots brewing. The more destitute heated up water for tea pulled from the bark of nearby birches. A few lay on blankets reading and smoking a pipe. He'd never seen anything like this in Parsons, Kansas. There were bums and transients who made their way through his little town, but they were more migrant workers who drifted with the seasons. These men had no place to work and nowhere else to turn.

Had he unknowingly joined a force of men cast into a well of desperation? Harry stopped and tried to soak in the landscape as if taking one big gulp of moonshine. He had trouble comprehending how these men lived. It was alien to him, yet to these men, it seemed like just another day. The camps of burlap and canvas stretched in spots as far as his eye could see. Harry wondered if the founding fathers had this image of democracy when establishing this place as the seat of government. Harry walked among these tattered men — his comrades — assembling here by some unseen force, drawn together with the same look of loss in their eyes.

Harry was looking for a familiar face. He wanted to reconnect with his men. However, this lot looked all the same. He wondered if anyone would recognize him now. Each man was gaunt, weathered, and beaten like a gnarled old tree. They all had the leathery look of life on the skids. Many had come by train with no place to call home.

Harry had thought himself down on his luck until he spotted one man, unmoving, simply staring toward the capital. He had the hollow gaze of a corpse. The rings under his eyes were layered deep and the hollow stare reminded Harry of the dead he'd seen in pictures.

A man in a torn jacket came up to him. He smelled sickly sweet. Before he uttered a word, the stench from his breath reached Harry and made him wince. The man's teeth looked like old farm corn.

"Hey Buddy. You just get here?"

"Yeah," replied Harry, backing up and trying to keep his distance. The man wanted to crowd Harry, and the stench of the man made Harry withdraw.

"Were you in France?" the man asked.

"I was on a sub."

The man eyed him. He didn't even know there were subs used during the Great War. "Ya don't say! Did ya sink any of the bastards?"

"No, we didn't."

"Sorry to hear that. You got any whisky for a soldier today?"

Harry felt that this man had said that line a thousand times. It had the rehearsed quality born of repetition.

"Nope. No whiskey."

The man continued to crowd Harry. "You gotta dollar for a vet? I sure could use some breakfast — a dollar?"

"No. Sorry, can't help you out."

Before Harry could finish, the man grabbed hold of Harry's arm. The thin fingers felt like those of a skeleton. The grasp firm but little meat restrained Harry's wrist.

"Come on, pal. We were in it together. Help a guy out. We were all brothers in this, you know?"

Harry tried to free himself without causing a scene. "Sorry, I have to go." The others in the area looked up, shook their heads and returned to their routine with a silent gesture, as if saying 'here we go again.'

"You got nowhere to go. You're one of us. Come on..." The man pushed him backward. For such a thin figure, the man had incredible strength. As he was being attacked, Harry couldn't help but hear the voice of the man resonate in his subconscious.

'You're one of us' rolled around and bounced off the walls of his mind with sickening clarity. He'd left what was left of his home and came here to fill that void that the war had produced.

Harry wanted to rejoin his fellows at arms and regain that piece of his life that was kidnapped during the war. Now, as this man pawed and clutched at him, he couldn't help but realize that the man was right. He had nothing. It was only a matter of time before the desperation would sink in and he would be seeking out some newcomer to assault in the hopes of getting something — anything.

A dollar wouldn't bring back the sanity. But in the moment of desperation, Harry saw himself in his assailant's eyes.

"I know you want to help a friend out." The man's eyes turned bloodshot as a wild gaze took over.

Before Harry knew it, the stranger had his hand down Harry's jacket pocket. Harry pushed him backward. The man fell to the ground and started yelling, "You son of a bitch! God Damn you, son of a bitch."

The crowd looked up for a moment, but didn't intercede on Harry's behalf or the stranger's. The thin figure started to get up. Harry took quick steps to distance himself from the troublemaker. This was hardly the welcome he envisioned when he left his home. He hoped there would be an organized group with discipline and leadership — like the military. But this was a mob. He kept looking back, checking to see if the stranger was following him. The cursing stopped, and the man appeared to have faded back into the general mill of destitute men that lined the street.

Harry thought it better to simply head for the capital. The general attire and cleanliness of the people looked better in that direction. He was on the outskirts by the river. He looked over his shoulder once or twice and determined he was safe.

He wasn't.

From the bushes, the man that had panhandled Harry attacked with a flanking dive that drove Harry off of his feet. As he hit the road, the wind went out of Harry with a resounding "Oomph." He didn't even have time to turn his head before the wild haymaker swings started. The first one connected with his nose which bled instantly and made his eyes tear. He instinctively put his hands to his face which freed up access to his coat pocket. The stranger dug deep and found the truck keys and wad of cash in his pocket.

It took a moment for Harry to recover from the attack. Harry tried to grab the man's ankle as the man quickly rose. Harry missed the mark as waves of pain ran to his brain.

The man turned and kicked Harry in the temple, sending darkness over him. He knew he'd been kicked a few more times, but his body had shut down from the blows. The blood ran thick along the road.

Those that had seen the event chalked it up to two hoodlums in an argument and walked on the other side of the street. Harry tried to pull himself up, but when he moved he couldn't breathe. Harry knew that he had some cracked ribs. He had to skirt sidearm-style out of the street.

He lay on his side wheezing. Blood mixed with spittle as he resigned that there was no way for him to rise to his feet. He'd lost everything. Harry had no idea how long he lay on the sidewalk. A fine mist started to fall and mixed with the blood as it trailed along the curb. He heard footsteps as women in high heels were escorted around the man curled up in a ball lying half in the street.

"My god man — are you okay?"

A young, dark haired man approached Harry from the opposite side of the street.

Harry looked up but could only vaguely make out the shape of the man's face. One of the swings had opened a cut over his right eye and blood was still oozing from this gash.

"Let me help you."

Though Harry was still in a state of semiconsciousness, Harry detected a slight accent in the man's voice. The man's white shirt was stained from a few days wear. The bottom of his pants were frayed. The man pulled Harry's arms and heaved him to a grassy clearing. With each tug, the searing pain ran through his ribs, along his chest and through his lungs.

The young man noticed Harry's torn trousers.

"Looks like you've been robbed. Let me get you some water."

The figure disappeared for what seemed like hours, but returned with a small bucket of water and a wet rag.

"Thank you," said Harry still unable to take a full breath.

He rose up with some difficulty to a sitting position. Pulling a rag out of the water Harry wiped away the clotted blood around his eye. "He attacked me and took my wallet."

Harry wrung the rag, dipped it in the bucket and squeezed a mouthful of water.

"Not a problem there old-timer. My name's Timothy – Timothy McCormick. And you are?"

"Harry – Harry Burrows. I can't..."

Timothy interrupted. "You don't need to explain to me. The town is littered with bad people around here. The skinny ones are the vets and the fat ones are the politicians. The fat ones take your money and smile to your face. The skinny ones rob out of desperation — the fat ones out of greed."

Harry laughed which sent pain through his chest. He started coughing as he sat forward. "Thank you, Timothy. You're a good man, Timothy. I can't repay...."

Timothy put his hands up. "No need to repay me. We both have nothing."

Harry sat unmoving. Timothy wondered if there was some sort of secondary head trauma that was now taking effect.

"I..." hesitated Harry looking at his ripped trousers, "I don't know what to do next."

"As for what to do next..." Timothy tapped on his shirt pocket looking for something. "I'm heading out on the next train. I'll be leaving tomorrow."

Harry didn't understand how Timothy's travel plans pertained to his current state.

"What? Not sure I follow you."

Timothy pulled out a piece of paper from his back pocket. It had been folded and refolded a number of times. Some of the ink had run together but the page was still legible. Harry took it from

Timothy. He squinted as he silently sounded out the words. His head pounded as he tried to make sense of the larger letters.

"Help Build a Path to the Future..."

Underneath the large print was an image of was men with their arms around each other. In front of them were pick axes and shovels.

"The Federal Emergency Relief Association is looking for men to participate in a program of rebuilding and developing a highway along the Florida Keys. We are looking for veterans who are willing to work for a decent day's wages. Living facilities and meals are provided. Veterans welcome."

Silent moments ticked by as Harry scanned the page. At one point Timothy wondered if Harry was illiterate and politely pointed to the title and started reading.

Harry spoke, "Is this a work program from the New Deal?"

"Yes, I believe it is. Came a long way, hitchhiking to Washington to catch the train."

Harry eyed Timothy. "You don't look like a soldier. You're too young."

Timothy replied, "I'm not a veteran, but I'm down on my luck. They're looking for a strong back. They won't turn me away."

Harry continued to wipe at his wounds. Timothy turned to leave. Harry spoke and Timothy stopped.

"Seems I don't have a lot of options."

Harry fingered the paper still sounding out the words.

Timothy turned and sat on his haunches.

"You don't look like you've been on the skids very long."

Harry replied, "Lost the farm, lost my wife..."

"Sounds like you need work."

"I do."

"Then I'll see you in Florida."

"Why the hell are you going? You're young. There's always work for someone like you."

"You don't know my family... my dad was a banker, but he drank. Women, booze, the crash... seems my family name is well known throughout town. I don't seem to be able to wash it away. The only answer is to head far enough away that no one knows my name. This seemed far enough."

Timothy helped Harry to his feet. Harry was slow to rise. He rested his elbows on his knees but stood to look Timothy in the eye.

"Thank you, again. You're a good man."

"Ahh, it's the McCormick blood." Timothy laid his Irish accent on thick. "Angels of mercy, we are. Now you've got the luck of the Irish."

Harry hobbled with Timothy back to Harry's truck. He broke the window to his own truck and took his duffle bag of clothes. He left the few tools. He wouldn't need them where he was going.

*Outlaws in our own land and homeless outcasts
in any other. Desperate men, we go to seek a
desperate fortune...*
- *Captain Blood*

Stone fixed his hat for the hundredth time. He'd
already burnt his scalp in the rich Florida sun. Now,
only the canvas of the yacht was saving him from
being roasted alive.

However, he put up with the inconveniences of
the wealthy to secure his own future. He smiled,
hung on and prayed this ordeal would soon be over.
He hated the water. But James Garwood wanted to
take out *Penelope*, a J-class sailboat he had built
for his personal use at the millionaire's club.

In the midst of the desolation of the Keys
between Florida City and Key West rose an isolated
yet exclusive getaway for the rich and famous. The
millionaire's club, otherwise known as the Long Key
Fishing Camp, rose along the beach with a sculpted
line of palm trees. The large white main building
hid the many small cabanas behind it. This main
building had a grand seating area for dinner and two
smoking rooms where men would retire to conduct
business behind closed doors while women chatted
about their state in life. It was a place where the
well-to-do could come and "get ratty" — hiring
fishing boats to take them out for the big game fish.
These men and women drank rum and pretended to
be the tough mariners who actually sailed these
waters for a living. They wanted to be like Papa
Hemingway without actually putting themselves into
harm's way.

The sun wasn't friendly to this elite crowd so
the summer found the millionaire's club all but
empty as spring ran into summer. The Vanderbilts
and other corporate moguls would only frequent
this place when the mosquitoes were gone and the
northern winters were cold. Those who stayed
during these hot and humid months were diehard
sailors. James was among those who allowed money

35

to make money while he monitored his affairs between sailing jaunts.

The sleek sailboat cut through the water in the stiff wind. Stone promised himself that he wouldn't defile *Penelope* with his morning coffee and croissant as James adjusted the traveler. The yacht heeled over to a steep angle and Julius Stone concentrated on breathing deeply to avert the disaster of retching on the varnished wood.

Penelope wouldn't find itself racing like its sister sailboats. This one was for show. James was a tanned athlete who was born from wealth and paraded it wherever he could. He was married with four children, but *Penelope* was his latest toy. The name also happened to be the name of his flesh-and-blood mistress. Such was the decadence of the rich.

"I guarantee a sizable return on your investment." Stone took another deep breath as James swung *Penelope* around. "With your investment and the pool of funds I've already acquired, Key West will be the paradise of the rich. The time to buy is now, before the prices soar."

James didn't answer. He was looking up at his telltales, wondering if he should trim the mainsheet to pick up speed. A few others were on the water today. Most of the rich who stayed on into the spring had their boats out, whether powered or sail, during this playtime before lunch.

After he was satisfied, James turned his attention to Stone. The bronzed man had a white shirt which billowed in the breeze and made him look like some movie star. Indeed, some of the movie producers who frequented the millionaire's club in Matecumbe said the same thing. James considered the amount of work and time required to appear on the silver screen and humbly declined.

James seemed to be constantly dickering with some odd line or finessing his course and not giving Stone the proper attention Stone thought he deserved. Patience was not in Stone's makeup. He

36

was rapacious and hated pandering to the likes of James. Stone felt entitled to such wealth and considered anyone with more money an impediment to his goal.

"Before I plunk down a dime I want to know what kind of numbers we are talking about. Normally, I wouldn't give you a second glance, but you have the backing of the government, and that makes your offer a little more enticing. I'm not a fan of Key West. Too damn far away from the mainland if you ask me. But I'm listening."

"I can guarantee a ten percent return on your investment in three years. Much of this, of course, depends on how eager you are to make more money. I'm already buying up properties right and left. Hell – they might have to change the name from Key West to Stone Key as far as I am concerned. I have some properties on the line that might interest you."

"You say you're going to build the highway all the way to Key West? How long is that going to take?"

"Two years."

"Are you crazy?"

"We can use the coral for the block for the bridges. There's no need to haul in cement. It's already here. We've got a labor force five hundred strong and growing."

James jibed the boat to run with the wind as he headed back toward the Millionaire's club. This settled the boat and killed any breeze. Within a minute, Stone went from being seasick to being a sweltering sponge. He had no clue why anyone would like to venture out like this. It didn't seem to bother James who locked the wheel and sat directly in front of Stone. Now James was ready to talk business.

"Sounds like a long-shot. What about the weather? You know — the hurricanes."

"We get the crowds in winter. During the summer, only the hired hands will be around to keep up the paint jobs. The only thing we have to worry about during the summer is keeping Papa Hemingway happy. As long as the bars are open, that'll be no problem."

The two chuckled.

Stone continued. "I plan on buying property around his house. We'll set up tours there. There's a lighthouse nearby. We can go there, too. It's the American Riviera. But you have to act quickly. I have some properties on the line — two on the water which would suit you just fine. We could build a dock for Persephone." Stone ran his hand along the boom.

"*Penelope*," James corrected.

Stone had absolutely no properties on the water. He was making it up as he went along. The only thing he was sure of was his plan. Now that he had the labor force in place to build the road and he had effectively blackmailed governor Sholtz, Stone could start selling properties to the wealthy at a significant markup. The profit he made from bilking the rich would provide him the resources to acquire more properties for himself. He'd even gone as far as obtaining some of the vets from the highway labor force to work on refurbishing the "conch houses," as they were called, for sale back to his investors at a significant markup. This was all, of course, in the name of government improvements. It was a government subsidized coup.

The suggestion of a home on the water in Key West piqued James Garwood's curiosity.

"On the water, huh? Is it near a marina?"

Stone smiled, "Why right around the corner. You could wake up, roll out of bed and land on the deck of *Penelope*." He patted the boat like a mother pats a baby's bottom. Stone knew the implication. *Penelope* both as a boat and a mistress could reside in Garwood's little hideaway in Key West.

James smiled, knowing that he couldn't pass up this opportunity.

"If you don't deliver, that little island won't ever let you leave." James nodded to Stone letting the implication of the statement settle in.

"Trust me," Stone replied as he pulled out his handkerchief and rubbed the sweat off his brow.

*Men are not prisoners of fate, but only
prisoners of their own minds.*
-   *Franklin D. Roosevelt*

The train came to a hissing stop at the lower
Matecumbe station. The building was an oasis along
a line of sand, coral and mangroves that connected
the small dots of islands from the Florida mainland.
It was a whistle stop with a small water tower and
feeding pipe to refresh the steam powered
locomotive on its way somewhere else. The building
and deck spanned little more than the length of one
of the large engines it served but was the first
human construction after miles of saw grass, palm
trees, and tropical scrub.

After traveling for so long, Harry wondered if he
reached the end of the world. There was a breeze,
but it blew hot and moist through the open windows
of the coach. It was a far cry from the cool gray sky
of Washington DC.

He'd left the center of government with a
bloody mouth and a bitter soul. Harry hoped to find
answers, not in the bonus money he deserved, but
in the hope of finding answers to the deeper
questions which rose up through his sense of loss.
What was wrong with him? How can he get back to
his old self — his old life? Would he ever be able to
reunite with Elizabeth?

He saw the turquoise ocean waters in the
distance where the sky drew a straight line along
the water's edge.

Turning and looking out the other window, Harry
saw the gulf waters through the rows of mangroves.
The little manmade rise upon which the train rails
were set was the high point of this slender
countryside. It was only a few feet above sea level.
Harry had never been around so much water. He was
accustomed to the flat terrain of acres of farmland
that stretched to infinity — not a thin pencil of land
dividing the vast blue expanse. The great dust storm

in which he once lived was quite the opposite of this watery world.

Were it not for Timothy, Harry would still be joining the ranks of the destitute finding a reason for hope in Washington, DC. He was still bruised from his beating, but the pain had diminished to a dull nuisance. The men in DC were a lost rabble on the verge of becoming a mob. Taking Timothy's advice was a way to continue his quest for answers and find work besides. At some visceral level, it felt like the right choice.

Here, on this train, the men looked liked him, but had an expectation of better things. The "New Deal" was the possibility for redemption, and Harry wasn't going to miss the opportunity. It was the possibility of escape that drew him here. It was the hope of work. It was the change on a grander scale that lit the furnace of expectation in destitute men.

It was a new place, it was a new adventure. It was another "Over there…"

As the hiss of the train spelled the last breath of the great machine on its long trek to this alien landscape, Harry wondered if, after he'd saved some money, he might even try a living here. Maybe he could beg Elizabeth's forgiveness and invite her to start over. It was a different kind of rugged life that he would have to learn.

He pondered how life would be different on the water. Other than the small pond, his was a life forever grinding the dirt. Maybe with a job and the hope of prospects he could win Elizabeth back. It would take time. He wondered if he could transplant the flower of his life from the dry dustbowl life to this place. Everything was green and blue.

This was his first thought of hope in a long time and it felt good.

The train gave one last little lurch as the brake was set. Timothy was the first to rise.

"I think our President sent us here to get us out of his way." There was trepidation in Timothy's voice as he craned his neck out of the window. "I suppose that's why the government issued us oneway tickets. This place is so remote, I don't know if I'll ever make it back again."

"Some of the men said you can find a good time in Key West," replied Harry. "Maybe you'll like it here. I was told it costs us two bucks to get down to Key West. That's where the train ends. We'll have to go sometime."

"You got two bucks?"

Harry laughed. He pointed to his ripped pocket where the thief stole his wallet. Timothy put a hand on his shoulder.

Timothy said, "I heard some of the vets saying that if you blow your money in Key West, you can get a ride back on credit."

Harry chuckled. "Well, you gotta pay the loan back. If you spend it all on liquor, you'll be breaking up rocks down here forever."

Harry grabbed his bag and stepped off the car. No sooner had he taken couple of steps than three waiting National Guardsmen pulled him aside. They wore tan boots, a matching belt and cap cocked to one side. The guards looked young enough that they didn't yet need to shave. One of the guards grabbed Harry by the hand.

"Excuse me sir, we are authorized to detain you and check your bags."

"What?" exclaimed Harry. The youngest of the three was already trying to pull the single bag from his clutches. "This is mine."

"We're under orders. If you don't comply, we'll have you put in jail. Please face the wall."

Harry didn't know what to make of the police force welcoming committee. He was stunned into submission. He'd done nothing wrong. He hadn't shaved in days and looked as bad as any of the other men who either ignored what was going on or submitted on in compliant silence.

42

Two of the guards held him and began a pat-down. He looked over and saw that he was not the only one receiving this treatment.

"Many of you vets have brought liquor across state lines. That just won't do," one of the young officers stated in a commanding voice like a small dog protecting its porch.

Harry was innocent and this treatment was making him mad. He couldn't take it anymore. Harry turned away from the wall and, sticking his elbow out as he spun, slammed his elbow against the temple of the restraining guard. The one who was rummaging through his bag jumped up and grabbed his rifle which he'd carelessly laid on railroad deck.

The armed guard was tall and lanky. He raised the butt of his rifle over his head threatening to strike Harry in the face.

Harry didn't flinch. He squinted but made no sound. For a moment the two stood motionless like Chinese Samurai statues.

Harry had just arrived and wasn't going to let anyone destroy the ounce of hope he held in his heart. He'd been knocked down in Washington DC and he wasn't about to be dragged down again.

Harry mustered the will to stand against the treatment he was facing. The guard saw a hungry anger in Harry that caused him to slowly lower his rifle.

With defiance, Harry broke the silence that pervaded the deck of the train station. Everyone stood motionless. Even the breeze had abated into the stillness of the moment.

"You're pointing the wrong end of that thing at me if you plan on gettin' me to back down. I ain't no coward. None of us vets are."

The other men turned toward the younger guards. There was a quiet collection of force as each vet drew closer to the outnumbered guardsmen. The tension was visible on the sweat of each vet's brow. The vets didn't know each other's name, but the war had forever made them one unit.

The guard Harry cocked with his elbow stood up and said, "No. You are worse. Around here you are nothing but dog shit. You smell and you're good for nothing. We don't want you here. Go back to Washington."

The man spit at Harry. He wanted to hit him in the face, but the man was short and merely managed to soil his jacket. Harry didn't bother to look. He kept his gaze fixed on the man with the rifle.

A large black pickup with a wooden bed rolled up the road. The rickety sides of the bed wobbled and looked like they would fall off at any moment. The vehicle barreled at breakneck speed, threatening to run directly into the platform. At the last minute the truck spun and stopped within inches of the base of the stairs leading to the station. A plume of sand and dust blew onto the platform distracting the escalating conflict.

The man at the wheel jumped out and hopped from the rough coral ground to the train platform in a single bound. When the National Guard saw him, they turned but didn't move.

"Howdy boys," said the man to the mass of men pairing off for a brawl. The Alabama accent of Fred Ghent was unmistakable.

"Looks like we got us a new haul of workers trying to make a decent living in Purgatory. I am glad to see that the Guard is doing their job to keep these men sober. Ha ha..."

Ghent was out of breath but he continued, "However, we have much work to do and I'd like to get 'em settled in."

The Guard backed away like mean dogs before their owner. Ghent was short and red-faced. He wore blue work pants and a grey long-sleeved shirt that was frayed and thinning.

"Gentlemen, get your things and hop in the back of the truck." As he said this, he spied the young man with the rifle. "Johnny? You don't want to be causing trouble. Aunt 'El wouldn't be too happy to find out you've been mistreating the vets."

Ghent stared at the young man and dared him to respond. His words were short and to the point. The young man lowered both his rifle and his gaze. The men started toward the truck. Harry picked up his bag and shot a glance at the young guard. The young man refused to return Harry's gaze.

As Harry passed, Ghent put his hand on Harry's shoulder. "Sorry about that, mister. Didn't catch yer name."

"Harry — Harry Burrows."

"Welcome to the last place you'd ever thought you'd be, Harry."

Ghent looked into Harry's eyes and read the pain that he'd seen in the throngs of others he invited off the platform. As a vet, Ghent empathized with these men. These were his people. As the head of safety for FERA, Ghent was used to breaking up brawls and sobering up men. More than that he saw the quest in the souls of those who'd been abandoned. With each train, new vets arrived. Some were down on their luck. Some had lost it all. Most were suffering years of loss. Some were simply broken.

Tim was sitting close to the cab of the truck and glanced up at Harry as he climbed aboard the flatbed. Tim said, "Nice welcoming committee, huh?"

Harry had been deeply troubled by the war and subsequent downfall in his affairs but, as he looked at the others in the truck, he wondered at the destitute state of the strangers joining him. There was always some food on the table at the end of the day back at his farm. They were emaciated and smelled of old potatoes. Some of these men looked way older than their years. He'd slept most of the way on the train and had Tim as his companion so he'd not noticed the state of the others. Their clothes were tattered, and a few of the men resembled scarecrows in a cornfield.

After the initial skirmish, he thought the men would be introducing themselves. These men kept silent. Harry looked around. Only a few caught his gaze and returned eye contact. Some had looks of lost hope, others harbored suppressed anger.

One man however stood out among the crowd. He seemed to barely fit into his clothes. This man was twice the size of the others next to him. His firm, strong frame rippled through the seams of his blue denim shirt. When Harry met his gaze, he smiled and nodded. Harry returned the nod.

The Black Ford truck sped down the isolated road that paralleled the railway. The breeze felt good against the sun which beat directly down on these new arrivals. The engine revved as Fred Ghent accelerated over a small bridge. Conversation during this trek was impossible between the crunch of the crushed coral roadbed and the growl of the motor, so Harry simply took in the landscape that raced by and sized up the men who would become his coworkers.

The large man who stood out among this lean crowd sat back and put his arms out along the slats of the truck. As the large man reclined back, the sun caught the ring on his finger. On the ring's face Harry noticed the combined square and compass of the Masonic Order.

The truck veered off the main road as Ghent pulled away down a small incline. Timothy's bottom hurt from the lengthy train ride, and now it was being punished further by Ghent's driving and the crude path leading down this small incline. As the truck passed a large group of palm trees and overgrown saw grass, the camp came into view.

Cleared of all vegetation, this section of barren landscape was filled by row upon row of small bunk houses neatly arranged in military fashion. Each were identical to the next. They were half the size of a boxcar but not as high. Each had two "windows" — cutouts in the frame with a piece of cloth to keep out the bugs and rain. The tin roof was painted black — for no apparent reason as it only made the living quarters unbearable during the day.

In front of the bunk houses was a large mess hall with an attached tent on the side. The water tower seemed taller than it really was because everything else hugged the ground. A set of railroad tracks ran to some large metal storage containers by the water tower.

All but one structure at the camp had the same faded whitewashed look about it. Standing in stark contrast to an otherwise drab and functional campsite sat a faded carnival tent at the base of the road. The red stripes had faded to pink but were still visible. The carnival tent's canvas ruffled with an inconspicuous breeze still beckoning invisible children inside. The tent had holes and obvious sign of wear. It had been bleached by the relentless Florida sun which baked the campsite in the noon day heat. The slight wisp of wind offered no relief serving only to carry the humidity from the water inland. This time of day even breathing was a chore.

Harry gazed at the camp and wondered if this was a temporary stop before arriving at some other final destination. The place appeared hastily assembled. It wasn't what he'd imagined. He thought there would be a large communal flop house. He looked for a brick and mortar office.

Though the middle of the day, Harry noticed that there were a large number of men who seemed to be ambling around the campsite with no intention of working. Along the camp's edge, two men sat on crates facing each other on either side of a barrel. The top of the barrel had a hand-painted checkerboard. A half bottle of whiskey sat between the opponents. Neither moved, each either lost in strategic thought or simply petrified as their

47

brains baked in the midday heat. Three men stood under a single palm tree sharing a cigarette and vying for the best spot in the shade.

Ghent pulled up to the large carnival tent. Timothy barely made out the name "Benchly Circus" in faded red letters. Only the outline of the letters remained. Time and the elements washed away the inner colors of the text.

A man in white shirt and khakis with a clipboard sat behind the table ready to process the crew of new arrivals. Behind him a few men organized large wooden boxes of clothes, mess kits, and lanterns.

"End of the line boys – Welcome to Camp Three – Upper Matecumbe. Everybody out!" said Ghent as he hopped from the truck. He came around to the back where the travel weary vets stood on the truck bed and stretched before hopping down to their new home.

"Form a line at the tent. We'll get you registered and assign you a bunk house. Thanks to our President and the New Deal, you'll get a new set of work clothes. We'll have chow in about an hour. Congratulations, you are now an employee of the U.S. government."

He paused as he pulled out a Lucky Strike and lit the cigarette. He threw the match on the ground and took a deep draw. Exhaling he spoke as smoke billowed out of his nose and mouth.

"Trucks leave at 8 A.M. sharp so, once you get your assignment, make sure you don't miss your ride. You don't want to walk. I'll see you this evening."

"So this is it," said Timothy lining up behind Harry.

"I reckon," responded Harry.

Harry could feel a presence behind him. Timothy felt it as well. The large man stood behind Harry and dwarfed those around him. Harry looked over his shoulder. "You cast a pretty big shadow. Didn't know someone planted a tree behind me."

48

Harry grinned and hoped the large man would return a smirk. Harry had encountered trouble when he first arrived in DC and again the moment he set foot on Florida soil. The man smiled and shot out his hand. "Buddy Brickman" The man had the look of a brawler and had the accent of a man fresh from Brooklyn.

Harry turned and shook Buddy's hand trying to match the firm grip, but the man's strength prevailed.

Timothy stepped up to the desk and registered. The man with the clipboard eyed him suspiciously. Timothy's youthful appearance seemed out of this place. Most of the vets were in their forties. He was in his late twenties. Where many of the men had the leathery look of a rough life, Timothy had a baby face which made him look younger than his years.

"Name?"

"Timothy McCormick"

He smiled as he said his name but the smile quickly vanished as the man with the clipboard returned an angry scowl. Timothy was a civilian volunteer, not one of the vets on the dole. Timothy was an outsider among this line of hardened war heroes. The man with the clipboard jotted Timothy's name while another man in blue pants and a stained white t-shirt eyed Timothy up and down. The man then turned and started picking clothes from a myriad of unorganized boxes. As he went from box to box, the ash on his cigarette which dangled from his mouth dropped onto the government issued work outfits. Timothy wondered if the whole camp would catch fire as the result of this man's carelessness.

The man took the clothes, threw them on a table and folded them with both military precision and speed.

Timothy thought, "This must be his job. With hundreds of men already at the camp and hundreds more arriving every week, he's gotten good at what

49

he does." The man in the stained t-shirt deftly tied the package together with a belt, cinching it tightly.

"This'll do ya. It's three days worth. Should last you 'till the end of June. We'll let you know if ya get to smellin' too bad. We're short on water down here. Have to import it from water tankers on the train."

"Thank..." Timothy stopped because the man already eyed Harry and had turned to get another package prepared.

"Bunk house thirty-two is your new home." The man with the clipboard pointed behind him with his thumb. "Back there and to your right."

Timothy grabbed his things and headed to edge of the carnival tent. He stepped from the shade into the light and realized how incredibly hot the Florida sun would be while working on the road. He wondered if there would be anything left of him after a day of labor because, even in this short moment of exposure, he could feel the sweat rolling down his back.

Harry was assigned the same bunk house. The two met at the tent's edge and headed toward the rows of hastily built structures. The small structures were lined behind the mess hall. The bunk houses were raised off the sand and coral about a foot by cement blocks. Harry wasn't sure if that was to keep the insects out or to prevent wet shoes during a high tide. The whole place was built along the water's edge and seemed as though it could be submerged with a heavy thunderstorm. Harry wondered if the same kind of violent flooding storms attacked this flat land like it did in his Kansas home. If so, he thought the small rise which separated the floorboards from the ground would be little help.

A single step led up to the door on the other side. There were no signs indicating which bunk was theirs. Harry and Timothy went completely around one of the bunk houses looking for a number or some indicator that they were close to their home —

bunk thirty-two. Others, like them, were wandering around with their personal suitcases and fresh work clothes. They all seemed lost, meandering around the camp, with each growing listless in the heat of the day.

Two men emerged from around the corner of one of the shacks. The men were disheveled, but had the leathery look of having been down in Florida for a while.

Harry interrupted their conversation. "Excuse me. I'm lookin' for bunk house number thirty-two. Can you help me out?"

"Sorry pal," answered the man closest to Harry. He looked thin and wiry. "Just got here."

Before Tim or Harry could ask another question, the two men turned away.

After a complete lap around the bunk houses, Timothy spotted a group of men heading for the mess hall. "Hey! Excuse me..."

One of the men slowed and looked at the two. "Sorry pal just got here."

He turned and rejoined the group.

"But I didn't even ask you a question! Hey! Can you tell me where bunk house thirty-two...."

Timothy's voice trailed off as the group entered the mess hall.

"I'm gettin' hot and tired. Nobody seems to know much of anything around here," said Harry. He stopped walking, and looked down at his dusty shoes. "We should go back to the tent and ask for more specific directions."

"I've got a better idea," replied Timothy.

He turned and entered the nearest bunk house. Harry followed him inside.

A short naked man was sitting on a makeshift cot looking at pictures in a magazine. He covered up his erection and started yelling as soon as Timothy entered.

Quickly glancing around, Harry noticed that there were three cots in the room with barely enough room to maneuver. The occupants of this

51

small space had built makeshift shelves over their respective beds to keep their clothes.

"Goddammit! Get the hell outta my house!" the short man yelled.

Timothy remained cool and calm, ignoring the business that man had previously been attending. "I'm sorry sir, my name is Timothy McCormick and it appears that no one around here seems to know the location of building thirty-two."

"Get the hell out of my house!" The anger in the man had redirected his attention from his personal business and thus diverted his concentration. Timothy wondered how long he'd been at the task "at hand."

Timothy simply smiled and laid his luggage on the bed next to this man. "It appears that there are no signs and no one seems to be of assistance, so I'm afraid I'll just have to unpack my things here."

"Goddammit!" The man's face was turning red and the blanket had fallen exposing the flaccid lost cause. "That is Clyde's bunk. Get your things and get outta here."

With all of the politeness of an Irish house servant, Timothy responded, "I'd be glad to, sir. All I need is directions to bunk house thirty-two."

The defeated man looked down and then looked up again. "Aw shit. Three rows down. Take a right and it's the second one in. They're lined ten in a row, idiot."

Harry remained silent and watched Timothy.

"Why thank you sir, I appreciate your help." Timothy stuck out his hand in thanks to the short man. He then thought better of it and put it in his pocket. Harry bellowed loudly at that gesture and the two men left the small building laughing aloud as they exited.

They shut the door and the expletives flew from inside the shack and disappeared in the freshening breeze that seemed to come from nowhere.

With both direction and purpose, the two headed for their bunk. A pale man rounded the corner and asked, "Hey, I'm looking for bunk house fifty. Can you give a guy some direction?"

Harry opened his mouth but Timothy was quick to interject, "Sorry pal — just got here."

The man seemed despondent, having heard that from everyone else he asked. However, Timothy added, "But there is a gentleman in there that would be glad to offer a hand in helping you find your bunk house."

Harry chortled, but stifled it like a sneeze during Sunday prayer.

The two entered their bunk house and noted that it looked amazingly similar to the one they'd previously visited. There was only one shelf on the far edge of the shack and a short stout man with thick white hair was unpacking his things. He was bent over, putting his shoes under the bed. He straightened and turned as he heard the creak of the door.

"Hello!" the man said.

"Hey there, is this bunk house thirty-two?" asked Harry.

"Yep. Had a helluva time finding it. Had to go in the mess and ask the cook," the man replied as he wiped his hands on his trousers.

"Yeah. Seems that there's a running joke around here, and we're the butt of it," said Harry.

The man stuck out his stubby hand. "Elmer — Elmer Kreisberger."

Elmer radiated joviality. This was partially due to the fact that the heat had turned his cheeks red, giving him more than a passing resemblance to Santa Claus minus the beard. His shirt was completely soaked in sweat and he heaved to catch his breath in the broiling enclosed space.

"Harry Burrows — and this is my friend Timothy McCormick. Seems we're gonna be your bunk mates."

"Yeah, I think I saw you get off the train. Are you the one who took exception to the guard at the station? That took some nerve. Word gets around. I bet you'll be in a fight before the weekend. Trouble stirs trouble ya know."

Elmer reached behind him and pulled out a flask from under his pillow. It had once been shiny but from constant use had tarnished. The ruddy man took a swig and offered it to his new bunk mates. The two declined.

Harry said, "Yep. Seems I'm already getting a reputation. I ain't lookin' for trouble. It just seems like it finds me."

"Hah!" said Elmer. "That sounds like something a cowboy would say in one of the westerns."

Elmer bowed his legs and stood with his finger gun aimed at Harry. With a cowboy drawl Elmer repeated Harry's line, "I ain't lookin' for trouble. It just seems like it finds me."

He broke from the cowboy character and slapped Harry on the back.

Elmer's voice changed to a more serious tone, "I guess this is our outpost on the great frontier. I just hope to God that I can find a place to get some more to drink around here."

Elmer turned red as he said, "Those fools at the station took most of my liquor. I had quite a stash. I hear they sell beer here, but that just makes me piss all day. I need hard liquor or a good bottle of hooch."

"I could do with a bottle myself." Harry nodded and winked. He hadn't had a drink in days and his body craved it. He wondered if that was why he had a headache. He also noticed his hands were a little shaky.

"I'm true to my Irish whiskey," added Timothy, joining the conversation.

Elmer took another swig, refastened the cap and stuffed the flask back under the pillow.

"I'm originally from Baltimore," said Elmer.

"Well! We're almost neighbors." Tim's face lit up. "I lived just southwest of there?"

"Oh yeah, where?" asked Elmer.

54

"A little town called Frederick."

"I've been there. Now ain't that a small world."

"I'm from Kansas. Left the farm. The whole place had turned to dust" Harry looked down at the floor with a growing despondency. He brushed at the sand that had made its way inside.

"Government took the farm, huh? Sorry to hear that. I think we all got a story like yours, mister," said Elmer. "But now we got a job and three squares a day. So – I can't complain."

Harry looked up and into the eyes of Elmer. In the quick glance there was a moment of understanding. Elmer hadn't shared his war story, but the eyes conveyed the same feeling of loss. Until now, Harry was very much alone.

As they unpacked the three maneuvered awkwardly around the small, hot enclosure.

"Either you're lying about your age or you are drinking from the fountain of youth," said Elmer to Timothy.

"Just looking for decent work."

"You running from the law?"

The thought hadn't occurred to Harry. He took Timothy at his word.

"No — not the law. My past — my father's past."

"That's a sentence you'll never be able to serve. Family reputation runs generations."

Elmer took another swig from his flask. He held it out to Harry who, this time, took up the offer. The alcohol went down rough and Harry had to swallow twice to get it down. He passed the flask to Tim.

"I'll vouch for him. He's a good man," interjected Harry as he put the last of his things under the bed. "He picked me up when I was down. Tim's a good man."

The smell of cooked ham wafted into the bunkhouse. Harry hadn't realized how hungry he was. He tried to remember the last time he ate. The smell grew thicker as a bell, the universal call for chow, rang through the camp.

The mess hall was a flimsy, quickly constructed A-frame structure filled with narrow handmade rectangular tables that ran in long rows. At the far end of the building, the blueprints for the massive construction project were tacked to the wall. The line for chow was filled with men who'd returned from a half day of work. These were men who'd been at the nearby motor pool. Their job was to repair broken trucks and small construction equipment. The smell of the cooked ham mingled with the smell of body sweat, grease and the chalkiness of crushed coral. The new arrivals stood out in their "civvies" — the clothes they arrived with or the newly pressed and unstained work clothes.

Tim and Harry sat down together with their roommate Elmer. Buddy Brickman, the large man with the Masonic ring, parked opposite them at the table. The volume in the room doubled as the men sat down and conversation and the clinking of silverware echoed off the walls. Harry couldn't remember when he'd last had a decent meal. Even the canned peas seemed like a delicacy.

A disheveled man sat with the group. His hair was black and slicked back, hiding the thinning spots.

"Welcome to Matecumbe, gentlemen," the man barked. "M'names Stuart Krebs. Seein' as you're new, I wanted to let you know that you'll be joining us for some welcoming festivities behind the mess hall after dark. Wouldn't want you to miss it."

"Festivities?" inquired Elmer. He was intrigued. He hoped it involved drinking and at least one member of the female sex.

"Yessir," Krebs continued. "Y 'see the government has given you the provisions you need to work around here, but you'll be needing some necessities that aren't on the government docket."

"I hope that means you have some Irish whiskey around," said Tim.

56

"Call it whatever you want. It'll clean yer pipes and give you a good night's sleep. You'll need it. The place gets so Goddamned hot around here, you need a snort or two before you hit the hay or you'll be nothing but a wet puddle in the morning and no good to anyone. Most of the teetotalers around here end up part of the bridge. Seen at least two of them collapse myself. Didn't know if they just fainted, or they chose to take a swim in the cement. Now they'll be holding up highway one for the rest of eternity. You'll want to drink as much as you can, and the water here ain't for shit. Tastes like rust and gives your the trots."

Krebs deliberately knocked the glass of water by Tim's food. The water spilled into his lap. Tim jumped up as Krebs laughed.

"Jesus!" Tim cried. Krebs laughed.

"We got a runner coming to take care of you, so don't be late."

Harry was confused. "Runner?" he asked.

"God, you sound like one of them backwater boys from the sticks! Yeah – runner. I suppose '*Yer Paw*' made some hooch in the barn? Well, we get ours from a local on a boat. He runs the stuff up and down the coast for all us dough boys." Krebs took a large bite of the ham. "God damn this is good. Couple of weeks ago a reporter came by to check up on us. The government got wind of it and sent down real food. I hope it don't run out any time soon."

"So it sounds like you got us something to drink. Glad for it. I'm parched. I had my eye on the gas canister by the motor pool," said Elmer as he chased some peas off the table.

"So what about ladies? Will they be joining us tonight?"

"Ladies? Are you kidding? Even the dogs don't stay around here after the sun goes down. There ain't no ladies except the locals and they know better. If you want sex you gotta head out on the train and make for Key West. There are a couple of whore houses there that'll take care of ya. But stay away from the Indians and the niggers. They got disease. If you ain't careful you might wake up with your arm chopped off with a machete by some jealous husband. The regular women ain't that great either, but close your eyes and they can be anybody you want 'em to be."

"If you're lucky Mabel Gray might bring a boat of leftovers over here if work is slow. She knows when the boys get payday and shows up occasionally, but don't bet your cock on it."

Buddy got up, having finished his meal.

"Damn you're big. You box?" asked Krebs.

"I've raised my fists a few times."

"We got — er well — a bit of a boxing club. It is a wagering event. I'd put my money on you."

"I grew up in the streets," said Buddy with his Bronx accent getting thicker as he reminisced of his younger days. "Had a few street brawls. I came out with a couple of cuts and bruises, but I held my own."

"Street wise... I like that. There ain't rules when we box 'cept the match is over when the other guy falls down in his own blood. You up for that?" Krebs raised his eyebrows.

Buddy looked down, remembering a few close calls as a kid. He returned his gaze to Krebs and said, "Unless you got a ringer at this camp, you best put your money on me. Haven't kissed the ground since I was young."

Krebs smiled and winked. "Gotta love this guy. Can't wait to see your skills."

The noise level fell as the crowd devoured what was left on the table.

Buddy left with his dirty dishes in hand.

Harry turned to Krebs and asked, "So what is the plan for work tomorrow?"

Krebs answered, "Oh you'll hear the spiel in a little bit. Ghent'll let you in on everything. Funny thing is, you ain't gotta do a god damn thing around here. If you want, you can sit in your bunk all day reading the funny papers. You won't get paid — but'cha won't get fired."

Tim was surprised, "What? Won't get fired?"

"Fired?" Krebs let out a snort. "We got a hundred men who don't do a damn thing. You ain't never gonna get fired here. They *can't* fire you. What would they do? If they do fire you, you complain to the press... and the last thing the president wants is a service man, pressed to work in hell, complaining to the masses about their poor treatment. They got us all where they want us — as far away from Washington as possible. We can raise as much hell down here as we want and nobody gives a damn. You'll get your pay whether you break your back or sit on your ass and push a broom in a circle. Just like all the other government employees. Hell, I make three times as much gamblin' down here as I do haulin' coral blocks."

Buddy returned and stood at the end of the mess hall staring at the drawings that were nailed to the wall. The renderings of the bridge connecting Lower Matecumbe to Vaca Key had weathered edges and the corners had started curling. The moist air had started to mold through the paper. Little green spots randomly dotted the margins.

Buddy stared at the images on the wall like a cat transfixed on its prey. As he focused intently on the diagrams he turned his Masonic ring around on his finger with noticeable agitation.

Harry looked at the man looming over the drawings and blueprints. Having finished his meal, Harry stood up and joined Buddy. For a moment Harry said nothing, looking both at the drawings and at the mesmerized Buddy. Harry's eyes darted between the schematic drawing and the artist rendition trying to summon the mystery in the drawings that had Buddy hypnotized.

Harry glanced back at Buddy and then returned to the images but failed to see what held Buddy's gaze. Harry opened his mouth to inquire, but Buddy spoke without taking his eyes off the images.

"Pal, this project is doomed to fail."

Harry was surprised by Buddy's comment.

"What?"

"I'm from New York. I've seen my fair share of bridges. For a while I was a riveter. Been on some of the tallest buildings in the world. I've seen bridges from twenty stories up, inside and out."

"Yer pullin' my leg, right?" asked Harry.

"Nope. Wouldn't kid about a thing like that. But I'll tell you one thing. It'll never work."

"C'mon. You mean some team of designers made all of this, we got hundreds of men toiling in the sun, and with a glance of them papers on the wall you can tell me that they got it all wrong." Harry chuckled, hoping that Buddy would laugh and let Harry know that he was just kidding.

"Take a close look at that bridge," started Buddy pointing to the picture.

The image showed a graceful arc of concrete rising from the azure blue water. The black road lined the top of the massive edifice as it curved from one island to the next. The perspective of the drawing made the road seem all the more majestic as red and blue cars zoomed along the pristine tarmac. With art deco finesse, the artist's hand paved a virtual future filled with the promise where trains became a thing of the past and families packed their things and drove wherever they wanted. Harry squinted and moved closer, appreciating the artist's conception, but the problem still eluded him.

Buddy continued, "See, when we came over on the train, we had to ride over a bunch of trestle bridges, right?"

"Yep."

"Well, we got the same kind of bridges — trestle style — in New York. This one — well — it isn't a trestle bridge."

"So?"

"Whoever thought this one up designed land based bridges. That giant wall of concrete is going to limit the flow of water between the islands."

Harry scratched his head. "I don't see how that's a problem. The thing is huge. And looky here..." Harry pointed to open arches. Sailboats were passing between them. "The water can move through there, just like the sailboat."

"You ever see a bad storm blow through something like this?"

"I'm from the Midwest. We got summer storms all the time. I saw a tornado once."

"No, it's not like that. You see, I'm talking massive amounts of water trying to get through that little hole." Buddy pointed at the sailboat in the blueprint threading the needle of the massive wall of concrete.

Harry tried to defend the drawing. "Well, the scale of that thing is bigger out there. On this little piece of paper, it..."

"No, I'm talking millions of pounds of force against this bridge. It'll never stand in a hurricane. They've stopped up the flow between the Gulf and the Ocean. You think water is something that just flows in and out. Well, if you jump – or fall – off a bridge — its like hitting concrete. Men don't drown when they jump off a bridge - they break their neck. Now imagine a force like a thousand trucks pounding against a wall like this."

Buddy waved his finger along the bottom of the picture of the concrete bridge.

"The water's gotta go somewhere... either the water wins and the bridge collapses, or the bridge wins and this whole place floods. You see – a hurricane can move tons of water in a second."

Harry had heard about hurricanes, but he had no frame of reference for understanding the power of this force of God. After what seemed a persuading argument he refused to believe that Buddy knew what he was talking about.

Tim joined the two ruminating over the papers tacked to the wall. With his typical joviality, Tim put his arms around the two men and said, "Contemplating the next wonder of the world are we?"

"It's a wonder alright," replied Buddy, spinning his ring.

"Seems this man has some doubt about the viability of the project upon which we are about to embark," Harry said like an old professor.

Timothy replied, "It wouldn't be the first time I've been sent on a fool's errand. I'm just happy to be gainfully employed at the moment. If they tell me to pick up a rock – I'll pick up a rock. If they tell me to put it down – I'll put it down. Simple as that..."

He burped and continued.

"I just hope there isn't some embarrassing initiation for the newcomers. I don't look good in a dress and wig. And I certainly don't want to be wearing one around this lot."

Buddy broke from the images and shook his head as he walked out of the mess hall without a saying another word. Harry wondered whether the brooding Buddy would start walking north, away from the work that lay undone. He seemed genuinely disturbed by something that the government had approved. Harry was sure that a team of designers had reviewed and debated over the plans.

Timothy turned to Harry, "Seems he's in a bit of a mood. I've never seen a man get sullen so quickly."

"I do believe he is ruminating over his decision to come here."

"Well, tonight we can do a little forgetting. You up for it?" asked Timothy.

"Sure thing. I need a snort."

I have to believe that when things are bad I can change them.
-    *James. J. Braddock*

After sunset, Harry, Elmer and Tim took the kerosene lamps from the bunk house and joined the crowd that gathered behind the mess hall. The night buzzed with a variety of insects that seemed to know the newcomers and created a living cloud which feasted on the blood of the rookies. Timothy swatted the team of menaces that aimed for the back of his neck. When he withdrew his hand, there were streaks of blood from the merciless cloud that swarmed about the camp.

Some of the men set a bonfire along the beach in a fifty gallon drum. It crackled as sparks flew up and out toward the moon filled sky. Many huddled close to the flame. They weren't seeking warmth for the evening was sticky and hot. The men drew close to dispel the buzzing bloodsucking demons.

As the three walked toward the crowd, Harry lit a Chesterfield and offered one to Elmer and Tim.

"Nope, never took a fancy to tobacco," said Tim.

"Suit yerself," replied Harry.

Elmer took one and thanked Harry. The two lit up and the smoke from the cigarettes dissipated the insects as they joined the crowd.

There was a distinct smell of kerosene and citronella. Already, some of the group was well inebriated. Bottles were passed back and forth. The trio spotted the man called Krebs and joined him.

"Ahh... more of the Florida virgins. Welcome!" He passed the bottle to Elmer.

Elmer looked eagerly at the bottle and took a hearty gulp. He closed one eye, curled a little and started clucking and flapping his elbow. His face instantly became flushed. As the spirits dissipated

63

he let out a "Whoo hoo! God I needed that! Yip! Yip!" and handed the bottle over to Harry.

Harry took a sip and swallowed. Instantly the fire water burned his throat and sinuses. He'd had moonshine before, but this was a swill that tasted more like gasoline and rubbing alcohol. He coughed once, swallowed hard and passed the bottle on. He wanted to be polite, but he knew that if the bottle went around again, he would simply put his lips to the opening and only consume a few drops. If he needed paint thinner, he would know where to get it.

Tim took a large gulp, gagged and coughed violently. The men around him laughed.

"Damn, you brought your son here to do a day's work and he can't seem to hold his liquor," said one of the men.

"He ain't my son."

"He ain't one of ours." There was malevolence in the voice of the man. "He hasn't been in the trenches, and he can't drink worth a damn."

Tim wanted to speak, but couldn't get his breath. Words tried to come out but the damage was done. He coughed out a few incomprehensible syllables, but any coherent reply was destroyed by the burn rolling down his throat. Harry patted him on the back to loosen the hooch that had lodged in Timothy's lungs.

"He's a good man," said Harry defensively. "Tim got my back in DC and I'll stand for him."

Krebs joined in, "Yep. He's a young one, but I'll bet he doesn't whine half as much as you women."

The other vets backed down. Krebs was sharing a bottle with the newcomers. His clout and support were the baptism of Tim's acceptance and initiation to the forlorn tribe.

Harry was glad that Krebs was backing Timothy. If things would've turned violent, Harry would have gladly taken a blow for Timothy. But he'd seen enough hatred over the last few days. It left a bad taste in his mouth.

Harry's head felt light. He looked at the bedraggled men wearing ill fitted clothes. Some had hats with a weathered brim. All were dirty and scroungy just like him.

It was a place for misfits, and he belonged. The bottle came around and he was feeling a little loose. He took a larger swig than he should and the heat worked its way down to his stomach. He inhaled which seem to ignite his lungs with a soothing warmth that matched the evening swelter. He heard a little buzzing in his ears that wasn't coming from the mosquitoes.

As the booze was passed around the general conversation became louder. One of the men took a nearly empty bottle and flung it into the fire. The bottle broke and fire roared high. The small band cheered as the flames soared out of the drum.

Someone shouted and pointed out to the watery darkness. The men erupted with joy. Harry squinted to see what the ruckus was about. Timothy heard the sound of a distant motor over the never ending hum of the insects.

Without any running lights, the flat boat made its way toward the men. Some of the rabble started whooping and hollering. Others danced around the fire and spit some of the alcohol into the bonfire which barked back with tongues of blue light.

Silhouetted by a gibbous moon, two dinghies paddled toward shore. The men were ready with ropes. As the boats neared they tossed the lines and pulled the small craft on land. Two children about the age of fourteen started unloaded cases filled with bottles of various sizes. Some of the men crowded the little ones ready to offer a hand, but a man who until then remained in the shadows fired off a shotgun. The sound rippled off the water and settled the thirsty mob. The workers backed off as the old man stepped out of the boat and onto the beach.

"If you are thirsty I got your drink. If you're already drunk you get to the back of the line."

Some of the men dropped their money in their haste to join the ranks in the front of the line. The two boys stood still like silent soldiers before the cases. They, too, had rifles which they pulled from the rafts. They stood in silent vigil surveying the chaotic frenzy. Two men started brawling for a spot near the front. Other men, rather than breaking up the fight, pushed them from the line and started taking bets on who would be the victor. One of the men grabbed an empty bottle and smashed it across the other's face. Blood splattered into the darkness and the man crumpled to the ground.

Elmer's eyes went wide.

"This looks too good to pass up, I'll see you folks later," said Elmer as he sauntered off, checking his baggy pockets. He disappeared into the line, and the sound of glass bottles clanked as the vets toasted away their paltry earnings.

A crack of lightning sparked across the blackness out to sea. Another followed turning the distant sky momentarily purple.

Timothy and Harry looked at each other and the crowd cheered as natural fireworks heralded the evening's festivities. Bacchus was making his arrival known as the growl of thunder raced along the water.

Krebs shouted, "All hail the power of the almighty to render the sky electric! I do believe we need to make an offering to appease this omnipotent rumbler."

Some in the crowd mumbled obscenities and generally ignored him. Yet Krebs continued, "Come one come all, we are going to have a fight tonight! We have a big new boy in town that I want you all to get to know!"

Krebs pulled Buddy by the hand to a clearing. "I give you Buddy Brickman — a New York street brawler who has yet to taste defeat."

The crowd quieted and became interested. Those who still had some change from their purchase of libations gathered to make bets. As if on cue, the men formed a large circle. One of the brought a soiled shirt and tore it in half. He started wrapping Buddy's hands.

Harry stepped up to Buddy. "You don't have to do this you know."

"I've seen these men and I could take every one of them. I enjoy a little sport." Buddy dug into his wrapping and twisted off his Masonic ring. Buddy turned to Harry and said, "Hold this for me."

"Jimmy! Hey Jimmy! I want to introduce you to your new friend."

The crowd whooped and hollered at Jimmy's name.

"Buddy," started Krebs with all of the theatrics of a carnival ringleader, "I know you won't let me down tonight. I want to introduce you to one of our family members. Jimmy! Jimmy where are you?"

A man of great size stepped through the crowd. He wasn't quite as big as Buddy, but he seemed fit. Jimmy wasn't wearing a shirt and his muscles rippled as he stepped toward Buddy.

"Jimmy Conway – meet your friend Buddy."

Conway stepped forward. He looked at Buddy and smiled. "Man – you look familiar."

Buddy heard the New York accent. "I'm from the Bronx."

Jimmy grabbed him by the shoulder and gave Buddy a hug. "Hah! Good to meet you Buddy – I'm from Brooklyn. After we pummel each other, I'll buy you a drink. Good to have a fellow New Yorker in our midst."

Krebs, frustrated at the pleasantries broke in between the two. "Okay ladies, you can kiss later. Right now it's time to show what you're made of."

As if on cue lightning and a roll of thunder belched through the darkness. The clouds thickened causing the moon to temporarily dip into blackness. The men responded by lighting ground fires in the corners of the improvised ring.

"First one to kiss the dirt loses — and I ain't talking about losing your footing. Try to keep this honest, gentlemen. Lets wager folks!"

All the newcomers looked on as money changed hands. The empty pockets used their newly acquired alcohol as collateral. A few train tickets entered the growing pile. Men moved from one location to another to support their makeshift contender.

"All right! Take your corners."

Buddy backed toward one of the blazes. Harry asked once again, "You sure you want to do this?"

"I guess you farm boys didn't scrap much. I'm up for it — cooped up in the train too long. I gotta stretch my bones." With that Buddy craned his neck and practiced a few quick jabs.

"We ain't got rounds, no time limit, and if you want to chicken out, all you got to do is drop your guard and let the other guy put you to sleep. Have at it, boys!" Krebs stepped from the ring as the surrounding men yelped with excitement.

The two each took a defensive posture and circled around the ring, sizing up any opening. They ducked and weaved at the nearly undetectable motions of their opponent's aggression. The crowd simmered down waiting for the first blow. Both smiled a little as they dodged and bobbed.

Jimmy stepped forward and Buddy countered to the left following with a quick jab to the face. Jimmy read that and followed with a blow to the ribs. Buddy let out a "whump" realizing that Jimmy Conway had a great deal more strength than Buddy had assumed. Jimmy tried to follow with a left cross, but Buddy stepped back throwing up a block.

Some men drank while keeping one eye on their money and the other on the fight. When their favorite ducked, a number of the spectators imitated their movements instinctively.

Jimmy stepped in and delivered two more quick jabs to the midsection. They lacked the power of the first and Buddy was prepared. Buddy again stepped left and connected with an arcing swing to the face.

The crowd erupted with the exchange. Timothy yelled, "Come on Buddy! Keep your guard up!"

Harry wanted to yell advice into the ring, but he didn't want to distract his friend. Instead he tilted the bottle he'd gotten from the boatman.

The two fighters backed away, both mentally reviewing the initial foray. Jimmy stepped forward and Buddy parried to the left. This time Jimmy was ready. The right cross came unseen to Buddy with a force that made his ears ring. It landed on the corner of his mouth and he tasted blood immediately. The sight of blood sparked the crowd like a wild pack of dogs and the lightning and thunder elevated the intensity of the event. It appeared that God was watching the contest as well.

Jimmy came close and started pummeling Buddy's midriff. Buddy, however, wasn't going to give up. He sacrificed his ribs for an opportunity for a quick upper cut. Jimmy sensed what was coming and backed away. Buddy connected, but it wasn't a definitive blow.

Buddy came in and clinched. He saw his own blood on Jimmy's chest as Kreb's broke them up.

"No time for dancin' boys! Keep fighting!"

Buddy was worse for the exchange. The sweat from his brow got in his eyes and stung, but he dared not blink. Jimmy was a little rattled at the uppercut. Jimmy stepped back as Buddy lunged for an all out assault. His hands were high, and the jabs came straight at Jimmy's nose. Two connected in rapid succession, but an equal number of hits once again took its toll on Buddy's ribs. Jimmy stepped back and shot a wad of snot full of blood on the ground.

The crowd whooped at the site of the reigning campsite champ hocking blood. Even the evening rumrunners were cheering their favorite. To an outsider, one would have thought the two had some longtime grudge. Both were intent on bringing the other to the ground.

Blood was pouring out of Buddy's mouth as he huffed. He was wheezing as he tried to take a deep breath with his bruised ribs bitterly complaining with each inhale. Jimmy's nose had grown since the last exchange as two lines of red ran to his clenched mouth. Both men's blood glistened in the fire of the night and the once white wrappings on their hands were now soiled to burnt sienna.

Timothy looked on and said, "They're going to kill each other."

Harry said nothing but looked on with a tensed jaw. He both loved and hated what he saw.

They two pugilists looked like they wanted the round to be over, but this wasn't an ordinary fight. With a few quick breaths Buddy came again at Jimmy. Jimmy stepped sideways and landed a cross to Buddy's face. Buddy mustered a full body cross to the ribs, which sent Jimmy flying backwards. It looked as though Jimmy would stumble and fall, but he kept his footing. Buddy lunged at the opportunity and carelessly dropped his guard to protect his now black-and-blue ribs. Jimmy saw this and came with a straight punch which landed on Buddy's right eye.

This stopped Buddy in his tracks.

Jimmy returned with another cross to the temple which spun Buddy's head more than one would think anatomically possible.

Buddy backed up. Blood was trickling into his eye that was closing rapidly.

Jimmy came in and offered a few jabs to the midriff. Buddy could barely breathe. Jimmy finished with a right cross that sent Buddy tumbling to the ground.

"Get up! Get Up!" came the cries from Buddy's corner. "Goddammit – move!"

Buddy tried to pull himself, but his ribs complained and he again dropped to the ground.

Krebs ran into the ring and raised Jimmy's hand in victory.

The crowd was delighted by the spectacle. Other brawls immediately broke out for those who lost their month's salary.

Harry ran to Buddy. "You okay?"

Buddy coughed and tried to get his breath. "Yeah, I took a helluva beating." Buddy's eye was completely closed. He struggled to get on his elbows. Harry helped him. Separating himself from the fans, Jimmy came over and assisted Buddy to an overturned wooden box now empty of bottles.

"That was a good fight, Buddy."

"You pummeled me like it was nothing."

"Krebs didn't tell you?"

"Tell me what?"

"I was a heavyweight contender. I was going for the title before I fell on hard times. You held up pretty good there. You gotta watch your elbows. You opened up too much. I bet you'd have taken me if you covered a little better. You fought as good as Jack Britton... we played by the rules, and it took me fifteen rounds to finish him."

"A heavyweight..." Buddy started to laugh. Doing so started a spasm of pain, so he tried to squelch the laughter.

"A damned ringer — I shoulda known."

Krebs came over. "You okay boy?"

Buddy answered, "Yeah, I'll be a little sore for a few days, but I'll be okay. Sorry I lost your money."

Krebs replied, "Who said I bet on you?"

The liquor was flowing freely now that the main entertainment was over. Harry had two bottles — one in his tattered jacket pocket and one in his hand. He was getting drunk. But tonight he wasn't drinking alone. Buddy, sitting next to Harry, had become something of an instant hero. Even though he lost the fight, he gave Jimmy a bloody nose. No one before had even ruffled Jimmy Conway's hair.

Those who lost their money to Buddy still offered him a consolatory drink. He looked like hell, but after the generosity of his new found fans, Buddy felt little pain.

The small barge was emptied by the thirsty crowd and it silently floated away from the rabble as men sang, fought, danced and drank. Krebs walked past Harry and Harry tugged on his shirt.

"You guys do this every night?"

"Nah – only when it's dark."

"What? Oh – ha!" said Harry, leaning forward. "I'm not sure I could do this all the time."

"What else ya gonna do? We try to do something special when the liquor boat comes. Your friend there didn't disappoint," replied Krebs.

Timothy joined the conversation. He'd gotten some whisky. At least that is what the label said. With a slur, he tried to enunciate his words, so he would be understood. "Sir, I plan on working. I plan on developing skills down here."

"Good!" replied Krebs. "I'll make sure you work with me. I'll teach you how to move block on the rig."

"Excelle... Exc... Wonderful," said Tim staggering as he laid a hand on Kreb's shoulder.

Krebs laughed and chimed to the newcomers.

"Welcome to hell, ladies..."

We're not here to stay; we're on a short holiday.

Life's Just a Bowl of Cherries — Gershwin

"Goddammit Odie – where's my damn truck?"

Harry and Tim arrived to a red-faced Ghent. Ghent wasn't the kind of person to run, but the speed of his gait made Ghent look ludicrous as he approached the incredibly tall and thin man named O.D. King. The two exchanged some heated words before Ghent mounted the driver side of a large flatbed.

"Climb aboard boys, you'll have to hang on to each other 'cause it seems a couple of vets took my truck."

"They stole it?" asked Tim.

"Nope – borrowed it. It seems they wanted to have words with the president — want to give them a piece of their mind, so they hot-wired it and are headed north."

The assembled men chuckled. This seemed to diffuse the anger in Ghent. Apparently this wasn't an isolated incident. Ghent laughed at himself and shook his head.

"Don't worry. They won't get past Panama City. They don't have money for gas. It'll be back here tomorrow. Until then boys, hop on board."

Tim, Harry and a collection of the new arrivals were sent to a site where they were digging the limestone coral to create the bridge. Rising from the low level vegetation were two behemoth machines — giant dinosaurs belching smoke and making a horrendous racket.

Ghent got out the work detail he and some men drew up earlier that morning.

"What are those things?" asked Harry pointing to the large cranes.

Ghent stood with pride.

"They are what makes this whole operation possible."

Ghent looked down at his paperwork.

"Harry, you'll be working as one of the mechanics tending to these machines and the other equipment here. I'll introduce you to the foreman a little later."

Once again Ghent returned to the paperwork. He pointed to Time.

"And your pal here will be tending the bucket."

Ghent walked from the road to the worksite. There were huge pits where the coral had been exhumed for the project. Trucks were parked in a line waiting to receive the stone that would be refined for use on this gargantuan project.

"Y'see this is where we're making the block for the bridges. Instead of bringing in concrete, we're using what God gave us to cut block. You folks," continued Ghent pointing to a group of men "are going to lay the seam."

Ghent bent down and picked up one of the digging irons from a pile. A broad strip of white paint lined each iron. "All you gotta do is follow the lines that have been marked and dig down. When your diggin' iron reaches the white line, you don't go any deeper. Make sure that you don't cheat me on the depth. If you do, the block will be short, and we can't use it. If we can't use it, you'll have to dig out another one. You understand?"

"The machines here will break the bottom of the rock and haul the block onto a flatbed where it goes to build the bridge. Get outta the way of the machine though. You wouldn't want a two ton block smacking your noggin. Three men did that and never got up again. These machines are part of the government's glory to reuse what it has. They were originally digging in the *Culebra Cut*."

Ghent waited and squinted at the men hoping that someone would enlighten the others. He saw the blank stares on all of the men's faces. He'd done the spiel before and paused to see if anyone would speak up. No one did.

"The Panama canal boys! Remember that? Now you can share in another part of living history. We're paving the way to the future. Let's get started."

Tim joined Kerbs. He climbed up the ladder which led to the cab of one of the large machines. Krebs wasted no time getting started.

"It's not hard to figure out when you get going. Basically, We take the scoop and shove the base of the block along the seam. It breaks along the bottom and then we can lift it out," said Krebs. Krebs looked at Tim with a look of suspicion.

"Most of the folk down here are much older. What brings you down here kid?"

Tim didn't consider himself a 'kid.' Tim replied without hesitating, "My prospects up north weren't looking too good. I decided that I was destined to become a hobo, so I jumped this train to Florida."

Pointing to a lever behind Krebs's right elbow, Tim asked, "What's that do?"

"That's a ginisten."

"What?"

"A ginisten," replied Krebs as a matter of fact. He swung the large arm forward and the whole machine vibrated as it penetrated the limestone. Timothy had to hold tightly or be thrown as Krebs jerked the sharp edge of the mammoth bucket and slam it into the rock in fits and starts.

"What's a ginisten?" asked Tim still confused.

"It's connected to the gronesteel." The machine lurched forward under the weight of the large stone now swinging through the air toward the flat bed truck.

Krebs removed a Lucky Strike cigarette from his shirt pocket. He lit the new cigarette from the fading stub he'd finished. Closing his eyes for a long draw caused him to overshoot the awaiting truck. The large rock teetered as he made the adjustment.

"Shit," he said as the fresh cigarette bobbed in his mouth. He tossed the spent cigarette without thinking and Tim had to dodge the lit projectile.

Tim took his hand off the control deck when Krebs pulled down on the lever. Physics took over any control Krebs possessed as the large behemoth shook with the wayward swing. The cab spun to compensate for the two ton rock. Timothy lost his balance and failed to grasp the cab frame. He bounced out of the cab, off the ladder and landed on a large exposed drive shaft. The spinning section took part of his shirt instantly ripping it to shreds and threatening to consume him as well. He instinctively pushed off the rotating mechanism and landed on the rocky ground with a huff. A puff of the white dust choked Timothy as he inhaled from the fall. He coughed violently which only made his chest hurt more. He looked up at the machine towering over him. The arm stopped and was making its, now much slower, return to the flatbed.

"Goddamn boy, where did you go?!" came the voice from above the protesting machine.

Tim looked carefully overhead before getting back to his feet. He climbed up to the cab which was now filled with the smoke from a man who mindlessly sucked away at his cigarette under the stress of the moment.

Tim returned to the cab.

"What the hell happened to you?" asked Krebs. He gave him a quick glance, noticed the torn shirt, and followed with a quick, "You okay?"

Before Tim could answer, the machine lurched again as Krebs positioned the large stone over the truck. Tim didn't answer as Tim kept his focus on the levers Krebs was using to finesse the boulder. He pushed one with a red ball attached to the end and the bucket dumped its load from a few feet over the truck. The machine hurled backward, but Tim wasn't caught off guard this time.

The bang as the stone landed on the truck resonated through the whole quarry. The truck looked like it would be smashed by the impact. It rocked but reluctantly accepted the load like an overburdened burrow.

"I'm fine," said Tim with a tinge of anger in his voice.

"What?" said Krebs, the bobbing cigarette acting like a drunk orchestra conductor with each spoken word.

"...Oh yeah. Good thing." Krebs continued, "Last week a man fell off that broken digger over there. Got his hand caught in the cam shaft on the way down. He got a one way ticket home after that. Now everybody's gonna call him 'Lefty.'"

Krebs shot Tim a glance and looked at the torn short.

"Maybe you got lucky 'cause your Irish."

Krebs turned his attention back to the next line of stone that had been prepared. "Maybe that's what we should call you – Lucky. Lucky charm. Four-leaf clover. Something like that."

The truck that had been loaded belched smoke from its exhaust as it tried to break the inertia with the heavy load on its back. The wheels didn't turn at first as the engine revved in first gear. Finally, the wheels started slowly moving and the vehicle was on its way to the unfinished bridge.

"See, if you ever gotta take out the stone, make sure you point your truck in the right direction *first*. If you try to turn a corner too sharp, you'll blow the outside tire, guaranteed. Then the whole truck collapses. The front axle will break. You got about two-seconds to dive out of the cab before the rock comes to bury you in the driver's seat."

"You know how to paint a pretty picture, Krebs."

"This ain't work for the faint of heart. If you don't have the gumption to do the job, you'd better go home to mother."

Timothy was turning red, more from Krebs than the escalating heat or the hot metal of this gargantuan machine.

"Look friend," Timothy began. "I know I'm not as old as you. But I'm here to do my job. And right now my job is your job. You gotta show me how this thing works. I'll watch you all day and get the hang of this machine. I promise, but it would help if you showed me a little respect and answered a few of my goddamned questions."

Pointing back to the lever behind Krebs's right elbow, Timothy tried to get Krebs to explain. "Okay, that's a ginisten.. ginisten... and it works a gronesteel. But I have no idea what that is. Unless you tell me what it *does*."

"How the hell should I know? I was making it up as I was going along. I have no idea what that does. Never messed with it. You shouldn't either. Aw shit... you're cut."

Krebs pointed to a spot where some blood had matted along the torn shirt. The cut along the lower part of the ribcage made a dark spot that grew slowly. Tim looked down and pulled the shirt away from the injury. He looked down under his shirt and then turned back to Krebs.

"Don't worry about it. It's a scratch. I didn't even notice it."

A series of dark insects had taken notice and began lighting around the blood.

"Boy, you are new here." Krebs slammed the levers into a neutral position and the beast came to rest. He stood up and climbed out of the cab. He climbed a short section toward the rear of the engine. He returned with something that looked like a metal watering can.

"Here. Pour this on the wound and soak your shirt 'til the blood comes out." He handed Tim the can. Tim took a sniff.

"It's kerosene."

"Yep, best goddamn stuff on God's green earth. Kills the mosquitoes, and keeps you from getting gangrene. Trust me. You want to soak your wound. Infection around here is a given. Tend to that thing at chow time."

Tim put his free hand under the cut to catch the kerosene as he poured it over his wound. It stung, but Tim knew better than wince.

"Whoa, don't use it all up. I need that to prime the motor."

While Timothy was instructed on the operation of the metallic beast, Harry was learning the internals on the second machine which had broken down. His hands and shirt were already a mixture of dirt and grease. These behemoths were much larger and more complex than anything he'd seen on the farm or at war. But the old man at his side was patient with him.

Ed Sheeran could size up a man in a moment. He saw Harry as another vet down on his luck. But he knew he was a hard worker. Someone at camp had said that Harry worked on motors, so Ed took a chance on him. Most of the useless vets Ed delegated to smooth the gravel on the road, or brush the tar, but he saw something in Harry's eyes that only another hard worker could identify.

"It took me a month to get these things in working order. When they arrived, they came in pieces and they had half rusted through. They break down quite a bit. They're old, but they do the job."

"Looks like there's a leak in the hydraulic for the lift mechanism. Why don'tcha let me work on that," said Harry.

Harry struggled to get his hand in an awkward position to loosen a lug nut. "Ugh – dang thangs tight." With a heave Harry pushed loose the coupling.

"Good job," said Ed without looking.

"Thanks," replied Harry as he took out a knife to cut away the portion of the piping that had cracked. "Looks like we'll be digging away half the island to build the highway."

"We got another site north of here, too."

"So, you been here long? You come down on the train?" asked Harry.

"Hah – no. Been doing this sort of thing for quite a while. I helped build the bridges for the train, the Florida extension, almost thirty years ago. Had a helluva time. Lost a lot of friends."

Ed stopped what he was doing and stared out over the water.

The sky was a mixture of quickly moving clouds and sun. The breeze that stirred returned Ed from his momentary repose.

"They blew away."

"Blew away?"

"Yeah – had a terrible boss in charge of the men at the time. He was arrogant — never let nobody finish their sentence. He always had to prove he was right. Left the men stranded when the hurricane came through."

"Sorry to hear you lost some of your friends. Guess it was an act of God – huh?"

Ed stopped working on the machine and looked Harry squarely in the eyes.

"No sir — over a hundred. We knew it was coming, but the boss didn't let the men go. We knew it was bad because of the conchs and the crabs."

"A hundred died?" asked Harry, bewildered.

"More."

"The conchs..." began Harry as he wiped his hands with a dirty rag.

"That's what you call the locals around here — 'Conchs.' They all said it was coming. The barometer don't lie."

"And the crabs — are they people who aren't 'conchs'?"

"Nope," Sheeran smiled. "They're those little armor plated critters that walk sideways with their claws up in the air."

Ed put his hands over his head and made a crab like claw gesture. The two laughed.

"So you talk to the crabs?"

"Nah. I just watched them. They're all over the place. You can't drive ten feet before crunching one

80

under your wheels. But before the storm hit they all scampered over to the gulf. Thousands of them — all at the same time. They were like rats in a sinkin' ship. They clacketty clacked across the coral. Never seen nothing like that before in my life."

"Never experienced a hurricane," said Harry

"You don't want to. Trust me. I've seen enough of them. If the weather gets bad around here, we'll pack the equipment close to the mangroves or float 'em on the water inland. Then we'll find cover. You gotta find a strong shelter."

Harry nodded, but had no real context why the equipment would be trouble. It was large. He'd seen a truck toppled by a tornado, but this equipment was much bigger. By the sound of it, Ed had been thinking about what to do for a long time. He'd seen the senseless loss of life as the storm raged on. Since then, he'd pondered how he would ride out the next one.

"If a bad one hits, you stick with me. I'll show ya what to do."

Harry nodded and the two returned to the broken machine.

The only thing that could spoil a day was people. People were always the limiters of happiness except for the very few that were as good as spring itself.

  -   *Hemingway*

"Get outta my goddamn house!" yelled Hemingway spitting in rage.

A man had sauntered up the front yard and into his private residence.

"I'm – I'm *so sorry*. Mr. Hemingway, I had no idea." The man waved the pamphlet he was carrying as if it was evidence of his innocence.

Hemingway glanced at the rifle on the wall. That was enough for the man. He stumbled out of Hemingway's house with a stiff rapid gait that made him look like he was racing to the bathroom to take a wet shit.

The man, making his embarrassing exit, dropped the pamphlet he'd been carrying. Hemingway picked it up and was about to crumple it and toss it in the wastebasket. Instead, he paused to look at it. The contents displayed a diagram of Key West with sites numbered and identified. He saw the lighthouse, the marina, and his own home listed among the identified locations.

Hemingway's face turned red when he saw the markings on the page. His house was among the stops along a walking tour of popular attractions! But what really got his blood boiling was the fact that this was not some commercial enterprise. This was a government published document. The tour had been prepared and his house had been labeled on it without his consent. He scanned the page and saw the name of Julius Stone signed at the bottom. Stone had made this tour guide part of a government issue for every tourist arriving in Key West. With the weekend just starting, he wondered how many other intruders would stroll up to his home without a second thought.

The idiot tourist had long since vanished, but Hemingway opened the door and shouted. "I'm going to build a goddamned wall! I'm fencing this place in!"

He turned and shook his head. He was the only one present at the house but still engaged in his solo dialog. "I'm going to need a drink."

He grabbed his hat and stepped outside. They'd done some road construction and had pulled up the brick under the old road. If he found where the city workers dumped them he could buy them to fortify a wall between him and the weekend invaders.

The intruder made him mad. He needed a drink. Normally, he'd head to Sloppy Joes.

"No," he thought. They probably put Sloppy Joes on the map, too. He would head to Pete's Pub. Most of the tourists would be afraid of that part of town.

"I definitely need a drink."

The sky had turned fiery orange with licks of sulphur yellow along the edges of the high cirrus clouds. As the train passed over the bridge to Vaca Key the passenger cars seemed to float over nothingness. The low rail guides couldn't be seen from the passenger car windows.

The Friday train arriving at Key West was usually busy. However, tonight they were packed. The vets had been paid, and they hopped on the southbound train for a night of drinking. The standard tourist family had no idea that the train would be filled with raucous, foulmouthed drunks who'd baked their brains for a week in the hot Florida sun. They passed the bottles around as the train rocked and clacked over the rails on its way to the end of the nation.

One woman in a white knee length dress and striped blouse was traveling alone. Though the heat wasn't abated by the breeze from the journey, she still wore a white cloche hat and white gloves. She clutched her purse and tried to make herself invisible. This was impossible with the vets eyeing her and making comments under their breath.

One of the vets, drunk and uninhibited, decided to strike up a conversation.He left his cadre of men, who snickered as he slid next to her.

"Hello there, miss," he started innocently.

She squirmed and returned the pleasantry. "Hello."

She looked down, sending the physical signals of a woman who didn't want to be bothered. The man continued, ignoring her body language.

"Why miss, I am a veteran of the Great War. Some considered me a hero. I was in France as bombs went all around. But now, well, I am here building our future."

"How nice," she curtly replied.

"In fact, I take personal pride in what I am doing."

She looked out the window and shifted in its direction. He reeked of booze and three day old sweat. She blinked as the wind coming through the window threatened to blow off her hat. She put her hand on it and tried to find rest in her discomfort.

He slid closer.

"You see we're building a road." He leaned back and looked at the men in the rows behind him and winked. "Aren't we boys?! We're building a road to the future!"

The men laughed and nodded. Some made rude gestures behind her back.

"In fact, I am working on a bridge. It is a huge bridge that spans miles." He took a swig of the bottle he had at his side. He offered the bottle to her.

"No... No thank you." She bit her knuckle.

The man continued to press forward. As those behind laughed and made snide commentary.

"Indeed, the bridge, I consider my own."

"Is that so?" she said. She wanted to rise and leave but the man blocked the way.

"Yes... It is quite an erection." He smiled at her and showed his teeth. One of his front teeth had chipped and the others were stained. The smile had a sinister look.

Two of the men in the back were laughing hysterically. One started punching the other and then himself.

"Jane!" He said, mimicking Tarzan the ape man.

"Tarzan!" He continued, punching himself.

"Jane!" He said, punching the man harder.

"Tarzan!" He repeated, punching himself as he reenacted the movie.

"Dead in a minute," said the man who received the punches. He punched the other man in the stomach and knocked the wind out of him. The wheezing was mixed with laughter as they both rolled back and forth together.

"I would love to show you my erection sometime. It is the eighth wonder of the world." The man smiled and touched her leg.

"Oh, you brute!" she smacked him with her hand bag, rose and headed for the next car.

He grabbed her ass as she marched over him. She squealed but kept moving and didn't look back.

She felt vulnerable in every car as the eyes of the men with the same greased stained outfits leered at her.

Harry, Buddy and Elmer sat in a car filled with their fellow workers as the woman entered their cab and found an empty row. The three men, too, had started drinking, but were nowhere near along the lines of becoming fools as others in the compartment behind them.

Elmer brought enough spirits for everyone and they drank as the fire in the evening sky disappeared and the stars dotted the night sky.

"It gets dark quick here," said Harry.

"Yeah," started Elmer. "I heard a rumor from a sailor in Key West. He says that if you are on a ship and you look at the sun sinking on the water..." he winced and pointed at the horizon.

"... Look at the little sliver as it just sinks on the horizon. When the sun disappears — sometimes there's a green flash."

"Horseshit..." replied Harry. He took another swig of whisky.

"No! It's true!"

"Yer a goddamn liar!" Harry laughed and put his arm around Elmer.

Buddy who sat in front of them added, "No, Harry. It's true. I heard that in New York from the big merchant ships that come in. There is a green flash that is supposed to be magical or something."

"Horseshit... horseshit...." Harry exhaled and with the last little breath repeated, "...horseshit."

Harry didn't want to know anything about a green flash. He wasn't interested in fairy tales.

"I talked to Sheeran about the hurricane. Now that's real. I wonder if I'm gonna git to see one." Harry's Kansas accent was thicker with an alcohol induced slur.

"Never seen one myself. Hope we get to," added Buddy who sat in his own row on the opposite side of the aisle.

"Maybe it'll blow away the damn mosquitoes. Look at my arm." He held out his arm which was scared with pinprick wounds.

The men laughed at the large man who usually ended a night with something bloody, bruised or broken. He never complained after a fight. Yet here he was concerned over the lost fight with the tiniest of the vile Florida bugs.

The train rolled to a stop at the station in Key West. The three staggered off the platform and were met by the warm breeze filled with the smell of ocean air, open fire cooking, and debauchery. To the three men, it smelled wonderful. They didn't have a lot of money, but were hoping that someone more inebriated and wealthier would buy them a round. Before they left, the trio made sure they'd already purchased their return ticket.

Some of the vets made a bee line to the nearest whorehouse. They didn't have to walk far. Harry, Elmer and Buddy made their way toward Duval Street. Along the way, they came across a whitewashed building with iron work on the second floor. A man was pissing off the top story trying to hit any unwary pedestrian. The woman on his shoulder was laughing, one large breast jiggling as it poked out over the unbuttoned blouse.

Another man stood leaning against a telephone pole. He'd passed out, but somehow found a way to remain balanced in an upright position. His shirt was stained from where he retched.

"This place looks interesting," said Buddy.

Harry hesitated. "Kinda seedy, don'tcha think?"

"It's Key West! C'mon!" said Buddy.

He slapped Harry on the back. Harry stumbled and nearly fell, but caught himself.

"I'll keep an eye on ya. Don't worry. I got friends. Two of 'em."

Elmer and Harry assumed Buddy was talking about them. Harry held up his fists. The Masonic ring glowed as though it had a life of its own.

"See? Two friends."

They laughed as they entered Pete's pub. The smell of the place was an odd mixture of sickly sweet alcohol, cigars and unwashed men. From the outside, it looked as though it should've been condemned. Inside looked better. Along the walls were booths. A curtain rod hung over each one but the curtains had been torn or were missing. A mirror was mounted behind the bar along the far wall. Tables of various sizes were scattered throughout the establishment and people were huddled around them. Some of the luckier ones actually found a chair. Others, with a cigar in one hand and a drink in the other, leaned over to hear the table's conversation.

A number of vets from the train found the locale and had already ordered their drinks. In one corner there was a couple vacating a booth. The three made their way and sat down. Without hesitation, Elmer stood back up. "I'll get us something to get started."

He disappeared into the crowd. Along one edge of the bar, a large group exploded with laughter. The bartenders were busy. The vets mixed in with the locals and sailors. It was an odd lot this evening as a large crew from a fishing trawler was spending money from their catch. They were as drunk as the vets and were arguing and posturing.

Elmer returned with three beers. "This round is on me, gentlemen."

"Thanks," said Buddy.

They each took a long draw on the bottle.

"What's going on over there?" asked Harry as he pointed to a particularly raucous group.

"Oh! Papa Hemingway is at the bar. He's telling stories," said Elmer.

"Papa who?" replied Harry.

"Ernest Hemingway..." Elmer looked at Harry who had no clue who this Hemingway character might be. As if saying it slower would help, Elmer cocked his head like a confused dog and carefully repeated, "Ernest Hemingway — the famous writer."

"You mean like Zane Grey?" said Harry.

Buddy laughed out loud. "You mean you never heard of Hemingway?"

"Well... I don't read much." Harry started peeling the label off the bottle. "I learned to read real good while I was in the service, but it was a chore to keep up with it. Never heard of Mr. Hemingway. I read Westerns mostly."

"You'd like his writing. He's simple. He doesn't write stuff that's hard to read."

Buddy took another swig of his beer and pointed in Harry's direction.

"He's been there. He writes about war. He can tell you about it."

"Really? He doesn't just make it up?"

"Nope," said Buddy. Looking like a hitchhiker, he pointed his thumb in the direction of the bar and asked Elmer, "He's really sitting over there?"

"Yeah, go see for yourself."

"Funny... I've never met anybody famous. I walked the streets of New York – nothing! Since I been down here in the middle of nowhere, I met a boxing champ and now I'm going to meet a famous writer — strange world." Buddy got up and went over to the bar.

Harry finished his bottle. He sat silently contemplating his struggle to read. This led to the memory of books he left behind on the farm and his love – Elizabeth. For long stretches while he worked, he could forget her. It was the nights where he agonized and lamented over his treatment of her. She was justified in leaving him. He hoped that one day he would win her back. However, he knew the emotional wounds went deep. She didn't understand his behavior. Neither did he.

"Hey there, Harry! You look like you lost your pet dog!" said Elmer.

"Sorry, Elmer. Just thinking about the past."

"We drink to forget the past."

Buddy returned with a man with an open shirt and thick beard with a bottle tucked under his armpit. They were each carrying medium-sized glasses.

"Welcome to Key West, gentlemen. I'm Ernest Hemingway." The man sat next to Harry, and Buddy slid in beside Elmer.

"I told Mr. Hemingway," Buddy began.

"Papa..." corrected Hemingway. "Just call me papa."

"Papa," Buddy repeated. "I told him that Harry never heard of him."

Buddy put a glass filled with the dark amber drink in front of each of the men. Hemingway put the glasses and bottle on the table.

Buddy was acting like a starstruck kid when he said, "He said that he wanted to meet you, Harry. He even bought us a round."

"Rum, my friends. It is the drink of the house. They smuggle this from Jamaica. It is the best you'll find anywhere." Hemingway raised his glass. "To the men who served."

The others raised their glass and drank the sweet fiery substance. It went down smooth, and it warmed their insides. Harry never had rum before. It was sweeter than whiskey, but he liked it.

"So, you're Harry." Hemingway pointed to Harry. "I'm Hemingway, but you can call me papa."

Hemingway put his hand out.

Nervously Harry responded, "You're the writer. Yessir. It is good to meet you. Not much of a reader, but I hear you are the best."

Harry wiped his hand on his shirt before extending it to Hemingway.

"Well, I've been told my writing is too simple, but I write it like I see it," replied Hemingway shaking Harry's hand.

Harry took a hefty gulp of the rum. It burned on the way down in a good and soothing way that only a drinker can know. The heat radiated through his body and gave him courage to say, "I like to read westerns — you know — Zane Grey. I read *Forlorn River* twice."

"Hah! I went fishing with Mr. Grey. He loves the Keys," said Hemingway as he paused to look deep into Harry's eyes.

"Really? You know Zane Grey?"

"Yes, I took him out on *Pilar* just a few weeks ago. He caught a nice sized grouper. After that he went home, but he stays at the Long Key Fishing Camp on a regular basis."

"I never met anybody famous before," said Harry.

"I'm a little embarrassed that I ain't read anything you wrote."

"Hell, I can't remember half of what I've written. Especially after a glass of this…"

Hemingway winked at Harry and drew deep on his glass of rum. He turned to Elmer.

"I'm sorry, I don't think we've been introduced?"

"Elmer. Thanks for the drink."

"Hey, it isn't free. I want to hear your stories. So Harry, you spend time in the trenches?"

"No sir. I was on a submarine."

"A sub? You're the first vet working on the highway that I've talked to that was in the water. Did you see any action?"

Harry shifted a little. "No, not really. Almost got sunk, but the German's torpedo circled around and missed us."

"They sank their own sub?"

"Yessir."

Hemingway laughed. "See? Now there's a story. What about you Elmer?"

Elmer, usually the most jolly of the group suddenly turned serious. "Got lucky." Elmer spun his glass slowly on the table moving it like someone divining spirits from a ouija board

The group waited as Elmer began recalling his tale.

"My regiment in the 106th Infantry was wiped out."

Sweat formed on Elmer's brow as he lifted the rum for another drink. When he set it down Hemingway refilled Elmer's empty glass.

"I went in the trenches and came out without a scratch. With all the shrapnel flying around, I don't know how I didn't get killed."

He paused and sighed.His left eye winced as he went back to that place.

"We were at the Hindenburg line. The trench was tiny. Two-by-sixes leaning against the cold earth. Some of the shells that fell short buried us in dirt, they landed so close. I couldn't hear anything but a high pitched whirr."

"The sergeant was right next to me. I looked up to see if I could get a sight line on the enemy. We took turns doing that. It was the sergeant's turn. The artillery almost took his head off. He flew back, hit the other side of the wall and landed in my lap. I had to scrape pieces of him off of me. Pieces of his head were everywhere. There was one detached eye that stared back at me."

"Things went foul — you know? The men got to a point where they didn't care. They didn't cover. The just shouted 'Comrade' and fired. They stood up and emptied rounds. We bandaged those that were still alive."

There was an inner turmoil that resonated in Elmer's words. He wiped the sweat from his face.

"I wasn't a coward."

He paused to look at the men for some kind of confirmation. Silently they all acknowledged the unspoken bond.

"I unloaded until I ran out of ammunition. I couldn't hear a damn thing. I didn't know that the tank arrived 'till it almost ran over me. I high-tailed it to the tank. When it was disabled by shrapnel, I ran back to the front line. Borrowed guns and ammo from the dead and just kept shooting. All that shrapnel and I never got hit — not once. I don't know how many I killed that day. People on the tank got killed. I ran in the open and didn't get a scratch."

"Eventually I was picked up and made it to the rear. I was the only one left."

Elmer took another swig from his glass.

"I was the only one left. They all died."

He breathed heavily.

"Lucky? Maybe so. Maybe not."

He was having a conversation with his inner demons.

"They brought me back to the infirmary. Why? I don't know. Wasn't hit."

"I asked for more ammo so I could go back out there, but they said no. I got behind the lines and found out that two other men had survived from my company. They didn't get out without a lot of bloodshed."

Elmer swirled his drink. "You see? I'm lucky. Real lucky."

He sounded like he was trying to convince himself as he repeated, "...real lucky. It's like I *can't* die. No matter how hard I tried."

Tears were streaming from his face.

Hemingway reached over and patted him on the shoulder.

"We're all damned in some way," said Harry.

"Damned indeed," added Buddy.

Hemingway filled everyone's glass. He lifted his over his head and toasted, "To the damned!"

"To the damned!" they all replied as they clinked glasses and poured the ambrosia down the back of their throats.

As soon as they set their glasses on the table, A raucous argument broke out between a sailor and a vet. It was an instantaneous crescendo of words which was soon followed by blows. The vet had been injured and had a wooden crutch which he swung wildly to keep the sailor at bay. The sailor wielded a knife but couldn't make advances without being smacked by the crutch. The vet swung away and knocked a round of drinks off a nearby table.

"Hey! Take it outside!" yelled the bartender. Some were taking sides as the blood lust rose in the room. Others were laying down bets.

"I need some help. You're a pretty big fellow, Buddy. Mind giving me a hand?" asked Hemingway.

"Sure thing."

All four men stood up. Hemingway walked behind the sailor as if he was trying to leave. Harry partnered with him. With quick reflexes that betrayed his size, Hemingway grabbed the sailor's arm and pulled it backward, trying to pin the sailor in an arm bar. Harry swung around and grabbed the knife, smothering the sailor's ability to break free and possibly injure the famous author.

93

Simultaneously, Elmer and Buddy went after the drunk vet. They weren't as efficient at subduing him. He saw the hulking frame of Buddy approaching and took a quick swing. Buddy saw it coming and weaved as the crutch flew past his head. Elmer was coming up on the rear. He went to grab the man around the neck and put him in a choke hold but Elmer was shorter than the vet. A quick elbow from the vet slammed into Elmer's ear, boxing it and hurling him to the floor.

Buddy continued to advance but the vet was already on the backswing. The crutch collided with the side of Buddy's face. Any other man would have instantly been rendered unconscious. The crutch smacked Buddy so hard that it snapped in two with splinters of wood flying in all directions. The bar let out a collective "Oh!"

The vet was astonished at the remnant that he held in his hand. Buddy was dazed but shook it off and hurled himself at the man, yelling "Don't you do that!"

The man's eyes went wide as Buddy body slammed him. Elmer who was behind the vet grabbed the man's shoulders more to keep his balance than to render any form of assistance. The three of them toppled to the floor with Elmer on the bottom and Buddy on top. Now with the opportunity available, Buddy leaned back and delivered his signature right hook. The man's jaw look like it broke, but the dislocated jaw popped back in place and his eyes rolled back in his head. The man went slack.

Under the strain of both the unconscious vet and Buddy, Elmer wheezed out, "I appreciate you giving me a hand. Now could you please help get him off me?"

The four men dragged out the sailor and vet and hurled them into the street. The bartender came out from behind the bar holding a pistol. He pointed it at the two defeated men who only now were shaking off the cloud of unconsciousness.

"If you come back in, I'll use this on both of you."

As an incentive, the bartender shot the pistol into the air. He turned to the four men, nodded his head and said, "Thank you, gentlemen. Drinks on the house."

"Well," said Hemingway. "I haven't had a better invitation all night. You joining me?"

They didn't hesitate to return to their booth.

There's a little island named Cudjoe,
I lived there once...
It was all so long ago...
No dreams of a highway to link
The archipelago
With a North land some called "The States."
The keys all jade and emerald green,
A chain of precious jewels
Laid on a sea of ultramarine
Blue, a different shade of blue...

-    *Lily Lawrence Bow*

The wind died down before sunrise on Saturday as Timothy woke from his bunk. A squall came through in the middle of the night, which rendered any notion of a full night sleep fruitless. He didn't join his friends in Key West because the week had left him exhausted. The idea of a weekend of drinking and with the inevitable return to work was overwhelming. Even his Irish blood couldn't handle the stress of a weekend without sleep, a debilitating hangover, followed by morning of hard labor.

He'd hoped to find a night away from the snoring of his bunkmates, but nature decided to replace Elmer's basso profundo snores and snorts with a dialog of thunder. The rain dripped through the tin roof and ran down the walls of the place he now called home. The downpour came in sheets, with undulating regularity. For an hour the pelting deluge sounded like a hundred clashing cymbals punctuated by the bellowing roll of a timpani gone mad. Just as quickly as it began, the rain stopped as if God simply turned the handle of some celestial spigot. The silence that followed was almost as eerie. The night wore on with the on again, off again, maelstrom. Timothy never experienced such dramatic meteorological turn of events. The sun wasn't above the horizon yet, but he wanted to get an early start on his free day in this strange land.

He hoped that this day's weather would be less violent than the night's cacophony.

After dressing, he made his way to the edge of the mangrove forest. He refused to use the toilet facilities at the camp. Anyone within a hundred yards of the place either started to gag or fell victim to thousands of voracious insects. Instead he relieved himself along the wall of vegetation of wide dark green leaves with the white and purplish stems. He'd been warned about alligators though he'd never seen one. He really didn't know what they looked like or how big they were. The vets seemed fanciful in their description of this animal with its big mouth and large teeth. One of the myths that surfaced was about a man from camp who went out at night and was never found again. The crew suspected that he was eaten by an alligator. A week later they caught one of the monsters and opened him up. Inside were the remains of the man, mostly intact. It seemed more fairytale than truth so rather than getting sick in the putrid latrine, he decided to take his chances with these, as yet unseen, monsters. He felt the mangroves gave him better odds.

Tim knew last night's squall would calm the regular breeze which ran along this narrow stretch of land, allowing clouds of mosquitoes to have free rein later in the day. Timothy wasn't immune to their wrath and thought it better if he left the camp early to find some isolated refuge along the railway. The puddles which formed from the night's rain would only increase the number of the blood sucking insects and flies that plagued the men. The early hour worked in Timothy's favor. The bugs mellowed in the cool air with only a few stray flies keeping him company as he made his way out of the sleepy camp.

He'd thought about catching the morning train to Key West, but decided to save what little he had left of his money and instead see what the local color looked like.

The Atlantic, sun, and clouds painted a pastel portrait of reds, yellows, and pinks that ran across the big sky. Toward the Gulf side, the royal blue of pre-dawn held the darkness in a loose grip. His feet crunched under the crushed coral of the raised area of the rail which was the high spot along Lower Matecumbe Key. As the golden orb crested over the water, it brought a wave of heat born from the waters of the Atlantic. Timothy start to sweat, but the slight breeze kept him comfortable.

The rows of hastily built shacks were now out of view as Timothy continued his trek along the rails. The locals, who lived in modest homes along the road paralleling Flagler's railroad, came out to greet the dawn. They gave a quick wave and put their hand to their brow to better see who was walking this time of morning. The "Conchs" — those who eked out an existence in this place wore long pants, long shirts and long dresses. Most wore hats and those who stayed outside for any length of time kept netting to put over his or her face should the need arise.

Prior to the hundreds of men arriving at the camps, this tight knit community knew every soul on the island. The locals were a tough crowd, surviving with only limited water and planting on impenetrable ground. The brackish wells barely kept the Indians alive only a few years ago. The white man tenuously won the battle, but the real victory came with the southerly movement of industrial progress. With the advent of the railroad and electricity, it was now possible for some of the islands to break the inertia and begin the slow move toward modernity.

Most of those who lived here now served the rich who came here to fish or sail along the pristine Atlantic which was replete with big game fish. Many of the less wealthy tourists stayed in the Rustic Inn or Matecumbe Hotel before eventually ending up at Key West.

The normally friendly locals were upset with the invasion of hundreds of veterans on their land. The nights had been silent and now were punctuated with fights and drunken revelry which spilled into their tiny neighborhoods. The local's quiet life was disturbed by the constant sound of machines as the large black line was being constructed which laced together the small disparate spots of land between the greater blue world that surrounded them. The Conchs now had to lock their doors at night, which meant they had to go to Homestead to purchase a lock.

Along the Atlantic, Timothy noticed a spot where the Mangroves parted. On the other side of the roadway, a small cove of still water rippled with the slightest wisp of wind. It seemed to glow with iridescent hues, reflecting the golden light of the rising sun. There was no blue. Instead, the water seemed like a stew of emerald capped gold. Along the edge, a small spot of sand arced like the white crescent of a fingernail. Its appeal was overwhelming. It called to him to stride out to the horizon and beyond. Timothy headed toward spot for a moment of repose. The water rose and fell with small, almost imperceptible lapping, beckoning Timothy to step away from his terrestrial bondage.

He'd never gone swimming in the ocean before. Stepping on the soft sand, he sat and stared toward the horizon. There was a moment of fear and trepidation. He looked around for anyone else who might witness what he was about to do. No one was around. He slipped off his shoes and dug his feet into the soft cool sand. He wiggled his toes. He stood and took another look around. He was modest and didn't want to attract attention. He slipped behind some mangroves and began to undress. He slowly entered the water. It was cold compared to the warming day, but it was quite refreshing.

He stepped further, determined that he would get in the water up to his waist. He couldn't remember the last time he bathed. The sand was on a gentle incline which forced him to venture much further from shore than he originally thought.

The water was cool, but not alarmingly so. He paused, hesitating to dip his genitals into the cold. With one quick movement, he dropped to his knees, sinking in the sand as he did so. He arched his back and immersed himself completely. He rose up, as sparkles of water droplets flew off of his black hair. He was only in for a second, but he gasped for air, more from the invigorating baptism than from lack of breath.

The sun cleared the horizon turning the morning's gold to silver as the sky turned a pale blue with wisps of dancing clouds high overhead. Timothy had never felt so energized. He got on his feet and dove forward, swimming out further to chest high water. In the crystal clear Atlantic he could see small fish scurrying past his legs. He dove under and opened his eyes, but was disappointed that all was a blur. It stung his eyes and he rose and wiped the salt away.

When he was a boy he'd known some fisherman, who'd fitted the bottom of a box with glass and caulked the contraption with wax. He knew that when he returned to camp he'd try to reproduce the box and return to this spot. Colorful creatures of yellow and black seemed curious of this new human in the water, and attempted to sample the hair on Timothy's leg which undulated in time with the ripples on the surface.

He tried to swim to the bottom, but was pushed to the surface by unseen forces. He was buoyant, and wondered how people could drown in the ocean. He took a few deep breaths and tried to swim as long as he could with his face in the water. He puffed out the spent oxygen and tried it again and again. There was some strange "rightness" to being out here. He passed the point where he could put his feet on the sand. The land seemed a mile away, but Timothy wasn't afraid. In fact, there was a peace that he'd not known for years. It was as if the water was saying, "You're home now."

He'd drifted south of his entry point, and made effort to line himself back up with the shore line. It was tougher than he thought. The current was strong and he had to exert himself to make headway.

He dove down again, trying to grab some of the exposed coral and sea grass. He popped back up and noticed he'd drifted still farther from shore. A momentary panic filled him as he wondered if he strayed beyond the point of return. He kicked hard and made his way slowly back to the sand. Only when the tips of his toes scraped sand did the panic abate. He wouldn't be so careless next time. With his feet now firmly planted he let the motion of the water pull him slightly this way or that. He closed his eyes turned his head skyward. The salt dried on his face and he could feel it crack as he smiled. He wanted to stay here all day.

He didn't know how long he lingered in that one spot, simply "being." There was no anxiety and no pain. The water had dissolved it into the boundless ocean. Opening his eyes, he slowly focused on shore.

He was not alone.

An old truck stopped on the road. He paid little attention as he took a deep breath and tried to swim underwater as far as he could. He kept his head down at an angle until his muscles cried for a fresh breath. Arching his back, he turned toward the light and surfaced. He expected the stranger in the truck would have moved on. Timothy blinked and wiped his eyes. Focusing back on the road, he couldn't tell if his mind was playing tricks, or if the most beautiful woman in the world was hailing him. The white blouse was in stark contrast to the long black hair that hung down and moved with a life of its own in the morning breeze, hiding a colorful scarf carefully tied to hide her breasts. The knee length skirt displayed her sensuous curves. He waved back at her. She kept waving, and only after a moment did he realize she was saying something. His ears were filled with water and all sound was slushy and muted. He stuck his finger in his right ear, trying to clear it out.

"Hello!" he yelled from the chest high water. He stepped forward, trying to discern what she was saying.

"... you're a brave man," she said. He didn't catch the first part, but was astonished at the statement, thinking that he had, indeed, entered some kind of fantasy, where this goddess would be so openly flirtatious. Maybe she was a mermaid, caught on land, waiting for someone to carry her back to the sea. His head was swimming with the fantasy of his new found love of water.

He repeated, "Hello, I'm sorry, I didn't hear..."

She interrupted him. "Get out of that water!"

Confused, he asked, "What? Why?"

His mind rambled back to the stories of alligators. He wondered if he was swimming in their lair. Suddenly, the reality of the dangers of this place was sinking in. He started forward.

"Alligators? Are there alligators here?" The water kept him from moving quickly, but he started toward shore.

"No. You don't need to worry about alligators that far out. But you are a brave man to be swimming with sharks."

"Sorry, sharks?" This was a complete mystery to him. He'd heard of sharks, but knew nothing beyond the name. He wondered if the yellow and black fish nibbling at his leg hairs were some sort of dangerous shark.

"Yes! Those are shark infested waters in the morning. The sharks head toward shore until later in the day. Then they head out to sea."

Timothy had no context for understanding what she was saying. Was he in trouble? Where were the sharks? He walked toward shore.

"You should be okay, this close to shore, but don't venture out beyond waist deep."

"Are they dangerous?"

"The sharks? Generally no, but they feed here in the morning. If there's nothing around, they may consider you a snack. However, I guess the water is a little cold today. You're not dangling too much bait." With that she giggled and put her hand to her mouth.

"What?" The moment was lost on Timothy until he realized he was standing in knee deep water, completely exposing himself to this complete and utterly beautiful stranger. He dropped down and sat in the water. This made the beautiful stranger double over in laughter. She wasn't the least bit shy. Timothy didn't want her to leave, but found that he couldn't approach her in his current state.

"Thank you for the warning. I'll heed your words. Umm..." It seemed somehow inappropriate, but he asked, "What is your name?"

Moving the hand from her mouth, still chuckling, she answered, "Aella."

Not thinking he heard properly, he said, "Sorry?"

Slowly and a little louder, she carefully said, "Aella. It's Greek."

"My name's Timothy. Timothy McCormick." He started to stand, his instinct and training as a gentleman taking control, but he remembered he was nude. He paused and returned to his sitting position.

"You need to be careful in these waters. They'll charm you to death. I've seen more than one body float ashore. There's no current here, but if you get out too far, you could get in trouble."

Timothy had a sample of the current but chose not to share that he knew exactly what she was saying.

"Sage advice, Aella. Thank you. I've never been swimming in the ocean before."

"You're from the work camp, aren't you? You look a little young to be a vet."

103

"Not from the Great War — no. But the work here is good and I'm making a living."

"No, you're not. The president sent all of the bums and hobos on a train for Florida. He wanted them off his lawn. You're doing slave labor. That's it. How much money have you saved?"

Timothy wanted to move, but felt as though Aella had him in check. He couldn't stand, and he was on the defensive, ignorant and completely disarmed. "I just got here, so I really...."

"How much?" she interrupted.

He paused, swishing the water with his hand. "I haven't saved any money, yet."

"You drinking it all away?"

"No. I'm not a drinker by nature."

"You have an Irish accent. I can hear it. I thought you were all drunks."

"Look, ma'am," Timothy started.

"...Aella. Call me Aella."

"I've seen a few Greeks staggering in the streets. I'm just trying to make a buck in hard times."

"Well, you're not going to make it digging in the dirt. I've no compassion for you all down here. I've seen your work ethic."

At that, Timothy stood up. Even though he was stark naked, he wasn't sitting down for such an unjust assault. The water dripped from him as he raised his arm and pointed at her. "You have no idea what I, or any of these other men, have been through. You don't understand them or me. I'm no bum. I'm a hard worker! I'll not take such insults from a stranger. Aella, you don't know me...."

She started laughing. It caused Timothy to hesitate, "You don't know me, or what I'm capable of."

He was trying to be serious, rebutting the slander she cast in his direction. But it was as if he was talking to two different people. She now seemed like a giddy schoolgirl.

104

"What are you laughing at?" He tried to keep the fire in his voice, but her smile was contagious.

"Obviously, when I strike a nerve and you are willing to defend yourself..." she pointed at him, "... you get your point across."

Timothy looked down and realized that he had become physically excited while arguing. He sat down in the water again, which only made Aella laugh that much more. They both started laughing together at the situation.

"Aella, I know this is probably too late to ask, but could you turn around so I might get dressed? If I have any hope of continuing an intelligent conversation it may be better conducted while I'm wearing clothes."

"You know, if you were any other man, you would have asked me to take off my clothes and join you. It seems you have a modicum of a gentleman in you. Perhaps you are careless but not crude."

The thought had, indeed, crossed his mind. But his upbringing forbade uttering such a suggestion. She turned around as Timothy headed to shore. She could hear the soft padding of his feet along the sand.

A crazy idea came into Aella's head.

With her back turned toward him she said, "Say, how about joining me. I'm heading to Homestead for some supplies. I need a strong back. I can't make any guarantees, but in the mean time, I might be able to find you some real work."

Pulling on his trousers, Timothy replied, "I'd like that." It was his first lucky break he'd had in a long time.

"You know anything about the ocean? Been on a boat?"

"Yeah, occasionally. My parents took me to the Chesapeake during the summer"

"Hmmm... well, I can't say we have a spot for you, but the busy season is about to start and we could use an extra hand. We'll see how you load and

105

unload the truck. You won't get paid today. Consider this an interview. I'll introduce you to my father."

Completely dressed, Timothy made his way back to the road. "What do you do?"

"Oh, we're mostly spongers, but we work with the 'millionaires club' and help out with tours, fishing outings — things like that — when the season starts." Aella rounded the truck. "Hop in."

"What's the millionaires club?"

As the two got in the truck Aella responded to Timothy's question with a question of her own.

"While you've been scratching in the dirt, have you seen any sails on the horizon?"

"A few," Timothy replied. Aella jammed the truck in gear and spun northward. Timothy grabbed the lip of the door by the rolled down window. Aella took no notice how fast she was barreling along the road.

"Some of the early birds head down here about this time. Labor Day is when they start coming down in droves. But we get some early takers. Those rich folk who want to go out and catch big game fish — swordfish, grouper — that sort of thing. They pay a pretty penny for knowledge of wreck sites. That's where all the goliaths hang out. Because we sponge dive, we know all of the good spots."

"I don't know a thing about sponge diving."

"My father is one of the best."

"So he goes underwater in a suit?"

"Yeah."

Aella laughed and looked at him in a way that he didn't understand. She had the look of a mother looking at her child.

"He uses a suit and a dive helmet. My father showed me this world when I was a child. He built a small diving bell for us. Unless you see it for yourself, you'll never know. It's a completely different world. In fact, life around here is far different than anything most people have ever experienced."

106

"How so?" asked Timothy.

He brushed his hands through his hair as the wind from the truck blew it dry.

"Water is something that most people don't think about. We think about it every day. If our cisterns run dry, we have to get water carted in from Panama City. If the current is strong, we know that fishing is going to be a problem; diving becomes treacherous. Then there are the storms like the one last night."

"I'd never experienced a storm like that. It started and stopped in an instant. Then it would start up again without any warning. The thunder raged throughout the night. We've had storms up north, but I never knew anything like this."

Timothy was intrigued. Looking both left and right, Timothy could see they were riding on a very narrow strip of land. Bella splashed through the large puddles that dotted the roadway.

"That was nothing. Hurricanes are the worst."

"So I've heard. I hope I get to see one."

"Bite your tongue!"

Aella yelled as she looked at Timothy. Doing so caused her to swerve. She had to correct the wheel quickly as they left the tarmac, and the right tire bounced through crushed coral. "We had a hurricane miss us in 1931. The waves were treacherous. We lost power, of course, but we were cut off from the mainland for two days because a bridge collapsed by Snake Creek. We'll be going over the bridge. I'll show you."

She pointed toward the vast Atlantic. "Even though a hurricane might be hundreds of miles away, you still feel its effects."

Timothy had no context to understand what Aella was talking about. But as she talked, he watched her hair dancing around the open truck window. She was beautiful. She was unaware he was staring at her as she described the effects of weather on their home, boats, cars, and the conchs' livelihood.

"... the storm surge can decimate the sponges and disrupt the sea life."

"You seem to know a lot about the weather."

"We all do. You can't live down here and not be aware — daily — of the weather. Everybody has a barometer."

Timothy had seen the barometer in the mess hall. He never paid much attention to it, but Sam Cutler, manager of the campsites, was in charge of monitoring it. Next to the thermometer and barometer he penciled in the information four times a day. If a storm approached he made phone calls and dispatched men to make precautions. Sam was a nervous sort, always ready to pull the plug on teams when he thought the clouds amassed and the thunder rolled. More than once, Sam had called men off the worksite for a five minute squall. During the cloudburst the men proceeded to drink so there was no hope of having them return after the sun shown brilliant.

"You get to a point where you think you know what is going to happen. That's when Mother Nature turns on you with a surprise. That's what happened with the hurricane. A lot of people died that day."

The land seemed to grow in size as they headed north. Suddenly there was more land than water. It had been a while since Timothy was on the mainland. He'd grown accustom to seeing the big blue in every direction.

When he lived in Maryland, Timothy knew the Appalachians and could always navigate with that frame of reference in his sights. Here, the land was flat providing no landmarks to judge distance. The palm trees looked bigger than they really were because they soared over the bushes and shanties that dotted the level landscape.

Homestead seemed like a metropolitan empire compared to the stark work camp. The short period that Timothy spent with the vets had already altered his notion of reality. He'd started becoming one of them. Separated from normalcy, and flung

108

into a cadre of desperate vets, he'd lost his
bearings for ordinary community life.

This beautiful woman sitting beside him and the
brick buildings and sidewalks seemed more like a
dream.

"Are you okay Mr. Ireland?"

Timothy, who'd been looking out the window,
came back from his ruminations. "McCormick...
m'last name's McCormick."

"I think Mr. Ireland suit you better. I'm calling
you Mr. Ireland."

With a mock exasperation Timothy said, "Just
call me Tim."

She smiled and looked at him with eyes that
warmed both his body and soul. Most of the other
Conchs he'd seen down here had been hardened by
the life. She hadn't. She glowed as if charged from
the Florida sun.

She drove past the local hardware store without
slowing down.

"The hardware store..." Timothy pointed behind
him wondering why they didn't stop.

"I said we were getting supplies. I didn't say we
were going to the hardware store." She smiled.
"You do have a good back, don't you?"

"Are you going to ask me to haul a boat out of
the water and put it on the truck?" He smiled.

She looked at him with a very serious face. "Oh
no..."

She couldn't help herself and smiled as she
continued, "Hauling a boat onto the truck would be
far too easy."

He tried to discern whether she was joking. He
couldn't tell. He was getting nervous. He didn't
want to let her down. In fact, he would move
heaven and earth to impress her.

The dust swirled as she turned onto an unpaved
road and followed it through a patch of nothingness.
There were no signs. Only a row of telephone poles
gave any clue that this was leading anywhere.
Almost lost in the gray of the sand and coral, the

two arrived at a concrete building that sat on the edge of the water. It was a converted gas station. There were no business signs identifying the location as operational, but a number of large trucks were parked on one side.

He thought she was going past this structure when she slammed on the brakes and plunged the truck into reverse. Backing through the plume of dust, Timothy swallowed the chalky air and stifled a cough. She put her hand along the back of the truck's seat. Her hand brushed the back of his neck and he leaned back, hoping she would put her hand around him. She, however, was focused on backing the truck to a large open loading area.

A man emerged from the dark interior. The man's skin was roasted to the color of walnut. His black hair was filled with gray powder. He had a cigar in his mouth that looked like it had resided there for some time. The end was soggy, and he spit out part of a leaf as Aella slowed and then stopped. He came forward and opened the door.

She jumped out with a girlish hop.

"Aella!" yelled the man opening his arms for a hug. He was dirty from top to bottom, but she didn't hesitate to grab him with the same verve that he grabbed her.

"Sal!"

They embraced like long lost family.

Timothy got out as the two parted.

"It is so good to see you. I have what your father has ordered."

Tim heard the man's thick Spanish accent. Sal tossed the cigar on the ground. She put her hand on his shoulder in an air of familiarity. "Sal, I want to introduce you to my new..." she hesitated for a second and went on "... friend. His name is Timothy McCormick."

Tim stuck his hand out. "Good to meet you sir."

Sal returned the favor, and the man's grip forced Timothy to exert quite a bit of return force or have

110

his hand crushed. "Hah! An Irishman. Welcome Timothy!" He laughed.

"What's so funny, Sal?" asked Aella as they entered the building.

"We have quite a worldly group with us three. A Cuban, a Greek and an Irishman all together in this place and time. I know there is a joke here somewhere, but for the life of me cannot think one up... at least not one fit for female company."

Sal's passion for life exuded from his pores. Timothy couldn't but help smile in the man's company. It was as if Sal was given a double portion of the stuff of life.

He motioned the two young arrivals into the warehouse. It took them a moment to adjust to the change in light.

"Here they are."

Sal gestured along the inner wall where twelve rows of concrete disks lay neatly stacked. The concrete disks were about an inch and a half deep, and a foot in diameter. Two holes were drilled in the middle.

"Perfect. Thank you, Sal."

She nudged closer and gave Sal a sideways hug. He pulled a fresh cigar from his shirt pocket. He bit the end, spit it on the floor and lit the stogie.

"For you, I made a few extra... no charge."

She hugged him again. "You're wonderful, Sal. I brought Timothy to load them on the truck. We might hire him. But I want to see if he can pull his weight."

"Are you down here working on the road?" asked Sal.

"Yes."

"You seem a little young to be a vet. Hard times?"

Tim was getting tired of the same question, but he answered politely.

"Yes, it was an opportunity I couldn't pass up."

"Better than the alternative," Aella added.

After turning to Timothy, she said, "Time to start loading."

He looked at the stacks and realized it was not an easy chore. However, he wanted to make a good impression. He grabbed an armful and headed to the truck. She walked with him and pulled the handle, lowering the back so he could load the disks on the bed. He sat and swiveled and then moved forward to put them in the back of the empty bed close to the cab.

He looked at the disks as he carefully laid them down.

"What do you think they are?" Aella asked as she followed him back to the stacks.

"Hmm... buttons for some giant at the end of a beanstalk?"

The two laughed because they did resemble some large buttons. Timothy thought for a while as he grabbed the next stack. His back was already wet with sweat from the first load. By the time he was done, he'd be a wet mess.

"I haven't got a clue, sorry."

"I didn't expect you would."

Aella grabbed one of the buttons. "You remember what my father does for a living?"

"Yes, of course. He dives for sponges. Are these weights?"

"Good guess — but no."

"I give up."

"We have a little inlet where we dock our boats. It's about twenty feet deep. In some spots it's only eight feet deep. The current is light. What we're attempting has been done before by others, but we haven't tried it. You see, sponges are living things. We take a mature sponge and cut it into egg shaped bits. Then we tie them to the disk through these two small holes. We just use regular twine. It disintegrates as the sponges anchor themselves to the concrete disks. They grow on the disks. After a few years, we can harvest them. Because they're on the disks and not anchored to the coral, it's a lot easier to get them on the boat. My father won't have to hunt for more sponges. We can guard these against the sponge poachers who sometimes follow our boat."

"Sounds like a good idea. I hope it works." Timothy finished loading that stack and was heading back for more. Each load seemed heavier than the last, but other than his wet shirt, he wasn't about to let on. His manhood was at stake.

Sal looked on, smoking his cigar. He smiled at Aella and she returned his glance with a smirk. She'd saved the Cuban the trouble of putting the disks on the truck. Sal had a hydraulic lift and Aella knew it, but she chose to keep that detail hidden from Timothy who was wiping his brow as he returned for more.

Only after he'd loaded the last of the disks did he let out a big sigh. His back hurt and his arms were chaffed through his shirt.

"You did a good job. I hope you have enough energy to unload them all. My father is going to be angry with me for picking you up in the first place. You'll have to prove yourself to him. He is much less open than me."

Timothy's muscled ached, but he knew he'd be able to recover on the return trip. He smiled at her and said, "I'm fine."

She knew he was lying, but didn't let on.

With the disks loaded, her business here was done. She hugged Sal.

"I'll see you, soon."

"Take care of yourself 'little storm.'"

He hugged her back.

She and Timothy headed to the truck. With the work and the sun in full force, the day felt like a furnace. Timothy's mouth had gone completely dry.

She started the truck and put it in gear. The vehicle protested and refused to leave as fast as it had arrived.

"So, why did Sal call you 'little storm'?"

Aella smiled. "Because that is my name."

"What?"

"Yes, Aella means 'whirlwind.' My father named me Aella because I always moved in my mother's stomach. He said later that the name stuck because I was always into something and always talking."

"Hah, so you are a storm. I can believe that." Timothy chuckled.

"Don't get any ideas. In Greek mythology, I did battle with Hercules."

Timothy didn't know what to say. His first thought was to ask if she'd won, but thought better of it. He believed she could be a goddess. He imagined that she was in a white toga instead of her white blouse and scarf. He had to stifle the thought, lest his body betray him.

"What does your name mean?"

Timothy paused. He had no clue what Timothy meant. "Well, the McCormick clan runs many generations in Ireland. We have our own tartan, you know."

"Tartan?"

"Yes, it is the pattern which identifies our family."

"A cloth pattern?"

"Yes on our kilts."

"Kilts?" She eyed him up and down. "You have a kilt? Do you wear it at the campsite?"

"God heavens, no!" replied Timothy.

"Well, you don't seem too shy about exposing your legs — or any other part of your person for that matter."

She snickered as she remembered his shenanigans along the shore.

In the warmth of the day, he still felt the heat rise as he blushed. He marveled that she seemed so at ease with him while he seemed so awkward with her. She was in command, and he knew it. Yet, he didn't mind.

They rambled back down the highway, only stopping to refuel. As they passed the campsite,

Timothy said more to himself than to her, "Home sweet home."

"That isn't home, you know."

"Oh – sorry. Yes, for now that is my home."

"Home is where you settle down. Home is where you make a name for yourself. That is just a place. It is a place for people with broken dreams and a lost cause."

"Well, for some. But there are men there who are trying."

"All I've seen are men who are drinking and fighting."

"I don't think you would understand."

Timothy was trying to be polite. He shifted in his chair a little. He was trying to avoid controversy. Aella pressed forward.

"I haven't seen a single person in that camp who wasn't somehow deranged. They've lost touch with reality. When I take the train, they badger me without fail. I hate the train now. I'd take a boat to Key West before I'd take the train, and it is all because of the vets."

Timothy was a little upset. "Look – I'm there with them every day. I see what they're going through. I know what they've seen."

"Yeah, but you're not a vet."

"They're not deranged. Society let them down. It's hard to explain, but I think I understand their point of view."

"This is America. We choose our destiny. We decide our fate."

Timothy shook his head.

"I'm sorry Aella, but I disagree. These men have tons of courage. They stick together as one. They want to better themselves. Yes, I'll admit that a lot of the men are — I don't know — changed by the war. They can't unsee what they've seen. They can't undo what they've done. They drink to forget the purgatory that they now live."

"So why don't they just get a job?"

"It's not that simple. Even though you can't see the enemy — these men are fighting. They're fighting their past. They're fighting for their future, and many are just fighting to stay alive. A lot of these vets haven't had a square meal in months 'till they arrived here. They've been disowned by the very government that took them from their homes in the first place."

Aella didn't respond. She'd been on the receiving end of the vet's rude behavior too many times. She had no idea what was spinning in these men's minds.

"You rarely read about the everyday hero in the newspaper. You only hear about the common criminal."

Timothy wanted to get his point across, but he felt he was failing.

"There are a lot of average Joes out there doing what they are supposed to do. They are *building the highway to the future.*"

Aella laughed. "I'm not sure Matecumbe is the future."

Aella took a turn which led through a mangrove forest. The plant growth was thick and seemed ready to consume the road at any moment. Part of the road had a living tunnel which eclipsed the light. It reminded Timothy of the stories he read about the Amazon when he was young. He'd always wanted to get away to some distant and foreign land. He never knew that such a place existed within the United States.

A bump and splash brought Timothy back to reality as the vegetation opened to a large turnaround. The far end of the loop met a wooden dock with a small shed attached. In a patch of sunshine a weary porch roof wrapped around a dark green house. The shed on the dock seemed in better shape than the house. Nets, buoys and yards of rope lay coiled around mechanical contraptions of all shapes and sizes. A large boat was tied to the dock. Its hull, too, was painted the same color green.

Brizo was painted in bright white letters along the bow. Two men were on the boat, tying up the day's work. A line of sponges hung out to dry. Both men were bare-chested, tanned and muscular. One man was coiling a long hose onto a spool while the other swabbed the deck.

The man working the hose saw the truck and stopped what he was doing. He bounded from the boat onto the deck as he had done a hundred times.

"Aella! You are home."

"Papa, I have the disks. Sal said to say 'hello.'"

The two hugged. Aella had always been her father's little girl. Even now that she was a woman, when she was with him there was a girlish spirit which rose in her. He taught her the love of the water and how to thrive in this challenging land.

Timothy emerged from the truck. His back hurt from the inactivity of the trip. He winced as his feet touched the ground, but he told himself that he wouldn't show any more pain until the evening. There was a bottle of whiskey at night that would help him stave off the muscle cramps.

"Who is this?" asked Aella's father suspiciously.

"This is Timothy McCormick. He helped me load the disks. He has offered to help me unload them."

Aella was nervous. She knew her father wasn't always kind to strangers.

"Timothy, this is my father Nikolas Tethis."

Timothy shook the man's hands. They were rough and calloused even after a full day immerse in water. Timothy made sure to look Nikolas in the eye.

"Pleasure to meet you, sir."

"Welcome. So you've loaded the disks and are here to unload them — yes?" the Greek accent was much thicker with this man than Aella. Timothy had to strain to understand.

"Yes sir."

Nikolas paused as he looked at Timothy from top to bottom. Aella looked at the ground and bit her thumbnail.

"You are doing a lot of labor today. You expect to get paid? Yes?"

"Uh – no sir. I talked to Aella and I'm – well – I'm not getting paid."

"So you work for free?"

"Generally sir — no."

"Most men expect to get paid to work. I expect to get paid for work. So you think that you will get paid?"

Put that way, Timothy felt like a fool.

"I was walking along the road, and Aella picked me up and asked if I would help her."

"So you are good Samaritan. I think you expect to get paid." He looked at Aella.

"My daughter has nothing to offer you. Do you understand me Timothy?"

He repeated himself a little slower.

"My daughter has *nothing* to offer you."

Nikolas ran his hand over his thick black hair.

"I – I understand that sir."

"You are wearing the clothes of someone working on the road. But you are much too young to be a veteran of the war. So why are you here? Why are you not — where are you from?"

"I am from Maryland, sir."

"Why are you not in Maryland, then?"

"I was looking for work."

"It seems you have found the work, though I suspect you will be going hungry if you work for free. I want you to unload these disks and put them on the dock. I will pay you for your service."

Once again Nikolas repeated himself.

"*I* will pay you. Do you understand?"

"Yes sir. Though that is unnecessary."

"I disagree with you, Mr. Timothy McCormick. That is *very* necessary."

"Papa – he is a nice man who..."

Nikolas put his hand up and waved it back and forth.

"The world is full of nice men. I am sure Timothy is a nice man. That is why I will pay him for his work."

Timothy wasn't sure what to do. He wanted to see Aella again but knew the score with her father. With nothing to lose, Timothy spoke up.

"Mr. Tethis, I know that I am just a common worker on the road, but I have been nothing but a gentleman with your daughter all day. I have been looking for work for months and this opportunity to work on the road was my last hope. Should anything better arrive, I'd jump at the chance. But I would rather work for free than not work at all."

"Especially for one as pretty as my daughter."

Timothy felt like this would be the last time he would see either of them, so he set the record straight.

"Yes, your daughter is beautiful."

Nikolas was surprised the man would come out and be so blunt.

"But I made an arrangement with her and not you. I will unload the disks and be on my way. I will honor my contract with her. I have none with you. If you have anything else to say, please be brief because after I get these disks unloaded I must head back to the camp. I'd like to be back before dinner."

He folded his arms and waited for the heated rebuttal. But none came.

Nikolas raised his eyebrows. "I don't understand the logic of a man who would rather work for free with a woman as his boss rather than get paid by a man who opened his wallet. But I will honor your commitment with her, and I'll make sure you get back to the main road."

"Papa," said Aella, embarrassed at her father for being so overbearing.

Timothy turned grabbed the disks from the truck bed. He stacked them and heaved them without showing how heavy they actually were. He passed Nikolas who eyed him up and down again. "You have a bad habit of picking up stray dogs, Aella."

He made sure Timothy heard him.

"He isn't a dog. He's a nice man."

"You have never been careful. He isn't worth your trouble."

"I want to find him work outside the camp. I thought maybe he could work at the fishing lodge."

"Does he have any other skills besides breaking his back? Can he sail? Does he know about diving?"

"No – I suspect he doesn't. But he *is* a hard worker. Papa, look at him. He is working hard."

"I see him. I see him looking at you every few seconds. You need to find a rich man from the fishing lodge — someone like — what is his name..." Nikolas rattled his brain for a name. Finally it came to him.

"James – James Garwood. He is a rich man."

"Ugh!" cried Aella. "He is a married man — or at least I think he is. They are all married or strange."

Nikolas couldn't argue. He shook his head and acknowledged, "This is true."

She shot a glance at the man unloading the disks. "Timothy is — different."

With a skeptical tone Nickolas dared to ask, "Different, how?"

"He has a tender heart, yet he is strong. He works with a good attitude. He is poor. But many good men are poor. You cannot judge a man by his wallet. You have to look into his soul. He has been a gentleman. He doesn't smell like alcohol. Look at him. No, papa, really *look* at him!"

Nikolas felt that he may have been too harsh on the young man. He'd seen the outfit of the vets and made assumptions. He was overprotective of his daughter. He knew that she was someone to be guarded. She had the same radiant face of her mother when he fell in love with her. She was wooed by most men that crossed her path regardless of age or marital status.

120

"Okay. I'll let him on the boat if he needs a job. I would rather have him close to me rather than too close to you. But during the week, he stays with the other vets. I'll pay him five dollars to work on the boat."

Aella snuggled up against her father. "Oh papa, thank you."

Timothy was in agony. His muscles were cramping. Even his face was cramping. He was wearing a half smile and pretending that the work was easy — it wasn't. He could feel his legs rebelling in tight twists of muscle every time he bent down to lay a few disks on the other. He wanted a drink and a hot bath. Tonight he wouldn't have either. As soon as he returned, he would find a tall glass of water and then collapse on his bunk.

Having unloaded nearly all of the disks, he paused a moment to take in the still water and the palm trees. Something jumped in the water sending a series of ever widening concentric circles toward the shoreline. The insects had started to sing their late afternoon song, offering a pulsing rhythm of chirps and buzzes that mingled with the soft lapping of the water along the shore.

Brizo rocked against the dock and squeezed the old tires that were strung off the starboard side of the boat. The homemade "fenders" were truck tires that had gone flat years ago. Nikolas believed in reusing everything.

Aella glanced over at Timothy while he took a moment to reflect on what he saw. She knew what he was thinking. She felt a connection with him the moment she saw his face. Timothy was looking at the water with longing. This was a connection that she held as long as she could remember. She wondered if he had seen the broad ocean when a tempest brewed. She wanted to get to know him, but also wanted to heed her father's caution.

Nikolas proceeded to board Brizo and prepare for another outing tomorrow. While he checked the compressor, making a few adjustments with a wrench, Timothy reorganized the last few disks in neat rows.

Nikolas looked up and nodded. There would never be a "thank you" or "job well done" from this man. The nod was the best compliment anyone would ever get. Having laid a tarp over the compressor, Nikolas jumped onto the dock and approached Timothy.

"I spoke with Aella and we agreed that if you wish to make real money, you can come back tomorrow and help me on the boat."

Though Timothy wanted a day of rest, he would find a way to recover during the week. He wanted to be part of Aella's world. He had no idea if she would be on the boat tomorrow, but even sharing the same objects — being in the same space, was reward enough.

"What time shall I be here?"

"What? You didn't even bargain the price? You want to work for free tomorrow?"

"You said you would pay me. You are an honest man. I trust you. You will pay me what I am worth."

Nikolas paused. He looked into Timothy's eyes to see if he was telling the truth. Nikolas believed in the saying, 'the eyes are the windows to the soul.' He saw an honest man in Timothy's eyes.

"Hmm. Five dollars. That is what an *honest man* pays an unskilled worker."

Timothy wasn't about to bargain.

"What time shall I be here?"

"The boat leaves at six. Be here on time. If you get here late and the boat is gone, you will not get a second chance. I do not want a drunkard on my boat. If I smell whisky on your breath, I'll cut you up and use you to chum the water."

For a second, Timothy thought Nikolas might be telling the truth. But after a pause, Nikolas smiled. Timothy matched his grin and the two chuckled without unlocking eyes.

"I'll be here."

"Papa," said Aella. "Timothy has been working all day. I hate the thought of him walking all the way back to camp. Can I give him a ride?"

Nikolas fidgeted.

"Yes, you can take him back and drop him off on the road. Do not drive the truck into the camp. Unlike your new friend, the vets are a vicious lot. God knows what they would do to a pretty girl. Take him and drop him on the road — do you understand?"

"Yes, papa," she replied as she stifled a grin.

Nikolas had one more offer. "Timothy – you have done a day's work. Would you like some water or a strong drink like whiskey?"

"A glass of water would be wonderful," replied Timothy without even thinking. Only after he answered did Timothy realize the question was a test.

"Aella, be kind enough to get this young man a glass of water."

She stepped into the house which left Nikolas alone with Timothy.

"I want you to know that I have protected Aella all of my life. There is something special about her. I think you see that in her. Many men have come here and made their advances. Some of them have been rich — some poor. If you treat her with respect, you will have my respect. If you do not, I will come after you like a rabid dog. Do I make myself clear?"

"Yes sir."

"Good – I see some fear in your eyes. When Aella returns, you will smile like we have had a pleasant conversation. But know this — the ocean can hide many things...."

The screen door slammed as Aella brought a glass of water.

Timothy smiled and looked at Nikolas who matched the false grin. Aella could see their face and knew something was up. However, she respected her father and didn't press the issue.

123

"Thank you."

Timothy took the cup and drank. The brackish water had never tasted so good. He was getting a headache on top of the other pains that circulated around his body. The refreshing drink quelled the throbbing that was starting to rage in his head. He could drink a pitcher, but chose not to appear greedy.

Timothy returned the empty glass to Nikolas.

"Time to go, young man."

Aella and Timothy got in the truck. She sped toward the main road.

"I know my father seems like a harsh man. He really isn't. Once you get to know him he can be quite charming. He is a hard worker. He built everything you saw back there. He took a machete and cut the opening for this road."

"Oh – I know. He's a sweetheart."

Aella's eyes opened wide, and the two started laughing. She took the main road a little slower than normal because she wanted to spend as much time with Timothy as she could.

It seemed like an instant had passed as they reluctantly arrived at the campsite. She pulled off to the side of the road.

"Thank you for rescuing me from the sharks today."

Aella smiled. "Thank you for helping me haul the disks."

"Will you be on the boat tomorrow?"

"That is up to my father. But I'll try."

"Good. I'll be there."

"... on time."

"Yes," said Timothy. "... on time."

Timothy started to get out of the truck. He paused, turned and gave Aella a peck on the cheek. She smiled and blushed.

He closed the door and said to her through the opened window, "Take care of yourself — 'little storm.'"

He smiled at her. She dropped her head and looked at him with eyes that conveyed a thousand emotions all stirred together.

"Have a good night."

Timothy walked down the road that connected to the campsite. He heard the truck roll away. He'd have another night to himself. The other guys were spending the weekend at Key West. It was a good thing. He was going to get some more water and head to bed early. He had a long walk tomorrow and knew that he may not get to sleep. His head was still swimming in the memory of Aella's beautiful eyes.

It's a very, very dead place because it has died several times. It died as a resort of pirates, then as a house of smugglers and wreckers . . . then as a winter resort boomtown.

- *Robert Frost*

Timothy started walking before sunrise. He wasn't going to be late. In fact, he thought he might be an hour or two early. He really hadn't slept, nor did he want to. The image of Aella's face surfaced, and he held on to every smile, smirk, glance and profile he could. She was the embodiment of beauty. He recalled every detail — the dark hair blowing as she drove the truck and the sweat that built up along her neck as she watched him load the disks.

Sleep was intermittent as he was wrenched from sleep in the middle of the night when his muscles cramped to the point that he cried out in agony. Had his bunk mates not been away in Key West, he would have startled them to their feet with his cry of pain. He rubbed out the charley-horses and eventually got a few hours rest. The desire to join Aella for another day, hour, or minute was enough motivation to get an early start.

The predawn was eerily quiet as he crunched his way down the long road in lower Matecumbe. Even the insects had stopped their undulating chorus. A tern was the only sign of life as it spun a lonely arc in the purple sky. He worried that he wouldn't recognize the turn off the main road in the low light. The landscape repeated itself with a plethora of palm trees, small pines and mangroves. There was no change in the grade of the landscape. Everything looked the same.

It was hard for Timothy to tell which houses were abandoned and which were occupied. He strained to remember the path to the small inlet. He saw the dark opening surrounded by the vines, scrub and trees. It was nearly pitch black and for a moment he thought he'd taken a wrong turn until the path opened to the familiar dock and boat. Nikolas and another man were loading the boat with supplies. The other man was older than Nikolas. This man was carrying a series of long poles with hooks at the end. Nikolas was hauling some small nets with something attached to them.

"Good morning," Timothy called out. The older man waved.

Nikolas stopped what he was doing, stood up straight and bellowed, "Why good morning, Mr. Timothy! I half suspected that you would not be here this morning!"

"Why is that?" asked Timothy as he walked toward the dock.

"Because, the only thing I see at the camp sites are lazy drunk veterans who don't know about a day's work. But then you aren't a veteran. Perhaps that is why you are here — though I wonder if there is not some other reason."

"I am here to work. You said you would pay me a fair wage."

Even in the darkness, Timothy could tell that Nikolas didn't believe a word of it.

"Humph," replied Nikolas. "There is much to do. Get those supplies over there."

Timothy picked up what appeared to be a single pile of sailcloth. Instead, he found a complex outfit. Two gloves fell from his grasp. Under the outfit was a brass helmet. Timothy had read the Jules Verne novel and wondered about those men who could walk under water. As he picked up the various boots, gloves and accoutrements, he realized that he was in the presence of someone who had actually *done* what he'd only fantasized about. Nikolas had walked in the alien world beneath the sea.

For a moment he'd forgotten about the real reason he'd come. As he loaded the gear on the boat, he looked at Nikolas with both awe and respect.

"So you'll be heading under the water to get sponges today?"

Without stopping what he was doing Nikolas answered, "Yes. I will be getting sponges and other things."

"Other things?"

"Yes, there are many spongers. Many of them have left for Tampa. There are some who are still here— some are poachers who follow me to the best locations. Sometimes, I have to waste gas to get them to go away. Still, even the sponges are not enough anymore. I have to look for shells or artifacts that I can sell."

"Artifacts?" asked Timothy. He remembered a number of books from childhood that included pirates and buried treasure.

"Yes, many boats have sunk out there. I can find old planks, bottles, and sometimes even gold coins. I take it to the store, and the tourists sometimes buy — sometimes not. Mostly, I keep the gold coins."

Timothy returned to the dock and got the two brass helmets sitting like golden beheaded skulls looking out to sea. Nikolas grabbed them from him before he even got in the boat. Timothy thought that they must be quite valuable. Nikolas handled them with great care.

"Go to the house and ask Aella to bring the lube jar. She knows which one to get."

"Right away." Timothy shot out of the boat. He headed to the house and gently rapped on the screen door. The main door was open, but it was still too early to see inside.

"Hello? Aella?"

A woman appeared at the door. At first, he thought it might be Aella, but she was older.

"Oh hello... you must be Timothy."

"Mrs. Tethis?"

"Why yes."

She had brown hair — not black. She was older and her frame was thicker, but the same radiant beauty emanated from Aella's mother. She was not Greek like Nikolas. She looked like she was German.

"You can call me Margaret," she continued.

"Oh — um — yes – I need. Err, could you..." Timothy was totally disarmed. He took a breath and continued. "Ma'am, your husband requested the 'lube jar.'"

The woman smiled, "Just a moment."

She headed back into the house. She returned with a large paint can whose top had been beaten closed many times. The lip of the can was caked with what looked to Timothy like bacon grease. Timothy took the pail and started toward the dock.

"Morning!" came the call that startled Timothy so much he almost dropped the pail. He'd barely blinked and Aella whizzed by him. She was wearing a loose dress that anywhere else might have looked scandalous. On her, it billowed around her frame and hugged her in spots that made Timothy's temperature rise. She glanced back tossing her dark hair in the process. She winked, smiled and skipped toward the boat. It was just a second of recognition, but it made Timothy stop in his tracks.

The older Greek man and Nikolas were conversing in a tongue Timothy couldn't recognize. Their Greek bantering was as constant as their synchronized preparations. Aella joined in the conversation that flowed like a symphonic trio. Timothy climbed aboard as the music of the ancient language was passed between all but Timothy.

Aella moved to the older man. She took his hand and said, "Timothy, this is Alexander. He doesn't speak English. He is a friend of the family and helps on the boat. He has been working for us since I was born."

Timothy's name was book-ended between the unintelligible introduction. Alexander shot out his hand. It was leathery and one finger was bent in a way signifying a break that had never been properly reset. His grip was painfully strong, and Timothy tried to return the grip as best he could. The older

Greek sailor nodded as if to signify some unspoken acknowledgement of manhood before returning to the nets.

Nikolas primed the motor with three quick pulls on a cord and started the engine. It roared to life with a billow of black smoke against the pastel sky as if to send out the alarm that it was officially morning.

As he did so, Timothy looked out to the channel toward the open ocean. A large splash disturbed the water.

"Whoa! What was that? Was that an alligator?"

Aella laughed, "No. That was a seal. There are a few of them around here. I don't see as many anymore. Either the sharks get them, or fishermen kill them for their oil. There is a small family along the rocks that jut out of the opening over there." She pointed to a small crag that extended from the thick vegetation. As the boat neared the rocks, he could see the massive dark figure plop back up on the rocks with two others who lay still, undisturbed by the boat's presence. Timothy looked back as they passed by the seal family. The small wake of the slow boat sent small wavelets lapping against the rock. Timothy was mesmerized that any creature with fur could exist in the Florida heat.

Nikolas gunned the motor as they headed to open water and cut the wheel sharply to port. Timothy grabbed the nearby post. Aella and Alexander looked at him and smiled. Just as quickly he turned the boat back and did a quick "S."

"What's he doing? Is he drunk?" asked Timothy.

"No. He is avoiding the reef."

There were no markings warning of shallow water. The other three on the boat instinctively knew the underwater topography. The coral outcrops could rip a boat's bottom and sink it in minutes. Timothy looked over the rail and saw a hint of darkness against the blue. Anyone not familiar with the coral could never get into the inlet without severe damage.

"We'll be helping father get his suit on."

As if Alexander understood the young woman's English, he stood up and took the wheel.

Nikolas came back and took off his shirt. Underneath he had a thin tight undergarment that exposed his stiff muscular frame. He sat down on a wooden bench. Aella got the lard can and pried it open with a screw driver.

"Get some of this and start spreading it on his arms, like this." She grabbed a handful and started massaging his arms, covering his elbows and armpits. Timothy felt a little self conscious as he stroked the man's arm with the slippery substance. Timothy's mother had always called bacon grease lard, but this was more like a petroleum jelly. Aella moved to his neck and applied the slick substance there. She then started applying some to his legs.

Alexander locked the wheel, came back to join the other three in the ritual. The older Greek then hoisted the thick pant legs into position and the two helped Nikolas into the unwieldy outfit. Alexander grabbed the weighted shoes and started lacing up the boots over the canvas legs.

"We put the lard on papa to keep him from chafing. The sea water is terrible on the skin, and if we didn't put that on, the suit would turn him into a bloody raw mess."

The sun rose above the horizon spilling golden sunlight onto the glistening water. It was refreshing to Timothy to be away from the smell of the land and all of the bugs that had pockmarked his body. The ocean breeze felt wonderful the boat dipped into a wave sending a cloud of mist that ran from bow to stern.

Alexander returned to the boat and made a few adjustments to their course. Timothy wondered how he knew where he without land as a frame of reference.

After nearly twenty minutes of finagling gloves, boots and the outer skin of the diver, Alexander raised the helmet and placed it on the now heavily sweating Nikolas. The Galeazzi helmet was fastened to the suit with a series of wing nuts. Three portholes provided him the window to the world which had been Nikolas' livelihood for the past thirty years. The helmet sported the dual images of Italy on one side of the manufacturer's plaque and Florida on the other. Nikolas would have rather had Greece emblazoned on the shiny brass dome, but Italy was close enough.

"This seems so cumbersome. How can anyone get anything done in an outfit like this? It looks like he'd sink to the bottom like a stone and be stuck there."

"I have never been in the suit, but papa tells me that this is his uniform for the undersea world. He can move easily. You see, he has to have the weight on his boots, otherwise he would float to the surface."

"Really? With all of this he's wearing?"

"Yes, The ocean is strange that way. You need the weight because your body is built to float. You remember those seals you saw when we headed out?"

"Yes."

"Well, they are cumbersome on land. They have to skirt along their belly. They grunt and roll around on land. They look very uncomfortable, but in the water they glide through it like a fish. They can turn and dive with a push of their tail. What seems bulky, big and uncomfortable on land works well underwater."

Alexander headed to the wheel, cut the motor and dropped anchor.

"Help me hook the net on papa's back."

The two maneuvered a large ring with two brass projections onto a plate along Nikolas' back. The rods slipped into two holes. As Nikolas stood, Alexander handed him a knife and a long spear.

"Are those for the sharks?" asked Timothy, now timid and fearful of the creatures.

132

She laughed. "No. He uses those to cut and load the sponges into his net."

The floorboard clunked as Nikolas took a few baby steps toward the opening along the port side of the boat. Alexander hooked up the hose to the back of the helmet. Timothy moved in to help but Alexander pushed him away.

"Only Alexander is allowed to hook up the air hose," said Aella. "This is papa's lifeline. He trusts no one else."

"Not even you?"

"No. I am a woman. He thinks that is only a job for a man. You will know you've gained his utmost trust if he lets you connect the air hose."

Aella moved toward the bow. She paused along the post by the overhang and slipped out of the dress that she was wearing. Timothy looked on and swallowed hard. She was wearing a bathing suit that exposed her phenomenal frame. She was shapely in the red swimsuit. Her legs were long like the Athenian goddess of her ancestors. She smiled back at him. Only then did he realize that his mouth was open in stunned amazement. He clamped it shut and Alexander chuckled at the scene.

Aella Tethis turned the brass crank to prime the motor. She pulled the choke in a position for starting. Timothy couldn't stop looking at the beauty bent over the machine. She took care to make sure everything was in order. This compressor would supply air for her father. She checked the oil, air filter, and a myriad of other smaller details to ensure its proper operation.

Timothy couldn't take his eyes of Aella. The bust line of the swimsuit was cut way too low for her father's approval, and the covering that ran below the hips revealed a set of slender legs that many movie stars would envy. Her dark hair was pulled off her neck and beads of sweat ran in small droplets following the wonderful curves of a woman endowed with a beauty that made the Gods envious. She defied ever trying to maintain ivory

133

skin. Her Greek complexion coupled with the Florida sun made that impossible. Often, when not helping her father, she would take an afternoon and sneak a boat to an empty hideaway and swim without the bathing suit. The sun performed its magic on her skin while she explored the shallow waters off Plantation Key.

Aella tweaked the fuel/air ratios of the compressor until she was satisfied everything was ready. The pistons on the machine glided in rhythm, sending the precious air to her father.

Nikolas could feel the motor through the soles of his lead filled boots. This was his cue. He jumped into the water and as a mass of bubbles erupted back to the surface.

Timothy turned his gaze away from Aella to the man who could be seen descending to the sandy ocean floor. Though they'd traveled for twenty minutes and the shore was but an indistinct pencil line, Timothy was startled to be able to see with such clarity to the bottom. Surrounded by the brilliant turquoise blue, he could see the fish moving around dark spots that dotted the sandy floor.

A small breeze picked up which caused the boat to swing on the anchor line.

"Pay out the hose line," said Aella.

Timothy grabbed the line and started dumping it overboard.

"Not too much. That's enough. You don't want to have the line rubbing against the coral. Make sure you only pay out enough so papa can move freely. If he comes back, haul in the hose. Try not to let it scrape the rail."

She joined him watching the man thirty feet down as he cut pieces of the large barrel sponges. With a flick of the pole a piece would fly off. He would then spear it as it floated and put it in the net behind his back. It was a methodical surgery that he'd performed with practiced efficiency.

"Papa came to America in 1900 when he heard that the Florida coast had gold and silver washing up on its shores. Though it turned out to be an exaggeration, he used his skills with breath holding to plumb the waters in search of sunken treasure. He soon found out that the gold was scarce, but sponges were plentiful and in high demand. It wasn't long before he had his own boat, and he soon was obtaining the latest technology which would allow him to remain underwater for hours."

"Really?" said Timothy intrigued.

Aella was proud of her father as she watched him. Timothy imagined her as a young girl, bent over the rail as she was now with her elbows on the rail and her chin in her hands, looking down at her father.

"Starting with a diving bell, he explored the reefs and shallows up and down the Florida Keys. He partnered with an import/export business with Andros Sofokleous, a distant relative who traded anything. Andros engaged equally in legal and illegal trade, with the indifference found in a ruthless thug. Nikolas distanced himself from the seedier practices of Andros, choosing instead to focus on objects from the sea."

"Papa made a name for himself. At one point, he had three boats and a number of men working for him, but then the sponge trade died here. Some of his men tried to steal the business away by poaching the sponges. We fell on hard times. He almost lost *Brizo*, but used every cent to keep her."

She patted the railing of the boat.

"Only Alexander stayed by his side. The others went to Tampa, or left Florida to find work elsewhere."

She payed out more of the air hose as Nikolas slowly moved to another sponge.

Alexander looked as the two stood close together. Nikolas had instructed the older man to keep an eye on the couple. He rolled a cigarette and lit it up. He didn't understand a word they were saying, but could tell by their body language that the two were destined for love.

"Help me load the pool."

"Pool?"

"Yeah." In the middle of the boat was a deep opening. She grabbed two buckets with lines tied to the handles. Normally, Alexander would have joined Aella in this operation, but he saw the two love birds had things well in hand.

The two dipped the buckets over the rail and hauled the water to the boat, dumping it in the opening.

"We don't fill it up all the way — only about half way. We keep the sponges here. We clean them a little so they don't smell foul. When we get back, we'll cut and clean them some more."

Alexander rose. He grabbed a pole and connected it to a hook. He extended it over the bow. Anticipating what would come next he moved to the bow and waited.

The sponge net was full. Alexander used the pole to unhook the ring on his back.

Nikolas pulled out a leather pouch he'd stored around his weighted belt. The diver held it over his head. With a large exhale he filled the leather pouch and connected it to the net.

The sponge filled net rose to the surface as the leather balloon assisted it to the surface. Alexander leaned so far over Timothy thought he would have to pull the man out of the water. With a quick flip of his wrist he grabbed the net and pulled it to the boat. The three helped pull the dripping sponges out of the net. They carefully placed them in the pool to keep them wet. Aella cleaned off the living portion of the sponges in the buckets. She showed Timothy what to do and the two continued the process.

Alexander tied a quick bowline with a weight and tossed the net back into the water. Nikolas took a few slow deliberate steps and retrieved the net. The suit would be cumbersome for most but Nikolas was soon back to slicing and loading the net with more of the sponges.

"When my mother and father married there was no school, no hospital, or grocery store unless you were willing to trek northward to Homestead. Papa almost lost everything, including his life when, in 1908, a hurricane of devastating power raked across the keys. He awoke to the sound of the wind howling like a ghost. He ran out of the cabin to find the surf cresting over the small rise, inundating the mangroves. His boat was totally lost, along with the short dock — another sacrifice to the Gods. Papa had never seen such power in the weather. He vowed to be more careful and heed the warnings of the locals. He learned some of the tricks they used to determine when a storm was coming. He bought a plot of land from the Russell family and built a sturdy house, choosing to run pilings into the coral for support. He bought a bigger boat, and began to expand his operation, hiring some of the best workmen from the railroad."

"What about you," asked Timothy. "What was your life like?"

"As a child I learned to sail, operate a power boat, fix just about everything mechanical and revel in the paradise and remoteness of this unique place. At an early age my feet became very rough because I was always running barefoot over the hot sand and rocks."

"Mother taught me English and mathematics, while papa taught me to speak Greek and taught me its history. Every opportunity I got, I would join papa on the boat. Sometimes, I stowed away instead of staying with mother. Papa would be mad but never for very long."

Alexander stood up moved to Aella and spoke.

"It's time to add more gas to the compressor," she translated. She went down the hatch and returned with some rags. "Wet these in the bucket."

Timothy did what he was told. "What are these for?"

"If we spill any gasoline I need you to sop it up quickly. If we spill anything, it clogs the intake valve. We don't want papa breathing the fumes."

Alexander pulled out a big metal canister with a large nozzle. Timothy stood close to the old man. Though Timothy had never seen him take a drink, he could smell the alcohol on Alexander's breath. It rose above the smell of the gasoline and mixed with it. The old man opened the cap and poured. He had to stand on his toes because of the gravity feed of the fuel system. As he tipped it, a few drops missed the opening. Timothy heard the hiss and quickly applied the rags. They sizzled as he suffocated the fumes. The old man pulled out the nozzle and a few more drops hit the engine. Timothy moved in and took care of them as well.

The day repeated itself as each played their role in caring for the man in the water and the sponges in the boat. The only surprise was a net with two large grouper. Alexander looked at them as they flopped around on the deck. He took them and put them in with the sponges.

After being submerged for hours, Nikolas tugged on the air hose three times, signaling that he was coming up. Timothy felt like he was getting in the way of the routine. Alexander and Aella knew what to do and when to do it. The only contribution to getting Nikolas on board was when he and Alexander grabbed Nicolas and hauled the weighted diver up onto the deck. Alexander twisted the wing nuts on the helmet and carefully pulled it over Nikolas' head.

Nikolas leaned back and took a long draw of air. He shook his head which was wet from sweat. He rubbed his face with a gloved hand. Aella unlaced one of the gloved hands and before she could get to the other, Alexander handed him a flask. He took a long draw and said a few words of thanks before uttering instructions in his native tongue. Alexander went to the cockpit and started the motor.

They were off to another site.

An intelligent man is sometimes forced to be drunk to spend time with his fools.
-    *Hemingway*

Harry was awake before the others. He had more of a nap than a night's sleep. His head had been spinning from the night of whiskey and rum. He woke once with his heart racing and his body covered in sweat. Harry forced himself back to sleep rather than face the possibility of retching in the author's home.

After Hemingway invited them to his house, Harry had pretty much forgotten the rest of the night as the alcohol took over. The house was fabulous. He remembered finding an overstuffed chair that faced a number of deer heads. After that Harry woke with his head craned back, a sore throat from heavy snoring, and a room of passed out bunk mates. Hemingway was nowhere to be found. With only a few hours sleep, Harry still felt the drunken haze and lethargy of its effects.

He stepped out to the courtyard and headed toward town. Harry knew that some fresh air and a short walk would help drown the last vestiges of the drunken coda. A few cars rolled down the road, but the place, for the most part, was abandoned. It was Sunday and Harry knew there was a Catholic church service on the other side of town.

Salvation was not on his list of things to do this morning. He hoped there was a place he could get some eggs that would drown the cotton mouth and a cup of coffee that would clear his head.

Along the water, the boats bobbed and rocked with the gentle surf. A few men were out making repairs on their vessel. The sailors looked much like Harry. They had lived a watery version of the hard life. The grease on their hands and creases in their face told the story of hours on the water only to return without a single salable fish. Their hands spoke of days when the motors wouldn't crank or started with a black plume of ominous smoke.

"Farming is farming," thought Harry as he kicked a small rock down the road. He conjectured that when the fish were plentiful, the market price fell. When fish were scarce, the struggle to meet demand made the fisherman's life a never ending battle. He looked back at those men with a sense of kinship. His family farm was gone. He'd left it for this strange place and traded one kind of hard work for another.

Harry felt that the struggle of farming or fishing was bound with the fight for survival. Though he'd read the Bible and gone to church as a boy, he never subscribed to the notion that struggling was part of the path to redemptive glory.

He'd seen too much senseless suffering for that. He thought about his beatings that he got as a boy. No, God had nothing to do with the suffering of man.

But the new environment provided new opportunities that farming never could. Harry smiled remembering what he could of last night's revelry with a famous author. Papa Hemingway, too, was broken having seen the carnage and blindness that war creates. The author joined their ranks in the war that continued in each vet's head. Hemingway, his new friend, would write about the pain as a way to exorcise himself of those demons that haunted soldiers' dreams. Writing was Papa's redemption. Harry thought he might try to read one of the man's novels. It was a unique circumstance to know the man behind the pen.

Up ahead he heard some men calling out. The sounds of saws and hammers broke the tranquility of the morning. Back in his home town, no one except the dairy farmers worked on the Sabbath. He turned down Caroline Street and saw a truck filled with two-by-fours. Two men were working on a rooftop. Two more men were at street level replacing rotten floorboards on the porch of a baby blue two story home. The home had a covered porch on each floor. Along the second story a man was strapped to the post as he leaned far out over the sidewalk, his feet barely resting on the grooves that decorated the post. The can of paint dangled behind him threatening to land on the head of any unsuspecting passer by.

As Harry approached the workers, he realized they wore the same uniform issued to all of the vets in Matecumbe.

"Hey there!" yelled Harry.

"Hey!" replied the man strapped to the post. One of the men repairing the porch looked up and gave a nod and wave. Harry approached the two men at the stairs.

"Well, looks like Uncle Sam has you working on Sunday! Up north at Matecumbe they give us the weekend off."

"We're gettin' paid double on the weekends, so we work through as much as we can. Half the crew don't give a shit, but this team knows a good hard earned dollar." The man placed a nail on the newly replaced board and sunk it in two swings. He repeated the feat and then stopped to engage the stranger.

"M'name's Harry." He stuck out his hand.

"Elijah – and this Tommy."

The other man tipped his sweat ringed hat.

"I didn't even know they had vets working this far south. I'm part of the crew paving the road."

"You mean paving *the way to the future*," Elijah grinned and sent an elbow to his buddy, Tommy.

"At least that's what all the billboards say."

"I'm sorry?"

"Yeah – all ya gotta do is look around, and you'll see 'em. Fliers from Julius Stone. He's made a ton of 'em."

"I haven't..."

"Keep walkin' pal, and you can't miss 'em. Half of 'em are layin' in the road. Storm came through four days ago and tore some of 'em down."

"I'll keep an eye out. So what's the government doing fixing houses?" asked Harry.

"Well, seems Mr. Stone hand selected some of us with previous construction experience to come down here to keep the trash and stink off the roads. But he also got us doing some of his own handyman chores. Got three crews workin' on somethin' or other around here."

"So you're telling me, Elijah, that this Julius Stone guy is in the government, and he's having you make repairs?"

"Yep, you got it. We're really not supposed to say, but Stone gets us to fix up his houses. Stone sells 'em, and we get a little kickback in addition to what they're payin' us. So we get five dollars a day, and then we get extra on the side. But we were told we can't tell anyone, so don't go spreadin' the word."

Tommy gave Elijah a stern look as if to say, "You idiot. Keep your trap shut."

"How many houses does this 'Mr. Stone' have?" asked Harry.

"Hell if I know. Alls I know is he keeps us hopping from place to place. The guy is never here, but he is still a hard ass. He's hired some of the vets as foremen to crack the whip. Good thing though, if I need anything, even if it is something out of the ordinary, you can bet it'll show up on the next train."

"We were redoing one of the houses down the road, and we needed a new capital..."

"Capital?" Harry interrupted.

"Yeah – it's the top piece on a column on the porch. This house ain't got one, but it..."

"Okay – I get the idea."

"Well, I pull one that ain't rotted away and send it to Atlanta on the train. Three day — *three days* — later we got four of 'em." Elijah pulled a pack of Lucky Strikes from his pocket and lit one up.

"Woodwork, ironwork, nails, boards, paint — you name it. It's here. How about you?" Elijah took a long draw on his cigarette. He closed one eye as he blew out the smoke through the side of his mouth as a matter of courtesy for Harry.

"I fix machines. Mostly the big ones."

"What? Like big trucks?"

"Nah – mostly specialty machines. We got some really big cranes that cut and haul rock for the bridges."

Harry was hoping that Elijah would offer him a cigarette. He didn't, so Harry hunted his pockets for his pack. He found it in the back pocket. They'd been flattened, but were still useable. Elijah handed his cigarette for a light.

"What I heard is — you all ain't gonna finish the road."

"What?"

"Yeah – that's what I heard," said Elijah

"I ain't heard anything like that. We've been working all day building the bridge and paving the road." Harry scratched his head. This was news to him.

"Seems our government is gettin' some flack about you boys on the road."

"Nah – we're workin' harder than ever."

"You ain't the only one. They got a huge crew at the hotel."

"Stone own that one, too?" asked Harry.

"Yep. He's buyin' up properties so fast that people are just raising the prices and putting them on the market 'cause they know he'll pay top dollar."

"So I guess we'll be finishing that road, so Mr. Stone can fill up that hotel," replied Harry.

Elijah stood up, went to the truck and pulled off another piece of wood.

"Well, I gotta go find me some breakfast."

"There's a little dive about a half mile down the road. You can get eggs or grid fish. Whatever you want."

Harry thanked the men,waved and walked on. He wondered what the construction workers knew

that he didn't. That thought was quickly replaced
with the smell of bacon.

Key West
Where the tropics really begin
There is all-year fishing
There has never been a frost
You can go to sea in your car
- *Julius Stone Florida Keys Brochure*

It was Sunday, but he still chose to have a skeleton crew at the office. He was dealing with the crisis. Julius Stone took the presidential memo balled it up and hurled it in the general direction of the trash can. Sarah Beller, Stone's secretary, opened the door and let out a muffled cry as the paper came flying her way.

"Oh!" Her startled look faded when she realized what was coming at her. "Mr. Stone, a Mr. Sheldon is here to see you now."

"Fine, fine — send him in." She could see that Stone was in a foul mood and opted to back out of the door rather than turn around for fear that another wad of paper might hit her in the back of the neck.

"Dammit, dammit, dammit," cursed Stone under his breath.

Ray Sheldon entered the room. He held his hat in his hand. Sheldon never owned a suit, but he did have a Sunday white shirt he rarely wore. He'd donned the shirt, which rubbed his neck raw. It was the only part of his body that wasn't calloused from his hard life as a foreman.

Sheldon had worked on road projects for the last thirty years. He only had his work boots, which were dusty and scraped. He hoped he wouldn't scuff up the woodwork in Stone's pristine office. Ray Sheldon was part of the Works Commission until Stone requested he be transferred to the Federal Emergency Relief Administration Highway One road project.

"Have a seat, Mr. Sheldon." There was no handshake. Stone gestured to the chair.

Sheldon wasn't a fan of bureaucracy and hated being told what to do. He could feel his blood pressure rise.

"I'm putting you in charge of the Keys road project, Sheldon."

It was already a done deal. Sheldon knew this coming in. He still had to fill out the paperwork in the secretary's office but He was looking forward to heading to the Keys. He was going to try and squeeze in a quick trip to Key West as a kind of honeymoon for his new bride.

"Well, my history speaks for itself. I'll get the job done right."

"I don't care about getting the job done right. In fact, I could give a shit if it gets done at all."

This stunned Sheldon. "But – I thought you were the one that…"

Stone interrupted, "Yes – this was my project. I sent the men down there. But they're nothing but a bunch of psychopathic lazy asses. Seems their griping got to the newspapers."

Sheldon nodded. He'd heard a rumor of the poor conditions. He knew a couple of men died.

Stone's eyes went big as if to say, "You don't get it?"

There was a moment of awkward silence before Stone clarified, "You get it? The reporters got wind of the conditions and interviewed some of the men. This started swaying the political climate. Now the reporters were trying to lay blame on the Administration for the woes of the men down there. Instead of being a disciplined work force, they're saying we sent them down there to get rid of them."

Sheldon tapped his hat on his leg. He hated small talk and chose to get to the point. "Well didn't you?"

Stone chuckled. "Well, let's just say it was a 'social experiment.' We got men building a camp in the Appalachians called 'Shangri La' and the men there are living in the cabins they built, under a

147

canopy of mature maples and oak trees. No one knows about these men. You know why? Because the men in the Appalachians understand a hard day's work."

Stone was frustrated with himself for even bringing up the conversation. "Seems hard labor isn't for the bonus Army after all. Florida is a train wreck."

Stone leaned forward and rested his arms on his desk. With the tone of an angry dog he said, "Look Sheldon – the president told me I have to get all of the vets out of there by November. We're shutting down the highway project."

Stone knew that the failed highway project would mean his dream of the straightaway to Key West wasn't going to happen. The houses he'd purchased would be sold at a fraction of the cost had the road been completed. He'd already started his contingency plan by investing in the next great American tourist attraction – Cuba.

Sheldon could feel himself go flush. He was a man of discipline. He was rarely wrong. He knew he could whip the men into shape. The other two who were running the operation, Ghent and Cutler, didn't possess the skills and fire needed to complete the project. Though he wouldn't say this to Stone, Sheldon thought he might be able to finish the highway by November. He wasn't just going to let the men drink themselves to death and destroy this opportunity.

Stone continued, "We're sending some social workers down there to assess the situation. Those men are nothing but a bunch of drunks — drunks I say!"

Sheldon thought, "Social workers — touchy feely types. I know how to get the men to buckle down."

"In the meantime, I need you to make the best of things down there. Keep them healthy, happy and safe."

"Thank you, sir. I'll do just that."

The two men rose and Sheldon left the room, closing the door behind him.

"Dammit," Stone swore under his breath again. He was already concocting a way to unload the properties he'd acquired and shift the funds to Cuba. He wanted to keep all of this off the books to avoid taxes.

Sheldon headed down the steps of the government building. Parked illegally at the bottom of the stairs was his burgundy 1932 Cadillac V-12 Convertible Phaeton. The distinct leather brackets on the spare tires held the rear view mirror mounts. The multiple headlights and the general sheen of the vehicle turned heads. It was one of the few luxuries that Sheldon permitted himself. Sitting in the passenger seat was a Gayle Colvert, a girl of twenty-seven years. She had dark hair curled at the bottom. She wore a white dress with a rose print. She was almost half his age but Sheldon felt no regret. He never did.

It was a fleeting thought, but this day was the first anniversary of his first wife's death. As he took his place in the driver's seat, he turned to Gayle and said, "Let's get married. We're heading to the Keys."

She laughed, reached over and hugged him. As he drove away, she still clung to him and giggled as he sped down the road.

The palm trees clatter in the stiff breeze like the bills of the pelicans. The tropical rain comes down to freshen the tide-looped strings of fading shells

-   *Florida – Elizabeth Bishop*

It was dark by the time they secured the boat, unloaded the sponges, and stored the gear. Nikolas had few words as he headed into the house for a quick bite. Tomorrow he would repeat the laborious process. Alexander finished swabbing the deck and went inside as well.

A crescent moon backlit the silver and blue clouds moving slowly above the silhouette of palm trees. The water reflected the moon's curl. Small ripples inherited the luminescence sparking against the ink black sea.

Timothy was surprised how tired he'd become after a day on the water. He was able to offer only peripheral assistance, but the haze in his head reassured him that he would be the loudest snoring member of his bunk once he and his bunk mates returned to the camp.

"Thank you," said Aella, reappearing after she had gone into the house to change. She emerged wearing a white dress that appeared to be lit by the power of moonlight. In one hand she carried a kerosene lamp. In the other she had a sandwich and glass of tea on a small tray. "I know this isn't much, but it will tide you over until breakfast."

"Thanks," he took the glass and sandwich. She lay the tray on the ground. He took a bite. "Oh... this is good." He didn't know if it was chicken or turkey. He was so hungry that he didn't care.

The two walked slowly on the dock.

"I know we've only known each other for two days, but I feel like I've known you my whole life." Timothy wanted to say more, but he felt it was too soon. The last thing he wanted to do was to jeopardize their relationship by being too forward.

He mustered the courage to say, "This weekend has been a whirlwind. I wish I didn't have to go back to the camp."

They stepped up onto the dock and walked to the end. Aella sat, dangling her bare feet in the cool water. Timothy set his glass on the doc, took a few steps back, took off his shoes and quickly plunged them in the water. He didn't want to offend her with the smell. These were the only shoes he had, and the long hot summer Florida days took their toll.

The water was refreshingly cool. They both sat in silence as they drew circles in the water with their toes. It wasn't an awkward moment like so many silences between new acquaintances. This was a time of shared peace and tranquility. The songs of the natural evening serenaded the couple.

Aella finally spoke, "It was a good day."

Timothy replied, "Yes. In so short a time, so much has changed. I love this place. You showed me something about Matecumbe that I never knew. And you, Aella..."

He searched for the words, but she stopped him.

"I think I know what you are going to say. But I want you to realize that when the road is done, you'll be gone. It breaks my heart to think that you'll be living somewhere else, and I'll never see you again. I don't want to start something that we both can't finish."

He leaned back, feeling the daggers in her words. His emotions were running at an all time high, and he ached for her. Yet, he still kept his presence of mind to speak intelligently.

He wondered if she felt as he did.

"Up until this weekend, I didn't want to stay. Now I don't want to leave. I'll never be like your father or Alexander, but all of you have shown me something that I'll never forget. No, I don't fit in around here — at least not yet. But something lured me here, and I can't help but believe in fate."

She smiled, leaned back and placed her hand overtop his. It was warm and soft. She turned toward him and smiled. The moonbeams caressed her face and illuminated her beautiful smile. He fought the instinct to kiss her.

Reading his mind, she replied, "I think you just need time. Things change. We just need to be patient."

We have to distrust each other. It is our only defense against betrayal.
- *Tennessee Williams*

Ray Sheldon didn't waste time tearing into the leadership.

"Look – you've built railroads and I've built highways. It's what I know. We're gonna finish thing by November. You gotta get your men off their ass and start tarring. We've got a deadline."

"I'm sorry, Mr. Sheldon, It can't be done. If we could double the civilian team, then maybe..."

Ed Sheeran was trying to be as polite as possible. He was insulted by Sheldon's intolerance of the circumstances.

"It is simply a matter of application of force and proper leadership. If you don't feel up to the task, I'll find someone to replace you."

Ray Sheldon said this not to demean the elder Sheeran but to apply some incentive of his own. Sheeran however hadn't felt good about Sheldon's appointment. He'd heard he was a dictator and knew of his threatening tactics.

"We have to think about the men. They're not just a bunch of coolies. I don't have the authority to..."

Once again Sheldon interrupted. "I have the authority. No – I *am* the authority. Starting tomorrow, I'll iron this thing out. In the mean time, you think about how you're going to manage your teams. We're finishing by November – come hell or high water."

Sheeran turned away before bringing the conversation to blows. Under his breath he said, "Before this is over we'll see a little of both – I'm sure."

Ghent assembled the men after the evening chow. He'd warned them that this was a mandatory meeting, but still many of the men had left to carouse or find a fight somewhere. The man standing next to Ghent was red faced and seemed awkward standing up there. He fidgeted with the keys in his pocket, jangling them and rolling them around. He hated any kind of public speaking.

"Gentlemen, this is my replacement. I want to introduce Ray Sheldon. He'll be taking over while I manage the project from the mainland. I want you to show him the same respect you've shown me. He's got the skill to complete this project on time and under budget. I'll be heading to Hollywood, Florida where I'll oversee the operations and be in touch with Ray, and members of the highway commission."

The men clapped politely.

"Thank you gentlemen," Ray's voice was too loud. He cleared his throat and continued a little more subdued. "I want you to know that I have years of experience here in Florida working on roads. I know how to get the job done — and done right. Some say I'm a taskmaster, but I know what it takes."

The last thing Sheldon was going to do is tell the men that the whole operation was going to be shut down. He wouldn't even tell his close subordinates. That time would come. Sheldon had his own agenda. He was going to finish the highway.

"Gentlemen, I'm glad to be part of the team. We have a daunting task ahead of us. I understand that the civilians are at the worksite at 7:30 and you don't arrive until 8:30. Is that correct?"

There were nods and some murmuring as Sheldon continued.

"We are veterans of the war, and we need to show them that we deserve respect. So, starting tomorrow, we get there the same time they do. No exceptions. I don't care if you're in charge of a digger or a broom. We are all going to shape up. We know what it took to get the job done in the field. Consider the highway to the future as the front lines."

Sheldon felt that he had the crowd, now. He was demonstrating his skills to engage the men in the military discipline they so long desired. The crowd, however, felt quite differently. Ray Sheldon thought the murmuring was approval — it was not.

Sheldon continued, "Along with that, I'm temporarily suspending the sale of beer and alcohol on the premises. I don't care what you do on the weekend. But while I am in control, we're not putting up with a bunch of drunks on the worksite. It is a danger to your personal health and the health of project."

The murmuring got a little louder. Some of them hissed. Now Sheldon was attacking the one thing that made their jobs palatable.

"I expect the best from you men. Thank you."

Ghent stepped forward. He didn't realize that Sheldon would be making any changes. The news about drinking was a shock. Ghent had heard rumors that Sheldon had come to close the place down. The word was unofficial, but he knew his move out was part of that deal. Now Sheldon was making drastic changes only hours after arriving.

It was awkward, but he had to support Sheldon lest his dissent foment a mutiny. "These are good words. Thank you, Mr. Sheldon. Any questions?"

A voice from the back asked, "What are you going to do about the toilets? You making any improvements around here?"

Sheldon hadn't inspected the campsites. He'd only inspected the job sites.

"I'll make sure they are usable."

Harry stood up.

"What about the hurricanes?"

Sheldon stepped forward. "How many hurricanes have you seen this year?"

A few of those who'd been around said, "None..."

Sheldon responded, "...problem solved."

Sheeran followed up, "We're in hurricane season. These things crop up. You gotta..."

155

Sheldon interrupted and pointed at Harry, "You there, are you part of Sheeran's group?"

Harry answered, "Yep."

"See here... I am an expert on the weather. I've seen a hurricane or two. Have you?"

Harry started turning red and sat down, "... no sir. But like Ed said..."

Sheldon didn't let him finish. "I have provisions for the hurricane. If one hits we all meet here at the mess hall. We'll go in an orderly fashion to the train station where a train will pick us up."

It sounded like part of a corporate plan, but Sheldon was improvising.

He pointed to Sam Cutler. Cutler, a stickler for processes and protocols did a double take. Cutler had been working with Ghent on formulating a hurricane evacuation plan using the company motor pool. The train was all news to him.

He didn't like being out of the loop. Cutler monitored the weather and was in charge of notifying the leaders. It was his responsibility to get the evacuation rolling. If he didn't know the new plan, how was he supposed to account for the men?

"We have a train on standby in Miami, isn't that right Mr. Cutler."

"Umm...," came Cutler's immediate response. "I don't..."

"In fact, I believe we have two. I'll double check that." He gave Cutler a nod as if to say, 'we'll deal with this later.'

Ed Sheeran asked, "How long will it take to get one of these 'stand by' trains down here."

Sheldon answered, "Four hours — tops."

No one believed him. There were some guffaws at the statement. They'd been on the rails heading north and south. Inevitably somewhere along the way the train stopped. If they were heading to Miami or Hollywood they'd need to replenish the locomotive. Everything took time: getting a head of steam, linking the cars, checking the rails in the city, and the odd tree or cow that found its way along the track. All of these and more chalked up at least six hours from start to finish. Yet Sheldon played his speech as if he'd rehearsed the whole scenario. Cutler was taking notes and no one else believed the new boss. Most of the men stopped listening when they found out that their new boss just took away their beer.

I think we consider too much the good luck of the early bird and not enough the bad luck of the early worm.
        - Franklin D. Roosevelt

Harry was working on the pneumatics of one of the great beasts that cored out the coral. The previous night's introduction to Ray Sheldon put him in a bad mood.

He climbed the arm of the leviathan. Two large wrenches, screw drivers, clamps, and some larger parts were tied to his belt with twine. They dangled and hit structure with a clank as he maneuvered ever closer to the leaking pipe. He'd wrapped his hands with spare rags because the metal was too hot to hold on to with bare skin for any period of time. He left his fingers free, so he could hand tighten some of the bolts as he made the fix.

It wasn't long before he finished the work and started scrambling through the iron grid work. Sheeran watched amazed at how quickly a man of Harry's age could maneuver down the massive arm. Harry hopped to the ground and met Sheeran.

"She's ready to go Colonel," said Harry.

"We're missing a man. Krebs is nowhere to be found."

"You want me to hunt him down for ya?" asked Harry. He brushed the sweat from his brow that left a swath of black grease on his forehead.

"I'll call the mess hall and medical tent. If he's not there I'll check his bunk. Maybe he's sick."

"Sure. Take my truck." Sheeran handed him the keys.

After Harry made the calls, he headed over to the camp.

It wasn't uncommon for the vets to go AWOL after a drinking binge. Stuart Krebs was a heavy drinker and considered an unofficial leader among men. His leadership took the form of evening brawls, hooker visitations, or gambling. Though he was the master of ceremonies for the night's

158

debauchery, you'd find him one of the first for breakfast before work the next day. SO, his absence was a problem.

Harry walked down the rows of identical shacks and knocked on Stuart's door. There was no answer. He knocked again and listened, wondering if Stuart had passed out on his cot. He knocked one last time before he turned to leave.

It was a muffled cry that made Harry turn around. He wasn't sure if it was human. It sounded weak and too high pitched for a man. Harry checked the door and it was unlocked. Opening the door he was blasted with a wave of heat. The noonday sun had turned the place into a furnace. A shirtless Stuart Krebs lay on his back on the bed. There was blood on his bed where he'd bitten his tongue. He was panting like a dog. A white froth dribbled from his mouth.

"Oh shit!" was Harry's first response.

Harry rushed at Stuart whose eyes were rolled back in his head. Though the bed was wet, Stuart was bone dry. Here in Matecumbe Harry had quickly learned about the advanced stages of heat stroke and dehydration. Stuart was pale and looked near death.

"Stuart! Stuart!"

Stuart didn't respond. He was panting lightly and turned his head looking like a man possessed.

Harry grabbed Stuart's legs with his left hand and cradled his neck with his right. The skin was cold and clammy. He kicked the door open and jumped down the single step as he carried the body outside. Deciding it would take longer to try and get Stuart in the truck, he ran to the medical tent adjacent to the mess hall.

The small tent was attached to the mess hall because Carl, the cook, doubled as the camp nurse.

"Carl! Carl!" yelled Harry as he stepped in the tent. Harry laid Stuart on one of the cots. Carl, a large black man, came running in. He still held a

159

carving knife and was still wearing his stained apron.

"What is it?"

"I found Stuart like this. He was in his bunk. I think he's dehydrated."

"Okay. We got to get some fluid in him."

"I'll get some water," said Harry.

"Go ahead, but we gotta start easy. I'm getting some oranges."

Harry lifted Stuart up and tried to get him to drink. The water entered his mouth and dribbled down his exposed chest. He tried again with the same result.

Carl came back in with orange slices that were left over from breakfast.

"He's not drinking," said Harry. "He's shakin' and breathin' funny."

"Lean him back," said Carl.

He put an orange wedge in Stuart's mouth and shut Stuart's mouth by grasping his jaw and pushing upward like a nutcracker. He opened his mouth and pulled the wedge out.

"Gimme another," said Carl.

Harry handed him another. Carl repeated the process. By the fifth wedge Stuart started responding.

"Give him a little water," said Carl, "but not too much. He'll hurl it back up if you give him too much."

Stuart started speaking, but his words were incoherent.

"What's he sayin?" asked Harry.

"Hell if I know," responded Carl.

Harry tried to get him to drink water, but he tried to chew it like the oranges. His eyes rolled back in his head and he stiffened up.

"What the hell is going on?" Harry cried.

Stuart went stiff as a board before collapsing.

Carl cried, "Oh hell!"

Carl slapped Stuart on the face repeatedly to get him to come around. "He's seizing!"

Stuart tightened up and started shaking violently.

Carl yelled to Harry, "Help me hold him down."

The two did their best to keep Stuart on the cot. For five minutes the two wrestled the shaking frame. Harry couldn't believe that this was a human being, much less his friend. As quickly as the fit started — it stopped.

"Is he dead?" asked Harry.

Carl leaned down to his chest and face. "No."

Carl leaned back. As he did so Stuart's arm flopped in his lap.

"Oh shit... no" Carl stopped and looked down at Krebs.

"What? What?" asked Harry with confused alarm.

"I gotta get him some heroin." Carl pointed at Krebs' arm. It looked like it was attacked by a line of mosquitoes but a distinct line ran along one vein. Some of the injection points were black and blue.

"You mean Stuart's a junkie?"

Carl stood up and headed to the locked medicine cabinet. He pulled out a ring of keys. "Yep, and he's not the only one."

"What?"

"Yeah, only last week one of our own took his life on the rails. He'd been shooting up. He just waited until the train came and waltzed out with open arms."

Carl pulled out a syringe and loaded it with a small dose of the drug. He wet a rag and cleaned Stuart's arm. He then tied off his upper arm and plunged the syringe. Stuart moaned.

"I'm not sure if I'm doing the right thing or the wrong thing here. From what I've seen, the symptoms for having too much or too little of the drug results in the same thing. The men know I have the stuff here, but I hide it in a different place every night. Nobody but me knows where it is. It's one thing to drink yourself silly, but this stuff will turn you into a walking nightmare."

161

"So you knew Stuart was a junkie?"

Harry saw Stuart relaxing as the drug took effect.

"No clue. Sometimes you can spot 'em — other times not. I always thought Stuart was a heavy drinker — just like most of us. But he always had his wits about him on the job. He never missed."

"So what happens now? Does he get sent home? Does he go to the hospital?"

"Hah - no. We'll get him back on his feet in a day or two. Then he's back to work."

"What?!" Harry was astonished that they would let a heroin addict operate heavy machinery.

"The government sent us down here for a reason — and it ain't to build a road or bridge. If we went by the book, half the men would be sent home on the next train."

Stuart let out a soft moan but remained asleep.

"So we're just sent here to be forgotten."

"Yep. We got a oneway ticket, remember?"

Harry looked at Stuart Krebs with pity and anger.

"You gotta start cooling him down," said Carl. "Be right back."

Carl ran into the mess tent and returned with a bowl of water and a rag.

"Start washing his head with this. Then move to the neck and armpits."

The sunken eyes and pale skin reminded Harry of the man who attacked him in Washington DC.

Harry wondered what happened to that man. Did he die? Was he a junkie? Harry knew despair but not to the extreme depths that would make him stick a needle in his arm and become the Krebs he now witnessed.

"I gotta get dinner started," said Carl as he got up and started heading to the kitchen.

"There's a full moon and a high tide this afternoon. Sometimes the water rolls into the kitchen. I want to make sure I got the stove stoked and everything off the floor. Keep an eye on our pal, here."

162

"I will," replied Harry. "I need to call Sheeran — let him know what's goin' on."

"No. You'll keep your mouth shut about it. Tell him that Stuart was sleeping off a bottle of whiskey. If Sheeran catches wind that Stuart is a junkie, he'll have him spreading tar. Krebs is a good man. I don't know what happened today, but his world is wrapped around operating the big machine. You gotta give him another chance. Taking him off that line will kill him faster than the heroin."

Harry pondered the circumstance. The last thing he wanted was Stuart behind the giant rig while he was drugged out of his mind. But perhaps that was already the case. There were a number of men who had to drink in order to regain a semblance of normalcy. They worked better drunk than sober. Harry wondered how many others were hiding this, or some similar, dark secret.

He sat and watched Stuart rest. The canvas of the tent moved with a whisper of wind.

"So where's Krebs?"

Ed Sheeran was upset. He hated Ray Sheldon who had put some impossible deadlines on the old man's shoulders. With Timothy working one machine while the other remained idle, only half of the work was getting done. There was no way the crew would meet Sheldon's insane quota.

Harry finally returned to the worksite. He'd rehearsed what he was going to say to Sheeran.

"Krebs is a good man. Seems like, down here, we all have those moments."

"Drank a little too much? I'm not surprised," said Sheeran. He let out a sigh but didn't stop working on the truck motor.

Harry was relieved that there wasn't a direct question. "Sometimes we go over the edge. He'll be back."

The two worked silently on a mixer motor. Sheeran's silence was a little disconcerting. Harry wondered if Sheeran knew about Kreb's addiction. If so — he wasn't talking.

Me? I'll take bourbon. It kills you slower, but a lot more pleasant like.
- Jack Thornton: 1935 Call of the Wild

Hotel Matecumbe was now the designated headquarters for the highway operation. It was only a few miles north of the primary campsite. The two story structure wasn't the most pristine hotel in Florida, but it provided four solid walls from which Sheldon was now conducting his work. Given his young bride, Ray knew it would be safer to stay here rather than a campsite.

The large hand-painted brown letters of the hotel were painted six feet high so those drivers who missed the ferry could head north in the dark and still find the place. The palm wood interior breathed a distinctive tropical odor when heat and humidity combined. It was a sweet smell like molasses combined with the smell of an oak cask recently freed of whiskey.

Sheldon called the men together to the lobby-turned-operations center for a progress report and assessment. Sam Cutler joined Sheldon in the lobby. The two waited, not sharing a word. Sheldon was immersed in the plans. Cutler looked on, but realized that Sheldon wasn't the sort of man to chitchat.

Fred Ghent stopped in on his way to Jacksonville and entered the building with a sigh. He'd heard rumors about the operation shutting down and felt like some of the failure to complete the highway fell on him. Being called north was, in his eyes, a slap from the government. However, for Ghent it was a mixed blessing. He wouldn't have to put up with the barbaric conditions. Ghent looked forward to playing golf or maybe even taking up tennis. Ghent, the last of the group to arrive, sat with the others in the lobby's overstuffed chairs.

Sheldon didn't waste time. "We gotta get this mess about the hurricane evacuation settled. I'm planning on taking some time to go away for my honeymoon and I want this behind me. I made some promises last night and want them put into motion."

Cutler had already set up a plan with Ghent. He spoke up.

"We'd discussed the idea of pulling some of the coral blocks to build a hurricane shelter at the camps. So we thought we'd put men in charge of the motor pool to get them out as part of the early evacuation. The drivers would have a key at all times. They'd load the men into the trucks. That way we didn't have to wait for a train."

Ghent nodded at Cutler.

"We always have men who straggle behind, or are in some kind of dispute with the others. For those remaining men, they'd take the train so we'd only need one standard train. If I understand you correctly, Mr. Sheldon..."

"We need to have a train or two on standby," interrupted Sheldon.

"What I'm saying is," continued Cutler, now a little more frustrated.

"I spoke with a Mr. Loflin at the train station in Homestead, and he said all we gotta do is call him and he'll put out the order to prepare the train."

"So, we have a train on standby at all times?" asked Sheldon.

"It appears so," said Ghent. Ghent wanted to let Sheldon know that a responsible evacuation plan existed that would take care of any immediate threat. "He said something about a 'standby fee' but I said, 'No!'"

"It's just one locomotive, right? With extra cars?" Sheldon's wheels were spinning. "Ghent, look — here is how I see things." Sheldon turned his body toward Ghent, ignoring Cutler altogether. Sheldon was talking to his peer.

"We don't want the men gallivanting north with company equipment. We can make a savings in gas if we call the FEC and let them know we're hauling all our men on the train. We'd save cash that way as well as wear and tear on the company equipment."

Sheldon left no room for debate. He didn't want this to be an action formed by a committee.

"A single train will do the job. This way I can account for the men."

Sheldon spun to face Sam Cutler who was flush with frustration.

"Cutler, you'll make calls and monitor the barometer. You let me know if anything is brewing in the Atlantic."

"Yessir."

Cutler had never been through a hurricane, so he had no idea how to determine if one was approaching other than the barometer and the reports from the radio.

"I'll get the number for the weather bureau. I here there's one in Miami somewhere. I've been recording the barometer and thermostat at the mess hall pretty much twice a day."

Cutler, who was prudent about following the rules admitted,

"Of late I've been a little lax in writing down the numbers. It seems that some of the men had grown an instinct about what kind of weather would blow in. Sometimes the locals would call and let the vets know that a storm was brewing. The problem of the weather was handling itself. Other than the regular squalls, the weather had been rather forgiving — as far as Florida Keys weather goes."

Sheldon clapped his hands once.

"Well, it seems we have this wrapped up. Ghent, I'm in control. You go on and head north. Next week, or maybe the following — Labor Day weekend — I plan on heading to Key West with my new bride. It is our honeymoon. Any objections?"

Ghent was surprised that Sheldon would take a leave of absence so soon after taking command.

Cutler was fuming over Sheldon's departure to the Keys. The nervous little man had been the administrative assistant all summer. Part of his

167

position required that he be at the camps during the weekend. He'd never been to Key West much less some of the local fishing spots. With Sheldon cutting off the ready supply of alcohol, the weekends would become near impossible to control.

"Before we go..." Cutler injected. He never had problems talking to Ghent. Ghent was easy going and pliable on any subject. However Sheldon already had Cutlers palms sweating.

"I heard a grievance committee was forming and would be meeting with Sheldon once they got their demands in order. First on the list was reinstating the camp-wide sale of beer and cheap spirits."

"I believe that the camp-wide prohibition will result in improved manners and reduced violence. End of story."

Cutler continued.

"Half the men were already standing in line at the local grocery store using their hard earned dollars to purchase a bottle of rubbing alcohol and some coke to wash it down."

"Some of the National Guard had gotten wind of the new rule and set up road blocks to prevent the vets from leaving town. Last night a vet to stole a truck from the motor pool and rammed the blockade."

Despite last night's incident, Sheldon felt the project was now being managed much better than Ghent. Ghent didn't bring the discipline these mean needed. That is why the building of the highway had faltered and failed under Ghent's control. These were soldiers of war who responded to the crack of an order, not the enthusiasm of a weak man.

Without responding to the news, Sheldon turned to Ghent.

"I hope you have fun on the mainland."

This was Sheldon's way of dismissing the Ghent for good.

Harry was one of four men who'd gathered together a list of improvements. He'd never considered himself a leader, but word got around about the night with Hemingway and soon he found himself repeating the story — those parts that he could remember. The men gravitated to Harry and started soliciting him to help set things straight with their new boss, Sheldon.

Harry would have never considered joining a grievance committee had it not been for the inspiration of the boxing champ – Jimmy Conway.

Conway noticed the hill that led to the main road was collapsing. The rains had taken their toll on the excavation.

Jimmy Conway singlehandedly hauled loose coral from the edge of the water and just started building. There were no requirements for it. There were no specifications. It was something that he did in his spare time. At first some of the vets made fun of him. Someone, early on, had knocked part of it down. But after a while, the vets came to respect "the wall." This also got Jimmy thinking how other parts of the camp might be improved.

"Harry, you and me, we got the other fella's ears," said Jimmy after another late night boxing match. Jimmy's opponent was already drunk so it was no contest. When the fight was over he collected his money and approached Harry.

"I think if we get the right guys together we can change things around here. Sheldon is trying to bully us around. Half the men are sick. I hear some are drinking the gasoline. But that ain't the only problem. We got sanitation issues. Hell – at high tide the water runs into the mess hall. With the new guy in charge, we got to take responsibility and let him know that if he wants us to straighten up, the government has to live up to their end of the bargain."

"Well, I'm not much for public speakin' and I can't write worth a damn."

"Yeah, but the men look up to you. We can get someone to write down our list of changes."

169

"Okay," Harry felt better about the request knowing he wasn't going to have to play secretary.

"I think we need to limit our list to a few items. If we throw everything at him, then nothing will get done."

Harry scratched his head as he continued, "I'm worried about the shacks we live in. Two of them lost their roof during the storm two weeks ago. I hear the hurricanes are a whole lot worse."

"Yeah, haven't seen one myself. Kinda lookin' forward to it," said Jimmy. "The guys who have been in one say I'm crazy. They say I've been hit in the head one too many times."

"I think anyone who goes up against you in the ring are the ones hit in the head to many times."

"Hell Harry, I've seen battle in France. I'm not gonna be scared by the wind."

The two laughed and started heading to the mess hall.

"I'll assemble some of the men. I got Krebs to help us out. As soon as he's done collecting his money we'll work up a plan. I don't want to sit on this too long. We gotta strike while the iron's hot."

The committee spent the next three days polling the men and coming up with a list of grievances. Sheldon and Cutler knew about it so it was no surprise when Sheldon received a request to meet about some changes the men want to put in place. He told them to meet him at the mess hall before work.

It was a strangely cool and damp morning for this late in the summer. A fog had rolled over the campsite which brought an unusual stillness to the whole place. The smell of bacon wafted through the camp and mixed with the smell of bitter coffee as Carl and his crew prepared breakfast. A few supply trucks arrived and were picking up the men before shuttling off to the edges of the new highway.

Jimmy Conway, Harry Burrows, Stuart Krebs and Buddy Brickman formed the quartet of the grievance committee. Jimmy chose Buddy to fill out the foursome not because he had any particular managerial skill, but because he was large and imposing. Jimmy felt that it couldn't hurt to have a little extra muscle when it came to the crew voicing their demands.

Sheldon was already in the mess hall stirring an ample amount of milk into this morning's coffee. He lifted the mug and blew off a head of steam. The storm door slammed shut behind the four as they came in to greet their foreman.

"Morning, gentlemen," said Sheldon just before he took a slurping sip of coffee.

"Morning Mr. Sheldon," said Buddy. He was already twisting his Masonic ring. The others nodded and sat.

"So what are we up to, today?"

Krebs pulled out a folded piece of paper. "Mr. Sheldon, we represent the boys. We're looking for some improvements to our living conditions and a few changes to the rules."

Harry looked at Ray and noticed that he was turning a little red. He wasn't sure if it was the heat of his coffee, or the notion that the men were trying to take control.

Krebs continued, "We wrote down the grievances that the men have — you know — the things that need changed. We figured that now you are in charge, we can come to you with our demands..."

Jimmy Conway interrupted, "Well, they're more like recommendations for changes to keep us all happy and productive."

Krebs corrected himself, "...yeah, that's right — recommendations."

Sheldon nodded but didn't say a word.

Krebs flattened out the paper on the table. "The men would like to see the following: first — they want you to lift the ban on the sale of alcohol on the premises. That was pretty much unanimous."

He stopped and looked at Sheldon. Krebs cleared his throat and fidgeted a little.

"There are more demands, but we prioritized them by importance. Booze seems to be number one. A lot of the men are gettin' the jitters. Some of these guys haven't gone a day without a drink in quite a while. I saw a bunch of guys trying to break into the utility closet to see what was in the cleaning supplies. They'll tear up their guts if they can't get a beer. One beer ain't gonna do anybody any harm."

Sheldon sat silently. The men knew he was a hothead. The word got around. They'd figure he would come for a fight. But instead he sat back and said nothing.

"Number two is the sanitation. There ain't a decent place to take a shit around here." Krebs looked at the other men and smiled.

Jimmy, who'd taken on the leadership role, clarified.

"Don't take this the wrong way. We want to help out. We'd be glad to dig a hole and build a decent set of outhouses. You can't use the one's you got. Between the stench and the bugs it just ain't safe. Heard one of the men got some kind of sick in his back from just shitting. That ain't right"

Jimmy looked up for some sort of acknowledgement. Sheldon nodded but remained eerily quiet. After a moment of silence between the two, Krebs reluctantly continued, "The men want a raise. You can't earn a livin' down here on the money we're makin'."

Krebs didn't want to open that to debate, so he rushed to the next item. "The men want the rules for hurricane evacuation posted. It seems like you changed up some of the rules and a bunch of us are confused. Harry brought this up the other day."

Buddy chimed in. "You mentioned that we'd be heading out by train. We got a lot of trucks. I don't see why we can't use them. Seems like a waste of

— well — if we gotta get out fast, I don't want to wait for a train."

The men stopped and looked at Ray. They figured he'd be tearing into their proposals — at least the one about the raise. He sat there in a stare down. Finally he spoke.

"Go on."

"We all want more water trucks. Some of the men have passed out tarring the road. It's hot work — especially this time of year."

The men nodded. "We're just looking out for our interests. A man can't roll tar if he's flat on the ground."

Ray didn't say a word as the men went through their demands. He occasionally sipped his coffee, but that was it. When they were done he leaned forward.

"Thank you, gentlemen for bringing this to my attention."

Ray's tone had the cool demeanor of a librarian giving directions. Perhaps what the men heard about Ray was wrong.

"Now as you know all of these things take time and money. That's time and money spent not working on the road. I plan to get this road built, and I'm going to do whatever it takes to get it done."

Harry replied, "Well, if you improve our living conditions and fund our wage increase, then we will get it done."

Sheldon was definitely turning red. The tone of his voice demonstrated a calm that was self-imposed.

"And if these demands aren't met?"

Krebs answered, "Some of the men will strike."

Krebs coughed and continued, "At least that's what I heard."

That's what Sheldon had expected. Here was the division and threats he'd feared would happen when Ghent left. Sheldon wondered how long it would take. He'd been in this position before.

"Gentlemen, I appreciate you coming to me with these..." he paused, "concerns. I want you to know that I plan on taking them under consideration and will let you know of any progress."

"What kind of timeline do you see implementing — say — the pay raise?" asked Buddy.

Sheldon smiled. It was an insincere smile that someone could easily have misinterpreted as a sneer.

"Well, that's the point. I am the foreman down here. My job is to get things done. It seems like you have me over a barrel."

Buddy twirled his ring faster. "No sir, we are partners in this."

"I don't see it that way. I see that if I don't meet these demands, we don't get the road done. Okay – look at it from my point of view. This is a government operation. You know as well as I do that the government doesn't work by one man — alone. Everything is done by committee."

Harry listened to Ray and what he said sounded reasonable, but there was an undercurrent that he didn't trust.

Sheldon swirled his coffee with his spoon and set the spoon carefully on the table.

"So I need you to do me a favor. I need you four to take my truck and head to Hotel Matecumbe. I'll get Sam Cutler to wire your demands — er — requests, to the appropriate authorities. We'll see what Uncle Sam can do to help us out. I can't make guarantees at this point but I'm sure we can get the ball rolling. Cutler is the one to take care of that sort of thing. I don't know much about how the wheels in DC turn. I build roads."

The men looked at each other. Sheldon had made his point.

"So you think we can get these things done?" asked Krebs.

"You gotta tell the men to give me time. The government wheels roll slow around here. It takes a while to get paperwork from here to DC But if you

174

get your demands to Cutler, I'll try to expedite the matter. Sound good?"

Krebs bought in first. "Sure thing, boss."

Krebs looked at Harry for some kind of insight on Sheldon. Harry shrugged his shoulders.

Sheldon lifted his hip, jangled some keys and pulled them out of his pocket. He handed them to Krebs. "Gentlemen, Cutler may have to have you fill out some paperwork. Okay?"

The four looked at each other. It seemed simple. This was far easier than any of them imagined.

"Let's meet again in three days time. I'll give you an update then." Sheldon stood up and walked to the edge of the mess hall. He opened the door and flung the bitters from the bottom of the coffee outside. The other men looked at each other and rose.

The truck was dilapidated but functional. Jimmy and Buddy hopped in the bed while Krebs and Harry got in the cab. Harry drove. The wheels spun and loose coral sprayed back toward the mess hall as the truck made its way to the road.

"Well, that was easy," said Harry.

"Yeah – a little too easy if you ask me," replied Krebs pulling out a cigarette.

The four ambled north. It was only a mile from the campsite when they came across two cars on the side of the road. The young men wielding rifles wore the unmistakable garments of the National Guard. As the truck approached the men walked into the road. One put his hand up.

"Goddamit. I hate these fools," said Harry.

"Well, we ain't drunk and we ain't speedin'."

Harry slowed the truck. He didn't want to stop. Something in the back of his mind told him to break through the road block.

"Morning gentlemen," said one of the young men. Harry couldn't recall if that was the boy who accosted him on his first day in Matecumbe. "Can I ask you all to step out of the truck?"

"Why's that?"

"We have been stopping the vehicles because a number of vets have been drinking, and we have been authorized to confiscate all liquor. Also got a call that some vets stole a company truck."

Harry shook his head. "It's not even nine in the mornin'! Ain't nobody's drinkin' this early. We didn't take no truck."

"Please exit the vehicle."

"C'mon. Here – smell my breath." Harry leaned out of the window and blew. Krebs started laughing.

Buddy and Jimmy jumped out of the bed and crowded the man by the driver side window. Two other National Guards pointed rifles at them.

"Stand away from the truck!" The youngest squinted as he pointed the gun at Jimmy.

"Goddamit!" Harry swung open the truck door quickly hoping to hit the man by the window, but the man jumped back in the nick of time. "We ain't drinkin!"

Krebs got out.

The men were surrounded by the guards. Another member of the guard looked in the truck. He pulled out two bottles from under the seat.

"Hey, this is the boss's truck. That ain't mine."

"Gentlemen, you'll have to come with us."

Jimmy stomped the ground. "We are not going anywhere! This is a setup!"

Two guards pointed their rifle at him.

"Sir, you'll have to settle. You are all under arrest."

Krebs was the first to say it, though the others were thinking it all along.

"Sheldon set us all up. He called the National Guard. He put the booze under the seat. That's why he had us take the grievance to Cutler. He knew all along."

"I can't go to jail," said Krebs.

Harry knew why, but he didn't say anything. He'd seen what happened to Krebs when he didn't shoot up. Both knew there was the potential that Krebs might die behind bars.

176

"We'll figure this out. Somebody will come get us out."

Buddy Brickman spoke up, "Yeah – but nobody knows that we're going in. We never told anyone else we were heading out. Sheldon did this. We'll rot before anyone else finds out."

"Dammit!" yelled Krebs.

The guard hauled the men away in two vehicles they'd parked behind the mangroves. They drove to Homestead where there was an adequate jail. The four men were put in a cell that was eight by eight. They were the only ones in the entire jail, but the guard chose to keep the other cells empty and crowd the four men together, just for spite. The local sheriff arrived a few hours later. He was an older man who walked with a limp. It looked like his right leg was shorter than his left.

"Hey boys, I hear you had a little hooch under the seat - stole a truck."

"No, we didn't steal no truck. The booze wasn't ours. We were set up."

"Oh yeah, I've heard that one before."

"You can't keep us here."

"I'm not doing anything. You took care of that. The Guards were just doing their duty."

Some of the south bound locals saw the events that transpired on the road. It didn't take long for the word to spread quickly throughout the camp that Sheldon had the four men arrested.

Timothy was the first to take action. He knew he didn't have any bail money. He hoped that a local with a little more history in Florida law would be able to solve the problem. He thought of going to Nikolas, but felt that his relationship with the man was tenuous at best. He didn't want to jeopardize his relationship with Aella. Besides, Nikolas wasn't that kind of man to be front and center in the community.

He opted to go to Ed Sheeran and let him know what had happened.

Ed was on the barge he kept tied along a canal near the dig site. He'd kept the canal boat in top shape. It was often quicker to haul the trucks and various machinery over water than it was by land. It only took one disabled vehicle to snarl traffic and prevent delivery of large machinery. He could also haul a number of vehicles at a time with a minimal crew.

Tim relayed the story.

"I can't believe it," said Ed shaking his head in disbelief. "Sheldon's got some nerve. Damn, those aren't the men I want to see incarcerated. Trust me; there are plenty out here who should be locked up. They're no better than animals. But Harry? C'mon, you know as well as I do that he's a straight shooter. He's troubled, but he's really got a heart of gold — not to mention that he can fix anything out here."

Timothy agreed.

"Look, Timothy – let's get done the day's work and we'll head up there and see what we can do. I can't make promises, but I'll see if I can't pull some strings. Sheldon thinks he's proving a point. All he is really doing is alienating everybody. He's setting up for war. Between you and me, Sheldon's nothing but an arrogant ass."

Timothy smiled, "Yeah, you can sometimes look at a person and size them up. I thought the same thing."

The humidity shot up around the jail with storms threatening all around. The musty smell, the thick atmosphere and incredible heat wilted the four otherwise hearty men. For the last few hours each man contemplated their individual fate as they hunched over on the wooden benches.

"How long you think it will be?" asked Krebs after what seemed like hours of silence. The question bounced off the concrete walls.

"How long 'til what'?" asked Buddy Brickman. He'd taken off his shirt and was using it to wipe his

178

head. Because of his incredible size, he seemed the worst of the bunch. Sweat rolled off of him and made puddles on the floor.

"'til they come for us. You know — to let us out." Krebs was starting to fidget.

"Who's gonna come for us?" Brickman replied. "Hell – who knows we're here? Sheldon did a pretty good job of conning us. I don't care if I get sent to jail. When I get out of here, I'm gonna punch him right in the nose."

"I'll hold him for you," added Jimmy as he stood up to stretch. He took the cue from Buddy and took off his shirt.

"I mean, they ain't just gonna leave us here, right?" Krebs asked.

Jimmy was getting annoyed at Krebs. "Look," he started. "Sheldon put us in here 'cause he's the boss and we were a threat. He doesn't want us comin' back and stirrin' up trouble. He'll let us out when he thinks we've learned our lesson."

"So, how long do ya think?"

"Dammit! Who knows! Maybe a week. I just hope the sheriff comes back with a pail of water for each of us and some food," Jimmy yelled.

"We're not a bunch of God damn animals!" He stood up and pounded on the bars.

"So, a day? You think a day?"

"Shut the hell up, Krebs!" Jimmy's temper flared as a roll of thunder shook the building

Krebs muttered, "I'm sorry. I'm sorry. I'm sorry."

Harry looked at Krebs. He wasn't trembling, but he noticed that Krebs wasn't sweating like the rest of the men. His face was ashen.

"We're all on edge," said Harry.

Turning to Harry, Krebs said, "I gotta get outta here. I can't stay cooped up in here."

Harry replied, "I know." Harry looked Krebs in the eye. "Trust me, I know."

There was a wordless passing of understanding. That moment of connection calmed Krebs. Harry nodded a silent, "I know."

"Where the hell are they," demanded Ed Sheeran as he bolted from his truck. Sheldon was on the road with the surveyor. Sheldon had one of the many books of blueprints out on the truck hood. "Where are the men you had arrested?"

Sheldon couldn't help but smile. "What are you talking about?" He hid the grin as best he could.

"You know what I'm talking about. You had four men arrested this morning."

"I did nothing of the sort. I heard of four men who were arrested because they had liquor in their stolen truck. I suspect they'd been drinking. Serves them right."

"Dammit Sheldon, these men are the leaders. You don't just lock them up. Word's gotten around you know. You think you're under control, but you're not. This isn't how things are done down here. I need those men onsite. Where are they?"

"They're in jail where they belong."

"Panama City? Homestead? Hollywood? Tell me or you'll have an army of men at your doorstep. They're already talking about a work stoppage."

Ray stepped forward so he was nose-to-nose with Sheldon. "Is that a threat? I can send you home if you don't like it here."

"You have no idea what you're doing. The men are about to mutiny." Sheeran turned away and started walking to the truck. He heard Sheldon kick the truck.

It was dark by the time Timothy and Sheeran arrived at the jail. The two brought a change of clothes for the men. The sheriff was waiting for them when the duo walked in. Sheldon had called ahead, fully aware of coup.

The four men perked up when they saw Timothy and Ed enter the jail.

"We're here to pick up the four men."

The sheriff didn't get out of his seat. "I was told by Mr. Sheldon that we are to continue to hold these men until I hear word from the National Guard. They'll not budge until then."

The sheriff folded his arms in a defensive posture and leaned back.

Sheeran's intensity was palpable.

"You have to understand that Ray *is not* in charge. He may think he is, but the men that are building the road are an army — one of the best armies ever assembled. These four men you have incarcerated represent the leadership of the army. We're talking about seven hundred men. They are all out there."

Sheeran pointed south and then put his hands on the desk and looked into the sheriff's eyes. There was a seething cauldron behind Ed's words. Those in the room had never seen this side of the old man.

"They have done *nothing* wrong. You know as well as I do that they weren't drinking. This is all part of one man's stupid quest. Do you understand my point? I would hate for an insurrection of seven hundred men to befall this outpost of humanity. There aren't enough rifles to stop them. Our government has trained our soldiers well."

The sheriff thought for a moment. He'd never been in this predicament before. The old man stood back and watched as the sheriff's wheels spun. A storm was brewing among the group of men. They had a cause — their cause — and these four men would be the martyrs.

The sheriff felt the oppressive weight of Sheeran's words. These weren't just four men stirring up trouble, they were the advance of a greater force. Ray Sheldon was just one man with a grudge. The sheriff silently got up and unlocked the cell.

"Go on. Get outta here. Ya learned your lesson. Go on, now. All of ya — git."

"Goddamn – goddammit. You let them go? Who gave the order ? Never mind."

181

Ray Sheldon slammed down the ear piece on the phone nearly knocking it off the wall. He turned to Cutler.

"Can you believe that? That ol' redneck let them loose. And do you know who was there? Ed – Ed Sheeran. I'd bury that old man in the bridge if I could get away with it. Okay. We gotta diffuse the situation before the word gets around. Let's figure out a way to take those men out of the picture for a while. I don't want them to think they can get away with this. Any ideas?"

"Give in to their demands," Cutler blurted out the statement before he could even think about it.

"What? Are you crazy?!" Now Sheldon's rage was turning to Cutler. Cutler was tired. He was to the point of giving the whole thing up. It had been a hot summer and now the whole operation was unraveling. He'd heard from Ghent that Stone had given the order to start shutting the place down. Sheldon was not following orders — not exactly.

"Look, there are some benefits to giving in." Cutler knew that compromise was the only answer.

Sheldon interrupted.

"I'll never give in. Send them adrift out there with a bottle of rum and a six shooter. We'll see how long they last."

Cutler sighed. "If the men get drinking again, they'll be in no condition to rebel. You remind them that if they don't work, they don't get paid. They are all so hard up for liquor, they're drinking the degreaser. You lift the ban and the crew will be high and happy."

Sheldon considered it for a moment.

Cutler continued, "You've got Labor Day coming up. Give the boys a break."

He was normally unreceptive to any other ideas, but this one made sense. He had no other recourse.

"Okay. But we got to keep those jail birds from talking."

Sheldon sat down next to Cutler. In the lobby of the Hotel Matecumbe the ticking clock made the thought process difficult. Sheldon picked up the list of demands that the team had written down. After a moment a smile came across his face.

"There!" Ray poked his stubby work-worn finger at the page. He then tossed it carelessly in the direction of the table. The paper fell short and wafted to the ground.

"What?" asked Cutler, bending down to retrieve the list.

Sheldon stood up.

"They are worried about the God damn weather. So we'll give those rebels a chore."

"Chore?"

"Yeah – simple. They are worried about hurricane preparations. We'll pull the four men and put them to task reinforcing the shacks. We'll get them putting crossbeams on the living quarters. They'll be done in a couple of weeks. By then we got Labor Day and the whole crew will have forgotten about them."

"Sheeran won't be happy."

"To hell with him."

Sheldon spat on the carpet.

Cutler knew the crew. He understood what that assignment would mean.

"If you take away Timothy, Krebs and Harry you got critical men off the big equipment. Sheeran will be the only one trained to work it. The bridge work will go much slower."

Sheldon headed for the door and turned back for a last word to Cutler.

"Have Sheeran train someone else. Hell, we're not even supposed to be doing this. We're just here to make them happy."

I ask you to judge me by the enemies I have made.
   -   Franklin D. Roosevelt

It was a gamble that wasn't paying off. Julius Stone was struggling to keep this long comb over hair on his sweaty head. His hat had already started smelling of mildew. That was the nature of this place. Key West robbed everything of its life. Whatever lived down here was deep in decay. Had he known the exorbitant costs to bring his plan to fruition, he may have never started. Word was starting to get around the tropics that the highway planned was doomed by the drunken vets.

"I tell you, it is a wonderful home, Mrs. Prichard."

The woman was wearing a dress that was both too conservative and too warm for this climate. They'd come by train to Key West. Clarence and Lucy Prichard were part owners of the American Fruit and Banana Company. Clarence had the sense to wear a linen suit, which was now stained in the armpits. Lucy was from Virginia and had never seen a palm tree.

Clarence was looking for better trade routes and cheaper docking fees. Work was going to tie him up in Panama and Honduras for a few months. Because of the nature of his work with company, he'd often had to leave his wife of thirty years for months at a time.

Somehow word had spread that during their separation Clarence hadn't been faithful so Lucy insisted on joining him in his trek south.

She thought Key West was the answer. Clarence said it would be too hot. She was used to the oppressive Virginia summers and thought she knew what to expect. Having arrived in Key West, she felt drunk with the heat that was burning her scalp though the small hat perched on her head.

Stone had been giving them what he thought was a royal treatment by putting them up at the hotel.

"It is a wonderful home. Look at the iron work."

The vets had done a good job hiding the imperfections. Stone knew where to look. Some of the porch wood was rotting. Stone was short on funds and materials were scarce. He had them paint the porch a rich robin egg blue. He stepped carefully and guided the two inside.

Stone was looking to do a little better than breaking even. These two should be an easy mark — but he was getting frustrated.

"Oh my!"

Lucy jumped as a cockroach scurried across the hallway floor.

"Just a Key West bug. We spray the houses but sometimes one gets by." Stone tried to stomp on the critter, but it changed direction and made a beeline to the white moulding. It disappeared under moulding and raced into the bones of the house. Stone wanted to curse out loud but stifled.

"I don't know Clarence," said Lucy. She was beginning to think the whole idea of coming down this far was wrong. Clarence was a good man, despite his habits.

Stone retaliated. "Oh Lucy..." Stone took her hand and patted it. "This is a lovely home. It has been recently renovated. I don't want to let this one go, but I'm afraid that I have to settle some debts and need to liquidate this very special home."

This was at least partially true. James Garwood had purchased one of Stone's homes at a premium. However, during the last storm, part of the roof had blown off. Stone was in such a hurry to close the deal that he hadn't paid close attention to the legal documentation. James Garwood, the rich socialite who loved sailing the Florida waters, had maintained his fortune because he was legally careful. Part of the contract on the house included a clause which acted as a warranty the house against structural damage for a year.

This left Stone stuck with paying for everything.

"Mrs. Prichard, I have a reputation around this island."

That too was partially true. But the reputation was far from stellar.

"Honey, this was your idea," said Clarence squeezing her hand. It was a veiled argument that had been brewing between the two for months.

"Well," she started, realizing that he wanted her back in Virginia. "It is actually quite nice."

Stone smiled. He squeezed her hand again.

"You have to trust me. The road is almost near completion. Once that happens, even if you don't live down here, you'll be able to rent it out to all of the vacationers that will be thronging to this piece of paradise. Consider it an investment in the future."

It was a statement that Stone had, at one time, believed. But he knew the score when it came to the highway. Now he was taking his funds and placing it in a better bet. Key West would always be a place of decay and home to the decadent. It would remain broken and bankrupt. It was a dream that turned sour and Stone knew he had to resurrect himself. He was going to be a Phoenix rising from the ashes. But he knew he had to unload the real estate that was already starting to putrefy.

"I like it, honey," said Mrs. Prichard. She released her hand from Stone and grabbed her husband's. He smiled uneasily.

Stone knew he had made the sale. It was one less property. He was ready to invest in a sure thing. Away from government control, a mere ninety miles away was a short ferry ride to the next vacation paradise for Americans frustrated with the unfinished highway along a stretch of nothing. From Miami he already invested in the shipping industry and purchased some real estate in a venture that couldn't fail — in Cuba.

186

With a scratch of my pen I started this work in Key West, and with a scratch of my pen I can stop it-just like that...
- *Julius Stone*

Sheldon held out hope that he could finish the road. He'd allowed the vets to start drinking again. The boys seemed happy, but the work was going slower than he anticipated. He'd kept the lie of hope alive in the vets. But before the Labor Day weekend, that lie came crashing down.

Ray hadn't been informed they were coming. Ghent hadn't called him, nor had he received word from Julius Stone. Yes, they knew that he was aware the place was being shut down, but they hadn't told him when the social workers were being sent to talk to the men.

It was a parade of fancy black Chevrolets that arrived among the palm trees. He'd never heard of Harold Henderson and his band of cronies. They, of course, had assumed the men were aware of the closure.

Cutler was upset that Sheldon was nowhere to be found when the social workers arrived. Cutler tried to call Sheldon earlier in the day. Cutler had gotten a call and heard that the men were on their way.

Sheldon took a little time to sneak off for an afternoon of sex with his young bride. It was near dinnertime before Cutler could finally get in touch with Sheldon. By then, it was too late.

When word finally got to Sheldon he spewed a sailor's tirade that made Cutler cringe.

"We're here tonight to help you work out your problems and help you relocate," said Harold Henderson. He'd dropped his coat over a chair revealing arm pit stains that ran nearly to the cuff. He left his tie on.

The men in the mess hall looked at each other with confused faces. A few of them chuckled at the suits.

Sheldon was still racing down the road as the message was being relayed.

"I'm sorry guys," said Cutler. "I hate to bring you the bad news but we're closing up shop down here."

The place erupted.

Harry stood up on the bench. "What?! But the road isn't done!"

"I know, I know," said the government employee.

"You know how it is with the troops and the government. You are going to be compensated and we'll give you travel money so you can return home."

Timothy yelled what the others were thinking.

"This is our home!"

Mr. Henderson put up a hand to calm the rabble.

"Come on guys!" said Cutler.

"It is still your home," Henderson replied. "We need your help to work on the road. We're not closing down until November. Until then..."

A violent undercurrent of resentment was brewing in the mess hall. The social workers folded their arms as they looked at the crowd which appeared poised to pounce at any moment. It was at that moment that Sheldon came barging through the door. Some boos erupted from the rabble.

"Hey – settle down goddammit!" Sheldon's face was already beet red. He gave Cutler a sideways glance that could kill. It was a mask and everyone in the room knew it.

Normally, Ray Sheldon didn't smile. But there he was stepping up with a grin on his face as he faced the vets. The smile was plastered there with contempt.

"Boys, I gotta tell you — this came as quite a surprise to me! Ha ha — But like good soldiers you've been given your orders."

Someone in the back yelled, "Bullshit!"

The crowd erupted with laughter. A few veins on Sheldon's neck rose up and started pulsing.

"Aw c'mon," he said trying to diffuse the situation, "now we got a deadline. I'd like to prove, and I want you to prove too, that we can finish this thing. Let's double our resolve."

Krebs leaned to Billy Brickman, "I want to double my drinking. This is the hottest month of the year down here. He's gonna try and kill us all."

Brickman nodded in agreement.

The leader of the men in suits and ties stepped up, "These social workers are here to help you."

Brickman couldn't take it anymore, he stood up. His massive frame loomed large as he stood on the bench. "We have busted our asses down here to get the work done. We've been paid shit. We get eaten alive by mosquitoes. We've given up our real homes for a life down here. Now you're telling us to go home? Where? To What? You got jobs for us 'cause nobody wants us. That's why you sent us down here in the first place."

The man had anticipated this retort.

"The government is still committed to you..."

"Like our bonus?!" yelled Harry.

The men laughed and nodded. It was starting to get out of control. Sheldon pointed a finger at Harry.

The government man spoke up. "Look – this weekend I spoke with the Florida railroad. They have given you all a discount on tickets. It's a two dollar trip to the keys and four to Miami. Payday is Friday."

"And I suppose you are bringing in some female government employees?" asked Elmer.

The crowd laughed but there was a malicious tone in their chortles.

"We have planned a series of job placement..."

Someone in the back started singing *Brother Can You Spare a Dime*. It was off pitch until a few others joined in...

They used to tell me I was building a dream, and so I followed the mob,

When there was earth to plow, or guns to bear, I was always there right on the job.

They used to tell me I was building a dream, with peace and glory ahead,

Why should I be standing in line, just waiting for bread?

Sheldon could feel this getting out of hand. He motioned to the leader of the social workers.

"You and your cronies would be best served to leave about now," He put a hand on his shoulder as the volume increased.

Once I built a railroad, I made it run, made it race against time.

Once I built a railroad; now it's done. Brother, can you spare a dime?

Once I built a tower, up to the sun, brick, and rivet, and lime;

Once I built a tower, now it's done. Brother, can you spare a dime?

The men left to the anthem that had taken on deep reverence. Some of the men didn't know the words, but others had it emblazoned on their hearts. Each could feel the pain of the other. It was an invisible connection that drove these men to the end of America. They were the lost boys who had discovered themselves in the humid heat of yet another forgotten cause.

The tenor of the music changed as they sang the next lyric. Some of the men were crying as they tried to, inconspicuously, wipe away their tears.

Once in khaki suits, gee we looked swell,

Full of that Yankee Doodly Dum,

Half a million boots went slogging through Hell,

And I was the kid with the drum!

Sheldon and Cutler left. As Sheldon left the room Krebs conducted the boys to the final refrain.

Say, don't you remember, they called me Al; it was Al all the time.

Why don't you remember, I'm your pal? Buddy, can you spare a dime?

The music ended. The troops had won a minor victory but were to ultimately lose the war. They would never finish the road. They would never pave the way to the future. Once again, the hard work of these now aging men would be lost in time. They were told to go home to a place that was now nonexistent. For a month they were to lick their wounds as they spread tar in the unrelenting heat. They were forced to relive the nightmare of rejection they'd suffered once already.

The group disbanded in silence, some with their arms around each other. There would be a night of drinking and reminiscing. They felt their spirit was taken from them. They were given until November to work on a road that would not lead to the future. It would lead nowhere.

Timothy was the first to speak as Harry and Elmer headed back to the shack.

"I'm not leaving."

"What?" Harry was surprised, but not startled that Timothy would opt to stay. "What the hell are you going to do?"

"I've been talking with Aella's father. There are a bunch of locals that work at the fishing club. They told me that I could probably get work there. A bunch of the millionaires arrive after Labor Day. I could..."

"You could kiss their ass," said Elmer interrupting. "You'll be a goddamn nigger working for the rich folk."

Harry interceded. "Hey, you don't need to be so mean to Tim. At least he's got prospects. Look at us old farts. We ain't got a pot to piss in. Timothy here has a job speculation and a woman to boot. He's the only one coming out on top."

"You gotta introduce us to your filly," said Elmer.

"Hah! I wouldn't bring her within a hundred yards of this place. Between the guys wanking in broad daylight and the others willing to do just

191

about anything to have their way with a woman, she would simply be a target."

"Well, you'll invite us to the wedding won't you?" asked Harry smiling at the proposition.

"Shit, he only met her a little while ago, now he's getting married?" Elmer slapped his leg.

"You know," Timothy started. "I know this sounds crazy, but I actually might."

Timothy imagined the two of them on the train as they were heading to Key West for their honeymoon. He saw her in a white dress and him in pinstripes.

"Look at him, Harry," Elmer said with a grin. "He's got a stupid grin on his face and a loaded gun in his pocket."

"Harry, I'd want you to be my best man." Timothy stopped the group as he put his hands on Harry's shoulders. "We've been through a lot since I saw you in DC."

"What about me dammit?" Elmer smiled.

"I'll let you pour the drinks at the reception."

"Only if I can hide a few bottles for myself."

Sheldon and Cutler raced back to the hotel.

"How the Hell did this happen. Now we'll never get those vets off their asses! What kind of boneheaded thing did Ghent or Stone or whoever the hell in the goddamned US government issued those asses to come down here..."

Sheldon took a breath. His face was so red parts were turning purple. "... and think they'd get an ounce of work out of the men after they closed this place down."

He'd been ranting the whole way to the hotel. Cutler was upset but kept quiet. He would be out of a job like all the others. Sheldon stopped his rant and took a few deep breaths.

"I'm goin' away this weekend. I hate to leave you tending the farm, Cutler. But now, I bet every vet is either going to Miami or Key West and getting fall down drunk. Hell, I'm going to join them."

Cutler thought about his fishing gear that, again, would go unused. He'd be baby sitting the camp when the vets would be at their worst.

"We gotta collect every key from the motor pool tonight. The vets'll be fixing to travel as soon as they get liquored up enough. We can't have them stealing government property. If you know anybody who's got a spare set of keys — take 'em. Get all the keys from Ed Sheeran while you're at it. We might have a mutiny before the weekend is out. We should also shut down the sale of liquor."

Cutler shook his head, "Nope. That didn't work before, and it isn't going to work now. Better to have them drunk on their ass, then going stir crazy sober. We won't be getting any more work out of them. Tomorrow they'll be doing what they want. This is the vet's playground for a while. Let them get smashed over the Labor Day holiday, and then we feed and clothe them. They're done — we're done."

Sheldon's rage was starting to boil over.

"Just get the keys."

Red sails in the sunset way out on the sea
Oh carry my loved one home safely to me
-    *Red Sails on the Sunset - Jimmy Kennedy,*
     Wilhelm Grosz

Timothy wasted no time getting to Aella. By now he knew the routine. He headed out before dawn. The air was pleasant, unlike the last few days. For a week the unrelenting humidity made work unbearable. This morning, however, a light breeze and cooler winds made the trip to see Aella tolerable. It was still the work week, but any hope of continuing the progress on the highway was past.

The prior night was an evening of drunken revelry. Two men had to be driven to the hospital because they'd stopped breathing after poisoning themselves with drink.

Buddy Brickman and Jimmy Conway celebrated another rematch. Buddy held his own against the contender and after five minutes of street brawling it looked like Buddy would, for once, be the victor. But Jimmy's ability to dodge and weave (and the fact that he was slightly more sober) allowed for a final set of punches to the gut which slowed Brickman's progress.

In the past, Timothy would have tilted the bottle with the others and screamed and chanted as the two mammoth men pummeled each other. But last night was different. Timothy had come down here on the government promise for work. But that promise had been broken. Many men drank to forget that their future was, once again, dashed at the mercy of the government they gave their lives to uphold.

Timothy, however, had come down with the promise of work. He found another outlet in the Tethis family. He worked on the boat and had gotten to know a few of the locals.

Timothy's arrival was a little late and he almost missed Aella and her father. They hadn't expected him during the week so there was no reason to wait.

194

As he neared the dock, he heard the sound of the motor. Timothy quickened his pace, trotting toward the boat as they were ready to cast off.

"Timothy! What are you doing here?" shouted the delighted Aella.

Nikolas shot him a suspicious glance.

"They're shutting down the project. The government is closing down the camps."

A look of concern grew on her face.

"Aella, we are leaving." Nikolas was getting upset. "Say goodbye to your friend."

"Papa wait!" she jumped off the boat.

"Aella!" yelled Nikolas as he throttled down the motor.

"One minute, papa!" There was a defiance in her voice that Nikolas never heard before.

Aella ran to Timothy. "So what does this mean? Will you be leaving?"

He looked into her beautiful brown eyes that already started welling up with tears. He smiled.

"No, I intend to stay."

Her shoulders relaxed and her smile matched his.

"Oh I'm so glad." She hugged him.

He stepped toward the boat.

"Mr. Tethis," said Timothy in a loud voice over the droning engine. "I was informed, last night, that the government is halting the road project. I plan on staying and working here. There isn't much for me back in Maryland. My hope is that I can work at the Millionaire's club when the season starts and the regulars start arriving. Until then, I would like to work for you."

There was a pause. Nikolas looked him up and down. Nikolas knew that Timothy was a hard worker, but his father instinct told him that Timothy would not be able to give Aella the kind of life that a father wanted for his daughter.

"Yes, yes... you can work for me. But only for a little while. I have Alexander. But if you are going to

195

become a sponger, you will have to talk with a Greek accent and not your strange Irish one."

Aella clapped her hands in delight and gave Timothy a hug.

"Climb aboard. We have a lot to do today. Today you learn what hard work is all about. Today you dive for sponges."

Aella and Timothy jumped on board *Brizo*. They had barely gotten both feet on the ground before Nikolas jerked the boat away from the dock.

Alexander had been below deck and came up as they headed out through the channel. He lit a hand rolled cigarette and, closing one eye, took a long draw. He took in the landscape. The Greek's face changed as he looked at the shoreline. He'd seen something that no one else saw.

Stepping forward, the man spoke to Nikolas.

"What is he saying?" asked Timothy.

Aella replied, "I'm not sure, I couldn't hear."

Just as quickly as Alexander materialized, he returned to the bowels of the vessel. The couple moved to the bow.

"What was that about, papa?" asked Aella.

"Alexander says that a storm is coming."

Timothy laughed. "Really? Look at the sky. It doesn't look stormy."

The dawn approached with a few cirrus clouds intermingling pink and purple. In a moment they became a phosphorescent maroon with no hint of malevolence.

Nikolas spoke. "Today we do some easy dives and stay close to shore. Alexander knows the water and the waves. He has a magical eye when it comes to the weather. If Alexander says it's going to rain, then it is going to rain. He told me the seals were gone and the crabs were moving inland. Storms are nothing to tempt. So we stay close to shore today."

Timothy shrugged, "Okay. It still doesn't look like bad weather. Look at the water out there, it is smooth as glass."

Alexander resurfaced and took over the controls for Nikolas.

"Today – young Timothy..." started Nikolas, "you will join me in Thalasa."

"Excuse me?" replied Timothy.

"The sea — the greatest place. The world is mostly water. We are made of sea water." Nikolas poked at Timothy. "And yet we do not have gills. At one time, I believe we did. What was his name.... the man... oh — the Beagle..." He turned to Alexander and rattled off his question in Greek. Alexander responded with his cigarette bouncing in his lips.

"Ah yes – Darwin... Mr. Darwin was right. We evolved from the sea. Some of us, especially the Greeks, have a greater kinship with the water. Perhaps we arose to land later than the Irish – I do not know."

Aella blushed and smiled. Her father was beginning to wax poetic. The old man seemed to be loosening up to her new Irish friend.

"You will join me in the depths. We will not be going deep today. But you will need to follow a few rules."

Timothy's stomach stated to turn. It was one thing to take a swim in the water. It was something else to watch a man gather sponges. However, he was now being asked to plunge into an environment that was not normal for a mammal, an Irish mammal, like himself.

"The first and most important rule...." Nikolas paused for dramatic effect. Timothy leaned forward in anticipation. Timothy was starting to sweat. "... is to breathe."

Timothy started to laugh, but he was the only one. Suddenly he was cognizant of his breath. He was embarrassed thinking the old man was joking with him. He was not.

"This is not a matter of humor," Timothy detected a tone of stern importance in Nikolas' voice.

"When you enter the water, it is human nature to hold your breath. But that is the very thing that will kill you. You must breathe. The compressor will feed you air. If it fails, Alexander will hook up a crank to the pump and churn the machine like he is making whipped butter. Trust me. It has happened only twice, but Alexander is the best man for the job."

Timothy could feel a small stream of sweat running down the back of his neck. He swallowed hard.

"The second rule..." Nikolas looked around and then back at Timothy. "... be aware of everything around you. You don't want to fall down. You don't want to let any other animals know that you do not see them. If you look at them, they will leave you alone."

Timothy thought about the first day he met Aella and the possibility that he might have been breakfast for sharks.

"We will get our suits on. Aella will help you. Watch what I do and do the same. Yes?"

Timothy was nervous. He ran his fingers through his thick black hair.

"Yes. What do we do first?"

"Are you wearing a bathing suit?" asked Nikolas.

Timothy blushed. "No."

"Do you have an undergarment that covers your privates?"

"Yes, I do."

"Hmm..." Nikolas thought. "Go below. Alexander has a duffel bag. Get his suit. He is larger than you, but it will be better than your undergarment."

Timothy went below and searched for the duffel bag. Odd parts, cans and machinery filled the cramped space each with the scent of oil and diesel. He found the duffel bag and the trunks. They had a drawstring so Timothy would be able to cinch them tight.

"Do you think he is capable of this?" Nikolas asked his daughter.

"I think he is capable — and more. He is a hard worker, papa. He is a good man who, like so many others, fell on bad times. We've talked, and I think he's come to know himself here."

Nikolas softened. "I want the best for you. I don't want your feelings hurt. He is a transient."

Aella turned to smell the fresh ocean breeze. The morning had come and everything was blue and silver.

She turned to her father and said, "We are all struggling. When you arrived, were you better off than Timothy? It is not what you have, but who you are. Timothy is a good man. I know it. You know that he wouldn't dive in the water if he wasn't trying to prove himself to you."

"He is still dry. We'll see if he gets his feet wet."

Aella smiled. "I know he will."

The trunks he wore were too large. It was obvious that Timothy had been wearing his shirt and pants while building the road. He was tanned on his forearms and neck where his skin was exposed. The remaining Irish-white skin glistened in the morning sun. He stood in stark contrast to the other golden-colored people on the boat. Aella tried not to laugh. The two Greek men looked at Timothy and made remarks under their breath.

Nikolas sat and pulled out his can of "lard," greasing his hands and feet. Timothy did the same. Timothy donned the canvas overalls that refused to bend where Timothy would like. Like the swimming trunks, the outfit that Timothy was donning was configured to a man Alexander's size. The canvas bent in at odd places. Timothy hoped that he wouldn't be all red and chaffed after the affairs of the day were over. He wriggled into the top portion of the uniform. Aella helped him the buckles and ties.

Alexander reached the destination where a mooring ball had been set. It was a popular place for fishing, but few came here for sponges. The Tall lanky man used a hook to grab the line and secured the boat to the ball. He came back to help Aella get the two ready for their immersion.

The Greek hoisted the weighted boots and dropped them with a thud in front of Nikolas. Both Nikolas and Timothy were sweating profusely now that the boat was idly bobbing.

"Aella, get us some water, please," requested Nikolas. She returned with a pitcher. Nikolas took a swig and poured some on his head. He passed the pitcher to Timothy who did the same. Timothy let out a big sigh as the water trickled down his back and front.

The two aquanauts smiled at each other. Timothy's smile, however, was mixed with anxiety and the growing pangs of fear.

Anticipating the Timothy's reticence, Nikolas asked, "What is rule number one?"

Timothy responded, "Breathe."

The boots fit loosely on Timothy's feet at first, but Aella pulled the laces tighter and tighter over a series of "lace ups." Two leather straps with buckles provided additional means of support for the heavy shoes. Timothy glanced down to see if the straps were made at the Bucheimer facility in his home town.

"Timothy – can you yawn for me please?" It was an unusual question from Nikolas.

"Umm – okay." Timothy opened his mouth and yawned so wide the back of his head hit the brass fittings on the collar. "Is there some special significance to this?"

"When you get in the water — yawn. Otherwise your ears will pop. It is very uncomfortable."

"Okay."

Timothy realized that this exercise was necessary. He'd seen Nikolas yawn on deck and assumed he was just tired from the early day. Timothy yawned again and felt his ears pop gently.

There was no turning back. Timothy was about to enter the water and the butterflies in his stomach were dancing wildly. His head was starting to spin. It was hot and that only multiplied the effect.

"Move slowly. You don't want to fall down. Breathe normally."

He wondered what else he should know. However, he had no context for asking pertinent questions. He knew that if he wasn't careful, he'd get woozy and hurl what was left churning in his stomach. Luckily he was still within eyeshot of the shore. He focused his gaze on the unmoving horizon. It was an old trick his father had taught him. This calmed his stomach but not his nerves.

Brizo rocked in a slow dance as a series of large swells made the craft tip. Some loose equipment rolled on deck. Alexander moved to the bow, lifted a hatch and tossed the anchor overboard. He didn't want the boat shifting as the two entered the water.

"This is it," thought Timothy. "This is one of two things — either Nikolas really hates me and he plans to create my demise underwater, or this is a test of trust."

The helmet, which was the last accoutrement to be attached, lay next to Timothy. It was different than Nikolas'. This was a crude assembly.

"I see you are looking at the helmet. I made it myself from a boiler. It was my first helmet that I used when I went sponging. I think it will still work. I haven't used it in years. You see, you are following tradition!"

Alexander knew the word 'traditio.' He lifted one hand and gave a hearty, "Oya! Oya!"

Aella leaned down and looked him in the eye. He smiled at her, but it wasn't convincing.

"Timothy – you are a brave man."

Alexander picked up a wrench and lifted the boiler-helmet. Aella gave him a quick kiss on the lips. This time Timothy's response was a real smile. He shot a glance to Nikolas who pretended to look out to the shore.

With a little maneuvering, Alexander lined up the holes and threads on the suit and helmet and started putting on the wing nuts. Aella moved to the compressor and started it up. The motor was much louder through the hose that ran out of the top of the helmet. He was breathing heavily as he heard the creak of the wing nuts being tightened. His field of view was limited to the forward window and the two smaller openings on the side.

Aella's face came into frame and she took up most of the small viewport. It was reassuring and Timothy's heart slowed a little. The heat was rising. He didn't know what was happening or what he was to do next. His breathing was heavy and he started to feel faint.

After a minute Alexander's face met Timothy's and he felt a pair of hands lifting him up. The suit was extremely cumbersome.

He stood and felt someone hand him something. He tried to look down and saw a feminine hand put the air hose in his grip. He saw Nikolas take a small leap over the side of the boat. The whirr of the motor sending him air was being silenced by the rush of blood flowing by his ears. He wondered if he would pass out before this adventure even started.

It was an act of will to take a step. The heavy boots clunked on the deck as he approached that space where the railing had been removed.

"Lord, help me," were the last words he spoke before imitating Nikolas and taking a giant leap into the great unknown. He instinctively held his breath and closed his eyes. He heard the sploosh of water, knowing he was sinking fast. He could feel the air hose being played out by someone on the surface. It was only an instant but his ears started hurting. He'd forgotten to yawn when he entered the water. He did so now, only to have both his ears crack with an equalizing pain. He opened his eyes just in time for his feet to find the sandy ground.

The viewport was quickly filled with Nikolas' helmet. Nikolas was gauging Timothy's response. He first checked to see if the young man was breathing. Next he checked to see if he was in agony. Finally, he checked to see if Timothy was scared out of his wits. Satisfied that none of these conditions existed, he left Timothy's small window to the aquatic world.

Through the portal, he gazed at a coral outcrop. A school of sergeant majors moved in unison among the purple fan coral that sprung up from the many crags. The yellow and black bands of the fish danced in and through the colored living landscape. A blue tang — its brilliance magnified by the bands of light that came from the rippled surface looked like living electric currents.

Timothy felt a tug. Startled, he turned and nearly lost his footing. Nikolas put a hand on his shoulders. The man's other hand was holding a large serrated knife. Nikolas looked into Timothy's eyes again and saw he was okay. Timothy put on a grin, his eyes squinting. Satisfied, Nikolas gestured for Timothy to follow him. They moved away from the rocky outcrop toward the sand which stretched into an abbreviated infinity. The sand was distributed into wavelet hills created by the regularity of the tide. The sun refracted and danced along the watery bottom with a light show radiating in strands of wonderful serpentine luminosity.

From the blue haze emerged what appeared to be a column. As the two moved closer the structure became clearer. Timothy saw that it was a large barrel sponge. In fact, it was the largest single sponge that he'd ever seen. He knew but never really comprehended that these were actual living things. Nikolas pointed to the base of the sponge. Timothy didn't see the object. Nikolas crouched down and pointed again. He then indicated something with two fingers and pointed again.

Timothy squinted and saw two thin curved antennae sampling the water and area immediately outside the sponge. The young man still had no idea what was attached to these projectiles. He looked at Nikolas and gestured the international sign, "I don't know."

Nikolas pointed and then quickly jabbed his knife into the hole. A sand plume erupted at the base of the darkness and Nikolas pulled out a large dark lobster. Timothy didn't know what it was at first. It appeared to be some insect-like monstrosity with its legs and arms unable to free itself from Nikolas' clutch. He'd only ever seen a lobster on a plate.

He'd always thought the claws on the lobster were bigger. These seemed small in comparison to the huge frame. Nikolas let the creature go and it awkwardly swam to the bottom where it scurried into the hole.

Nikolas then took the knife and with three quick movements sliced a piece of the sponge. He held it in his hands, showing Timothy the dimensions. Without looking, Nikolas tossed the sponge into the net that had been harnessed to his back. The Greek handed over the knife and gestured again how to slice the sponge. Timothy tried it and failed miserably. The sponge, though soft, was unyielding. Timothy hadn't put enough pressure and ended up cutting into the sponge like sawing into a piece of meat. Small pieces floated around his face mocking his feeble attempt.

Nikolas took the knife and showed him again. This time Timothy would pull and slice at the same time. The result was much better. He realized that the knife would only cut if he moved the blade while simultaneously pulling back on the sponge.

The piece he cut came out and floated in front of him. Nikolas nodded approval as Timothy tried to toss the piece into the net. It fell short. He grabbed it and placed it in the net. Nikolas pulled another knife at his hip as the two worked together. Timothy thought it strange that the cumbersome outfit on land wasn't so bad underwater. But the work was, by no means, easier.

They reduced the size of the sponge by half before Nikolas halted the operation. They moved to another sponge nearby and repeated the operation. Timothy noticed that as they hacked away at the sponge, other strange and wonderful fish came to share in the bounty. Multicolored parrot fish and angel fish skirted by grabbing a piece of floating debris. Timothy stopped and looked at the sea life that lived in such abundance and tight community.

By the time they moved to the third sponge, the two divers had attracted a large number of fish. Timothy had to swat them away to see his next cut. As he did so, the fish darted away and immediately circled back.

Only when a shadow crossed over them did the fish disperse. Nikolas stopped, looked up and resumed his methodical work. Timothy also stopped and looked. A large shark passed a few feet over his head. The gray beast shot around them and the animal's eye passed Timothy's field of view.

Timothy jumped back in fear and let out a yell. He lost his footing and stumbled backward. The beast was startled by the alien under the water. With a flick of its massive tail, the shark disappeared into the turquoise haze.

Timothy couldn't catch his breath. He lay on his back hyperventilating. He was waiting for the hungry beast to come and eat the human on its back. Timothy jumped when a dark figure appeared and grabbed his arm.

It was Nikolas. He helped Timothy to his feet and put the knife back in his hand. Only then did Timothy realize that his hyperventilation came from the fact that he'd fallen backward and landed on his own air supply.

Timothy was embarrassed. He felt he'd failed. He'd have to apologize to Nikolas. Nikolas looked at Timothy. Each man locked their gaze through the small windows in their helmets. Timothy saw that Nikolas was smiling.

This was his world. Nikolas felt comfortable here. The fish that kept him company were his pets. Nikolas, through that small portal, had a grin on his face and a softness in his features that were lost on land.

The hours went by quickly. It was hard work and Timothy was glad that he'd put lard around his hands. His elbows however were becoming chaffed from the resistant material and the repetitious act of slicing.

Nikolas called a silent halt and motioned toward the boat. Timothy could see the underside of the hull bobbing on the surface. Puffy cumulus clouds moved swiftly across the water's surreal ceiling.

Alexander dropped a line from the boat. Nikolas pulled himself, arm-over-arm, toward the surface. Timothy was, for a moment, at the bottom of the ocean — alone. The air compressor still amplified its life giving sound through the hose. A lone barracuda darted past as Timothy said goodbye to this wonderful new world.

Only as he was ascending did he begin to feel an emotion he'd never experienced. The fear had subsided and the understanding of the sea started to creep into his veins. He embraced a communion with the deep that only a few from the terrestrial realm had ever happened upon. He looked into its vastness and wondered what lay beyond that fringe of blue. There was more out there. There were bigger and stranger life forms. His imagination was getting the best of him. Schools of purple wrasse swam by bringing him back to his senses.

He started toward the surface. His arms ached from the cutting, so the hand-over-hand ascent along the dropped line was no easy task. When his head broke the surface, he could go no further. The weights on his shoes wanted to pull him back down. He was sweating heavily. It took all three of them on the boat to help lift Timothy onto the deck.

He had little grace as he pulled, squirmed and eventually rolled onto the deck. He was less graceful than the seals he'd seen along the shore. Now safely on the boat he sat up. There were still drips and rivulets of water on his portal, but he saw Aella's face which stared at him with a mixture of relief and concern. He smiled and gave a rough "thumbs up" sign with the heavy gloves.

Alexander started undoing the wing nuts. Aella helped. The two pulled off the homemade helmet and Timothy took a long draught of air. Alexander was the first to speak, "You okay?"

"Yes, thank you," responded Timothy, a little surprised at the question posed by the man who never before spoke a word of English.

"Very – very good." Alexander smiled.

Timothy knew that any other response would have resulted in the man's blank stare. Alexander had exhausted his mastery of English and returned to other tasks.

Aella snuck him another kiss as the others went about their business. Nikolas was already out of the top portion of his diving suit.

"You did good my young friend!"

"Thank you," Tim responded still a little winded from exerting himself in the suit.

"Did you like my pet underwater? He is my..." Nikolas was searching for the English words.

"... my guard pet. Like a dog. But it is a shark. It is my guard shark. He likes to keep me company. He scared you — yes?"

"Umm – yes!"

Nikolas turned to Alexander and started rattling off the narrative of the shark encounter. He even fell backward and held onto the line, gasping for air. Alexander laughed so hard that the cigarette dropped from his mouth, and he had to quickly pick it up before it became saturated with the sea water splashed on *Brizo*'s deck.

They dipped the helmets in the fresh water and put them in the sun. Aella helped Timothy out of the outfit. He scrubbed his hands with soap and washed them off in the sea water.

Aella brought up a huge basket from below. The first items were two unmarked wine bottles.

"If you want to be a part of our crew, you have to drink a real wine. This recipe comes from the Isle of Limnos. I have had to make a few modifications since the countries are so different, but the process is similar." Nikolas opened the bottle and took a taste. He passed the bottle to Timothy.

Timothy took a taste. The wine was instantly refreshing and had overtones of blueberry and chocolate. There was a buttery aftertaste that melded with the salt on his lips.

Aella pulled out some cheese and started cutting. She produced an olive salad and some chicken sandwiches. The sandwiches had a rich yellow sauce that was foreign, yet pleasing to his tongue.

"So how much more will we be harvesting today?" asked Timothy.

"We are done for the day."

"What?" Timothy was surprised. They never returned before sundown. It was only midday and the weather was perfect.

"Alexander says there is bad weather coming. He knows the weather. I think he is the grandchild of Anemi."

"But the weather looks fine..."

Aella put a hand on Timothy's wrist. Though Timothy wanted to get back in the water, it was not to be. After lunch they stowed the gear and pulled up anchor. The sky was still perfect but the breeze was starting to strengthen. There was no sign of bad weather.

As they headed back, it seemed that *Brizo* had to work harder against an invisible current. There was a distinct rise and fall of the water. It was more swells than breakers. Alexander gave Nikolas a grave look.

"Those two look like they saw a ghost," said Timothy.

"They are a strange pair. They seem to know more about the water than anyone else here. Even some of the locals haven't a clue and these two seem to feel it in their bones. They don't look happy."

As they idled back to the dock, Nikolas said to Timothy. "I will need your help."

It was the first time that Timothy actually felt like they had a bond. As if the immersion was a baptism and a rite that he'd passed, Timothy was now part of the crew.

"Of course," Tim responded. "Whatever you need."

"I need you to help me stow everything. A storm is coming and it is a bad storm. We need to make sure nothing is left un..." again the words failed Nikolas. "... we need everything in security."

"Let me know what you need. I am there for you."

Alexander jumped from the boat and pulled the line around the pier. Nikolas finished the job.

"All of the equipment must come off the boat and put into the house. I do not want it on the dock. It must be inside."

The crew started grabbing all of the gear hauling it to the house. At first they filled up the kitchen, then the living room. Coiled rope lay strewn across overstuffed chairs. The diving suits lay on the ground like severed corpses. Hooks, knives, and machinery occupied the kitchen table and chairs.

There seemed to be a million little cubby holes where something on the boat was stashed. Timothy noticed how high *Brizo* sat out of the water with all of the equipment now in the house. Nikolas came to Timothy.

"We are not done."

Though Timothy ached, he said nothing.

"We have to put those concrete disks in the water. Toss them over the dock here."

"What?" It seemed strange that He would want to toss the pile of disks away.

"Please – do as I say." There was a sense of urgency in the man's voice.

"Okay." Timothy grabbed a stack and started tossing them in the water. He could see a few shattered as they hit the bottom. Aella and Alexander helped the other two as they lined the bottom of the dock with the disks.

"If Alexander is correct, we could be in trouble if these start flying around."

Timothy didn't see that as possible. Each disk was about five pounds and now sat in twenty feet of water.

By the time that task was complete Timothy's back was ready to go on strike.

"And now — we have the dock house."

Nikolas opened the door to a room filled with miscellaneous maritime equipment, hardware and boards. It looked like a never ending task. Yet, the crew worked hard to get the equipment in the house. Timothy realized that this house did not, nor could not, have a basement. In Maryland it was odd to find one that didn't have a coal chute running to the furnace. Here, the coral ground was impenetrable.

Aella's mother worked around the equipment in the kitchen preparing a large feast. By the time the last piece was stowed and the boat was anchored in the middle of the inlet, everyone was exhausted. The sun was starting to set, but there was still no sign of bad weather. Timothy thought that this exercise was futile. He didn't understand and dreaded the thought that tomorrow he would have to lug everything back out of the house.

There was no table available, so everyone heaped the food on their plate and headed outside and sat on the edge of the small porch. They spoke little, each consuming second helpings. Timothy felt that wave of food induced coma taking over. It was magnified by the utter exhaustion of a hard day's work.

Nikolas got up and walked over to the barometer. He tapped it a couple of times. The barometer was the true test of the weather. If there was a change, the barometer was the prophet which foretold a storm's coming. The needle hadn't budged. If anything, it looked like it had risen a little. He turned to Alexander and spoke a few words. Alexander shrugged as he shoveled down his food.

"We need to walk, Timothy," said Aella before uttering a most unladylike belch. She smiled because, though she'd done this many times before, she had never done it in front of Timothy. She blushed.

Timothy was amused and replied with a satisfactory belch of his own. "Yes, let's walk."

"Aella, do not go out in the water. It is too dangerous. The tide is pulling out and the storm is drinking."

"Yes, papa," she said as she grabbed Timothy's hand. They walked under the tropical canopy along the driveway.

When they got to the road, Timothy asked, "What did your father mean when he said, 'the storm is drinking?'"

"Bad storms consume the ocean and spit it back out. If this is an ebb tide, then you get currents which could pull you out to sea. It is bad."

"Do you really think a bad storm is coming?"

"I believe my father."

"Is it a hurricane?"

"Who knows? I think he believes — yes."

She quickly turned off the road, pulling his hand.

"Where are we going?"

"Shhh!"

The two approached a thick mass of mangroves. It looked like an impenetrable wall of lush green and gnarled branches. At the base, there was a small opening just large enough for them to crawl through. Timothy's muscles ached and the food in his belly made it hard for him to crouch down any more. They passed through the thick brush; immature sea grass tickled them as they crawled through the small opening.

It was a relief when they emerged to an opening of palm trees and soft sand. The water lapped onto the small shoreline.

"They said that the Indians thought this was a sacred place. Grab some of those." She pointed to a large plant with, wide banana-like, leaves. He pulled three and she did the same.

The two spread the fronds out on the sandy shore. The water lapped lazily giving no indication of impending danger. Some driftwood had come ashore and whitened like the bones of some ancient creature. A line of seaweed marked the high tide of the day.

The two lay on the leaves facing each other. Aella's face seemed to soften as they gazed into each other's eyes. Her blouse was open and a single bead of sweat followed her neckline to the curves of her breasts. Timothy's body ached for her.

They stared, saying nothing — simply soaking each other in. Timothy could feel his heart quickening as he tried to sear every detail of this wonderful moment into his mind.

Without a word, he placed his hand on the back of her head and drew her in for a kiss. She closed her eyes and melted into him. Her lips parted and he leaned his body against hers. They embraced and he softly whispered, "I love you."

She pulled back and looked at him. Her brown eyes conveyed the same love, but she didn't utter a word. She traced the edge of his dark hair, around his ear and down his neck. She unbuttoned the first button of his shirt. He didn't realize that he'd been holding his breath. After kissing again they sat up. His hand moved to her neck and on to her blouse. He cupped her breast in his hand as if holding a precious jewel. She undid one button and pulled the blouse over her head. The golden skin was dotted with perspiration both from the heat and the passion. She was glistening like a goddess of her ancestors.

Timothy removed his shirt. They both stood and held each other in an embrace, each feeling the unspoken connection to the other. Her hand slid to the place where he'd grown hard. He let out a moan. He kissed her neck. As he did so, she arched back, small beads of sweat running down her chest.

She loosened her dress and it fell to the ground. She undid his belt and they both stood there looking at each other. They touched and explored each other — hands, arms, neck legs. They lay back down. Timothy climbed on top and felt for the soft separation between her legs.

She helped guide him in. She was so beautiful Timothy had to refrain with an incredible force of will not to climax at that moment. She rolled him over so she was on top, undulating and arching back, moving with the rhythm of the surf. She stopped and kissed his neck and chest. Each touch sent an electric fire through his body.

She looked at him and felt him inside her. His hands were strong as he placed them on her hips as the two moved together. He rolled her off of him and mounted her again. She could feel him move ever quicker as the two became lost in the act.

Both found satisfaction as they consummated their love for each other while the palms swayed in the freshening breeze. They lay together enjoying each other with their hands and mouth.

"You should put on your clothes, Timothy. You are going to get burned by the sun."

"You are amazing," replied Timothy. "Your body is incredible. Your skin was made for this."

"When I was a child, I would sneak here and swim naked. There was never anyone around. I'll admit that I still come here every now and then."

"Can we swim now?"

"We shouldn't go out too far. Papa said the current is too strong, but it would be safe to wade out a short distance."

The two got up and walked hand-in-hand to the refreshing water. They knelt down as the wavelets came up to their neck. Timothy could feel the slightest pull of the water and knew that Nikolas was right about the current.

"I never want to leave you. I never want to leave this place," said Timothy.

He kissed her.

"I want you to stay. I want you here — always," she responded.

He looked into her eyes and felt their spirits combined. He looked at her, so at peace and part of the space they occupied. He no longer felt like a stranger. He, too, had been accepted. He kissed her and uttered, "I'm home."

Jerry Travers: Are you afraid of thunder?
Dale Tremont: Oh, no. It's just the noise.
Jerry Travers: You know what thunder is, don't you?
Dale Tremont: Of course. It's something about the air.
Jerry Travers: No, no. When a clumsy cloud from here meets a fluffy little cloud from there, he billows towards her. She scurries away and he scuds right up to her. She cries a little and there you have your showers. He comforts her. They spark. That's the lightning. They kiss. Thunder.
- From the movie "Top Hat"

Sam Cutler, Ed Sheeran and Ray Sheldon were running a shuttle system between the camps and the railroad. It was payday, the men knew their time was here was over, and the Labor Day weekend was upon them. The atmosphere of the camp had changed dramatically. Even though it was both the Labor Day weekend and a payday, the camp was eerily quiet. The sullen nature of the men was a far cry from the usually chaotic bacchanal of the weekend. Sheldon expected trouble and didn't waste time to make sure the men knew he was in control. Sheldon made a call to Sheriff Maloney who sat on a bar stool in the mess hall with a rifle slung over his lap. This was another in a string of changes that filled the atmosphere of the camp with a sense of oppression and foreboding. The paymaster had a sidearm.

"Welcome to hell, gentleman," said Elmer as he stood in line. "Even a drink ain't gonna make this place any better today."

A few of the men grumbled.

"But I'm gonna drink anyway."

A few more chuckled.

Many of the men were heading to Miami or Key West. The trains were full of the men who had depleted their store of alcohol and were ready for

215

more. Others decided to stay. Their decision was due to depression, lack of money or an "in-house" store of spirits.

Elmer was among those who decided to stay. He'd saved enough money to last for a while as he headed north. This would be his last weekend at the camp. He wanted to say goodbye to Harry and the others. He'd raise a glass or three with them. He wanted to catch Timothy who had been noticeably absent. His courtship with one of the locals was a hot topic at the camp.

There was also the famous reuniting of Buddy and Jimmy in the ring. Jimmy had been giving Buddy some boxing tips. The two contenders were becoming equal rivals as they duked it out yet were best friends outside the ring.

This was a bittersweet moment for Elmer. He'd been nothing more than the town drunk anywhere else. Down here he was given responsibility. He'd done a little work and made a little money. From those on the outside, those with stable jobs and stable lives, it would appear that Elmer had achieved a small success. For Elmer, the camp had proven pivotal. Elmer now had something he'd never been able to claim — a marketable skill. He could help build a road.

Others may not have been able to make that claim. This place had broken more than a few. Some died here. Other men dried up in the sun — their spirits withering against the tide of yet another hardship.

Elmer looked at the men in line as they waited for their pay. He'd seen the same sullen look on these men as those he'd seen while he was in prison. The vets were, again captives and victims of circumstance. Some had an animal desperation about them. More than a few were broke with nowhere to go.

As soon as the news of the camp's closing was announced, some men snuck away to the motor pool to hot-wire the trucks. The keys were safely secured by Cutler in Hotel Matecumbe. Those that tried were caught and turned over to the National Guard and hauled north.

With the Labor Day weekend upon them, hundreds of the workers would seek refuge in prostitutes and bars far from here. Those that could run — would run. Those that stayed would try and bury their sorrow in the best way they knew how.

Harry was among those who felt their cause had come to an end. For Harry, there was just nothing left to believe in. The hope was gone. He'd looked for Sheeran to share his thoughts, but the old man was busy ferrying the revelers.

Harry walked among the large machines, now idle, and wondered if they would even bother to start them after the holiday. He walked down the road and looked at the broad expanse of concrete that was the unfinished bridge. Would someone else finish this monumental task?

Harry remembered the picture hanging on the wall of the mess hall. From his vantage point, it looked even more amazing. The water lapped up against the white structure that rose from the horizon as the structure stretched two stories high. He walked down the road that no car or truck would travel. A fishing boat had dropped a few lines near the bridge. A lone fisherman had his hat pulled over his face as he waited for a bite.

As Harry ascended the grand structure, he could see where the other camp had made headway on the Long Key side of the bridge. Harry could empathize with the unfinished bridge. His life had been a set of unresolved moments that ate away at his soul. He'd thought he would be able to claim at least one victory with the completion of the highway. But this was not to be.

He reached the edge of the highway. Rebar reached out like tendrils of some great beast hoping to embrace the behemoth from the other island. He sat down and dangled his feet over the edge. He could see the current flowing in as the water glistened diamond rays of sunshine into his eyes.

It was more than a passing thought. As he sat on the edge of the bridge, he wondered what would happen if he just scooted over the side. Would he hit the water and end it all? He remembered Buddy saying that the water was hard when someone jumped from this height. He couldn't be certain it would be his final act. He'd written no note. He said goodbye to no one.

But as he contemplated his own demise, he remembered the friendships he made. He remembered the adventures he had. In the midst of his pain, there had been moments of redemption.

There was more to his life than the failed accomplishments. He had, in at least in some small way, succeeded. Timothy, Elmer, Krebs, Brickman and Jimmy had become valuable friends. He came to know Ed Sheeran and created bond with his boss at a deep and personal level. Even if they parted company, he still carried the camaraderie that time and distance would never sever.

Harry pulled back and stood at the edge. He wouldn't jump — at least not today.

The whistle blew and the train for Key West made its departure. The sound was hollow and echoed through the palm trees as it made its way south. Cutler drove back to Hotel Matecumbe angrier than he'd been in a long time. He wanted to fish, but once again would be denied. Of course, he could just slip out back behind the mess hall and cast a line, but it wasn't the same as heading out into the big blue in the hope of catching some of the larger fish. Daily he watched other fishing boats motoring out to where the big fish live somewhere beyond the horizon.

With half the men gone, he thought he might sneak out late Saturday and row to a few holes that might bring in a better catch. He'd have to wait and see. Cutler was always torn between his desire to go fishing and sense of duty to the men.

After entering the lobby of Hotel Matecumbe, he looked at the cubby behind the desk. He'd long ago dismissed the need to wait for someone to come out and give him any messages. This had become his second home. He saw a note in the hole where he got his mail. It was a hand scribbled note from someone who had called from Jacksonville Florida.

Jacksonville, FL – 1PM, Aug 31

I received this from a weather man who called and wanted to relay the information –

Tropical disturbance of small diameter about sixty miles east of Long Island, Bahamas. Strong winds.

Beatrice

Cutler glanced at the note and made a mental map of the storm's location. It was far off. The message was rather vague, like many he'd received over the summer. Last week he received a similar notice and nothing came of it. Nonetheless, he would notify Sheldon.

He wadded the paper and threw it in the waste basket. He picked up the black phone and made his request to connect to the camp, hoping Sheldon was finishing up there.

"Sorry, he ain't around. Haven't seen him since this morning," said Carl. The cook and a few others were cleaning up from a rather light lunch crowd. "If I see him, you want me to give him a message?"

"Yeah, we got a storm advisory from the weatherman in Jacksonville. Let him know that."

"Will do."

Cutler hung up the phone. He tried to call the phone that was installed at the bridge worksite, but there was no answer. He tried a few of the other camps, but no one had seen Sheldon. Cutler wondered if the man had headed to Key West early.

Sheldon was outside packing up the convertible. Gayle had put on a white dress with blue pin stripes and a hat. She applied bright red lipstick. In that outfit, she looked even younger than her early twenties. No doubt men would make advances toward her in Key West. Many would mistake him for her father rather than her husband. At times he treated her like the girl she was. But having her was a way for him to feel young. Time was catching up with him, and he was fighting it all of the way.

"Did you get all of my things? I think you forgot one of the bags," she said as she pointed to each suitcase and mouthed the numbers.

"Honey – we're only going for the weekend. This isn't a month-long excursion around the world." Sheldon was upset. He had to throw some of the bags in the back as well as the trunk.

"Look – this is my honeymoon. I've been waiting long enough. It has been hot down here, and you know I hate bugs. Bugs – bugs – bugs. That's all I see all day. They crawl on the floor, fly overhead and get into, well, I won't even tell you where I've found some of those awful bugs. I just want to get away."

Sheldon snickered. "Gayle, I hate to break it to you, but I think they might have a bug or two in Key West."

"Ugh," Gayle raised and dropped her shoulders. Sheldon thought she looked like a movie star when she did that. "You'll just have to take me..." she thought for a second. "...on a boat. Yes, you'll have to take me on a boat to get away from the bugs."

"Yes dear."

Sheldon drew out his response. If he could get past the conversation portion of the honeymoon, he thought he might just have a good time. His bag consisted of a few clean shirts and a bottle of Kentucky whiskey.

They got in the car. Gayle leaned in and gave him a quick smooch as he started the car. Sheldon figured that he had tied up the all the loose ends. He'd given Cutler the number of the La Concha Hotel in Key West if Cutler needed to contact him.

With the news of the closure, he was glad that he wasn't sticking around. Sheldon told Cutler that if there were any skirmishes, Cutler was to let them duke it out until they were all a bloody pulp. That was no cause for the authorities. However, he wanted Sheeran and Cutler to make regular rounds. If any of the equipment was disturbed, they were to call in the guard. This was government property and that was an offense with stiff penalties and jail time.

The summer storms hadn't amounted to much so the thought of a hurricane wasn't on the forefront of his mind. It was the end of the season, and so such a storm was unlikely. He confirmed with Ghent about the train, and both agreed that all was in order.

It felt good to have the breeze blowing through his hair as the two raced down the highway. Sheldon glanced to his right and saw the large looming mass of concrete. This was the result of his leadership. It was a monument that he would have to leave undone. He was considering going back to Julius Stone and negotiating to get a civilian crew in to finish the job. He was already running the estimates through his head.

He would love to bring Gayle back down that road and open up the convertible on the long bridge.

"Hey, I heard that there is a movie called 'Top Hat.' Do you think we can go see a movie?"

"Honey, I'm not sure they have a cinema in Key West."

Ray only knew of bars down there. He figured there'd be some shops, but he never entertained the idea of doing anything but drinking and screwing. He put his arms around his wife and gave her a squeeze. As he did so, he passed a car and accelerated. He was pushing seventy miles an hour. He barely heard the honk from the slowpoke that was disappearing in the rear view mirror.

However, Ray's speedy travel was short lived. After only a few short miles, they stopped and joined the line of vehicles waiting to board the ferry. They sat as the cars were loaded one by one. Normally the engines of the ferry would be idling, but this time they were silent.

It was a three hour trip on the ferry from Lower Matecumbe to No Name Key. From there, it was a little over forty miles to Key West. Sheldon wanted to make it to Key West before sundown, so he could find a good place to hide his car. He didn't want it to get wet if at all possible. Storms blew in regularly on that little island. That's why he bought the alcohol before he left. He didn't want to traipse around Key West in an evening deluge and end up spending more for cheap liquor than he would in parts north.

If he was stuck at the hotel with Gayle – well the booze and the young wife was all he needed.

He slowly drove his vehicle onto the ferry and lined his car up close to the others. They got out and presented their tickets.

"Hey, why ain't the motors revved for the trip?"

The man taking the tickets answered, "The motors were running a little hot, so the captain called an all stop. The engineer is taking a look at them. We might get off a little late, but not too much. Nothing to worry about."

Gayle had already headed up the metal stairs to get a bird's eye view of the landscape. It was, at that moment, one of the highest vantage points for miles. Sheldon joined her.

"Look – look over there," said Sheldon pointing.

"You see that? There's the water tower for the camp. And if you follow the line south. There it is... there's the bridge."

"Where? I see the tower but I don't see the bridge." Gayle put her hand over her brow to cut down the sun.

"Follow the horizon. See? Over there..."

She spotted the two white rises. At first it looked like two clouds on the horizon lifting up from the land to the deep blue of the sky. They were unfinished. Sheldon was proud but he wouldn't be satisfied until both parts met in final glory.

With a rumble and a puff of black smoke, the first of two diesel engines rumbled to life. Sheldon wrapped his arms around Gayle. She placed her arms on his as the ferry trembled as the second engine roared. The smell of the fumes never bothered Sheldon. As the diesel permeated the boat, he took a long whiff. It was the smell of power.

Cutler looked around the desk at the hotel. It took a while, but he found what he was looking for. A box of silver thumbtacks lay hidden under a pad of paper. Like he'd done before when he'd received a call, he put a tack in the approximate position of the storm. He would track it like the others. There were numerous holes from previous pin pricks in the map that hung on the wall.

This mark was an isolated point on a very large map. But he was doing his duty. If there were any other notifications, he would follow the storm. On more than one occasion, he was able to keep the vets safely at work because he'd tracked the storm as it veered away.

Cutler then went out to his truck to check his tackle box — just in case.

Harry was walking back down the road. In the heat of the afternoon, the tar smell was as fresh as if it had been applied that morning. A line of cars were heading in either direction on the old road. Apparently a truck had broken down. This was as many cars that he'd seen along the highway in a week.

"Hey! Harry!"

Harry turned but didn't see the one crying out his name.

"Harry – over here!"

Ed Sheeran was waving. It was hard to see him. He was in his dungarees and a once blue shirt. Various stains had marked him so he was camouflaged against the mangroves. He was tinkering with a large diesel compressor that was mounted on a pickup truck. Harry returned the wave and headed over to see the old man.

"I heard the word about this project the same time as you or I would've let you know. I hope you know that."

Ed's tone was apologetic.

"I understand. It's not your fault. Hell, it's nobody's fault."

Harry kicked some of the loose coral that lay on the side of the road.

"Well, I feel responsible."

Harry heard the pain in Ed's voice.

"Ed, you know that the government is in the habit lately of turning tail on itself. One minute they got a sweet deal — the next they pull the rug from under ya."

"Well, I heard that it ain't official yet. Nobody's signed the order."

"The suits that came down sounded pretty official to me."

"I suppose. But I can't imagine that they'd let all this go to waste. I bet there'll be a civilian contingent coming here to finish the job. Heck, it might be government funded. Maybe Flagler's company will buy into it. Though – from what I hear they're going belly up."

"Well, you've been good to me. I appreciate that." Harry put a hand on Ed's shoulder.

"You got any prospects?"

"None at the moment," replied Harry.

224

"What I'm drivin' at is – I suspect whoever is working on the project next will need a few good hired hands. You know how to fix just about anything down here. That sea water makes everything rust fast."

"Ain't that the truth," said Harry. He looked at the generator. "Looks like that generator has seen some of it."

"Yeah, seems we've all gotten a bit rusty down here."

"I can't make any promises." Ed hesitated. "You see, I'm pretty much in the same boat as you are. Once this thing shuts down, I'm out of a job — just like you. But I've been doing this a while, and I know someone'll be looking for some good foremen and experienced engineers. If you ain't got anywhere in particular to go — stay a while. I'll put in a good word for you."

"I appreciate that Ed." Harry considered the fleeting thought he had on the edge of the bridge. It seemed that he'd not lost everything after all.

"You are a good friend. You know I lost the love of my life back in Kansas. If I could prove myself down here, maybe I could get her back. I dunno."

"You're one of the few I'd seen get better down here. I'd hate to lose ya." Ed stuck out his hand. Harry took it and the two shook as they looked into each other's eyes.

"Thank you Colonel."

"Hey, that's what friends are for." Ed said. "Oh, by the way – I heard a rumor."

"Oh?"

"Some of the conchs say a storm's coming. I hear it's a bad one."

"How do they know?"

"Beats the hell outta me."

"Did you talk to Sheldon?"

"No, he'd already left for Key West. I talked to Sam Cutler. He said the storm was far away. He checked the barometer and it hadn't budged. I told Cutler we need to get the train down here, but he said that Sheldon thought it wasn't a big deal. I'm not sure he even talked to the man."

"So what do you think?"

"I trust the locals. That's why I'm tellin' you."

"Do you think Sheldon ordered the train?"

"Hah," Sheeran shook his head. "Have you ever heard of Sheldon taking advice? Even if it is from a damn weatherman talkin' about the weather."

Harry shook his head. "Never. He's as dense as he is stubborn."

"So I know we got a lot of men out for the holiday and I can bet that most are gonna be three sheets to the wind tonight, but I'd like to get an early start tomorrow and haul this equipment to the hurricane channel and put it on the barge. Who knows what's coming, but I don't want to take any chances. You think you can muster a handful of men?"

"I'll do my best. How many? Four?"

"That'll do. We'll stow away as much as possible. Worst that can happen is that we have to get it all back out on Tuesday."

Krebs sat in his shack. From under the pillow he pulled out the last vial of heroin.

"This is the last time," he said to himself. He'd said those words before, but this time he meant it. He meant it the other times as well, but he knew he was out of money. With the program shutting down, he wouldn't be able to support his habit. He was a gambling man and knew the odds. They weren't in his favor. The "juice" slid into his blood. It felt cold and inviting. It stopped the pressure that was mounting in his head. His heart and breathing slowed. He was surprised that the effects were so quick.

At one point in his life he started using the stuff to get away from reality. Now he was using to hang on to it. He'd been on the edge more than once. He dreaded what was going to happen. He never knew when the tremors would start. He never knew when the ice picks would start stabbing at his brain.

He wanted to go to Key West but had missed the train. Maybe there he could have hustled more heroin. Maybe he would have taken a fool's money in a sucker bet. Most of the men were on to him here. Tonight there'd be the fight. He had a few dollars and he thought he might put them on the underdog. Brickman was getting better. The odds were against Buddy Brickman, but he'd seen how hard he was training.

Cutler had given up trying to find Sheldon. In his calls he did finally contacted Sheeran who was at the worksite. Oddly, Sheeran seemed to know more about the storm than Cutler, though Sheeran hadn't heard a peep from the weather bureau. The nervous Cutler looked at the single thumbtack in the map. He'd tracked the storms through the summer. Most took a circuitous route around the watery way and ended up God knows where.

On one occasion a storm married with a high tide and drenched the mess hall. The water lapped right into the kitchen but subsided without causing too much damage.

This time things were a little different. Cutler wasn't sure who was in charge. Sheldon had left without instruction. Ghent was north but still on the payroll. It seemed that by proxy he was in charge, though command hadn't been authorized to him directly.

He hated when there was ambiguity.

The phone rang. Cutler answered.

"I'm Clarence Goodall from the weather bureau calling with an update on the storm."

"Hold on a sec." Cutler scrambled to find a pencil and paper. "Go ahead."

"There's a tropical disturbance of small diameter centered near long Island, Bahamas, apparently moving west northwestward. The winds are picking up — squalling and possibly gale force near the center. We've issued a caution for the Bahama Islands and any ships in that vicinity."

"So is it strengthening?" asked Cutler.

"Hard to say. I am just going by the few ships in the area. The information is rather scarce. Some of the ships out there don't have an English speaking crew, so they're just sending us the numbers."
"Thanks."

Cutler hung up the phone and got out another thumbtack. He then picked up the phone and rang for Sheeran.

"Ed, I have some more information on the storm."

Cutler relayed the information.

"Sam, that thing's closer than I thought. What have we done for the men at camp?"

Sam looked at the barometer. It had actually risen indicating fair weather.

"It still doesn't seem like much. We've been through worse. And most of the men are gone."

"Does Sheldon know about any of this?"

"Hard to say. He's gone on his honeymoon. I haven't heard from him."

Sheldon watched a fishing boat hauling in a large tarpon. The water was teaming with fish and the fishermen were having a good day with the catch. Gayle was by his side watching the action.

"Do you think we could go fishing?"

"That's a man's sport honey. You can't fish."

"It looks like fun."

"It is. But it's hard work. It's not something for a lady." Sheldon tried to dismiss her notion.

She looked at him with slight disappointment. She didn't understand why only men could fish, but she resigned herself to the wisdom of her older husband.

She'd come from a struggling family and Ray offered her what she desired most — security. She was ignorant and immune to the problems such an age difference brought to a relationship. She

228

thought the sex was something dirty. On more than one occasion Ray, smelling of rum and sweat, had hurt her. She was warned by her mother of such a thing and so accepted it as normal. It was a sacrifice she was willing to make. With Ray, she could buy new clothes and drive a fancy convertible — well, she would if Ray let her. She thought he would — in time. She felt she could change him... of course, she could.

Maybe she could persuade him to take her fishing. It looked like fun. All of the fishermen on the boat were reeling in a catch.

As Gayle was thinking about these things the ferry lurched forward and backward.

"Ohh!" yelled Gayle. As the boat slowed she held on to the hand rail and giggled. "Did we hit something?"

"I don't know. I don't think so. But something's happened — we're slowing down."

Ray headed aft and looked at the frothy wake of the vessel. He noticed that only one engine was working. His face turned red. He wanted to be in Key West before dark.

"Goddammit!"

He returned to Gayle who was still perched over the rail watching the fishermen. The captain of the fishing boat was topside pointing at something. He'd spotted another school of fish making a run. He turned the craft toward the ferry. The men were topless and had their pants rolled up. From her vantage point they were all tan and muscular. Now she really wanted to go on a fishing trip.

"One of the goddamned engines failed."

As he said this, the other engine cut off. The ferry drifted.

"Jesus Christ – We're never gonna get to Key West."

Ray turned and looked around for someone in charge. He noticed a man coming from the wheelhouse. Ray made a beeline for the man.

"What the hell is going on?" he said stepping in front of the man's path.

"We're having a little problem with engine #1 overheating. Rather than tax the other engine we're going to make repairs, if you could..."

Sheldon interrupted. "You're gonna fix the problem quick, right?"

"We think it might be..."

"That wasn't a question. I'm on my honeymoon and I want to get to Key West."

"I understand. There are a lot of people...."

"I'm not a lot of people. I am a man on his honeymoon. Fix this goddamn ship and get me the hell off of here."

"We'll do our best."

Ray stepped aside. "Goddamn right you will. Maybe even better than that."

"So what did the man say?" asked Gayle.

"We'll be on our way within the hour," replied Sheldon. His face was still red.

"I hope we get there before the storm," said Gayle without looking at Ray.

"What?"

"I overheard some of the people saying there is a storm coming."

"Where?"

"Those people over there." She pointed to another couple who were walking toward the starboard side of the ferry.

"No," Sheldon caught himself. He said the word 'no' filled with the volume and timbre of a man reaching his boiling point. "I mean — where is the storm? Where is it supposed to hit?"

"Oh I don't know," She waved her hand to dismiss the point. "I just overheard them. I didn't..."

Ray had already turned. He headed up the stairs toward the wheelhouse. He knew they'd have a barometer there. It read 29.50. It looked like it had risen a little with the last reading marker somewhat behind the current reading. He hated the thought of a big storm hitting the keys this weekend. If the storm went north, he might be called back to work and his honeymoon would be ruined. If it tracked south, he and Gayle would get drenched, and their honeymoon would be washed out. The later prospect didn't seem near so bad, but it still would wreck the picture perfect weekend he'd envisioned.

Ray took a few deep breaths. He hated when things happened, and he wasn't in control. He couldn't fix the engines on the ferry, he couldn't stop the incoming weather, and he couldn't stop his damned wife from watching the shirtless fishermen.

*Never think that war, no matter how necessary,
nor how justified, is not a crime.*
- Ernest Hemingway

"Drunk" is a word like many words that describes a state of being. However, it fails in many respects to qualify any degree of drunkenness. To call someone drunk, means they've imbibed enough alcohol to change their behavior to the point that it is noticeable by a third party. Often it means the person who is drunk has started to exhibit loosened morals, slurred speech, or loss of coordination. Yet to call the men gathering after dinner drunk is like calling an opera star 'someone who can carry a tune.'

A collision of forces, both political and social made these men topple over the edge and define new meaning to the term "drunk." The force of men gathered behind the mess hall, as they'd done before, represented a state of drunkenness not seen since the days of Blackbeard in Jamaica. In a sense they shared much with the pirates of old. They'd both seen battle and longed for more glory. They wanted to take what they felt was rightfully theirs and, in their state of mind, were concocting ways of doing just that. Many wanted to sabotage the equipment and steal the trucks and make for DC. However, they'd heard those few who'd tried the task were now sitting in jail.

So they gathered in numbers to do that which the earlier pirates of this island had done. They were gambling away their money on a fight.

The only two men in the camp who'd not had enough drink to qualify as drunk were the two contenders – Jimmy Conway and Buddy Brickman. Yes, they both had some rum to deaden the pain but not the senses. Theirs was a mere sampling compared to the spectators. The vets gathered like wolves smelling blood.

Krebs was among them and was, once again, taking the bets. He'd put his hard earned money on the underdog this time. In fact, he'd bet everything he had. He figured that he could find a train north tomorrow and get the "juice" he needed once he got his money.

Both Jimmy and Buddy had been building a retaining wall at the edge of the camp. The leaders didn't mind them putting in the time, because they'd proven themselves useless in road construction. Each would find and haul the largest block of coral they could find. They didn't use wheel barrows. They didn't use trucks. Every rock that made this four foot high and two foot wide expanse that ran from the road to the camp was carried by hand. As the larger rocks became scarce each would travel farther and haul longer the heavy coral stones. They wore gloves, but the sharp coral cut into their forearms. They usually abandoned their shirts before 10AM, so their bodies had become dark tanned. Each looked more animal than man now — their hide much darker than the other vets.

The manual labor was done with joy. Each would tell the other how far they went to get the boulders they carried. Only after that long day would Jimmy and Buddy go off and practice sparring. Jimmy gave up some of his secrets, and Buddy learned the technique of a professional boxer. Both thought about heading to the ring once the shutdown was complete. Jimmy had the connections, and Buddy was willing to ride Jimmy's coat tails.

"You see," said Jimmy one night as they were about to start their sparring session. "With equal opponents, the more experienced will take advantage of knowing where the punches are going. An amateur wants to punch you in the face. Why? He thinks that is how you win a fight. He wants the knockout punch. He wants to see a cut over the eye. He wants to see a bloody nose. That is the folly of an amateur. He is so hungry for blood, that the

233

experienced boxer knows every punch the amateur is going to send."

Buddy was making a mental note of everything Jimmy said.

"But what the amateur doesn't know is that a body blow is like hitting someone seven times."

"What?"

"Think about our past fights. When I hit you, I'm going for your rib cage. If I connect you hurt. Now – every time you breathe, you have to move those muscles I just bruised. It's like hitting you seven times. I know you are coming for my face, so I cover. I don't care where you're planning to strike — all I care about is which side you are throwing your punch. If you come at me with a right jab I'm already sending my left fist to your gut. You might connect, but I've taken your power. You can't help but pull the punch when you feel me connect with your rib cage. Now that your hurt there — guess what — you are going to drop your elbow because it hurts to keep it up — at least for seven breaths. That's when I throw my left hook. You might stop it, but you have to extend the rib cage to do so. See?"

This was a far cry from the street brawling that Buddy did in New York. He knew how to suppress pain. He was quick on his feet, but he never thought about the psychology and the physics of the fight itself. Buddy never had a trainer. He only knew the streets. Buddy had learned the benefit of hard work while building the road and now his training with this contender might make a difference when he returned to New York — the land of concrete and steel.

Buddy internalized Jimmy's teaching and was ready to give it another go in the "ring" behind the mess hall.

"Harry," said Buddy as they headed toward the crowd. "Hang on to my ring."

"Sure thing," said Harry. The big man handed over the gold Masonic ring. It had gotten tight on

Buddy's finger in the heat so he struggled to remove it.

The government had reconciled with the men, in part, when they complained about a lack of recreational resources. Among the balls, badminton racquets, and croquet sets (these things quite useless in the coral ground) were sets of boxing gloves. Of all of the equipment, these were given to the two now entering the ring.

Some of the men howled like animals, drunk out of their minds, giving up their savings for the chance to win in the match up.

Buddy had used the jump rope for the last thirty minutes to get a good sweat going. Jimmy had run with a pack full of rocks on his back. Both were glistening in the moonlight. Each entered the homemade ring, bobbing and weaving in an effort to stay loose.

"Ladies and gentlemen!" started Krebs.

"There ain't no ladies here!" yelled a man from the back.

"Speak for yourself Sherman!" came Krebs' quick reply.

"There ain't no gentlemen here — neither!" said a man from the darkness. Krebs let that one go.

"Tonight is a special night. We have a Labor Day celebration like none other."

"Get on with it dammit!" yelled another heckler.

"This Labor Day – we are pleased to bring you a fight between giants!"

"Yeah!" yelled Elmer who had joined Harry's side. He had a bottle of whiskey and was drinking it like cold soda pop on a hot afternoon. A man beside Elmer was on all fours. He wasn't sick. He was just so drunk that he couldn't stand. Still, the man yelled as though he was somehow associated with the event. Perhaps he thought he was listening to the radio. No one offered a hand to help the man to his feet. Each felt that when the "dog drunk vet" did ultimately pass out, he wouldn't hurt himself on the way down.

"We have a timekeeper who is going to give us three minute rounds. Johnny, you brought your watch?" The man lifted it up.

"All right then, let's go!" yelled Krebs. The crowd erupted with joy.

Krebs stood by Johnny, the timekeeper who held up a "wait finger." When the second hand brushed the twelve he dropped it, and Krebs slapped two long iron pipes together with a loud clang. He didn't realize how the recoil would hurt his hands, so he dropped the bars and they rattled together as the two stepped to the center with gloves raised. Most didn't see the imperceptible nod before they touched gloves.

As with most opening first rounds the two sized each other by the minutiae of movement. The slight head dodge and change of footing told them each was aware of the other's intent. The two warriors exchanged equal jabs, both opponents now matched in technique. The crowd wanted blood so they started swearing at the two who seemed to be doing nothing more than waltzing around the ring. Krebs clanged the pipes together signaling the end of round one. This was followed by a series of boos from the drunken crowd. They wanted action. They wanted a brutal animalistic hunt, not the gentleman's boxing match that had been the first round.

Harry was in Brickman's corner.

"You okay?"

"Never better," said the large man.

"Not a lot going on in there."

"That's what you think."

The second round was a round of surgery. Jimmy anticipated Buddy's new techniques. Jimmy could tell that Buddy was thinking too much. He hadn't internalized the lessons. Each move was a half second late, and it provided the opportunity for Jimmy to get in the better part of the punches.

Buddy was getting frustrated with himself. He knew he was a better fighter than this. He could feel the blows to his side. He tried to drop his elbow on the incoming blows but they found their way in nonetheless. The pain was increasing as the round progressed. Buddy had to think of something new, something that Jimmy wouldn't be able to anticipate.

Buddy got a quick jab to Jimmy's left eye as the pipes clanged for the end of the round. There were hoots and hollers on both sides.

Harry said, "You didn't look bad out there."

"I think the crowd is getting bored." Buddy huffed.

Harry took a ladle of water and doused the fighter.

"You lost that round."

"Tell me something I don't know."

"What is the worst that can happen?" said Harry struggling to say something constructive.

"You get knocked down again. So why is this time any different?"

Buddy came up short for an answer. He'd trained harder the last few weeks and listened to his mentor. But, in the end, he was still the same Buddy Brickman who had learned to scrap in the streets with the best of them.

Brickman let Harry's words sink in. Buddy knew he very likely might lose. He ate the words because he knew Harry was right. The only way he could win was to resign to the possibility — the likelihood — that he would lose. But by opening up to the possibility, he could relax and just box. It didn't matter. He wasn't a contender. This wasn't a prize fight. He would use the tools that Jimmy gave him but he wouldn't rely on them. He closed his mental playbook and decided to let his mind and body decide freely how the next round would progress.

The pipes clanged and Buddy rose a different man. There was more spring in his step. He wasn't boxing to win. He was boxing because he loved to box.

A smile came across Jimmy's face. He could see something different in Buddy. Buddy shot out a jab. It was relaxed but it had a snap. He connected with the side of Jimmy's face.

Buddy changed direction and opened with a combination to the gut. One of the two strikes connected and Buddy pulled his guard up knowing that Jimmy was going to counter. There was a quick volley of punches one of which got through. It was intuition more than training at this point. When the punch came to the face, Buddy figured he had a fifty-fifty chance which direction it came from. He opted for the left side and threw a strong left hook to the body. It connected solidly and Jimmy gave out a 'huff.' Without thinking, he followed with a left jab that connected with Jimmy's eye.

Jimmy wasn't expecting the combination and the accuracy with which Buddy was now fighting. He'd not seen such skill since he was in New York. Jimmy parried and tried to counter with a body shot of his own, but it was blocked by Buddy's elbow and a swift move to the right exposed Jimmy's midriff once again. Buddy came in with another series of punches that left Jimmy gasping.

The crowd was going berserk. A few of the spectators started fighting. The smell of blood was in the air. It became palpable when Buddy connected with a barrage of quick jabs. Jimmy's left brow broke open and started bleeding freely.

Buddy thought about what Jimmy had taught him. If the eye is cut, move in the direction of the eye. Buddy started moving left. Jimmy had to overcompensate to see his opponent. Buddy kept jabbing left when he was in the blind spot.

The pipes clanged. The vets were jumping up and down like overexcited children.

Buddy plopped down in the wooden folding chair that was in the corner of the ring. He leaned back and opened his mouth. Harry pulled a ladle of water and drenched Buddy. He swished it around and spat.

Buddy shook his head and opened his mouth for more. Harry followed with another ladle.

"That was incredible!" Elmer came up and slapped Buddy on the shoulder. Others were either howling cheers or insults depending on the nature of their bets.

Buddy, feeling the energy he expended asked, "How'd it go?"

Harry responded, "You mean you don't know?"

"I felt good."

"You looked good. Keep it up. What got into you?"

"I realized that I'm not afraid to lose."

"What?" asked Harry pouring yet another ladle of water over Buddy's head.

"You told me I'm gonna lose."

"I never said that."

"Don't worry it's okay," Buddy smiled.

The pipes clanged again though it seemed shorter than the previous periods between rounds. Buddy hadn't fully recovered. He huffed as he stood for a round he knew would be brutal.

Jimmy met him with a touch of the gloves and started in with a rapid succession of head and body shots that left Buddy dizzy. No matter what Buddy did, Jimmy found a hole. Each punch took some energy from Buddy. He tried to rally and was able to reply with jabs. Only later in the round was he able to command and dominate. Jimmy was tired from the initial foray and started to fade as the round progressed. Buddy finished with a set of good combination mixing both head and body shots.

Both sides of the ring claimed victory for that round. Both fighters were tired. Jimmy normally finished off an opponent in three rounds. He was winded, and the men in his corner squeezed his brow to stem the blood that kept oozing over the eye. Jimmy wanted to win, but felt that, in this fight, he had finally met his match.

Buddy's chest heaved. He was sucking air while trying to get rid of the painful ring that buzzed in his head. His hands were sweating which made the gloves heavy.

Krebs slammed the pipes together as the crowds cheered. There was blood on both sides. Buddy had a cut on his cheek, and Jimmy's left brow still gushed bright red.

Buddy felt elevated getting this far with Jimmy. He'd never before been so long in a fight with this man. It was a matter of will, and though his body was hurt and weakening, his spirit was strong. In the midst of the pummeling, Buddy was going through a spiritual awakening.

"The good fight wasn't about bringing the demise of the opponent," Jimmy said to Harry during a training session. "It is a way to honor your opponent by fighting well. If you cheat, you are saying to your opponent that he isn't worthy of the respect of a good fight. If you don't give it your best, then you are saying that your opponent isn't capable and you are being easy as a sign of pity. So fight your best fight and you honor your opponent. If you win — then you thank him. If you lose — you still thank him."

The two touched gloves.

"Thank you," said Buddy quietly as they began the round.

The blows Buddy sent came in rapid succession. Jimmy closed up as best he could, but he didn't try to retaliate. He couldn't. The last right cross to the temple sent Jimmy sprawling to the ground.

The vets went into a state of frenzy. A group started chanting "Brick, brick, brick..."

Harry came into the center to steady the exhausted Buddy Brickman. Buddy waved him off as Buddy knelt and helped Jimmy back to consciousness.

"You fought well," said Jimmy as he shook his head and wiped the blood from his brow.

"I have a good mentor," Buddy replied.

"Thank you."

"I couldn't have done it without you," said Buddy. "Thank you."

At 9:30PM Cutler received an update on the tropical disturbance. The man had been listening to the radio, hoping for better news. The report was much like the other two, but the prediction was that the storm would reach Andros Island sometime early Sunday. The biggest difference was the additional notification that the weather bureau was posting storm warnings from Fort Pierce to Miami.

Cutler called the number that Sheldon had given him. He felt it important to let Sheldon know that he was on top of things. Cutler grabbed another thumb tack and pinned it on the board.

"Hello?" he said having reached the lobby of La Concha Hotel. "Mr. Ray Sheldon, please."

"I'm sorry, sir. Mr. Sheldon hasn't checked in. He has yet to arrive."

"What?!" Cutler was shocked. "Sheldon should have been there hours ago!"

Sheldon had just driven into Key West when Cutler was calling the hotel. He was fuming at the circumstances. He wanted to be both drunk and sexually satisfied by now. His intent was to get his wife in bed, have his way with her and then sneak out to some of the bars for a late night drink after she'd passed out.

It was late and both of them were hungry.

"I still don't see why we can't both go fishing." Gayle brought up the topic again. She was now less interested in actually catching fish than looking at the other men who would be fishing. She was totally unaware of Ray's anger.

"Jesus Gayle! What is it with fishing! Fish stink! They break the line! You're weak. You wouldn't be able to reel in a minnow if he gave a tug on the pole! Stop talking about fishing."

241

"But I want to go! This is supposed to be a place where *everybody* goes fishing. Even that famous writer lives down here and goes out fishing."

"Yeah – but he does that to get away from his *wife*!"

The ferocity of his voice scared her. She started crying.

"Oh – don't start crying on me. No – no – stop crying – right now."

Sheldon was trying to prevent his anger from turning into rage.

"Look – honey bun – we're both tired and hungry after that trip. Let's get something to eat. Look here…" Ray squealed his wheels and turned into the parking lot of a small restaurant.

"…We can eat something here. I'll get you a burger. Do you want a burger?"

Gayle moped, "Yeah sure… a burger is good — anything but fish."

Ray imagined slapping her but didn't. He got out and opened the door for her. The restaurant was once a cigar factory that shut down in the twenties. The restaurant only used half of the space, but an aromatic charm of the dried Havana leaves still emanated from the walls.

The waitress sat them down at an oak table with chairs that creaked when they sat. Ray decided it was time to change tactics. He wanted to charm his young wife. He looked around.

"Nice place, huh?"

Gayle was looking at the menu. Without looking up she said, "Yeah it's nice."

Ray scanned the room. A couple at the next table had split portions of the daily newspaper. Each was sipping coffee. The headlines dangled over the edge. The topic of the day? The approaching storm.

With the frustration of getting into Key West, Ray had dismissed the notion of the storm. He never really relied on what Gayle had to say. Sometime she just blathered on about things. He figured she overheard something on the ferry about the

242

weather. However, the paper confirmed the fact that a storm was on its way to the coast.

Ray couldn't read the details from this far away and he wasn't going to go and bother the couple. The waitress came back and asked, "Hey there. New in town?"

"Yeah we just got here," said Ray.

The woman eyed the two. She wasn't sure if the woman opposite the old man was his daughter, his wife, or a floozy he'd picked up along the way. The girl had a ring on her finger. The waitress thought the two looked odd together, like two jigsaw puzzle pieces that didn't quite fit. She wanted to make light conversation, but also knew that if she slipped, her tip would be less.

"There's plenty to do down here. You should check out the lighthouse tomorrow. There is a boat that can take you out to a deserted island where..."

Ray interrupted. "I think we are ready to order. Aren't you, dear?"

"Yeah," she said, putting the menu down.

"I'll have a burger with a pickle on the side," said Ray.

Gayle looked up at the waitress. "I'll have some fish sticks."

Papa Hemingway had been fishing most of the day. He'd taken a few of his friends. The conchs had talked about weather coming. That usually meant the fish were driven to the coast. He'd spotted some frigate birds diving in the turquoise waters and knew something was underneath. He hauled in a large Dorado. The crew celebrated, and Hemingway was feeling no pain by the time the sun set.

When he settled back in his house after a long day in the sun, Hemingway glanced at the local paper, *Key West Citizen*. The lead story warned of a weather system approaching. He looked at the barometer in the back yard and noticed that it had dropped significantly from the morning reading. He took off his sailor's cap and scratched his head. He thought about pulling his boat out of the water but came up with a better plan.

Not wanting his treasured boat, *Pilar,* to be damaged, he moved it to a deep water submarine dock at the navy yard. His popularity in these parts granted him certain liberties with the military as well as with the general public. The space wasn't occupied, and the deep trench meant less turbulence if the bad weather zeroed in on Key West.

Ray felt caught in a nightmare where you never seem to arrive at your destination no matter how hard you tried. Gayle wanted to send postcards to her family, so she had him stop by a drug store that was open late. While she fingered through the cards, Ray picked up the paper and read the article about the storm. He was starting to get worried.

They arrived at the *La Concha* Hotel four hours later than Sheldon had planned. He was mad about everything: the ferry, Gayle, the storm, and the fact that he'd be out of job in a few weeks.

When he finally arrived at the lobby, the concierge gave him the Cutler's note with the weather report. Sheldon took the note and decided to find out for himself how bad things were going to get.

They arrived at the room which overlooked the festivities of Duval Street. A jazz band was playing somewhere close and the music wafted up to their room.

"This is so romantic!" said Gayle as she plopped down on the bed. Ray opened the suitcase and pulled out the whiskey. He poured two glasses. Gayle was sipping hers as Ray emptied his in one shot.

"Slow down!" Gayle said giggling.

"I don't want you passed out on the bed — good for nothing."

"Don't worry, I'll be fine. You worry about yourself. Honey, before we can start the honeymoon, I gotta make a call."

"No! You can't work. We are on our honeymoon!" Gayle pouted. She knew that little pouty girl face worked to soften him up.

He smiled.

"I'll just take a minute. I'm just calling to get an update on the weather."

Ray dialed the number for the desk and connected to the Key West weather station.

"So what's the latest?"

The voice on the other line said, "Looks like it is over Andros Island, heading for the Florida Straits. It has a little kick but nothing major. The recorded winds are running about forty knots."

"Hey, could you do me a favor? I'm in charge of the vets in Matecumbe. If the weather starts getting dicey, I need you to give me a call. Can you do that? I'll be up a while."

"Will do." Sheldon gave him the number of the hotel and his room number. He had covered that base, so he could put it out of his mind.

"Thanks."

Ray hung up the phone and glanced at Gayle. She'd finished her glass. She wasn't the type to be able to hold her liquor and already he could see her nose getting pink. That would spread to her cheeks and she would start to giggle about anything.

She was pouring seconds for the both of them.

She lifted her glass and handed his over. She held hers up.

"A toast — to love!"

She pirouetted and sloshed some of the drink on the carpet before taking a swig.

"To love!" Ray felt awkward saying that sort of thing. It wasn't in his bones. But for her, he gave his best.

Gayle put her drink on the nightstand table. She moved over to the window and glanced out.

"It's so beautiful here. All the lights... the music."

She turned back to Ray who was already finishing his second shot of whiskey.

Gayle giggled, quickly looked over her shoulder and, right by the window, slipped out of her dress. The young girl with firm breasts gave Ray a coy smile.

"So what do you want to do on your honeymoon? Just sit around waiting for the weather man to call?" The moon was brilliant, shining over the naked girl's left shoulder. The backlit moonbeams made it look like the young girl had angel's wings. Ray had already forgotten about the weather.

I sailed away to Treasure Island
And my heart stood still
When I landed on the silvery shore
-   On Treasure Island - Tommy Dorsey

Ray Sheldon was startled awake by the phone's ringing. It was still dark outside. He'd passed out after a night of frolicking with his wife and a half bottle of whiskey. The phone sounded way too loud. He shot out his hand to pick up the receiver and knocked the half-full whiskey glass to the floor in the process. Gayle let out a moan, rolled on her side and took most of the covers.

"Hello?"

"Hello – this is Kennedy from the weather bureau."

Sheldon was still fumbling back toward reality. His mouth tasted foul and his head had that dull throb of only being half drunk and half awake.

"Umm – okay. Go – go ahead."

"We've been monitoring barometric pressures in the area and it looks like the storm is headed for the keys. There's been a drop here in Key West."

"How bad is it?"

"That's a little difficult to tell. There aren't any ships in the area, so I have nothing to go on. However the pressures along the keys are lower than parts north. You wanted me to advise you with any change."

"Thank you," Sheldon hung up the phone. "Dammit."

Sheldon knew that he couldn't wile away the weekend in a carefree honeymoon. He sat for a few minutes in the darkness. In the distance, he could hear hammering as store owners who received the same news were now boarding up their windows.

He reached for the phone and dialed Fred Ghent, his immediate supervisor who'd rested peacefully in Jacksonville.

"Ghent, this is Ray."

247

"Yeah – I figured you'd call. I heard about the storm."

"I'm in Key West. Cutler is manning the operations at Matecumbe. I don't know how bad it is. The weathermen don't seem to have a clue, either."

"Well, you best get back."

These were not the words Sheldon wanted to hear. Gayle would be furious.

"I hear ya. We got to set up the train. Most of the boys are out of town, but we got to get the others ready to roll out. I'll call the dispatcher to get the train ready."

"Don't worry about that – I'll call. You get yourself back to the camp. Give Cutler a call and let him know you're on your way."

Sheldon hung up the phone. He woke Gayle and gave her the bad news. She didn't want to get out of bed. Sheldon was already packing when she finally put her feet to the floor. They had to get to the ferry by eight. The two didn't have much time.

Fred Ghent called the FEC train dispatcher.

"We want to make sure that we have enough space for our boys to get out safe," Ghent said as he mentally went through the preparations the team had discussed. "We're going to need four or five more cars."

"Can do," said the operator on the other line.

"We're not paying for them." Ghent wanted to make sure that the failed road construction project didn't incur anymore unnecessary debt.

"Understood."

"How long is it going to take to get the train down to Matecumbe?"

"Well, it will take about three or four hours to assemble the cars and get the train ready."

"Excellent – thank you."

"No problem," the dispatcher replied.

Fred Ghent hung up the phone. He'd done his part — or at least that is what he thought. The dispatcher noted that they would need additional cars for the vets. However, Ghent had never directly ordered the dispatcher to prep a train. From the point of view of the dispatcher, the phone call was merely informational. Fred Ghent thought that the assembly was already being started. No train was being prepared for the evacuation — nothing was being done.

Sheldon called Cutler. Cutler had been awake on and off every hour of the night. He had nightmares of a hurricane. Having never been through one, his imagination was getting the better of him. He dreamed that he was blown out of the hotel into a swirling mass of destruction.

Jarred awake, he checked the weather reports and plotted the course of the meandering storm. Five thumb tacks were pinned to the map. He monitored the radio. He still didn't know if he was in charge.

When the phone rang he jumped on the receiver.

"Cutler, this is Ray."

Though he hated the man, he was relieved by the phone call. Cutler felt alone and abandoned in the midst of the growing crisis. He wasn't sure what he should do next. Having Sheldon on the line relinquished his burden of responsibility.

"Good to hear from you, Ray. Seems like we have a storm coming."

"Yeah – I'm heading back and should be there this afternoon."

Cutler let out a silent sigh.

"Okay, good."

"Ghent is taking care of the train. Make sure the men are ready."

Cutler really didn't know what "ready" meant. Should they pack? What about the camp? Cutler hated Sheldon and knew that if he started asking questions, he'd get a tongue lashing. Rather than hear the barrage of expletives come this early in the morning, Cutler decided to simply accept his charge. If he needed help, he had Ed Sheeran and others who'd been through a hurricane to give him a hand.

"Okay, boss."

Sheldon hung up the phone. Gayle was dragging her feet getting dressed. Sheldon had a gut feeling that time was now of the essence.

At the worksite Ed Sheeran was waiting for some men to arrive to help him move the equipment. Harry was the first one there, followed by Timothy, Elmer and Buddy. Buddy was limping a little not from any problem with his leg. His side had taken a beating and it hurt to put the full weight on his left side. He wondered if he had a cracked rib.

"I got a few of us to give you a hand," said Harry. "Do you really think a storm's coming?"

"Well – how do you feel today?"

"Huh? Umm – quite honestly I'm in a little bit of pain. Me and the boys had a celebration after the fight. I'll admit I drank with the best of them. Not the cheap stuff, though. So I'm hurtin'."

Ed smiled. "How about your knees and elbows?"

"What? Um..." Harry scratched his head. "I suppose it all hurts. My head hurts the most but everything is achy."

"Me too," said Ed. "But I didn't have a drop to drink last night. When you get older, you can feel it in your bones. Yep, my right knee is telling me that we'll have a blow sometime in the next forty-eight hours. All the locals feel the same."

"I still can't figure. In Kansas, we know when a tornado is going to touch down. The sky gets all dark and sometimes the sky goes green. You can smell the electricity in the air. But look around. It's a beautiful day. I don't smell nothin' but the salty air. It ain't too particularly hot, neither."

"A hurricane isn't a twister. Hurricanes take their time. You don't think they're going to amount

250

to much. We've seen some pretty bad storms come through, but nothing like a hurricane."

"I was working on the railroad when one came through. The foreman told the men to keep working. It was only a storm blowing through. I believed him. Just like today, the weather didn't seem to amount to nothing. By evening, there were only some light winds."

"The next day, we left for work, and the clouds were racing across the sky. There wasn't any rain. There wasn't any thunder — just a light wind which actually felt good. But it got bad real quick. The foreman told us to keep working. I turned chicken when the gusts started. I went onto the barge — told the foreman I was sick. From the time it took me to walk from the worksite to the barge hell unleashed its fury. I went into the barge and could feel the barge rocking as the wind whipped up so loud it sounded like the devil singing."

The men stood mesmerized as Ed told his tale.

"I never did see the foreman. He never returned to the barge. They never did find his body, nor that of thirty workers. They were blown clean off the face of the earth."

Harry swallowed hard.

Elmer laughed. "Old man — your giving us the creeps."

No one else laughed.

Elmer said, "There ain't going to be a hurricane. Nothin' is going to happen."

Harry was spooked. "Well, I feel it in my bones."

"That's 'cause you had a few pints of whiskey last night!" replied Elmer.

"Well, if your body hurts before a hurricane, I think it's going to be a big one," Buddy winced.

"So if a hurricane hits, what are we supposed to do?" asked Timothy.

"You find me — or one of the conchs. They know what to do. Who knows? It may pass us by. Maybe it will hit Key West."

"Well, if Sheldon is there on his honeymoon, good luck to him," said Elmer.

"He ain't on his honeymoon no more. I heard he'll be heading back," replied Ed. "But you guys just come and find me. Got it?"

The group nodded.

"In the meantime, let's clean up this place a little. Even if we get a glancing blow, I don't want the equipment to be out here in the open. Let's get it on the barge."

It was not easy work. Most of the rocks were honed with heavy sledgehammers and Iron pick axes. They loaded the pick axes and shovels in barrels and hauled them on the flatbed trucks. There were hundreds of shovels, brooms and spreaders that were located around the site. With that completed, the crew hauled the generators and larger equipment.

Finally, they ran the trucks up onto the barge which floated in a channel cut among the mangroves.

"I don't get it, Colonel," said Harry. "Why are we putting all this equipment on the barge? If the hurricane does come through, wouldn't the trucks be safer on dry land?"

"When the wind gets whipping, nothing is safe. It doesn't matter where you are."

Buddy stepped into the conversation. "Mr. Sheeran, I don't think anything is safe here. I've been saying it all along."

Ed looked in the large man's eyes and saw fear.

"What do you mean?"

"Follow me."

The crew stepped off the barge led by the large man. He didn't say a word. He didn't explain anything. He just walked.

In a low tone, Timothy cupped his hand and said to Harry, "You think the fight — you know." Timothy slapped his head and spun his finger. "Got a little crazy?"

"You don't remember, do you? I haven't forgotten the day we met the big guy."

"What do you mean?" asked Timothy.

Buddy stopped. He turned south and just gazed straight down the road.

It was a scene that Harry had marveled at the day before. The large white concrete structure shot up from the small island. A small causeway was cut into the wall of stone.

"We built this, and it might just kill us all."

It wasn't complete, but the large arching structure was already absorbing small swells that flattened out into whitecaps as the water tried to make its way to the gulf. The crew looked on silently. Each pondered what would happen if the floodwaters started raging from the ocean. The large bridge was not a passage to Julius Stone's Caribbean paradise. It was a dam trying to hold back one of the most powerful forces on earth.

Elmer was the first to speak. "I think I get your point."

"Yeah," said Ed eyeing the large structure. "I think the big man's right."

"So what are you going to do when we're done? You headin' out?" Harry asked Ed.

"Nope. I'm staying until I know everyone is safe. When we're done, you boys head north." Ed eyed the shore, mentally timing the incoming waves.

"I'm staying with you. I want to help."

"You're a good man Harry."

Cutler paced. He didn't know what to do in a crisis and he felt a big one coming. It was good that Sheldon was returning, but he wanted to make sure things were in order upon his return. He turned and glanced once again at the thumb tacks on the map. He knew Ed Sheeran had been through hurricanes and was making preparations in the field. But he didn't want Sheldon to think he was just sitting on his ass.

He called and halted any sale of beer on the premises. It might cause a minor revolt, but the vets would be sober when it was time to take them out. Sheldon would understand that. Still nervous over the decision, Cutler picked up the phone and dialed Ray Sheldon's boss, Fred Ghent.

There was no buzzing on the other end. The long distant circuit was not connecting. He tried again unsuccessfully. Cutler slammed the phone down.

"Damn! Damn!" He lifted up the phone and slammed it again for good measure. He tried to think of what to do. He thought of assembling the men in the mess hall, but some were in the field helping put the equipment away. Some were packing for a Labor Day trip. Some were recovering from the previous night's festivities. He was concerned that, should an emergency arrive, he'd have no way to herd all the vets together.

He felt like a schoolboy who had to take a test for which he'd not studied. He wanted to take action, but didn't know what to do.

"What if something happens to Sheldon if the storm hits? What was he supposed to do?" he thought as the questions and fear of command began eating away at his sensibilities.

He tried calling Ghent again. Once again, the line wouldn't connect. Others in Florida were making long distance calls and the limited number of circuits was being consumed by family members checking in on the holiday.

He tried a different number. This one rang.

"Hello, FEC."

"Hello, this is Sam Cutler. I'm down here in Matecumbe with the vets. I believe someone there spoke with my boss, Mr. Ghent. He checked about securing a train with extra cars."

"Yes, I believe that is correct."

"Well, we need to get the train ordered."

There was a pause on the line. Cutler could hear the man talking to someone, but the man had apparently put his hand over the phone, so he couldn't make out the dialogue.

"Who did you say this is?"

"I'm Sam," Cutler was so nervous he had to take a breath between his first and last name. "Cutler, I work here."

There was another pause before the man responded. "Do you have the authority to order the train?"

"No," replied Cutler. "Technically – no. I do not." He couldn't lie. Sheldon was still in charge. There was no official transfer of authority. Cutler couldn't get in touch with Ghent.

"I can't order the train without the proper authority."

"Okay," Cutler's palms were sweaty. "I'll get the authority and call you back."

Cutler hung up the phone. He paced as if pacing would somehow clear up the fact that he couldn't raise either Sheldon or Ghent. He tried calling Ghent again. There was no answer.

Cutler slammed down the receiver. He stared at the barometer. It was starting to fall.

Stuart Krebs knew he had to do something. He was out of heroin. He needed another fix. He hoped the storm that was supposed to hit would be his ticket. He heard they would be taking the train north. This was a well-timed free ride. He could sit in his shack and wait, or he could get out of the cramped walls which felt like they were closing in on him. He opted to walk.

It was quite a walk to the Hotel Matecumbe, but it was worth it. The day was pleasant. The wind had shifted a little and high cirrus clouds danced in the upper atmosphere. He arrived at the headquarters to find Cutler pacing.

"Sam," said Stuart as he entered the makeshift office. "What's the story on the weather?"

It was a topic that had begun to give Cutler tunnel vision.

255

"I've been tracking the storm here — see?" Cutler started from the first thumb tack and pointed to each one. "Then I've stopped the sale of beer at the canteens. And I'm trying to get the train ordered."

"You haven't ordered the train? Why not?"

"I – I don't have the authority."

This came as a bit of a blow for Krebs. He knew that the delay would mean the train wouldn't arrive for hours. Krebs would be cutting it close. He knew some people in Miami, but didn't know how his condition would deteriorate between now and then. He thought about raiding the mess hall and finding some sugar, candy, icing — anything sweet. That seemed to keep his mind and body from the jitters.

"So call somebody to get authority!"

"I've tried. I can't reach anybody."

"So what are you going to do?"

It was a question that had been bouncing around in Cutler's head for hours. The men depended on him. He didn't answer Cutler. Sweat formed on his brow as he fixated on the barometer.

The two honeymooners arrived to the dock on time, but the ferry was late departing from shore.

"You still owe me a honeymoon. That wasn't a honeymoon. That was a one night stand."

"I bought you dinner, didn't I?"

"Yeah, but you didn't take me fishing. We're coming back here and you are going to take me fishing." Gayle was upset. She paused.

"And dancing."

"I don't dance."

"I don't care. Take me to a club. I'll find a man who can dance. Maybe some of the fishermen know how to dance."

Ray hated the feeling that he "owed" anybody — much less his own wife.

The ferry pulled away from the dock, and Ray pulled away from his wife. He wondered if it was a mistake marrying someone so young. She wanted to go out and do things that didn't interest him anymore. He lit a cigarette, cupping his hands around the match because the breeze was brisk. He paused by one couple who sat in with their car door open. They were listening to the latest weather report.

"So what do you think, mister?" asked the man in the car. "You think were gonna get hit with a bad storm?"

"All I can say," replied Ray "Is that we may be getting out of Key West just in time. The storm is centered somewhere around Andros Island. If it keeps its course, Havana and Key West will see the worst of it."

The couple smiled. The woman said, "I hope so. We cut our vacation short."

"Yeah," said Ray. "Me too."

Ray wasn't certain that the storm would batter those locations. "These storms meander," he thought.

"The reports seem to indicate it is going to track south. I'm betting on it."

"I hope you win that bet," the woman replied.

Ray walked on, toward the aft of the vessel. Twin wakes from the motors parted in a slow V as the shoreline disappeared.

Timothy was beginning to panic about the storm. He wanted to be in two places at the same time. He was dedicated to helping the men load the equipment but wanted to be with Aella. He was worried about her. Not knowing what she was doing was driving him mad.

He'd loaded the last cement mixer on the barge.

"I gotta go," he told Harry.

"I know. There ain't much left here. Go."

"Thanks."

Timothy started down the road.

"Where's he going?" asked Ed.

"He's got a girl — a local."

257

Ed thought a moment. "We're pretty much tidying up around here. Take my truck. Get him where he's got to go and come back."

"Thanks."

Ed handed him the keys, and Harry spun off to catch up with Timothy.

"Hop in."

Timothy smiled and jumped in the truck.

"You really like this girl, don't you?"

"You have no idea."

Harry thought about his past. He remembered those years courting Elizabeth. All that time he had his life mapped out. He never could have imagined how things changed. He still loved her. But if he went back to her, he wouldn't be the same man.

"You know Tim?" Harry tapped his hand on the steering wheel. "Don't let her go. If you feel for her the way I think you do, don't let her go."

"You got any regrets?" asked Timothy. He'd heard the stories from Harry, but until now hadn't pressed him on the issue of his marriage.

"Hell," started Harry. "My life has been built around regrets. It seems I've let circumstances take control. I never should've left the farm. But life is filled with 'wouldas' and 'couldas.' Since I've been down here, I've learned it's what you do with the hand you're dealt. Seems like you got something ahead of you."

"I hope so. I've never felt so strongly for someone."

"So – you staying once this is all over?"

"Yeah – I think so. Maybe I'll be a Greek sponger."

"Not with your Irish blood."

The two chuckled.

"Here we are."

Harry stopped and Tim hopped out.

"So where are you going to be if this thing hits?" asked Harry.

"I hope I'm in Miami with a beautiful woman walking on the beach. How about yourself?"

258

"Hah! I'm not so lucky. I'll probably be playing cards with Sheeran and Elmer. Elmer cheats you know. But he still loses. I haven't figured that one out."

"See you after this is over my friend," Timothy stuck out his hand. Harry grabbed it and shook.

"I hate letting you go. You've been my good luck charm."

"Maybe the Irish luck has worn off on you a little."

With that Timothy turned and headed down the rough road toward the house. He wanted to hold Aella and get out of Matecumbe.

As he passed the thick line of overgrowth he stopped.

There were no vehicles at the house. The place was boarded up. The boat had been anchored in the middle of the inlet.

"Aella?" said Timothy, too quietly at first. He headed to the porch. "Aella!" He ran to the back, hoping the back door of the house was unlocked. Everything was shut tight. He went to the dock. Even the little shack had plywood covering the single small window.

"Aella!" he cried out again.

She wasn't there.

He ran to the small opening to the hidden beach. He crawled through the tight cluster of mangroves and emerged at the other side. He looked around and headed to the beach where they made love.

He was alone. She'd gone. She'd left.

He sat down on the beach and put his hand in the warm sand.

"Aella," was the single word on his lips that he let out more as a sigh than a call.

He dug his hand into the sand hoping to feel her warmth somehow trapped there. It was cold and wet. He pulled his knees to his chest and started rocking. He had no idea where she was. He wanted to be with her in safety.

"Aella!" he yelled at the top of his lungs.

He hoped he'd missed something. Maybe she left him a note. Maybe she left him some indication where she'd gone.

He raced back to the house, cutting his arms on the branches that hung low on the hidden path. He searched frantically for something — anything. He went to the edge of the dock where they dangled their feet. The water was clear and the disks were strewn about the bottom, but there was nothing else. The water shuddered in small ripples as a wind came through the opening from the sea. The wind blew Timothy's dark hair. He looked out to the water.

He felt the storm was coming. Like the locals, he *knew* something bad was coming. In the heat of the day, he shivered. A wisp of wind blew through his black hair.

With Aella gone, he didn't know what to do. It would be easy to return to the camp, but he would find no comfort there.

As he pondered his options the sound of coral being crunched by a vehicle drifted from the edge of the road.

He stood up and ran toward the opening.

The black truck rambled down the road toward the house.

Aella was driving.

He didn't even let her get to the house before he ran in front of the truck. She slammed on the brakes.

"Where were you?" She hadn't even turned off the ignition before he opened the door and kissed her.

"I met my parents in Homestead. They went ahead north to Miami. I couldn't stand not knowing if you were okay. So, I came back. I searched for you at the campsite. It took me a while to find out that you'd left there to look for me. I wasn't going to leave without you. Alexander says it will hit tomorrow. He's rarely wrong, but the barometer hasn't moved much. Everyone is saying the storm is tracking south."

"I was worried you'd gone."

"Hop in," she said.

She backed out of the path and on to the road — heading north.

"Where are we going?"

"You looked like a crazy person coming running up to the truck like that. My mama said that the best way to tame a wild beast is to feed it. So we're going to the Rustic Inn for a bite. We can make plans there." She put her hand on his leg. "Is that okay?"

A wave of peace washed over Timothy. "Sounds perfect."

Ray stood on the forward deck of the ferry. His wife stood by him feeling the breeze. Some clouds had moved in creating intermittent relief from the blazing sun. Ray was about to tell Gayle that he'd be heading to the office as soon as he dropped her off, but a screeching sound, like the wail of a wounded animal interrupted.

"Oh my God, what was that?" Gayle put her arm on Ray's

"Beats the hell outta me."

The boat slowed.

"Oh hell..." Ray stomped his foot on the deck.

"What? What? What is it?" Gayle looked worried.

"That sound? I think the shaft broke on one of the motors."

Ray turned in a huff to find someone in charge. The boat fired up its one remaining motor. For a second the boat turned to port, but the captain stabilized the rudder and the vessel took its slow course toward its destination.

"Goddammit!" yelled Ray.

Gayle caught up to him.

"We only have one motor. It's going to take us a helluva long time to get back."

"What about the storm?"

261

"Fuck the storm!" He yelled. Heads turned. He lowered his voice. "The storm ain't gonna hit us. It is going south. We're just going to be stuck on this god damn boat for a few extra hours."

It was the worst honeymoon he could have imagined. He just wanted to be home.

Cutler had been trying to call Ghent for hours. He tried the office several times with no luck. He tried Ghent's home with no success. He'd all but given up.

Ghent had been told that his job was coming to an end. He'd been replaced by Sheldon at the camps. But as most government jobs go — he'd figure he'd ride this the best way he could.

Lately, Ghent would go missing for a few hours at lunch, only periodically checking in at the office before heading home early. So it was little surprise that Sam found Ghent at the golf club where Ghent had become a member. Fred had been playing a round of golf. He'd sat down for lunch and a few drinks when the call came through.

"Ghent! I have been trying to get through to you all day!" Cutler was a nervous wreck.

"Sam, what's wrong?"

"Have you ordered the train? We need to get the men out of here."

Ghent could hear the anxiousness in Cutler's tone of voice.

"Calm down! Sheldon is on his way. He should be there by 1:00."

Cutler looked at the clock; it was almost 2:30. "He's not here! No one's here. It's just me. We gotta get the train."

Ghent wanted to reassure Cutler. "I called the FEC railway. They have a train ready to go. I talked to them. We can discuss our options when Sheldon returns. Relax."

Cutler was in no mood to relax. He felt Ghent was taking things too lightly.

"What do you mean, 'the trains are ready to go?'"

"They told me they have a train in readiness. It'll take three or four hours to get one down here for the men. We have plenty of time."

Cutler couldn't shake the nerves. This should have been reassuring news, but it wasn't. Little did Cutler know the information that Ghent gave him was wrong. There was no train on standby. The dispatcher had merely informed Ghent that it would take three hours to add additional cars and prep a train. Ghent misunderstood the communication. There was no train waiting to help the vets at all.

Sheldon could have been angrier. The ferry arrived three hours late. The time he was with Gayle cooped up on the ferry was taxing. He could handle her in small spurts — like after dinner at the end of the day. She was a needy little thing, and he felt like he often took on a fatherly role. Getting back to work was the best thing after the honeymoon debacle.

He'd put the top up on his convertible after he dropped off Gayle because it looked like it was going to start raining. He'd park it in the garage until it was time to leave. Unlike his orders for the vets, Sheldon had no intention of taking the train. He'd drive his wife north after the men were safely onboard. He arrived at the Matecumbe Hotel and walked into the makeshift office. He immediately noticed the map with the pins, the disheveled weather reports, and notes strewn about the place.

"There you are! I've been waiting for you," Cutler sighed when he saw Sheldon at the door.

"Hey there Sam, how are you doing?" Sheldon could see that Cutler was in a panic.

"How am I doing? How am I doing?!" Sam's words cut through the air and made the normally aggressive Sheldon back down. "You leave me here but don't authorize me to get the train when a hurricane hits! That's how I am!"

"Whoa – whoa – hold on." Sheldon put out his hand. "Take it easy there, Sam. Look outside. What do you see?"

It was cloudy and a light misty rain had started to fall. Other than that, the wind had died down.

"It looks like it's starting to rain."

"Yeah – that's all it's doing." Sheldon chose to take it slow. "Look at the barometer. It only dropped a little bit. If this is the hurricane, that thing would have gone down a lot more than that. You did a good job while I was gone."

"I called Ghent and made sure the train was ready. He said it was. I also closed down the canteens at the camps. No booze – I want those men sober when it's time to give the order."

"What? Over the Labor Day weekend?" In Sheldon's mind, Cutler had overreacted."We don't need to do that. The men work just as well half-drunk. This is their weekend. You can't take that away."

Sheldon called and had the sale of beer reinstated. Cutler knew that Sheldon had been through a hurricane. He couldn't remember the details of Sheldon's story about it, however. Cutler knew that Sheldon had a way of making things up as he went along. Had Sheldon really experienced a full-blown hurricane?

Sheldon was calm and relaxed . He was taking the news in stride, believing that the brunt of the storm would pass south.

He looked at the now gaunt and pale Cutler. "Sam – go home. Get some rest. I'm in control."

Cutler looked defeated. "Okay, Ray. See you tomorrow."

"Take care, Sam."

Sam Cutler walked out of the hotel. A swift wind had kicked up, and the rain pelted him as he made his way to his truck.

Sheldon shook his head. Everything had been cocked up since he decided to leave for Key West. He hoped his luck would change. He knew that

264

Ghent told Cutler that the trains had been ordered and were in readiness. Since things had been so screwed up, Ray decided to call the FEC railway himself and make sure everything was in order.

"FEC, this is P.L. Gaddis."

"Hey there, this is Ray Sheldon in Matecumbe. I'm in charge of the vets working on the highway and we've got an arrangement to get them out in the event of a storm."

"Are you authorized to make the order?" asked the man on the other side.

"Yes sir, I am. But I'm not giving the order right now. I'm just checking in to make sure everything is ready. How long would it take to get a train down here?"

"Well, if you order the train now, it would take about three to four hours."

"Sounds good. I'll let you know."

"Great. Let us know when you need the train."

Sheldon hung up the phone. He was satisfied that he had a timeline for evacuating the men.

But there was a problem.

Gaddis, the FEC Dispatcher made his time assessment on an immediate order of the train. The Northbound train had entered the station and it was still warm and ready to go. Gaddis factored the time to get the engine ready into the equation. With a cold machine and cars uncoupled, it would take far longer. Sheldon didn't have that piece of information because he figured the trains were in a constant state of readiness. Ghent indicated that there were two trains ready to roll at a moment's notice. This was not the case.

Aella and Timothy sat in the wooden booth at the Rustic Inn looking out at the rain that had been off-and-on. They ate a hearty late lunch and had been sitting at the booth for hours. They'd paid the original tab and were raking up another with coffee and extra biscuits that were too light and fluffy to pass up. O.D. King, the owner of the place recognized Aella, but didn't know Timothy. He came by repeatedly to fill their coffee mugs.

The hours passed as the two discussed their past. They were quickly deepening their relationship — building roots by finding those tangents and differences that help solidify a burgeoning love. Timothy talked about his life in Maryland. He talked about his father and about the struggles of his family going bankrupt.

Aella talked of her life on the water. She told of the times when she would take the boat to Alligator reef. Her father was always nervous because of the sharks, but they didn't bother Aella. She spoke of a fish that haunted the area.

"The goliath grouper," she said, "was as big as a car."

"We've been here for hours and never got around to discussing what we came here to discuss!" said Timothy. He put his hand on hers. "I hear the storm is tracking south. Even so, I want to make sure you're safe. I think we should go to Homestead at least. I would prefer to head to Miami – I think that would be safer."

"Well, that's not what Alexander said." Aella leaned forward. "He said it's going to be bad."

"Yeah, but the barometers and weather reports don't jibe with him."

"I've never known Alexander to be wrong. He has some kind of built in – I don't know – weather station in his head. I've seen him predict storms a week away. I trust him more than the weather reports. If he says it's going to be bad — it will."

Timothy didn't know Alexander, but he trusted Aella.

"So Miami it is then. Did Alexander say when the storm was going to hit?"

"Well, he thought it would be today."

Timothy wondered whether Alexander's weather station in his head needed an adjustment.

Aella continued, "That's why they left this morning. I was afraid I was going to miss you. I

266

thought you might have headed out on the train or something. What a surprise to see you running down the drive like a wild man!"

"Hah – sorry – I was going out of my head because I thought I missed seeing you."

Aella took a sip of her coffee.

Timothy said, "So do you have a plan?"

"We have some friends in Miami. That's who my family is staying with. I think they could house you somewhere. You may have to sleep on the floor."

"That's fine with me. So should we get going?"

"I think we'd be okay to head out tomorrow. Perhaps you and I could head back to the house tonight."

Timothy could not have asked for a better deal. "Of course!"

He reached over the table and kissed her.

They sat back and stared at each other. Timothy looked out of the window at the sun. The puffy clouds which brought them rain had turned copper as the sun started to find its way toward the horizon.

The sea was not a mask.
No more was she.
The song and water were not medleyed sound
Even if what she sang was what she heard.
Since what she sang was uttered word by word.
It may be that in all her phrases stirred
The grinding water and the gasping wind; But it
was she and not the sea we heard.*
-    *Wallace Stevens - The idea of Order at Key*
     West

What makes a monster? Monsters start as something ordinary. Add to that immense power and resources. Suddenly the worst that could happen — does. Like the vets in the World War, they were caught up as pawns in man's ever spiraling desire for power and wealth. Nature, too, has its monsters. Occasionally, a small storm will enter warm temperatures.

This allows the storm to drink up more water. But the resource for water must be present at the time the storm becomes thirsty. If there is water, the storm can grow.

But a storm's desire to survive cannot be found merely in heat and humidity. Often a large storm is torn apart by foes like upper level winds, land masses, high pressure systems and the like. Only if a storm is willing to arm itself and become a weapon against the counter forces will it grow.

Out in the Florida straits in the wee hours of the morning, this unnamed storm found both resources and power. In its greed to survive, it began whipping out circular forces of immense power. The slumbering counter forces were caught unaware. This greedy storm went unnoticed for the most part. No ships were in the area to see its strengthening greed. No land masses lay in its way to alert the public. It entered the Florida straits and chose to stay hidden by remaining small, yet powerful.

What was once a simple storm had turned into a monster.

268

I've thrown away my toys,
Even my drums and trains,
I want to make some noise,
With real live airplanes.
-   *Shirley Temple – On the Good Ship Lollipop*

Harry woke to take a piss. Like most, he wouldn't use the latrines. He preferred to walk across the camp and take his chances along the thin line of mangroves that grew along the edge of the shore. The clouds of morning were thick and gray, pressing down the air in a low swiftly moving ceiling. Harry could see wisps of mist blow onto land. The breeze was slight but constant and smelled of salt. What was normally a pastel ocean this time of day was now gray green and churning with black wavelets.

He finished his business and turned back to camp. Some of the vets had reinforced their shacks with two-by-four struts dug into the ground. He nearly tripped over a small unused pile of them as he shook off the cobwebs of a good night's sleep. Reaching a small clearing, he looked out on the water. He'd never taken the time to memorize the tides, but this looked like it was low tide. The sand extended out and a few starfish, caught unaware, lay in the wet sand. The waves were coming in regular rhythms parallel to the beach. He could see a few white caps on the edge of the horizon on what was normally a serene time of day.

He snorted and hocked his spit on a mangrove having finished his morning chore. It looked like the storm was here, and it didn't seem so bad — just like the weather man had said. Most of the vets learned about the coming storm at dinner time. Word spread quickly and the crew seemed excited to have their first taste of a real Florida hurricane.

As Harry turned and headed back to his shack, a wind came from nowhere, blowing with a low droning whistle like the sound of some distant train.

He wondered if that was the southbound hailing its exit toward Key West. But the wall of wind that followed confirmed his suspicion that the sound was not made by man.

He'd only taken a few steps when the sky opened with rain that angled against his back. He'd been in the strange Florida storms where one side of the road would be drenched and the other side completely dry. His back became instantly wet. The rain drops were like golf balls pelting the man as he hastened his steps back to the shack.

By the time he'd reached the door, the rain had stopped as quickly as it began. A shaft of light appeared on the water.

Sheldon arrived at Hotel Matecumbe to start an easy day at work. He figured the storm had tracked south, even though he felt the outer bands as he drove the truck. Sheldon parked the truck and headed into the hotel. The wind had kicked up a little sand so he pulled the collar up on his jacket as he headed inside.

Cutler had been in the office since 3:00AM. Unable to sleep, the nervous Cutler had pinned more thumbtacks to the wall. The meandering storm still seemed uncertain of its destination.

"You're up early, Sam," said Sheldon.

"Couldn't sleep."

"Apparently."

Sheldon pulled out the pack of Lucky Strikes and lit a cigarette. "As I see it, the storm is tracking south." He pointed at the map. "Just like I said it would."

"But..." started Cutler.

Sheldon interrupted. "But I think we'll make the order today or tomorrow. I'm not against getting the men out mind you. It's just that if this thing blows over, we got a whole lot of men we got to shuffle around, as I see it, about four hundred or so."

The 9:30 weather report had come in and warned of hurricane force winds. The report was broadcast on the radio. Sam had obsessively been monitoring it in the early hours of the morning. Sam wrote down the latest information. With a determined look he handed it to Sheldon. Sheldon read it as Cutler turned and put another tack in the map.

It was the smell of coffee that woke Timothy. Only then did he realize that it was combined with the smell of eggs and toast. His stomach was the first to make commentary on the delectable aroma wafting his way. He pulled on his drawers and padded down the stairs to the kitchen where Aella had prepared a wonderful meal.

"Sorry, we're fresh out of bacon or sausage."

He came up behind her and put his arms around her. She leaned her head back ever so slightly as she put her hands over his. They swayed slowly to music that was in their head. Neither one slept much. They made love through the night. In the darkness sleep was intermittent. They rested but throughout the early hours the would just lay talking quietly or watch the other rest.

"Don't worry about the bacon. Everything smells wonderful." He buried his nose in the nape of her neck.

Since all of the tables and chairs inside were filled with the sponging equipment, the two carried their food out to the porch.

"Papa was mad that I didn't go with them. But I think he saw in my eyes that I wouldn't leave you behind."

"When this is over, I want to find work at the fishing camp. I want to make a name for myself down here. When I can, I'll work for your father. I want to earn his trust."

Timothy was thinking about the future life he wanted to give Aella. He'd seen the fliers that Julius Stone had made about the future of the keys. Timothy believed that this would, one day, become a tourist Mecca. He thought about acquiring land

and simply holding it until the crowds arrived. Even though the road project was not going to go forward now — he knew it was only a matter of time. The railroad was here. There was electricity. There would be stores. Families would come to fish and enjoy the sunshine and warmth.

For now he would labor and save. He believed in Stone's image of the future of the keys.

"That will take time. But you have shown to be a hard worker — that's a start."

"We'll eat breakfast — clean up — and then head out. Did you need to say goodbye to any of your friends?"

"I'll see them when I return."

Timothy looked up and it appeared that the low hanging clouds were kissing the tops of the tall palms.

"Wow – the weather sure does change quickly around here."

"Yeah – we don't want to wait around too long."

They finished breakfast and cleaned up. However when they got to the bedroom to change, they decided that they still had a little time before they had to leave. Passion trumped common sense.

The freight train pulled toward the camp with a lumbering screeching metallic wail. This was normally filled with a freight car of supplies, but Julius Stone thought it better to let the camp use its current supply of food. With the vets gone for the weekend, he reasoned, the camp would have excess. Not knowing how bad the approaching storm would affect the supply tent, Stone ordered the supply car to be transported later in the week.

It was a regular sight that Ed would normally ignore but circumstances were different. Ed stopped what he was doing and hustled to the locomotive to talk to the engineers as the freight train came to a halt.

Harry saw the old man run to the train and marveled at his stamina.

"Hey There! Hey There!" Ed Sheeran yelled and waved his hand to get the attention of the men in the behemoth at the head of the train.

"Hello!" cried one of the three men in the locomotive.

The train was moving at a slow clip and Ed didn't wait for them to stop. He grabbed a rail and pulled himself onto the engine.

"We're expecting a storm to blow through. So I need you to do me a favor."

"What is it?" the man asked.

Ed explained, "Don't dump the water tank. Just take it down to the camp, but leave the water in the tanker."

Ed's mind was on the approaching storm. The camp's water tower was its main water source. Normally, the engineer would back the train down a side track to the campsite. He'd then hook the tanker to one of three holding tanks by the mess hall. The men would use a compressor to pump the water in the holding tanks to the tower. It was a simple process.

Ed worried that the tide and swell of the hurricane might inundate the holding tanks thus contaminating the water supply. By keeping the water in the tanker, the men had another fresh water failsafe.

"Can do," said the engineer. "Hey – your supply car is empty. You know that?"

"What?"

"Yeah – got orders not to fill it on the way here."

"Dammit!" said Ed banging his fist against the metal machine. "What if our food supply is contaminated and we're cut off?"

"Hey pal, I'm just following orders. I got the empty car here if you need it."

"Yeah – take the car and back it to the worksite. I can use it to store some of this loose stuff I've been gathering up."

"Can do."

Ed jumped down from the locomotive as it started backing down the slight incline toward the camp. He returned to the worksite.

"Hold up, men. Don't bother loading the truck. We're going to get a box car to put this in."

The men who were assisting Ed had made piles from the spare iron pipes, wire, rebar and small tools.

Harry said, "You know, I never thought of this stuff as a weapon. I should've though. When the twisters came through, I once saw a one by four piece of lumber shot through an oak tree. I wouldn't want to be around if a pipe was flying my way."

"Yeah, I should've taken better care of the worksite," said Ed.

They heard a bang, but wasn't sure if it was the train changing out the cars or a crack of thunder. The sound echoed off to the wind and was lost.

Moments later the train emerged and backed along a side track that paralleled the worksite. Two of the engineers got out and uncoupled the empty boxcar. The train pulled forward, and the lone black car stood among the two large trenching machines that couldn't be moved. One of the men from the train jumped out and ran back.

"Hah, almost forgot. This car wouldn't do you any good." The man stepped up on a protruding step which led to the door and got out his set of keys. A chain was wrapped around the handle which opened the large sliding door. He unlocked the door and slid the unit open.

"That'll do ya," the man said as he hopped back on the train.

The locomotive puffed and chugged as it started accelerating north.

"Well, I suppose we'll have to make the best of a bad situation," said Ed.

"What do you mean?" asked Harry.

"This was the food truck. The government didn't send us anything this week."

"Hell – the way the food tastes – I think they're doing us a favor," said Harry with a grin.

Sam got the call he was looking for. The weather center in Jacksonville issued hurricane warnings for the area. Now, he had the hard evidence that he'd been right all along. Sheldon had dragged his feet and it irked Sam. Sam wondered if Sheldon was delaying the evacuation to spite him. He never liked Sheldon since he arrived, and hated him even more now. But the latest weather report was vindication.

He took the report to Sheldon and shot it under his nose.

"I told you," said Sam nervously. "God Damn you Sheldon, I told you."

"You told me nothing. Nothing I already didn't know. We got two trains waiting..." Sheldon paused, glanced down at the note and tore it in two. "All right. We're outta here."

Cutler took another push pin and placed it on the map.

"I told you," the nervous man said under his breath.

Sheldon picked up the phone to call Ghent. Like Cutler had done, Sheldon tried many phone numbers to track down the tardy supervisor. He was not to be found.

Cutler couldn't believe it. "Ray – you go ahead and make the call. Call the train yourself."

"I'm following protocol. We've got plenty of time. The storm is at least twelve hours away."

"To hell with protocol! We're talking about men's lives! We gotta get them out!" Cutler stamped his foot. He looked outside as a squall ran through the area spreading sheets of rain against the windows.

"Look here!" yelled Ray not backing down. "I'm in charge here! "

"Remember that tomorrow! When this weather hits, those men had better be gone!" With that Sam headed out, got in his truck and spun onto the road.

He didn't tell Sheldon where he was going. Sheldon sat down in a huff. He could hear the rain pelting the hotel. The rain came in rhythmic swells.

He looked back at the map. Sheldon stood up and stared at the map with all of the thumb tacks tracing over the water in a meandering dance. He fingered each one from off of Andros Island, to the Florida Strait. He fingered the last one that Cutler put in place before leaving. Sheldon then traced a path from the last two thumb tacks to Lower Matecumbe.

Sheldon looked at the barometer. It had dropped significantly in the last hour. He returned to the weather report that he'd torn in two. He picked up the pieces and put them together, reading the information again. He retrieved a thumb tack. It completed the line that ran directly to Matecumbe.

Sheldon picked up the phone and tried a few other locations in an attempt to locate his boss, Fred Ghent.

Cutler was heading out to find Ed Sheeran. He knew that Sheeran felt the same about the hurricane. With Sheeran, he could get the men assembled and ready to board either of the two promised trains. A wind gust blew the truck into the other lane. He saw that a few inches of water ran along the road. The water took on a life of its own as rivulets ran perpendicular to the road. In one spot, the low road had small waves that broke on to the blacktop. Cutler couldn't believe how quickly things were deteriorating.

He arrived at the worksite. It appeared abandoned but a lone man jumped from a boxcar. He veered off the road. The truck slid over the rails as he stopped a few feet from the man who was loading the last few buckets of tension wire.

Sam rolled down the window.

"Ed!"

The man turned. It was Harry Burrows.

"Hey, Sam!" yelled Harry over the deluge. He was drenched. "Ed's in the boxcar."

Ed saw the truck and emerged from the large boxcar. "Hey Sam! Looks like the storm is breathing down our back! Is the train on its way?"

Sam replied, "Sheldon's calling Ghent. So it won't be long. The trains should be here soon. We should assemble the men and get them ready."

"We're finishing up. We'll see you at the camp."

Cutler, still angry with Sheldon said, "Ed – I want to go on record that I tried to get the trains here earlier. Sheldon..."

Sheeran stopped him. "You don't need to tell me about Sheldon. Once an ass — always an ass."

Cutler smiled.

Sheeran said, "You got the men at heart. You always have Sam. Go and get them ready."

It took almost an hour to locate Fred Ghent. He never did tell anyone where he was going. He figured it was as much his holiday as anyone else's. With the storm blowing to the South, he figured that Sheldon would be okay. The temper the man on the other side of the line told otherwise.

"Ghent! Where the hell were you? I've been trying to get a hold of you so we can get the trains ordered. The weather's turned for the worst down here. It looks like it might hit a little closer to home than I originally thought. I want to order the trains and get the men out."

"Okay – okay," came Ghent on the other line.

"Let me see if I can get a party line going. I'm calling the FEC Dispatcher now."

Sheldon waited on the line. This was proper procedure he told himself. Minutes passed with nothing. He hated waiting. When the connection was established Sheldon could already hear Ghent talking to the dispatcher.

"I don't understand..." came Ghent's voice. "I thought we were supposed to have two trains. Not one — two."

"Sir – I'm sorry – I only have orders for one train."

Ghent heard the click.

"Sheldon – Sheldon, are you there?"

"Yeah – I'm on the line."

"They're telling me that they can only get one train, not two."

Sheldon responded, "Then we'll need at least ten coaches and..."

He did a little mental calculation.

"...three baggage carts."

After a moment the dispatcher said, "Hmm... I can only give you six coaches..."

Sheldon knew that the men at the camp would barely fit into that many cars. It would be a tight squeeze. He worried that the logistics had somehow broken down.

Ghent said, "Sheldon, I'll meet you at the station. I'll go as soon as we are done here."

Sheldon – worried that there would be further delays asked, "So it is three or four hours from there to here, right?"

The dispatcher responded, "Correct."

Once again Sheldon hadn't asked the right question. As a matter of distance, it would take that amount of time to travel to Matecumbe. However, the time didn't include warming up the locomotive and assembling the cars.

Satisfied with the answer, Ghent said, "That's it then. Prepare the train and I'll see you later Sheldon."

"Okay," Sheldon hung up the phone and looked at the map once again. Ray exuded confidence and downright arrogance. He knew that it took a dominant person to lead. He'd done everything right. He'd trusted the weather reporters. If they were wrong, then all of his timetables were off.

Sheldon picked up the phone.

"Honey?" he said. "Get packed and head to Hollywood. Don't waste time. Get your things together. I'll send someone to get you out."

"What about you?"

"I'm staying with the men. I'll see you when I get off the train. It's on its way."

She was silent.

"Look – I'll be all right. I promise. I'm going to send Sam Cutler to take you and the other women north."

Sam was too nervous. He was overthinking the storm. Ray could get Sam out while making it seem that Sam was doing his duty. He didn't want Sam to spook the men. And, if Sam was right, Gayle would be safe.

Doubt.

He would have to bury that emotion before he met with the men. But it stirred in him. He cursed Cutler under his breath for planting the uncertainty in his mind. He resolved that not a man would be left at camp. He grabbed the keys and headed into the storm.

Krebs was packed. He'd been packed for almost a day. His diet, for the last twelve hours, consisted of candy and beer. He couldn't remember the last time he'd slept. He counted his gambling money and wanted to leave. He had slight tremors that came and went. He played a countdown in his head.

"Two hours and the train will arrive. Four hours on the train. That will be the hard part. Then another hour and I'll have my 'juice.'"

He looked at his suitcase and checked his money. Not satisfied, he opened his suitcase and counted the number of shirts, socks, and pants. Krebs closed the suitcase. He stood up and paced the shack. The rain rolled across the tin roof trying to disrupt the man's concentration.

He sat down again.

"Two hours and the train will arrive. Four hours on the train. That will be the hard part. Then another hour and I'll have my 'juice.'"

This was the sixth time he'd repeated this process — word for word — action for action.

Timothy and Aella headed north. What had started as a brisk wind in the morning became blustery and then wild. The palm fronds whipped around trying to anticipate the direction of the next gust. Fingers of grey and white moved quickly overhead in a race to the gulf.

Aella stopped before crossing the bridge to Indian Key.

"Open your door and brace it open with your feet." She said.

"What?" replied Timothy, not registering exactly as she requested.

"Open your door. Lean back in the seat and brace the door open with your feet as we cross the bridge."

Still not fully understanding, yet complying he did as he was told. She opened the driver side door as well. Some of the gusts tried to slam his door shut. As she put the truck in gear she steered with one hand while doing her best to hold her door open. It was a little easier for her as she was downwind.

As they crossed the arc of the bridge a gust blew across the water. The wind hit the truck with such ferocity that both of them thought they were headed over the side. However, because the doors were both open, there was less for the wind to punch. Only then did Timothy see the wisdom of Aella. Had both doors been closed, the truck may have been pushed off the slippery wooden bridge and into the water below.

On the other side both of them closed their doors as she jammed the truck into a higher gear and fled north.

"You've done that before?" he asked, amazed at her intuition about the gust on the bridge.

"Never," she replied.

"I'm a conch. Remember? We know the weather."

They passed the camp. Timothy gazed at the men heading to the mess hall. He noticed that a few of the smaller sheds were obliterated by the wind. Timothy now understood why the locals feared the coming storm. Even in these early stages of the hurricane's arrival, the wind had started to tear apart the flimsier buildings. As the wind carried the remains of the shanties, Aella did her best to avoid the debris that was blowing across the road.

"I think once we're past Snake Creek we'll be in the clear, but I'm not stopping until we are north of Homestead," She looked at him briefly and smiled before returning her attention to the road.

"What the hell?" Timothy was the first to see it. The North bound road was blocked off by three National Guard. They had two trucks parked at ninety degrees to the traffic. They were letting a black Ford sedan through. Aella slowed as she approached the soldiers.

"I'm sorry ma'am. We are inspecting every vehicle coming through," the young man said as he approached.

"We're trying to get out of here before the storm hits," she responded irritably.

"I'm sorry, but we can't let you through," the man said as he looked in the cab.

"Why the hell not?" she shouted.

"C'mon, let us through. We aren't causing any trouble."

"We have strict orders not to let any of the veterans out except by train."

"What?!" replied Timothy.

"You heard me," the guard said with an equally stern response. "No vets out of here except by train. Sheldon's orders."

"That's insane," said Aella.

"Look, we're driving to safety. You can't hold us here."

"Ma'am, you are free to go where you please, but the vet stays here."

281

"Look, I'm not even a vet. Look at me — how old do you think I am?"

"Sorry, you're wearing the uniform of a road worker. We can't let you through."

Just then a wide finger of lightning and a boom of thunder landed so close that everyone on the road jumped. The light and sound were almost simultaneous.

Aella tried a different tact.

"I know you have a job to do," she said with a softer voice. "A man of authority has to follow rules."

She smiled and winked.

"But I bet you have broken the rules a few times haven't you. So why don't you break the rules one more time and let me and this Irishman through, okay?"

"No ma'am. I'd be glad to let you through. That isn't a problem. But he has to stay."

She huffed.

"Dammit, I'm not a vet."

The guard poked his head in the window. "You look like a vet. You *smell* like a vet. I was told that there are vets hot wiring the trucks in the motor pool. I was told that the vets are only allowed to head out of here on the train. So either you hoof it back to the campsite or you wait here for the train."

"Aella, you've got to go. I'll catch the train."

"It's at least three miles back to the train station. You can't walk. The hurricane is bearing down on us right now."

"It's the only way. I'll get back okay. I promise. I'll see you in Miami. Now go."

"No!" She pulled his shirt as he opened the door to get out.

He spun around and kissed her. They embraced with a passion that equaled the tempest outside. They held each other. He whispered in her ear.

"I love you. I don't want to lose you. I'll see you in a few hours. The train must be on its way by now.

I'll hitch a ride with the boys and see you at the station. Wait for me there. I'll be out of here before the worst of it hits."

"You don't know what you're up against."

"Yes, I do. I've got someone to fight for. I've got someone to live for. I love you and I'm not going to let anything happen to you..."

She pulled back and gave him a stern look. He corrected himself. "To us... To us. But you have to go. Go now."

"I don't want to."

There were a few other cars behind hers waiting to pass. One of them honked their horn.

He stepped out of the truck and slammed the car door shut. Then he paused, turned, and jumped through the window for one more kiss.

"I'll see you soon."

Timothy headed south only allowing himself one glance to make sure she headed north. The sand that whipped up stung his eyes. He was grateful when the wind mixed with the rain. A few of the vets weren't waiting for the train. They'd packed their bags and started walking north hoping to hitch a ride with one of the conchs.

"There's a road block a few miles back. If you plan on hitching a ride north, you'll have to hide. Either that or change into the best civvies you've got." Timothy had to raise his voice against the wind.

"Why the hell are you trekking south?"

"I'm taking my chances with the train," said one of the two men walking north.

"Well, good luck to ya. Sounds like you've got it."

"And good luck to you, too," replied Timothy thickening his accent a little. He figured he had the right to bestow a little bit of luck. He'd felt like the luckiest man on earth in spite of the weather.

The mess hall was filled with men. Beside them sat canvas bags filled with their few worldly possessions. They tossed cards — playing for peanuts, cashews and pecans — while they waited for the promised train. Some talked about the weather. Others talked about women and booze. When the whirling siren of a wall of wind came in from the water, it howled across the mess hall like the cry of a wounded animal. The sound mixed with the pummeling noise of waves that broke only a few feet from the tent. It caused the men to pause their bets, their jokes, and their conversation. It was nature's turn to talk. Some men looked on in excitement. A few started to worry.

Two men chose to sneak to the motor pool and hot-wire a truck. The fleet sat abandoned and unmonitored , the keys under Sheldon's control. The vehicle sparked to life and the men drove off. They passed the camp and headed toward Matecumbe Hotel. An hour ago there had been six inches of water on the roadway. The men stopped as they looked at the road. Waves were breaking over the road. The tide had come in and the hurricane was pushing the water further inland.

"We have to time it. As a wave comes in we gun it. Hopefully, it will recede by the time we get to that spot."

The two held on to the dash as the truck plowed into the water. The truck sputtered and coughed as it gagged on the salt water. The two men could no longer see the road for the spray that washed over the hood of the truck. But momentum carried them to the other side before the truck died as the next wave washed behind them. They were safe. At least until they met the National Guard a few miles down the road.

Carl the cook used the canned beef and beans from the stores in the supply closet to put together lunch. With the help of some of the kitchen volunteers the team not only made a meal for the vets but also made sandwiches for their trip on the train. The provisions were low but it mattered little at this point.

The door slammed shut as a wet and wind-worn Timothy entered the mess hall. His skin was red from the irritating sand. He had a bruise on his cheek where some debris connected with him as it blew into the Gulf.

"Tim!" yelled Harry as he looked up from his cards. "You look awful!"

The men at the table laughed. Timothy shook off his soaked clothes like a dog after a bath.

"Just came to get a cup O' Joe before I gather my things."

"I thought you eloped with your girl," said Buddy.

"There's a roadblock north of here. The guards are turning vets back. They say we've got to ride the train. They wouldn't let me pass."

The coffee pot had long since percolated, but it was still warm. Tim filled a mug, took a swig and winced. He grabbed the sugar and dowsed a hearty helping into the cup. He exhaled a long sigh before taking another sip.

"So when is the train coming?" asked Tim.

"They say it'll be here in a couple of hours." Harry folded his hand and stood up, stretching.

"I've got to get changed," said Tim. He paused as he scanned the room to see who was present. "Hey – where's Krebs?"

Harry looked around. He felt a cold chill run up his neck.

"Good question..." he replied.

"I'll see if he's in his shack."

"I'll go with you," said Tim.

"No, that's okay... you go get changed, I'll get him."

Tim felt that Harry was hiding something by the terse nature of his response, but he didn't know what. Harry was usually a straightforward guy, so this reserved side of him made Timothy wonder.

Harry didn't go out through the main entrance. He headed into the kitchen instead. Carl was whipping up sandwiches as Harry grabbed him by the arm.

"I haven't seen Stuart Krebs, have you?" he asked.

"No, I figured he'd already left. Haven't seen him since... well I can't say I remember. There are so many men here I can't keep track of them all."

"Yeah, but he's a junkie. If he is in the state like we saw him the other day..." Harry pondered. "So you have more heroin?"

"I've packed up the medicine and put it in the ambulance truck. I didn't want it laying out here if the storm hits."

"Can you get to some?"

"Not easily."

Harry thought, then said, "Well, I'm gonna see if he's in his bunk. Maybe he's okay."

"Be careful out there. The wind is really getting fierce." Carl returned to his sandwiches.

Harry stepped outside and had to cover his eyes. The sand hurt his face as it hurtled through the air. Two of the vet's shacks near the mess hall had collapsed in the wind. He didn't offhand know who lived in them. Some of the flimsy timbers did cartwheels and rolled from the men's quarters toward the edge of the road.

Harry turned the corner and headed directly into the wind. He had to lean forward because of the constant force coming ashore. He remembered the water swells from the morning. He squinted to protect his eyes and looked at the same spot he'd seen earlier.

The landscape looked dramatically different. The water had crept past the mangroves, and whitewater breakers were washing ashore licking the edge of the shack encampment. Waves crested with a white lining fringe until it could no longer hold its upright frame and came crashing down too close to the mess hall. Harry could feel the mass of the ocean wave as tons of water gave way to land.

The edge of the land was white and frothy with foam that quickly blew away. Harry eyed the spot where Jimmy and Buddy had grappled in their last great fight. The spot where the men celebrated their respective victories was now completely submerged.

Harry turned and took a step up on the single step leading to Stuart Krebs shack. He beat on the door.

"Krebs?!" yelled Harry above the wind and rain. "Krebs?! You in there?!" He beat on the door with his open hand.

No one answered.

"Krebs!!" Harry yelled louder. "Krebs! I'm comin' in!"

Harry tried the door but it was locked. He tried it again to be sure, and it didn't budge. The shacks weren't built to withstand the force of the storm or the force of Harry's shoulder as he jammed his body against the locked door. The wood splintered on the other side and Harry tumbled forward, thinking there would be more resistance. Harry ended up on all fours inside Krebs' shack.

"Two hours and the train will arrive. Four hours on the train. That will be the hard part. Then another hour and I'll have my 'juice.'" The man on the bed mumbled as he rocked back and forth.

"Two hours and the train will arrive. Four hours on the train. That will be the hard part. Then another hour and I'll have my 'juice.'"

Krebs was oblivious to Harry's entrance.

"Two hours and the train will arrive. Four hours on the train. That will be the hard part. Then another hour and I'll have my 'juice.'" Krebs didn't see that part of his roof had blown off and the rain was coming down — ruining magazines and newspapers that he'd stacked in the far corner of this little place called home. Krebs eyes looked gaunt and lifeless as he repeated his mantra.

Harry grabbed the man's face and forced him to look into his eyes.

"Krebs! Snap out of it! C'mon, pal!"

The eyes took a moment to focus. They looked like a man half asleep, but finally closed in on Harry.

"Hey Harry, is the train here yet?"

"No, pal. The train ain't here yet. You look pretty bad. Where is your heroin?"

"Hey – I want to get on the train. I need to get my 'juice.'"

"Do you have any 'juice' here, Stuart?"

"Nope. I'm getting on the train and getting my juice."

"Stuart I need you to come with me. I know where I can get you some juice."

"Do you have some?"

"No, we have to go see Carl."

"Oh, okay... the train is coming..."

Harry interrupted. "Forget the train. We have to leave now."

"Is the train here?"

Rather than try to reason with the man, Harry played along.

"Yeah – the train is here. You don't want to miss the train, do ya?"

"The train is here!" a big smile came across Stuarts face. Krebs was met with a wet slap as the wind found its mark through the ceiling's opening.

"Let's go get on the train," said Harry helping Stuart to his feet.

A two by four from one of the shacks slammed against the outer wall startling them both.

"What about my bag?"

"I'll get your bag," replied Harry, having no intention of doing anything but helping Stuart to get to Carl.

"I can't give him as much as last time. This storm is bad and we might need it when we have a real injury. I'm loading this stuff back in the ambulance as soon as I can."

288

Harry looked at Krebs and then back at Carl. "Okay, you gotta help him out. He said that once he got off the train he can get his own 'juice.'"

"I shouldn't be doing this. Damn Harry."

"After the storm, we'll both work to get him clean. I'll take responsibility for him."

Carl stopped short of putting the needle in Krebs arm.

"We gotta get him through this storm. The locals say it's gonna be bad. Krebs is in no condition, high or sober, to handle what is coming. You damn well better keep an eye on him."

He plunged the syringe into Krebs vein.

"When's the train coming?" asked Timothy.

"Shouldn't be here before too long. I heard they had it ready this morning and they were just waiting for word from Sheldon and Ghent." Elmer said as he hid a card under the table.

"Good. I was turned back at a checkpoint along the road. They wouldn't let me through. I want to get outta here as soon as I can."

While the men were talking, the train was not on its way. In fact, the large locomotive was merely getting the final boxcars added in preparation for its departure. The wind had started kicking up.

"We're gonna have to be careful on the bridges with this wind," said the engineer as he spit a large wad of chew on the ground.

"What do you mean?" asked the tender.

The tender a large black man with incredibly muscular arms. He had his sleeves rolled up. He opened the furnace and checked the flame.

"If that wind is over thirty miles an hour we can't cross the bridge."

"What?" The tender's eyes went wide. "Aren't we supposed to be getting a bunch o' people out before the hurricane hits?"

"We won't be getting anyone out if we cross a trestle and are dumped over the side."

"We'd better get a move on, then."

"As soon as we're done assembling the train, stoke the flames and we'll make our best time out of Homestead."

Hours after the order was given, the train sent up plumes of smoke and the locomotive started huffing as it made its way south. The rescue train was finally on its way.

Sheldon joined the vets in the mess hall. Confident that Cutler and Sheldon's wife were on their way to Homestead, he could focus on the men. After all, they were his responsibility.

Ed Sheeran entered the room, scanning it to find Sheldon. He stopped when Elmer looked up and gave him a wave. Ed waved back and headed over to Sheldon.

"We gotta talk."

Sheldon didn't want to be bothered with the old man.

"Let me finish this hand," Sheldon said as he lifted the cards.

Ed grabbed the cards and flung them — face up — on the table.

"We gotta talk - now."

"Damn you, Ed," said Sheldon spitting the words. Sheldon looked at the men across the table. "I'll be back. Deal me out."

Ed walked over to the image of the bridge hung on the wall.

"Where the hell is the train? We gotta get these men out now. Have you heard that wind? The shacks are coming apart. The surf is about to hit the mess hall."

"What the hell do you want me to do? We ordered the train. It's on its way. The storms not gonna hit..."

Sheeran interrupted, "The storm is here."

"What the hell are you talking about?"

Sheeran put his arm around Sheldon. It was not a familial gesture. He turned him toward the windows facing the ever encroaching shoreline.

"Take a look — look at the breakers."

The water was fighting itself to race to shore. Where once there was rhythm, the sea now displayed a chaos of waves and breakers.

"What the hell are you talking about," Sheldon turned to return to the table. The old man grabbed Sheldon with unrestrained strength. Sheldon, once again, faced the waves.

"They're not breaking at an angle."

"What?"

"Look!" There was a threatening tone in Sheeran's voice.

Sheldon looked at the waves. It didn't mean a thing to him.

"I've seen this before. Years ago, it was the same thing. The leaders didn't respect the storm. They took their time and men were killed. It's the same thing — the same damn thing."

Sheldon remained silent.

Ed continued, "The waves are crashing directly onshore. That means that the hurricane is heading directly for us. The waves aren't angled along the shore."

Sheldon didn't agree. Sheldon now felt he had the upper hand. He raised his voice.

"You don't know *what* you are talking about. I've been checking the weather reports. I've seen the course of the storm. Sam has been tracking..."

"That is the same thing that happened when I worked on the train. They thought that the storm was tracking south. They told the men to keep working. You never saw the fear in their eyes as the clouds mounted. You didn't hear their cries as they died – I did! Who are you going to believe — some weather reporter in Miami? A weather man in Key West? Someone in Cuba?!"

"Just because of the waves?" Sheldon was still not convinced.

"When I came here, I was timing the squalls. When I left, the squalls were ten minutes apart — now they are three... Dammit Sheldon, we have to do something now."

"We'll be alright. I know..."

Sheeran drove his point home. He tried to steady his voice and slow his heart rate in an effort to make his point without seeming out of control.

"Take a look at the bridge." Sheeran pointed to the picture of the bridge. "What's going to happen when millions of gallons of water strike that bridge?"

Sheldon didn't reply. Ed remembered the days following the hurricane. He remembered seeing his friends who'd been killed. He put the thought out of his mind.

"The bridge is..." Sheldon stopped and thought about all that Sheeran had said.

Sheeran looked at the oddly silent Sheldon. Ed saw fear in the man's eyes. Sheeran turned toward the men. He spoke to the crowd.

"I'm going to need some volunteers to look after the equipment until the train comes! I need men willing to join me on the barge!"

Harry had his arms around the weak, but slowly rousing Krebs.

"You got two volunteers here," yelled Harry. Ed smiled at Harry. A few others joined them.

"If you go there, you might not hear the train whistle. It's better to stay put," Sheldon was still being contrary even after all of the evidence.

A group rose and joined Ed. The majority stayed put. Harry could trust Ed Sheeran.

"Buddy, Elmer, Jim – you're not going?" asked Harry.

Elmer looked at his cards and then looked up at Harry. "I've been in the trenches in France. I've seen some pretty horrendous shit. I just can't think that the weather is going to get the better of me."

Harry shook his head. "Buddy, you're not going to stay here, are you?"

"I think Jim and I are going to get on the train. We're heading north."

"Okay," said Harry a little sullen. "I'll see you guys when I get back."

"What's up with Stuart? He looks out of it."

"Weekend bender — he'd been drinking pretty hard," Harry lied. "I got his back."

Harry scanned the room for Tim. He remembered that Tim was getting his things. He had no time to fetch him.

"Take care of yourself," said Buddy.

"You, too."

Ed was waiting at the door as Harry looked up. He grabbed Stuart and headed outside. He glanced back at the men in the mess hall. He wondered who he would see after this was over.

As soon as the men left the mess hall, they were blown toward the truck. More men left the building than could easily be accommodated on a single vehicle. Luckily a water truck, used to hydrate the men on a hot work day, was parked at the edge of camp. Carl, having finished all the meal preparations, opted to drive the water truck.

Harry helped Stuart get in the bed of Ed's pickup. He piled in with the rest of the vets who struggled to keep the sand out of their eyes. The men's skin turned red from the onslaught that whipped all around.

Harry looked away and felt the sand on his neck as the grains moved down his collar and slid down his back. The sky lit up with a lattice of lightning. Harry never heard the thunder. It lit again only a few seconds later, but no bolts shot toward the ground.

The truck lurched forward and headed up the small incline toward the main road which paralleled the railroad tracks. The water truck followed behind. They'd only climbed a few feet, but it was enough to give Harry a momentary bird's eye view of the approaching storm. The cauldron of motion, both in the sky and sea, seemed destined to penetrate the small cove where the men had made camp and swallow the entire place.

The storm looked poised to strike. The wind, rain and violent surf were just the advanced armies of something worst to come. It boggled Harry's imagination as the horizon vanished behind the black of the coming menace.

This was the warfare that Harry had never seen. Now he was in the trenches with the men. Each took their fate into their own hands by making judgments on where they would be and what they would do. They could see their enemy out there now. Their foe wasn't faceless. It was a vast wall of atmospheric snakes that beckoned them to make a small mistake.

Harry saw the shacks one-by-one disintegrating. He wondered who chose to stay in the comfort of their small bed thinking they'd be safe. Had lives already been sacrificed? Harry turned away. He'd not prayed in a long time. There was no need. His father's brand of religion which included a belt lashing wasn't the god that Harry prayed to now. Harry prayed for mercy. He prayed for the safety of his friends and fellow vets.

Sheldon went to the end of the mess hall, picked up the phone and dialed.

Nothing.

He clicked the handle in rapid succession and tried again.

Still nothing.

He wanted to get in touch with the station in Miami, Homestead, and beyond. He wanted to know when the train would arrive. Once again, he tried. He only heard static.

Some of the men looked at Sheldon as he tried unsuccessfully to contact the outside world. A few second guessed whether they should have gone with the more experienced Ed Sheeran. Others pulled out beer or whiskey as the card games became more animated and the weather grew more fierce.

Though it was far from a high ridge, the two trucks were along an elevated point on the road where the winds whipped with increased vengeance. Ed gunned the truck toward the barge holding the equipment. The truck shuddered with the combination of the speed and the payload. Harry could barely make out the two large cranes. They swayed like two dancing dinosaurs. He saw the mangroves which marked the opening of the channel where the barge floated waiting.

Ed cut the wheel to head toward the barge. At the same moment a violent gust — the likes he'd never felt before — surged past the truck. It got up underneath the vehicle filled with men and spilled over on its side skidding in a wide arc. The men were ejected from the truck, rolling along the gravel and coral. The lucky ones were those along the right side of the truck. They were near the bottom of the pile and merely tumbled a few feet. Harry sailed through the air with the others but landed on a man rather than the hard coral. The man let out a "Huff" as Harry kept rolling. Harry smacked the back of his head as he finally slowed and stopped. He got up, checked himself, and shook off the growing headache from the lump on his head. Others were doing the same. Some were bloody, and one looked like he was favoring a broken arm.

Stuart was on his feet, now a little more alert as he helped someone else. Harry ran to the cab of the truck. Ed was pulling himself from the wrecked vehicle.

"I'm okay! I'm okay! Damn wind blew the truck clean over."

The men from the water car witnessed the event and stopped to help. Together the vets made the rest of the trek on foot as the squall eased. Those that could run made for the barge. Others, leaning on each other, hobbled or walked to the place that would be their sanctuary.

Harry looked at Ed who looked as though he aged five years in the last two hours.

"What are you staring at? I'm fine!" he said. "Get to the barge!"

"I'm not goin' anywhere without ya!" Harry replied. The rain had started again with marble sized droplets that rolled in ribbons across the flat landscape. Harry helped Ed were the last two to arrive at the barge.

Inside a group of locals, whom Ed had invited for safe-haven, had already started tending to the injured. The main cabin area smelled of coffee. Someone had brought a case of Coca-Cola which the men eagerly grabbed.

"This'll be our home for the next twenty-four hours or so!" Ed yelled above the banter of the crowd. "I've secured the barge against the coral, the mangroves and some equipment outside. We've kept the ties loose so don't be surprised if this swells through the night. It is supposed to. I've been through a hurricane on a barge before, and I'll tell ya – it is the best place to be in these parts."

The men in the mess hall pulled out more beer as they played cards while waiting for the train. Sheldon didn't know when the train would arrive, but he calculated that it would be there sometime between 4:30 and 5:30PM.

Elmer sucked down another bottle as he continued to lose money in spite of the cards hiding in his lap. As he laid down another losing hand the entire room stopped.

It was something more felt than heard. It wasn't an explosion or a crack of thunder. Had they been on the west coast those sitting around the tables would have said it was an earthquake. It felt like the earth moved. The compression was felt through the ground and in the air.

"What the hell was that?" asked Elmer.

"I dunno," replied Jimmy.

People looked around. Buddy got up, winding his Masonic ring. He moved over to Ray Sheldon.

"What was that?" Buddy asked.

Sheldon shrugged.

"Was that the hurricane?"

"I have no idea what that was," Sheldon peered outside but couldn't see anything. The sheets rippled against the window.

"Maybe it was a wave crashing down?" Buddy conjectured.

Sheldon pulled out a cigarette and lit up. "I don't think so. I felt it more than heard it... I have no idea what that was...damnedest thing..."

He pulled a long draw on his cigarette. Things were unraveling. He saw it starting slowly. Things like this usually did. The storm was bearing down sooner than he expected. The train wasn't here. Some of the men had defected and sought other means of protection. Yet, they were all under his responsibility. If one of the men died, it would be on his head.

Control.

He had to do something. He had no idea where some of the men had gone. Some simply walked north.

He stepped to the kitchen and released the hook which freed the bell Carl used to issue the meal call. The wind took the bell and started its clanging. He hoped that there would be some out there who would hear its toll.

He'd not been outside so hadn't seen the destruction of more and more of the flimsy structures. A gust of wind blew, caught the bell on the pole and tore it from its mast.

"Gentlemen! Gentlemen! May I have your attention?!" Sheldon cried in his practiced voice of authority. "We're going to have a meal. After that, we'll be shuttling you men to the railroad station. We'll board the train in an orderly fashion and be on our way. We only have so many trucks so we can't all go to the station at once."

The engineer decided to turn the locomotive around. It would waste a little time, but he would rather pull the cars down to the vets. He wanted the bright light of the locomotive shining forward when he returned. When he arrived at the station at Matecumbe he would disconnect and use one of the side rails to move the locomotive to the other side — headlight forward — on the return trip. Preparing the train would take time. But he was told the storm wasn't going to hit until later that night. With the light facing forward on his return, the bright light might catch debris that had blown onto the track. Being a little late at the station would be small consequence for doing the right thing.

But the train was still too far from the vets.

Timothy returned with his duffle bag and watched the men. His heart was far from this place. He wanted only to get away —to find his way back to Aella. He wanted to create a new life with the one he loved. The hurricane was a momentary evil that tried to separate them. He wondered how she was doing.

He watched his three friends, playing cards, drinking and eating the sandwiches that Carl had prepared for the train.

The men were loaded in shifts. Timothy joined the third group of men. They were commenting on how they could stay and ride out the storm. They puffed up and acted brave while the maelstrom swirled about them. They did what men have done before entering battle. They talked of stories past and their conquests. The men beat their chests to rise above the current fear they were facing. The Indians of the island had done the same thing with war paint and the beating of drums; they — like the vets — were mustering all their courage.

The storm demonstrated its fury as a piece of the mess hall sheared off in the high wind. The men went silent as the wood and tin on the roof screamed away. Timothy was glad to be leaving. The men were silent as they drove to the train station. The canvas covered truck offered little relief. The men on both sides fought to keep the straps in place. As they rounded the corner the wind shifted slightly and the stinging horizontal rain shot into the bed of the truck. The men on the end were instantly drenched.

Men exhaled sighs of relief as the truck finally made it onto the main road. The truck had a high clearance so it was unlikely to stall under the six or more inches of water that flooded the roadway. Ray couldn't gas the truck and go too fast because he feared the water would enter the intake and stall. A double wake, made by the tires, trailed behind in an ever growing double "V". Timothy wondered if the rest of the men would be evacuated by boat along this submerged roadway. At this point it made more sense.

The truck arrived at the train station. Tim grabbed his duffle bag and headed inside. The men were packed in and the place smelled of must and sweat. The entire place creaked and moved under the onslaught of the forces of God.

Jimmy, Elmer and Buddy moved to the opposite corner of the mess hall. The remaining men watched as the parts of the roof sheared off and the rains mixed with the incoming tide to wet the floor. It started as just a puddle, but Buddy noted how the water rose and ebbed as the sea met the edge of the camp and the sea water seeped along the floor in an ever growing area.

The three were among the last to head from the mess hall to the train station. Elmer was finally on a winning streak. Fueled by his inebriation, he cajoled the men to stay and play another hand.

"Damn, it should storm like this every day. As the weather gets worse, my hands get better!" said Elmer as he slapped down another winning hand.

"Shut up and play," sneered Buddy.

The men felt that they were enduring the hurricane that had finally arrived on their small smattering of land. They were the old warriors who had won once and were winning again.

"You could hear them screaming all night long. I mean just a screaming and hollering for help"
- Charlie Roberts

It came in a single wave. The first herald of the storm surge — the water that was sucked from the bosom of the ocean and spewed back on land in a wave that would not recede — made its debut. It started as a rumble. The men felt the mess hall shudder before the wall of water hit. It crashed through the windows and smashed down the wall in a wash of white foam and debris.

The mess hall toppled like a house of cards. The roof collapsed on the men who were waiting for the next truck to take them to safety. All but one far corner was now rubble, being crushed and broken by the massive wall of water. Those that survived were buried under the remains. The water swirled and churned and broke up the mess hall into lethal bits.

Hell had arrived.

The train stopped as the drawbridge warning lights flashed red. The boat was slow to make its way toward the Gulf. The tender had to keep the train stoked, but it would take even more time to bring it back to speed. They were already late because of the switch to the locomotive. Now they would be delayed further because of the drawbridge. The rain pelted the big black beast and steam rose on its warm parts.

The boat had passed but the bridge remained up as part of the protocol for making sure no other vessels were in the area as they churned toward the open section of the channel. Slowly the section of track lowered and the locomotive built up its head of steam. There was no contacting the vets to let them know the train would be at least an hour late. The power started returning and the eight large wheels slowly began their march south. The engineer hoped that the winds wouldn't be too high to cross the many trestle bridges from here to Matecumbe. If the wind was too strong, he'd have to brake and take each one at a snail's pace lest the whole train topple over the edge to the watery abyss.

The weatherman in Jacksonville confirmed that their estimates on the storm were wrong. The scant barometric pressure readings they were getting proved it was heading north of Key West. Sections of the keys had grown eerily silent. The storm more powerful than anyone anticipated. Its track was different than anyone expected. The rogue was making landfall and the weather man was unable to raise anyone along Matecumbe.

Sheldon watched the barometric pressure kept tumbling. He marked the pressure line on every trip to and from the station. Each time, the distance between the low point and the new low point became greater. He didn't need an indicator — the weather was telling him as much. He was almost done hauling the last of the men out of the camp. The train should have arrived by now. He glanced at his watch which he'd tucked under layers to keep dry. He left — alone — to complete the transport of the vets.

Buddy came around and choked out salt water that made its way into his sinuses and lungs. He shot out wads of the water and wanted to hurl that which he'd swallowed. He let out a groan and belched up a foul mix of gas. He felt like his chest was on fire. He had difficulty breathing, but he didn't think he'd broken any ribs. He pushed away splintered timbers that still swirled in the macabre soup. As he moved, a piece of tin cut into his hand. He didn't feel that pain as much as the slice along his leg. A piece of wood had jammed into his thigh. He removed it and the blood oozed slowly from the wound. A few nail sized splinters still remained and he pulled them out as well.

He was in a state of shock, not realizing what happened or where he was. The wind and rain tore at his shirt and broke off a button. That made the shirt open even more and in a matter of seconds the wind whirled, the shirt became airborne and his bare chest was exposed to the elements. He could see the deep black and blue that was still growing along his left side.

He rose up on his knees and arched his back skyward. A few men were running away. He didn't know why. Things weren't making sense. He saw human limbs and body parts among the chaos of debris. Water was churning through the remains like a hydra of white and grey. Forward and backward it slithered among the dead.

He'd been playing cards. He looked down and a jack of spades floated by.

His friends...

Where were his friends?

He'd been with Jimmy and Elmer. He looked up at the men who he'd seen running. They evaporated into the gray and black of unrelenting precipitation. The table where they sat was gone. He yelled to the men who'd run away. Were his friends among those who disappeared in the distance?

"Jimmy! Elmer!"

His words were lost in the wind.

"Jimmy! – Elmer!"

He cupped his hands and yelled to the four points of the compass.

"Jimmy! – Elmer!"

The sound of a man in pain came from somewhere beneath him. It was close. He stood up and tore at the rubble.

Nothing.

He was sure he'd heard a human voice.

Another wave crashed and washed up to his knees, submerging whatever lay beneath. It pulled back and he heard a gurgling sound — a human gurgling.

Frantically, he tossed the two by fours, rafter remains, tin, parts of chairs, and parts of tables. The white of a shoulder glistened wet as he flung yet another part of the mess tent. He didn't know who it was.

A large piece of the roof obscured the rest of the body. He grimaced and let out a yell more animal than human as he tried to pull the roof off whoever lay beneath. He was filled with adrenaline, and in this moment of crisis he summoned all his strength to pull back the large obstruction. Buddy twisted and shoved it to one side. It slammed down, and slid down the pile until a gust of wind threatened to blow it back onto him. Buddy gazed down at the man partially uncovered.

Staring back at him was Jimmy. His eyes were fixed and unmoving. The man who'd become his close friend and mighty adversary in the ring lay motionless. All of Jimmy's herculean strength was no match for the powerful force that bore down and broke his body as the mess hall collapsed.

"No."

Buddy looked down at the man who gazed up at the churning heavens.

"God – no."

Jimmy didn't blink as the rain splashed his eyes.

"Oh God – no – no – no."

Buddy started crying. His shoulders heaved up and down. There was no thought of self-survival. The loss was complete. He'd become a better man because of Jimmy and now there was no way to return the favor. There was only emptiness — a large blackness that covered Buddy's soul. His friend — and a part of himself — was dead.

"No!" yelled Buddy with a ferocity that was more animal than man. The clouds answered with a gut wrenching roll of thunder.

Buddy closed his friend's eyes. He sat still next to Jimmy's body as the hurricane swirled around him. The water rushed up and didn't ebb, but lingered. The storm surge continued inland unabated.

A groaning sound followed by a weak water-filled cough permeated the silence that followed the thunderclap.The sound came from Buddy's right. Someone was still alive.

Once again, Buddy tore into the splintered beams, broken walls, and roof to find who was still breathing.

A guttural sound and more coughing resonated from beneath a swirling pool of sea water. Someone was drowning.

Buddy moved a roof truss to find Elmer underneath. He pulled his head up above the water that was growing ever deeper.

"Ugh," came Elmer's first word after coughing up a mixture of sea water and blood. "Get me out!"

He opened his eyes and shook his head to get the water off his face. The rest of his body was still pinned beneath the rubble. It was a jigsaw puzzle to remove the rest of the wreckage of the mess hall. Large items lay over smaller ones all intertwined in a chaotic latticework. A small wave came over Elmer's face and he had to hold his breath while Buddy continued to work to free him.

"Hold on, Elmer!" cried Buddy. "I'm working as fast as I can!"

Pieces went flying through the air as Buddy pulled them up, broke them and hurled pieces aside.

"Hurry!" said Elmer in a panic. "Please – hurry!"

Another wave rolled over him.

Buddy freed up his legs and could now work on his shoulders and arms. He was working as fast as he could. Elmer tried to sit up and cried out in pain.

"Jesus! Oh God!" Elmer winced and lay back down.

Buddy stopped when he saw what he thought was the last two-by-four on top of Elmer. He was about to yank it out of the way, but stopped.

"What the hell! I can't — I can't get up!"

"Don't move!" yelled Buddy. His face went ashen as he looked at Elmer.

"What?! Help me, Buddy. Help me up!"

"Oh Jesus, Buddy! Don't move — don't say anything!"

"Oww!" yelled Elmer. "What is it?"

Buddy wondered if he should tell the man his condition. A two-by-four penetrated through Buddy's left side. A pool of blood swirled around him.

"What?! What?!"

"For the love of God Elmer – don't move."

For a second, Buddy thought he should pull the large piece of lumber through Elmer. He then thought that doing so would spell instant death.

Buddy listened to what he thought was another chorus of thunder. But it didn't abate.

"Buddy! We gotta go! – NOW!" Elmer lifted his head far enough to see the large white wall of water coming his way. This wasn't another small wave that Elmer could ride out with a breath of air. This was a tsunami like white monstrosity that was barreling toward them. It completely consumed the mangroves and tore over the debris.

Buddy couldn't finesse Elmer. Knowing he might die either way, Buddy yanked on Elmer's shirt with both hands and pulled. As he did so the wave struck them both. Buddy closed his eyes as the force drove them both up and away in a tumbling mass of debris and human remains.

Though he was twisting through the watery onslaught, Buddy didn't let go. He was afraid the shirt would rip and Elmer would be gone when the wave receded. Tumbling over and over, Buddy lost his sense of up and down. He bumped up against a number of objects. His lungs burned for air as he hurtled for what seemed like hours. Yet, he still held on to Elmer.

Finally his head curled and the back of his neck hit hard on coral. Instinctively he reached out and took hold. His free hand was being shredded by the coral while holding Elmer's shirt. He feared the rock he'd grabbed would give way but the object held firm.

The water washed back and Buddy took a desperate gasp of air. He looked back and pulled Elmer toward him. He'd been flung forty feet from the mess hall by the power of the wave. The next wave, not as strong, churned the mess hall like an out of control window blind.

He stared at Elmer. Blood trickled from his mouth. The three foot long two-by-four stuck out of both sides of the man. Elmer wasn't breathing. Buddy smacked him on the face.

"Elmer! Dammit! Elmer!"

The man looked white. He was perfectly still. His mouth lay open and slack. Sea water mixed with the blood. Elmer's eyes were closed and he was unresponsive.

"Elmer!" Buddy yelled. He shook the man at the shoulders. Water splattered from his mouth but there was no response.

"Elmer! Wake Up! Elmer!"

Buddy slapped him. Hoping he would come around. He looked at the large piece of lumber shooting through him. No blood came from the wound.

In only a few minutes Buddy had lost two of his close friends. He leaned against the retaining wall that he and Jimmy helped build. There were no more tears. A numbness of the surreal experiences put Buddy in a shock induced haze.

He sat next to his dead friend and looked out to sea. He really didn't focus, but something primal registered deep in his psyche. A second large broiling wall of green and gray brought him back to reality. It looked larger than the last wave and it was carrying a great deal more debris. He saw a

307

truck floating fifteen feet high on the crest of the white water. This wave was lethal.

Ray Sheldon headed back to camp from the station. He would be glad when the last men were brought to the station and the vets were safely onboard. Sheldon started to round the corner past the overgrown vegetation that shivered in the onslaught as he made his way toward the camp.

He couldn't believe what he saw.

The devastation of the campsite and the utter destruction of the mess hall sent Sheldon's heart into his stomach. A large wave rolled over what was left of the site. As it struck, the legs of the water tower crumpled, the connecting pipe broke and the storage container shattered as it was consumed by the large wash that buried what was left of the camp.

Sheldon got out of his truck and started running down the slight decline toward the camp hoping he could save someone. He stopped short as the wave pulled the water tower out to sea. Ray looked for any human motion. He couldn't discern the human and non-human remains.

"Oh God," said Ray. "It's not my fault."

He scanned through the rain and grayness. He saw what he thought were human figures running off into the distance.

"Wait! Stop!"

Perhaps it was his imagination. He squinted and thought he saw men running. The human figures dissolved into the rain and reappeared again. He was surrounded by the spirits of the dead, he thought. Ray heard the screams of the dead in the wind. He felt the cold touch of the deceased through the torrent. Ray turned around thinking there were people surrounding him. He was being taunted by the ghosts.

"It's not my fault!" yelled Ray to the rain.

"It's not my fault!" yelled Ray to the wind.

The ghosts disbursed and he was left with the natural elements that blew hard enough to knock him backward. He landed on his ass facing the water. The camp was submerged as the waters rolled in with increasing ferocity.

The man was dead and the waves slammed him into the wall again and again. Elmer was flotsam. He floated to the surface and his head slammed against the rock. The violence shook Elmer from his death. He choked and gagged and spewed water from his lungs. He opened his eyes and gasped for a breath. Fire and needles stung with every breath. The spark of life rose up deep within him. He clung to the rock wall as another wave rolled over him.

He knew he had to find higher ground or be swept out to sea. The large piece of wood that protruded from his stomach kept him from any vertical movement. The water washed away.

Elmer started to crawl.

Psychopaths
-   *Julius Stone referring to the vets in an
    interview from 1935*

He had been consoling his investors for hours.
He was deep in debt and the loss of a single house
might throw his hopes of reaping financial reward
out the window. He'd overbought the town of Key
West. Some of the richer clients were threatening
to sue when they found their homes were riddled
with soft, termite eaten boards. One woman fainted
when she opened her freshly stocked pantry and
found families of cockroaches nibbling at her soap.

The dream homes in paradise were painted
shacks that would be quite nice had Stone invested
to fix them properly. Now, he was facing several
promises of lawsuits. He'd bilked the wealthy of
their money and now they were turning on him. The
only thing worse than the lawyers was the gossip
network. The rich broadcasted Stone's name in
shame and now he was holding a number of
questionable properties he couldn't unload. He'd
not paid any taxes on his properties and he didn't
want the government getting wind of the illegal use
of the veterans in Key West.

He'd kept this from his wife, enticing her with
the idea of moving to Havana to start a new
enterprise there. He boasted to her that Key West
was such a success that he would expand his
investments abroad. He was using Cuba to funnel his
money in the event the U.S. got wind of his doings
and attempted to seize his assets. He saw all of this
in the light of "doing business."

The phone rang.

He assumed it was another disgruntled
customer.

"Stone here."

"Julius Stone – this is Fred Ghent."

"Ghent! Good to hear from you. Where are
you?"

"I am outside Homestead at the moment. I'll be helping coordinate the evacuation of the vets when they arrive."

"They're not out of the Keys yet?"

"No – we didn't feel there was a need."

"So is the storm hitting Key West?"

Ghent replied, "No, it started tracking north. I lost touch with Sheldon in Matecumbe."

"Oh – good," Stone breathed a sigh of relief. He hoped the storm wouldn't bear down on Key West. His investments were safe.

"Good?" Ghent didn't understand Stone's response. "The men haven't been evacuated yet and the storm is closing in on them."

"Oh – yes, of course." Stone backtracked.

"I'm sure Sheldon has things well in hand. Is the train on its way?"

"Yes," Ghent answered.

"Good – well I'm sure everyone will be all right."

"It is hard to tell. We've lost communication. We haven't heard about the state of the train. We only know that it was late leaving the station."

"Well then," Stone was still thinking about his property. "... there's nothing we can do. This is..."

Stone thought of something reassuring to say. "This is an act of God. Nothing we can do about that but wait it out."

"True. It is an act of God. I'll call you when the train arrives."

"Good. Thank you."

Stone hung up the phone. He sat down on his desk and opened a portfolio with photos and information about homes in Cuba. These homes were surely in better shape than those in Key West.

They are only human beings; unsuccessful human beings, and all they have to lose is their lives.

- *Hemingway*

Sheldon didn't know what to tell the men as he made his way back to the train station. His hands shook not from the wind and rain, but from the realization that he may have waited too long. Sam Cutler's scathing words rolled around in his head. He replayed in his mind the biting reprimand from Ed Sheeran.

"It's not my fault!" Ray yelled as he pounded the steering wheel. The wind blew his truck off the road as it hydroplaned up onto the railroad track. He overcorrected and pulled the left wheel off the track and nearly veered into the ditch on the opposite side.

"It's not my God damn fault! Where the hell is the train?!"

Ray didn't know what to say to the men. Should he tell them that the remaining men were killed? He didn't actually see anyone. Perhaps they got out. He thought he saw men running in the rain. Maybe they decided to seek shelter with Ed Sheeran. He couldn't say anyone had died.

Yet, his gut told him otherwise.

He pulled up to the station. The wind had torn away some of the wood slats that ran along the outside platform. He heard the entire building creak. The pipe leading to the small water tower used to fill the train was nowhere to be seen. The wood shingles were popping off the roof. The place was filled with men.

"Where's the damn train?!"

It was dark and the water by the station coursed over his boots as he sloshed toward the station. He glanced back and saw that part of the track was underwater. Two boxcars sat nearby on a side track. He thought that these might house some of the men that were running around in the storm.

312

Sheldon arrived and could barely close the door of the station because of the pressure from the outside.

"Sheldon, where are the men?" Timothy asked when Elmer, Jimmy and Buddy failed to appear.

"They found somewhere else to ride out the storm."

"Oh?" Timothy wondered why the men changed their mind. "Did they go with Ed Sheeran?"

"Yeah – I suppose."

Timothy looked at Sheldon. He'd gone pale with that response. He sensed there was something wrong.

"There wasn't anyone there when I arrived."

Timothy thought about Ray's curious response. Perhaps the uncertainty in his voice was due to the fact that he couldn't account for his men. This was true, but Sheldon wasn't letting anyone know about the devastation that he witnessed. Sheldon wanted to make sure those men under his direct control were led to safety. He looked around and tried to count the hundred or more men in the station. He wished he'd taken a count of the men that had gone with Sheeran. He figured there were about fifteen men who were left at the mess hall. Maybe there were more. There should be more men.

Did some leave earlier? Were some at the motor pool? Had some ....

Ray's mind was cloudy.

It sounded like a crashing wave slammed into the station. The wall of wind smashed windows. This was followed by a loud 'crack!' as some of the pylons that supported the train station snapped. The structure stayed upright.

The men, who'd been talking and ignoring the events outside stopped and froze as they felt the station shift under their feet. Something on the roof sounded like popcorn. It increased in intensity. Golf ball sized hail shot through the broken windows. The men huddled in the center of the building. Some of the slats gave way around the window as the window frame was torn. Shards of broken glass shot at the men with deadly speed.

"Where's the damn train?" said one of the vets to Sheldon. There was a threat in his voice. "Sheldon – where's the damn train?"

"I ordered the train and it should be here..."

Another blast of wind rocked the station. The men felt the entire structure sway and, like the mess hall, a corner of the roof sheared off. The hail was now pea sized, but it was mixed with huge droplets of rain. The entire place was getting wet.

Sheldon wondered if the station would be there when the train arrived.

"Sheldon! This place is coming apart!" Timothy yelled.

Another gust pulled half of the roof off. Part of the roof collapsed on the men. Sheldon knew they were in trouble.

"Men! There are two boxcars on the sidetrack. Let's make for those! They'll be safe!"

Sheldon led the way. As he stepped out, he had to leap over sections where the decking floorboards were gone. The supporting struts were the only thing that kept them from tumbling down the four feet to the soggy ground. Sheldon's truck lay on its side, the front wheel spinning as if a child had wound up a top.

The first boxcar was locked. Sheldon tried both sides but the doors wouldn't budge. He sprinted to the next one and opened it. Inside were five large oil cans and some building supplies. He ushered the men inside.

As one man made his way along the track he was lifted six feet into the air. He slammed down on the railroad track and rolled down the embankment on the other side. Two other men, whose friendship exceeded common sense, ran after him. They, too, disappeared over the other side searching in the darkness while the forces around them tried to swallow any evidence of their comrade.

Sheldon was too busy getting the men onboard to see the three men disappear. Sheldon wished he could call out to the other men strewn about the island. He didn't know their fate.

One vet, who decided to ride out the storm in his shack, felt it lifted off its foundation as the tidal forces started carrying him out to sea. The housing split open as he saw the tops of mangroves pass beneath him.

One man lashed himself to a telephone pole with his spare belt. As the wind tore away at the tops of the pole, the electric line came down and burned him alive as he tried to free himself.

Two men found refuge in a sewer pipe. It was safe from the onslaught of the elements until the torrent of water consumed both exits.

Some survived against all odds. One man was washed out into the gulf. As the wind drove him further and further from land he resigned himself to death. As he did so, he slammed into a train trestle. He clung to it and climbed. The barnacles tore at his wrists and arms, but he climbed. The man found a cross beam and wedged himself firmly along the angled brace.

Ray hopped up into the boxcar with the other men.

"Hey Guys!" he said. "It's not my fault. Look – I want you to know that it's not my fault. You know that. Right?"

Timothy, who was nearest Sheldon turned away. Most of them did the same. Some sneered a remark that was lost in the smelly confines of the boxcar.

Buddy didn't know where he was going. The shock of the whirlwind around him made him numb. He was now shirtless as hundred plus mile an hour winds blasted his skin away. He felt nothing. He climbed over the rail and fell. He saw one of the two large cranes twisted and gnarled like an old oak tree.

He passed a truck that had flipped. The man who was inside was crushed under the steering wheel. He peered inside and tried to recognize who it was. He couldn't identify the man. Buddy leaned against the wind and continued his mindless trek.

He couldn't keep his eyes open anymore. He stopped and wanted to drop right there. The storm had taken his friends. He wondered why it had not taken him.

Squinting, he made out the boxcar he'd filled with supplies and tools. He could find shelter there. He winced as small pebbles shot through his pants like pellets from a bb gun. He moved to the lee side of the boxcar. There he could finally take a normal breath. He didn't realize how much energy he'd expended as he fought to simply take a step. The boxcar door was closed. He pulled the handle.

"Hey! Close the door!" came a cry from inside. "Hey – is that you, Buddy?"

"Yeah!"

"What the hell are you doing out there? Get in and shut the damned door."

Buddy slipped into the dark interior where a number of vets had found shelter.

The train was slowly making its way south. As it did so, the weather continued to worsen. The engineer had to stop to clear debris that covered the tracks. At first there were simply a few palm fronds and a large branch or two. Now they were battling downed trees.

North of Matecumbe a telephone pole had splintered and fallen.

"We gotta move fast," the engineer said as the engineer and fireman grabbed two one inch diameter iron poles. They jammed the irons under the telephone pole and heaved in unison to free the rails.

The large black man who fed the flames of the locomotive bent his legs and threw himself at the iron rod. The pole bent and dug into the man's shoulder as he lifted up. The telephone pole slid along the slick track and thudded then rolled down the gravel.

The two mounted the warm iron horse and started down the track. They successfully removed the pole but failed to see the telephone line that had wrapped around the wheel of one of the cars. Only after they'd gone a few feet did the sparks fly as the wheel seized up with the cable firmly wrapped around the axle.

"Oh hell!" the engineer cried as he, once again, set the brake. The two leapt from locomotive and raced to the car with the locked wheel. Precious moments were lost as they cut the wire. The metal frayed off as the two pulled out the wire, foot-by-foot. The nearer they cut to the axle, the more tightly the wire was wound.

Having freed the train, the two took the extra time to walk the rails. Satisfied that the cable was clear of the railroad tracks, they mounted and rode toward the vets.

The barge rocked, but the machinery was tied tightly. A few of the people inside were mildly seasick. Harry gave them a Coke and a bucket. Ed Sheeran had spent years thinking about how his friends on the railroad job might have been saved in the hurricane years ago. He saw the same faces in these vets. These people were safe.

Some of the lines Ed used to anchor the barge snapped, but most held firm. Harry sat in the corner of the barge as it rolled and yawed. It reminded him of the days in the submarine. It was a feeling he'd lost in the intervening land-based years.

He remembered those days when he returned from his missions. It was difficult trying to walk on land with his developed sea legs. Only by drinking could he find some normalcy in walking through town. Returning to the sub was a return to a liquid gravity that he understood.

Harry felt the roll of the barge comforting where most felt fear. His head nodded as the bodies in the cramped space and the humidity of human confinement enveloped him in slumber.

The sleep was deep and complete.

"Two hours and the train will arrive. Four hours on the train. That will be the hard part. Then another hour and I'll have my 'juice.'" Krebs was struggling.

The small amount of heroin Carl gave him was a band aid to keep him functional for a short period. That period was beginning to wear off. As Harry slept in the corner, the pacing Krebs was tired of waiting.

"The train is coming. I know it. The train... the train... the train is coming."

Those around him thought that he was suffering from shell shock exacerbated by the hurricane. This was only partially true.

Even those of saner minds thought the howling winds were the whistle arrival announcement of the train.

Some wondered if they made the right choice to ride out the horror on a floating vessel. Yet, they stayed on the barge because the others stayed. It was group confidence and commitment born from the herd. Had they been the only one on the barge, each would have slowly gone mad.

But Stuart Krebs didn't share that communal peace. He couldn't. He could only live inside his own head which played back the mechanical repetition of a drug related loop. His brain was wired now to seek out the only resolution to his quandary — to seek out the chemical which would return him, at least temporarily, to a state of normalcy.

"The train... the train..." He paced through the crowd as if they didn't exist. "The train..."

The wind rose and rolled over the little island. It tore away the palm tree fronds. It ripped away anything that man had made. Any birds on the island were already blown way out to sea. Strange sea creatures that moments earlier swam the great

318

deep were now rolling across a railroad track. Separated from their world, these monsters of the great blue also felt the savage unfairness of a world inverted by a force unfelt for hundreds of years.

Ed Sheeran looked at the barometer. It exceeded the range marked on its brass frame. He took out his pen and drew a new line below the manufacturer's measurement. The storm was worse than anyone had imagined.

Krebs was oblivious to the storm. Yet, when he heard the howling wind with its low sonorous bellow, something deep within his consciousness rose up and heard the deep bellows of a church organ roll across the sands. Everyone around him heard Aeolus,the god of the wind, blasting in full voice. Yet Stuart Krebs – lost somewhere between heroin fantasy and altered reality — heard what he believed to be the whistle of liberation.

"The train! The Train!"

Once he heard the hundred-mile an hour wind song, he ran for the door. The room rose with a cry to stop. He launched himself into the dark abyss.

"Krebs!" yelled Ed Sheeran.

Krebs was gone.

"Krebs!" yelled Sheeran again.

The words rolled in Harry's subconscious and roused him back to the real world from his slumber. Harry shook off the cobwebs and forced himself to a heightened state of alertness.

"What happened?" said Harry to no one in particular.

"Goddammit – Krebs ran outside." Sheeran turned to Harry.

"What?"

"I dunno, he went crazy and then stormed outside."

Harry stood up. "I have to go get him. He'll die out there."

Ed Sheeran rubbed his forehead. "If you go out there — you'll die. This is the worst storm ever..."

Harry hesitated. "But Krebs..."

"He's already dead. He died years ago." Both Harry and Sheeran looked each other in the eye. For a moment even the storm seemed to go silent.

Harry knew that every second reduced the probability that he'd be able to save his friend. It was an opportunity to redeem what he'd lost in the war. He could give his life for another. Without so much as a goodbye, Harry pressed himself against the door and stepped into the enveloping blackness.

Had Krebs been in his right mind and the storm not blown him away from the remains of the railroad station, the addict might have arrived in time to catch the train. Its whistle was lost in mayhem of the night. However, those men stacked together in the boxcar saw the steam engine slow — a metal blackness defying the night.

Stuart Krebs crawled in the darkness. The wind rolled him over but he kept moving toward the sound he believed to be the train. His was a singular thought. He was oblivious to the weather that tore away his clothing. He didn't feel welts rising on his body as debris slammed against him. His mantra looped though his mind and obfuscated all else.

But, when the man felt the cold rod and wooden rails, he knew he was saved. He was going to get his juice. All he had to do was to wriggle along the rail until he found the train.

Elmer made slow progress. He hadn't died in the trenches in France – he seemed to have a gift for living. Other men with less of an injury were face down in the water. Through the pain Elmer made his way up the hill to the train track. There were other men there, each holding on for dear life. He lay on his side, unable to lie on his stomach because of the protruding piece of lumber that had shot through him. Those around him looked stunned. They couldn't believe that Elmer would be alive, much less mobile.

Harry questioned his own sanity as he headed out for his friend. The boat jerked and rocked as he leapt toward land. He miscalculated the force of the wind as it carried him twenty feet and nearly dumped him into the churning canal. He grabbed the ground and pulled himself to safety. A palm frond came from nowhere, traveling at a hundred miles an hour, and slashed his face. The wind wanted to tear open the fresh wound even more.

Harry saw someone on the ground ahead of him. The body was naked. He bent down and turned the man over. Harry recognized him as one of the locals who lived nearby. His left arm was wrapped around his back in an inhuman contortion. The man was dead.

Harry fought to right himself and move onward into the blackness. He kept his legs far apart as he took baby steps. He often bent forward into a three point stance when the wind gusted. It was hard work and he was making slow progress as he guessed at the direction Stuart would have travelled. Only when he tripped over a railroad tie did he feel confident he could find Stuart. This wasn't the main line. It was a side track.

Harry remembered this track when he helped Ed load the equipment into the boxcar. Perhaps Stuart would follow this, thinking it would steer him to the train station. It was the only lead he had.

Sheldon cracked open the sliding door of the boxcar and peered north eyeing the tracks to the stalks of wood that had once served as the pilings for the train station. The structure had been torn away piece-by-piece. Sheldon looked out every five minutes. The train was now over three hours late. He was running out of options. The road was totally submerged so the thought of using the vehicles from the motor pool was out of the question.

As he squinted into the dark Sheldon saw something in the distance he'd not seen before. He blinked to make sure he wasn't hallucinating. He wiped the rain from his brow and covered it with his hand to be sure. In the distance a red blinking light cut through the blackness. It was dim at first, like a fox's eye winking back from a car headlight. But the red light reappeared again and again.

"It's here!" yelled Sheldon as he turned to the men. "The train — the train is here!"

He jumped out of the boxcar on the sidetrack, stumbled and fell into the rising water which was now ankle deep. He pushed his way forward as fast as he could toward the remains of the station to get to the locomotive. The train stopped about a hundred feet from where the men had found refuge.

Engineer Haycraft stopped where the train station once stood. He wondered if anyone in the area was still alive. Only after the engineer stopped did he realize how dire the circumstances had become. He needed two things: to move the locomotive to the front of the set of cars, and fill the thirsty engine with water.

The large mechanical beast drank more water than normal on its trek to the campsite. It didn't have enough for the return trip. Normally he would refill at the water tower by the station. However, little remained of the station. The water tower had been completely obliterated.

Sheldon stumbled but kept moving toward the train. As he did so, the men followed and fought their way from the sidetrack toward their newly arrived salvation. They were ready to get out of the hell that surrounded them.

The water was rising. Sheldon was only half way to train and the water had risen to his knees. The undercurrent stole some of the men's shoes.

Things were no better over by the quarry where Harry had, hours earlier, loaded equipment into a lone boxcar. Like the station, the storm surge brought an ever rising tide near the quarry. On a normal day he would have easily been able to see the train's arrival — but this night was far from ordinary. He rounded the windward side of the quarry's boxcar and noticed that the door was locked and chained. He turned and headed to the opposite side. He banged on the sliding door. Someone opened from the inside.

Before he even saw the face, he saw the large Masonic ring of Buddy Brickman.

"Harry! – Damn glad to see you! Get in! Get In!" yelled Buddy.

The water was rising rapidly as Harry stretched out his hand and Buddy helped him up. Harry glanced back at the water which swirled around where his legs had been.

"Krebs?"

"Yeah," replied Buddy over the howling wind. "He's in the corner. He don't look too good. Keeps talking about his juice. He's been counting backward from one hundred — not sure what that's about."

"He's sick."

"I'll say. He is shivering and rocking back and forth. You came out in this to look for him?"

"Yeah – sort of. Look – the storm is getting worse by the minute. We all have to get out of here."

"Like hell!" came a voice in the darkness. Harry knew it wasn't Krebs, but he couldn't place the voice.

"How many we got in here?" Harry asked Brickman as he squinted into the darkness.

"Fifteen – give or take."

"We have to go to the canal and get on the barge. You'll all be safe there." Harry had no idea that the train had arrived and was ready to haul them to safety.

"I'm staying put!" came another voice from the blackness.

"I'm telling you, it's not safe here! Head south! Follow the tracks! Find the barge!" Harry pleaded.

The water rose and started creeping along the floorboards of the boxcar.

"What the hell?" Buddy looked down. "Guys we gotta go!"

Buddy opened the door to find the water had risen to the edge of the door of the boxcar. He guessed it had risen four feet in the span of minutes.

Harry listened and could hear the water lapping up against the side of the car. A rogue wave slammed against the boxcar. Harry slid out the opened door and into the water. He rolled on his shoulder and accidentally gulped down a hearty helping of the wretched sea. He tried to stand but there was an undertow which was dragging him under the boxcar. He again lost his footing. The coral and sand beneath his feet were moving in all directions. It was difficult to determine where the ground held firm.

Harry half stood and hurled the seawater he'd swallowed. He tried running toward the boxcar but the current was shifting the ground beneath his feet. The current was pulling him in all directions except toward the boxcar. To get any traction he had to sidestep, placing his body perpendicular to the howling headwinds and shuffling his feet. As he finally made progress, he paused for a second because, through the gale, he thought he heard the sound of men's cries among the mangroves or somewhere deep in the excavated cuts that were filling with water.

A burst of wind lifted the side of the boxcar facing the ocean a foot off the ground. It tilted up and slammed down on the rails.

Harry grabbed the door of the boxcar. He yelled to the men inside. "You gotta get out of there! The wind is too strong. The boxcar is going to tip on its side!"

The men knew Harry was right. Buddy and the others leapt into the water. They formed a line with Buddy Brickman leading. Each man held on to the belt of the man in front. Buddy charged onward feeling the rails beneath his feet.

Buddy looked back and called to Harry.

"Krebs is still in there. He ain't gonna budge. Leave him."

For a moment Harry thought of joining the line of men heading back to the barge. He stopped and looked into the dark opening. Krebs was still in there.

"C'mon Harry!" yelled Buddy.

Harry looked at Buddy then back to the opening.

"Go! Don't wait for me!"

Harry pulled himself up into the boxcar.

Timothy had stuck with Sheldon and now made his way to a passenger car with some of the other men. He was drenched and cold. The car rocked with the wind, but Timothy felt much safer on the train.

Looking out the window Timothy thought the train was already moving. It wasn't. The water rushing onshore gave the appearance that the train was hurtling down the tracks. There were no other landmarks to see so his mind was tricked into thinking that they were already heading north.

Some of the men sat with their legs on the chair. They were soaked, but this was the first chance they had of actually drying out.

"You're the man we've been looking for," said Sheldon to the engineer. "Time to go!"

"We need water!" yelled the engineer.

"That's all we got around here!" replied Sheldon. "We have to get out of the storm. Get us north and we'll figure something out."

The engineer spun the dials to open the steam valves. He pulled the lever to engage the wheels. The train lurched forward and jerked to a stop. Some men were thrown from their seats.

"Damn!" yelled the engineer.

"What's the matter?" asked Sheldon.

"The brake is locked."

"What?" asked Sheldon in disbelief. They were so close to being saved and the train was stuck in its spot — unmoving.

The engineer looked out one side of the locomotive and then the other.

He saw the problem and cried, "Shit!"

"What is it?" cried Sheldon above the wailing wind.

"Boxcar in the back blew over! I have a couple of empty boxcars on the line. The brake line is still coupled to it. If one car is immobile it automatically sets the engine's brake. We gotta decouple the boxcar or we're not going anywhere!"

Sheldon saw the boxcar on its side. The water had risen above the coupling.

The men couldn't hear what was approaching over the cacophony of the night. Neither could they see it through the sheets of pouring rain. But the wave was like a tall menacing figure lurking just out of sight. Everyone felt the sensation of an intangible and evil presence. Every instinct told them it was there. The prickle along the back of their neck, the involuntary flexing of their muscles, the adrenaline flow and the quickening of the heart told them something horrendous was bearing down.

Timothy looked out the window and reacted just in time. He ducked away from the glass as the thirty foot wave smashed through the car. Large timbers were pinned to the outside while coconuts and other smaller debris made its way into the cab. The whole car rocked to one side. It felt like it would tip over.

Timothy heard what sounded like inhuman screams as the water rushed through. The car righted as Timothy realized the screaming noise was the ripping of metal as the smoking car tipped on its side. The coupling tore loose and the large metal frame collapsed with the men inside under the wall of water. The wave didn't retreat back to the sea. It continued to fill the car. Timothy was completely submerged as he shifted and stood on the bench looking for his next breath.

Standing on his toes, Timothy's head broke the surface. A small bronze handrail ran along the top of the car. He grabbed it and pulled himself up to breathe in the pocket of air that formed above the window line. Others had done the same.

Timothy thought, "If we stay here, we're all going to die."

Sheldon was about to go and attempt to uncouple the boxcar when the wave hit. He held on for dear life as the wall of water rose into the cab and doused the firebox — the lifeblood of the locomotive. Sheldon realized that all of the men he tried to save were now at the mercy of the elements. They were going nowhere.

No one was more surprised than Elmer that he was still alive. He spied the approaching wave threatening to pull him to his death. The white chaos of the crashing aftermath rolled over him.

Completely submerged, he clung to the track. The force of the wave was so strong that the track itself rose up off the ground. Elmer held his breath and swayed and swung with violent pitching as the track broke from its ties and freely floated through the water. The wood penetrating his body made him more buoyant than the others as he floated up with the oncoming wave.

Just as he was about to give in and exhale his last breath, he broke the surface. He hyperventilated before another wave sent him under again. This one was much stronger than the first and he nearly let go. His hands had cramped into a closed position like an eagle holding a field mouse in its talons.

"Krebs?" shouted Harry in the darkness.

There was no answer.

"Stuart – this isn't the train. This is a boxcar but it isn't connected to the train. We *have* to go Stuart."

"Two hours... Two hours..." came a weak voice in the distance.

"Stuart! Keep talking..." Harry followed his way to the far corner of the boxcar. Stuart was sitting by two rolls of cabling. The man was pale and looked like death.

"Stuart – we have to leave we have to get the train."

"Is the train here?"

"Yes, Stuart." Harry had no idea if the train had arrived. He hoped it had. However, he'd be taking Stuart in the opposite direction.

"Thank you, Harry," said Krebs. Stuart looked up at Harry. His eyes were mournful, but by connecting his gaze, Stuart seemed to return to reality. "Harry, thank you. You are a good man. You came for me."

Harry didn't say anything at first. He looked at Krebs and said, "Stuart, I'd never leave my friends — my comrades. I've come to get you home safely."

Stuart continued to rock. "I'm sick, Harry. Real sick."

Harry was about to reply but stopped.

For a brief second the wind calmed and Harry heard something that he'd never heard before in his life. It was something that was more felt than heard. A great rumbling as if Satan was rising from the depths. The sound reverberated through the cab. It was frightening and indefinable. Whatever it was, Harry knew it was getting closer.

"Let's go Stuart!" Harry grabbed the man and jerked him up to his feet. "Let's get the hell outta here!"

The tidal force that came made all the previous rising water look impish. The monster wall of water was large enough to entirely wipe lower Matecumbe from the map. For a moment in time, the island simply ceased to exist. Sting rays, sharks, groupers, and starfish were cast from the Atlantic to the Gulf in a single upheaval brought on by the immense fury of this rare meteorological anomaly.

The wall of water slammed into the seventy-five ton boxcar and tipped it on its side. Gravity, the water and all the forces of the storm pushed the boxcar toward the worksite.

The strength pushed it over the embankment. The place where they'd excavated the coral for the bridge was now a thirty foot deep pool. The boxcar plunged into the massive pool.

Harry flew through the air and landed on the on his back. The only exit was now lying face down on the coral floor. The other exit was locked and chained from the outside. A large piece of machinery slammed against his left foot, smashing the bones and rendering it useless. It pinned him down as the water rose around him. He thought he heard a man's cry but it was muffled by the torrent of incoming water.

Harry had only one quick breath before being consumed by the inrushing water. Ignoring the sharp pain, Harry pulled his leg free and floated up, bumping his head against the opposite side of the box car. Harry thought he heard someone cry, 'help' but it was muffled as the water rose. There was no hope of finding the exit.

He swam and became tangled in wire he'd loaded onto the boxcar earlier.

"Harry? Harry, help me." The voice was weak.
"Stuart?"
"Harry?"

He found Stuart. He was breathing the last few air pockets that were leaking out of the boxcar. There was no more air. Stuart's last cry for Harry was the last word he would ever hear.

This was it. In the few moments remaining before his death, Harry thought of the recurring dream he'd had. All along he thought it was his death in the submarine. He only knew of the cables

329

and debris from his experience in the sub. His dream was a premonition not of his loss, anxiety and fear while serving in the war. It was a premonition of this moment.

Harry had saved as many lives as he could. He left the security of Sheeran's barge. This was his choice. As the water filled the last few breathable spaces, Harry thought of Elmer, Jimmy, Buddy, Timothy and the others. He hoped hid friends survived this ordeal. He'd never really prayed before. Perhaps this was it... a last prayer.

He felt his chest grow tight.

He inhaled.

The wave was massive. Buddy was tumbled by the curl which crashed on him and the men. They were all separated.He closed his eyes and thrashed his arms not knowing up from down. Something knocked into him. He turned to grab it hoping it was something that would float. It was the edge of the boxcar he'd just exited.

Had he let go he would have been carried out to sea. He rode the moving boxcar as it tipped into the abyss of the worksite. He felt the outer rail that ran along the boxcar as felt his way to the door. He knew Harry and Stuart were inside. Buddy found the latch to the boxcar door and tried to pull it open. Something rattled. He felt and found the chain that wrapped around the handle. He pulled on the chain but it didn't budge. He swam around and put his feet on either side of the boxcar handle and pulled with all his might.

Buddy's lungs were starting to burn as he exerted himself underwater. For the moment the current had abated which gave him greater freedom of movement. He kicked at the handle while holding the chain. The handle wouldn't open. He was beginning to go black as his oxygen starved body gave into the need for a breath.

"I'll let go, get a breath and swim back," he thought to himself. "Maybe I can find a crowbar or something."

He let go and drifted upward. The trip to the surface was longer than he expected. He thought he was only a few feet from the top but the surge had rolled in and made his trip to the surface an interminable task. He broke through and exhaled as a new wave broke over his head. Thinking he was nearing blackout he rolled on his back and arched up. The first breath was salty. Coming to his senses after nearly passing out, Buddy tried to regain his bearings. His friends were on the bottom, and he wanted to find something he could use to free them. But as he floated, he couldn't see land.

Even in the darkness Buddy could feel the tide returning, pulling him out to sea. His foot caught on a metal protrusion, but the current soon set him free. He was swiftly moving away from the worksite and the boxcar that had become the watery grave for his two friends.

The surge consumed the island. Only a few trees protruded from the swirling landscape. He tried to swim against the tide. Doing so kept him in place but rapidly wore him out. Buddy struggled to paddle toward a palm tree whose fronds were sheared away. He miscalculated the speed of the receding water and slammed his chest into the exposed trunk. It knocked the wind out of him. He almost forgot to grab hold as the flow pulled him away. He kicked and barely made his way back to the tree, clinging to it as the water slowly abated.

He had no time to grieve for his friends. He wrapped his arms and legs around the tree and hung on fighting the accelerating current. At one point he felt something wrap around him. Debris was constantly bumping and moving on.

He looked down and saw the upper-portion of a human torso facedown in the water. It was caught in an eddy and swirled around him. He tried kicking it away, but it kept returning, reminding him that death was all around. The corpse taunted him, reminding him that it only took one mistake, one slip, and he would join the bobbing inanimate flesh of so many veterans caught in this macabre meteorological anomaly.

Timothy stood on his toes breathing the remaining bubble of air as the next wave pushed the passenger car off the rail and onto its side. He and the other submerged vets were flung around, spinning wildly like broken toy dolls. They rolled over each other trying to find a way out.

Timothy swam to the rows of broken windows. He was smaller than many of the others trying to get escape. As he wriggled his way through the one of the broken panes, he cut his shoulder, chest, and hips on the shards around the window's frame. His clothes were shredded in the process. Finding his way to the surface he stood on top of the toppled passenger car. He gasped as he rose up on the boxcar in water that was waist deep.

A few others found some lifesaving openings. They and broke the surface, hurling up the ocean that tried to consume them.

He saw the locomotive intact and upright. The car ahead of his hadn't toppled but stood at an odd angle.

Timothy launched himself toward the upright car and grabbed the awning that stuck out above the doorway. He put his foot the coupling between the cars. He wanted to pull himself to the dry rooftop of the next car but couldn't. Between the cars the water was moving rapidly out to sea. It took all his strength to hang on. If he shifted his body position he'd lose his tenuous hold on the train and be swept out to sea.

He held his awkward position, his body cramping in the cold water. Every fiber tensed shooting relentless pain. His calves and back spasmed. His hands screamed for release.

Even with his body rebelling and the receding tide coaxing him toward the black watery abyss he thought of Aella. He wondered what she was doing. He recounted the details of their first meeting, their first kiss, and the first time they made love. It was the details of how she smelled, of her gentle strands of hair that brushed against his neck, of the laughter and how she cocked her head back when she did so that kept him strong.

Some ethereal siphon was pulling the water back to sea with ever increasing force. The ocean was very thirsty.

Even more now than before the current was trying to tear him away from the train. Timothy held firm as lumber, mangroves, and metal parts hit the railing of the train, bounced off, hit him and then got caught up in the ironwork of the upright passenger car.

Hemingway had been napping on and off throughout the evening. He'd checked the barometer waiting for the hurricane to hit. Showers doused the area, but they were the garden variety storm that lasted a few minutes before the celestial drain was turned off. The writer had been expecting a fierce blow to arrive, but the latest reading showed that the barometer was rising.

To be safe, he grabbed his light coat and headed out toward the dock. It was a holiday weekend, so the town was busy this time of night. The carousers were in full force. He instinctively ducked as he heard the sound of someone firing off a pistol — though it could have easily been a firework. Winding his way to the naval yard, he found his boat - *Pilar* - safe and sound. He boarded her and climbed to the sighting post at the top of the craft and looked out on the little city. It was lit up and a myriad of festive music blended together in a cacophony of brass and piano.

He thought about joining the crowd but decided to make it a quiet night. He wanted to be fresh in the morning. If the storm passed close enough, the fish would be running. It would be a choppy but fruitful day on the water tomorrow and he wanted to be ready.

He ambled back to his home for a good night's sleep.

Buddy could see the waters receding. From his perch high in the palm tree he could see the glint of railroad track above water. Part of the nearby road had also emerged. He slid down the tree he'd been hugging. His entire body ached as his feet found solid ground. He waded through the knee deep water until he found the high ground and planted his feet on terra-firma.

He tried to get his bearings but, other than the rail and the road which spanned the entire island, nothing looked familiar. He made his way to the road. He had been turned around so many times, he didn't even know if he was moving north or south. He was looking for something — a landmark of some kind that would give him an indication where he was. He wanted to find the cranes that once towered over the landscape as they moved the large block from the quarry to the trucks. He wanted to find the camp where he'd lost his dear friend Jimmy.

The wind was easing and he felt he could actually take a breath without labor. He could walk without being pelted by debris. During the course of the evening, he'd lost his shoes. The small bits of coral dug into the bottoms of his feet so he had to pick his way carefully.

"Is it over?" Buddy thought to himself. The winds were dying down and the treacherous waves had disappeared.

As Buddy walked along the road he stopped because the entire visage changed. As if someone hit a light switch, the entire island began to glow. Bathed in silver, each droplet captured the radiance of the full moon as it broke through the clouds. A million dripping pearls lit up, mirroring the moon's reflective brilliance. The winds which had ripped away buildings weren't strong enough to float a dandelion seed. A quiet descended on this space as if someone covered it with a warm quilt.

Buddy looked up. Overhead and to the west, Buddy saw something few humans have ever witnessed. Balls of lightning floated through the sky. Had it been one ball, it would have been an incredible anomaly. Shining brilliantly overhead, no fewer than eight large electric spheres danced together. Some winked out and others appeared. Those looking up on this little mauled island couldn't help but consider the supernatural forces that descended on this place. The ethereal balls glowed white, green and red as they played in the sky. One by one, they dissipated before relinquishing the night to the simplicity of moon and stars.

Buddy stood motionless as the last orb winked away. He would never understand anything about this night. Nothing made sense.

He'd mocked those who'd been through a hurricane. At one point, he admitted that he wanted to see one. He began to weep. So much had happened that he couldn't fathom how his life had changed. Only now was he beginning to contemplate the incredible loss he'd witnessed. Yet his tears were not only for the dead, his tears were for the living who survived this horror. His tears were for the loved ones who might never find the bodies of those washed out to sea. His tears were for the children with drowned parents. His tears were for those who would not be able to bury a body and lay to rest the confidence of death.

The big man wept for the pain of the lost lives of vets, lives not lost in death, but heroes who'd been forgotten by a government and generation. He wondered if this night would be remembered.

Would it be memorialized with vigils and moments of silence?

He forced himself to suppress these thoughts. He needed to find something or someone that would ground him in a world that he recognized. He solemnly walked down the road to the future.

Timothy stepped off the train. The first and obvious change was the cessation of the violent meteorological onslaught. The next was the emergence of the brilliant moon. What unnerved Timothy was the incredible silence. As the vets looked around, trying to fathom the change, the loudest thing Timothy heard were the droplets hitting the ground. Timothy noticed that it was hard to breathe. It felt like the hurricane had taken the very air around him.

Sheldon stepped down from the locomotive. He was stunned by the course of events. His men died under his watch. The man who stepped off the train was far different from the man from this morning. He'd always been a leader. He was not out to make friends. He knew what he had to do and he put himself to the task without reserve. But this — the death — the loss — the complete and utter destruction — was not his fault. It was *not* his fault. The words rolled in his head and tormented him to the core. Others would come down hard on him. He would easily be the one upon whom everyone else would lay the blame. The once demanding and confident leader of men was now broken.

Timothy approached Sheldon, "Is it over? Is this it? We made it, right?"

Sheldon drew his hand across his face as if wiping off pain and insecurity that had grown inside him. He had to adorn the persona of the man he once was — at least for a few days.

"No - it isn't over."

Timothy was stunned. The calm seemed to betray the words Sheldon spoke.

336

"This is the eye of the hurricane. We took a direct hit. We have to move fast. Whatever we can do to secure shelter for the next part...."

Sheldon stopped as more men emerged and drew close to him looking for leadership. Sheldon wondered how many more of those men gazing at him with their fear-filled eyes would make it through the night. He raised his voice to address the crowd.

He cleared his throat and mustered what little courage he had left.

"We've come this far. No one could have expected a storm as strong as this. No one..."

Sheldon fought to keep his strength for what he had to say next.

"But there is more to come. I hate to bear bad news, but what is coming is far worse than what we've just experienced."

The men looked on with a combination of disbelief and abject horror.

"The winds are going to shift. When you feel them, we need to find cover. Trust me. The rest of the night will be worse — far worse."

It was a death sentence, but Ray Sheldon knew that he spoke the truth.

Sam Cutler was pacing. He'd finally gotten in touch with Fred Ghent. He'd tried to contact the camp. He tried to call the weather bureau in Key West. The lines south of Largo were down.

Ghent figured the train arrived and all was going according to plan. When he heard from Cutler, Ghent decided he should head to the station and meet Cutler there. Something wasn't right.

Ghent assumed that the train would be waiting with the men when he arrived. He pulled into the large parking lot and headed to the station to find Cutler and a few reporters waiting for the train's arrival. It wasn't there.

Ghent swallowed hard. Something had gone terribly wrong.

"Ghent!" said Cutler, relieved that he wasn't worrying alone. "They're not here. You think the train had problems?"

"I don't know." Ghent stared down the line at the rails that converged into the darkness. "Something's not right."

Cutler's face looked grim. "I told you. I told Sheldon. I knew this would be bad. I had a gut feeling. I talked to some of the reporters and they said the storm was stronger than anyone first imagined."

"How could they know?" Ghent replied.

"There were some vessels out to sea that skated the storm. The captains radioed that the swells were unlike anything they'd ever seen."

"That hardly seems like proof about the intensity...."

Cutler interrupted, "There's another ship — the Dixie — or something like that — that got caught in the storm. They say no one has heard from them. They think it foundered in the hurricane."

Ghent went silent. "What if Cutler was right?" he thought.

"How bad do you think it got down there?" Ghent asked.

Cutler's nervousness permeated his response. "Look - Ed Sheeran told me that it would be bad. The locals knew that it was bad. We should've listened to the people with experience. We waited too long. The men have their flimsy shacks. Maybe they could've stayed in the mess hall. I dunno. But the train isn't here. Maybe the winds kicked trees on the track. I've been wracking my brain trying to figure out why the men aren't here. I hope to God they're all right."

Cutler was forecasting a worst case scenario. Little did he know that his imagination was a far cry from the reality the men experienced. He had no idea how bad things had become.

As the two men spoke their words, someone seated behind them in the darkness overheard their

338

conversation. The young woman silently wept as she waited for the man she loved. Aella had dressed herself to meet Timothy when he arrived. Her flowered dress shown in stark contrast to the gloom of the night.

She wondered to whom she should pray? She'd never really been indoctrinated to any one religion. Most of the locals who attended church went to the Methodist chapel. For them, there was a confusing trinity/one God thing that to her made little sense.

She preferred the Gods of her ancestors that Alexander and Nikolas spoke of as they watched the sky. This made much more sense. Each deity was in charge and responsible for their area. The Greek Gods were a mismatched team that seemed more "real" than the confusing Christian God or Gods (she never could figure that out). So she prayed for whatever God was in charge of the wind and water to spare Timothy and the men. She prayed that those who stayed behind emerge safe from whatever was transpiring.

She wanted to be with Timothy now. But, even in her concern and worry, she knew that tomorrow she'd reunite with Timothy. No matter the circumstances, she would find him.

Sheldon didn't have much time.

"Men – we have been through hell. But it ain't over. This eye will pass on and the storm will return with a vengeance. I want you to divide into two teams. We need to look in the area for survivors."

Sheldon pointed at the train. "The car behind the locomotive is still upright. This is where we'll meet back. We can find shelter here and with the locomotive. It's all we've got. Find all the men you can, but if you feel a puff of wind, don't wait. Get back here. Once it starts, you won't have much time."

The men understood. They'd seen the power and now respected it. They formed the two groups. One group combed through the other cars which had blown off the track. The others headed toward the camp not knowing its state. Sheldon kept that little secret to himself.

Timothy walked with the men staring at the track heading south. It looked like a Salvador Dali painting as it rose off the ground, swirling and melting back to the ground. The passenger cars lay at odd angles, defying gravity, poking out of the very ground that tried to consume them. Timothy was the first to spot the man leaning against the pretzeled rails.

"Elmer?" said Timothy, not sure if the man slumped over was dead or alive. "Elmer is that you?"

The man moved. Only then did he see the piece of wood shot through the man.

"Oh God – Elmer!" He rushed to the man. Elmer's breathing was labored. He was exhausted from holding the rail while the tide swept over him. Timothy ran and put his hands under Elmer's armpits to help him to his feet. Seeing the protrusion he hesitated and stopped.

"Elmer – should I – should I take it out."

Elmer took a breath. "I'm not sure."

Timothy grabbed the piece that extended out his back. He put both hands on the wood.

"Aaahh!" yelled Elmer. "Wait!"

Timothy let go and took a quick step back.

"Get me to the hospital."

"Sheldon!" Timothy waved. Sheldon saw Timothy and rushed over.

"Jesus Christ!" Sheldon stared at Elmer. He didn't know what to do for the man. "Can we get a stretcher or something?"

Sheldon lowered his voice and said to Timothy, "He's a dead man."

"Elmer is my friend. We've got to give him a fighting chance."

"Okay," replied Sheldon. "You grab his arms and we'll take him over by the truck over there."

Sheldon pointed to a truck which had turned on its side.

"I'm not sure we should move him."

"This storm isn't done with us yet. The truck is facing east-west. When the storm hits, the winds will be coming from the South. This will give him a fighting chance."

Ray and Timothy carefully moved Elmer to the overturned truck. With each tug to maneuver the injured man Elmer wailed.

The other men found the camp shattered and splintered. The men lifted and picked through the debris looking for any sign of life. There was none.

So soon after this violent ordeal it seemed a cruel task to make the men search among the dead for the living. Some of the men weren't looking at all. They moved around the camp with far-away stares, not believing the extent to which their world was destroyed. Some called out the names of their friends in the hope that they'd get a reply.

Buddy found the one untouched and unscathed human structure that the hurricane hadn't been able to annihilate. Walking along the road he paused and looked at the large unfinished bridge. The bridge glistened bright white as the moon reflected the monument to the veteran's hard labor. The two sides weren't touching, but seemed closer to each other than ever before. The winds had sandblasted the bridge to a polished finish. The rain washed it to a pristine white. What man had started, nature had perfected. Like the pyramids or the Taj Mahal, the bridge took on a holy aura.

Buddy wondered about the flooding that accompanied the hurricane. Was the flooding a result of this massive structure? Would fewer lives have been lost had this been built differently? He understood little about the hurricane. He only felt its effects and grieved at the loss of life.

In the months ahead, when the construction was completed by someone other than the vets, there would be people who would drive along the bridge and not give a second thought to the human cost. They would see the palm trees and pastel skies. They would race to get to the shore or hurry to the boat that was waiting for them. There would be impatient children badgering their parents to stop. And they would ascend the bridge without a thought about the laborers who toiled to erect this grand structure.

He stood at the edge of the road which led to the bridge. He was about to turn and try to find Ed Sheeran and the barge when he stopped.

The absolute quiet of the evening was broken by a rustling noise. Yet, the air was absolutely still. The wind wouldn't be able to snuff a cardboard match. But the sound was unmistakable. He remembered this sound in Brooklyn as a kid when October winds blew the multicolored maple and oak leaves onto the road.

The palm fronds which littered the road lay motionless amidst the growing sound. Buddy didn't understand. Then, a puff of wind blew his hair. It was like a woman standing next to him had blown in his ear. It was small and directed. Perhaps this is where the sound originated. Perhaps the storm was about to resume its onslaught.

The sound grew. It no longer sounded like leaves. It sounded more like a high pitched machine. He couldn't quite place it. The rolling rhythmic pulsing of the sound was like a factory with its pneumatics snorting high pitched steam as conveyers moved their products down the line. He wondered if it was a boat or barge with an odd engine. Perhaps it was a steamboat with its big wheel rolling along the Atlantic. He squinted to see if there was a boat silhouetted against the moonlit sky.

There was nothing there.

The wind began to blow again. Not with the ferocity of hundred-mile an hour winds, but with the gentle refreshing breeze often found here in the keys after the sun went down. He looked up and saw the clouds moving over the stars as one-by-one they winked behind the swiftly moving bands. They were moving faster than the surface winds would indicate.

Only then did he realize that this was but an intermission as the eye of the storm passed through. The sound which was out to sea was still a mystery, but Buddy felt something grow in the pit of his stomach.

The sound was coming from the sea, and it was no longer high pitched. It was the sound of a thousand people screaming. It was the sound of the horsemen of the apocalypse. Buddy couldn't run. He knew it was already too late.

The return of the ferocity of the hurricane brought with it a single secret weapon. Buddy watched as the massive tidal wave, white and menacing, rose up against the blackness of the sky. The clouds hadn't consumed the moon, so the eighty foot wall of water was in the spotlight as it smashed against the unfinished bridge. The water, with nowhere to go, rose up over the structure and changed direction. It was heading straight for Buddy.

In the last moments of his life, Buddy saw the bridge collapse against the titanic forces. The island would again be consumed by the sea. But this time it was not in a gentle dome of a rising tide — it would come in a single wave of torrential attack.

Ed Sheeran had stepped outside from the barge. He wanted a breath of fresh air. He didn't expect to see people. He assumed the train had picked up the vets and left. Yet as he looked out, he noticed a few men. He called out to them, but the strange air seemed to stifle any attempt at communicating over any distance.

He then heard the unique sound of a mega-wave. He'd heard it once before. He knew what was coming.

343

"Hey! Hey!" he yelled. "Quick! Come here! Save Yourself!"

The electric stillness ate his words. The men in the distance seemed to be looking for something. There were others who'd come out to see why Ed was yelling.

"Get back inside! Get inside – Now!"

Ed gave up on the men meandering around the island. He had to save those few who sought refuge on the barge. He ran inside.

"Everyone – Brace yourself!"

The men who were picking their way through the debris at the campsite were at one of the lowest points along the island. Beneath the debris, the small spit of land was still inundated by the salt water. Ray Sheldon stood at the edge of the road leading down into the camp. He had no idea how many bodies lay beneath the rubble.

Still very conscious of the momentary pause in the hurricane, he was not going to let any more men die on his watch. As soon as he felt the wind pick up, he'd get the men to higher ground and back on the stable parts of the train. His senses were on high alert. He watched and listened and felt for the menacing storm that tried to woo them into a false sense of security.

There were survivors. Some were badly injured; others were being tended for deep, large splinters from flying debris. A small group of men located the truck that had the medical supplies. The truck had been flooded so some of the supplies were rendered useless, but others were worth their weight in gold.

Sheldon didn't so much hear as feel something change. He couldn't put his finger on it. The feeling came up through his feet. Perhaps there was some subterranean movement as millions of tons of water shifted rapidly. Perhaps it was the hush he heard in his ear. None of it added up, but he heeded the feeling. Adrenaline shot through his body.

"Find Cover!" he yelled, still not knowing why. "Find Cover! Quick!"

He ran down the road to the camp.

"It's coming! It's coming!"

Timothy looked up at the man who seemed possessed by some deranged spirit. There was nothing to indicate the kind of violence they'd experienced would suddenly return.

Sheldon waved his hands. As he did so he looked for the few places where the men might take cover. "The fence! Hide behind the fence — and hold on!" He pointed to some vets who looked at him questioningly as the madman rushed by.

"Now!" Sheldon implored. It was a command they heeded reluctantly.

To the rest of the men he shouted at the top of his lungs "The water car! The water car! Get to the water car! – NOW!"

The vets had never seen Sheldon in this state. His wide eyes and flailing hands were unlike the cocky, self-assured man they'd come to know. But his change scared them into immediate compliance. They ran, not knowing why, to the water car which was still upright on the side track that led to the camp. It was one of the only things left intact. Ed Sheeran decided earlier that day to keep the water car filled and not to unload it to the holding tanks which lay in ruins. The filled tanker was one of the heaviest objects around and therefore one of the most stable objects in the area. The men tripped as they stumbled to get to the tank. Bloody knees and bruised elbows would not hold back the men as they converged on the single point.

Sheldon stopped short of the water car to glance out at the storm. The hydra of clouds were advancing quickly, snaking their way back now that the men were in a vulnerable position. He saw something which he could not at first believe. The distant horizon lifted up and arced higher and higher.

Now he knew the source of his terror. Somehow he had a premonition of what was coming.

"Hold on for your lives!" He yelled as he dove for the water tank's rail that surrounded all sides of the metal container.

The tidal wave slammed onto the island, consuming it in one gulp. The debris from the mess hall was lifted up and used as underwater torpedoes. One vet holding onto the water car had his back broken by a large truss rod. Yet, he still held on. Others were lifted up, having wrapped their arm around the pipe. Their arms were snapped and broken, yet they, too, still held on.

Timothy saw the wall of water explode and accelerate as it hit the small rise. He wrapped himself around Elmer and grabbed the muffler pipe on the overturned truck. The truck moved with the force of the surge and twisted along the edge of the road. It floated up, and the two men were carried with the two ton vehicle. The truck acted as a shield against the splintered timber spears that mingled with the churning water. The truck bumped down on the ground as the wave moved on to try and claim other lives.

With the tidal wave, the next assault of the whirling dervish winds returned stronger than before. With it came the rains, the thunder and the final fury of the hurricane. The storm held back the strongest weapons until now as it assailed the remaining vets. The few survivors banded together like they'd done in the trenches as the bombs were hurled, and the guns were fired. The men had been through hell once and were damned to do it again. Their lives had been spent developing the tenacity and spirit to fight against all odds. They were older men now and were called to draw upon the stuff they learned from their youth. They were always soldiers. Once again they mustered their courage in the face of overwhelming circumstances.

The heartless beast that was this unnamed Labor Day storm didn't care about the men. It was a natural force of destruction that could have landed anywhere. Because it had blossomed so quickly, it was still small in size. And, as it arrived with its arsenal of malevolence, it left quickly.

The winds eventually abated. The waters returned to the sea. The men who were left behind could now lick their wounds and begin to heal.

They used to tell me I was building a dream
With peace and glory ahead
-    *Brother Can You Spare A Dime - Bing Crosby*

Timothy sat motionless as the clouds, thick and dark gray swam slowly across the predawn sky. As the sun started to edge toward the horizon, those dark masses started coming alive. Dark purple clouds with streaks of fiery red lined their edges bringing them to life as like Elijah speaking to the dry bones.

Sitting motionless, Timothy knew he wouldn't have much time for reflecting on the grandeur of the big sky for long. He'd actually slept leaning up against the truck. Once the storm tracked out into the Gulf and the winds died, Timothy slumped against Elmer. Both of the men fell into that deep dreamless sleep of utter exhaustion. It was a short rest but it allowed his brain to compartmentalize "what had happened" with "what will come." He blinked and rubbed the salt out of his eyes. His whole body throbbed in pain, but Timothy didn't object. It was better than the alternative.

The sky lightened to that of dark pastels with the sun yet to peek across the horizon. A whisper of a breeze blew like a soft kiss across Timothy's cheek. Gold edging ran across the clouds overhead. The combination of colors and metallic sheen made the sky look like a royal promenade. Chariots and dragons passed overhead heralding the coming of the glorious sun.

Tears welled up inside Timothy. He swallowed them down as Elmer started coming around. Elmer's face was chalky and his eyes were sunken. It seemed impossible that a man with a two-by-four stuck clean though his body would have survived a minute much less withstood the wrath of the entire storm.

Elmer coughed and winced.

"Hey there, pal," said Timothy. "Help is coming. We'll get a doctor. They'll fix you right up. I promise."

Elmer inhaled. As he did so, Timothy couldn't help but hear the gurgling noise that came from deep inside. "Tim..."

Elmer turned his head and smiled. "There ain't no doctor that is going to come and patch me. You know that."

He took another labored breath. "Don't make promises you can't keep."

Timothy didn't know what to do. He didn't want to lose his friend. "Look – as soon..."

Elmer interrupted. "Tim..."

Timothy stopped talking.

"You know what you can do for me?"

"What? Anything – you name it."

"Go and find me a beer. That's all I want. Find me a beer."

Elmer smiled. He slowly raised his hand and patted Timothy on the shoulder. With little more volume than a whisper, Elmer said, "go... go..."

Timothy stood up. "I don't want to leave you." Timothy knew why he was being sent on a fool's errand. "I'll just stay here. When the rescue comes..."

Elmer shooed him with his hand.

Sadly, Timothy complied.

"I'll be right back."

Elmer responded, "I know, I know..."

Timothy walked toward the nonexistent canteen. There was no beer for Elmer. He walked away and didn't look back.

Elmer looked at the sunrise. He thought of his home in Baltimore. He wondered if the sun looked the same there.

His face a blank stare, Sheldon walked along the edge of the campsite taking in all that surrounded him. At night he'd could only see the broad paint strokes of devastation. Now that the sun was rising

349

he could see details that eluded him earlier. Along the edge of the mangroves torsos, arms, and legs lay strewn as if tossed my some malicious child. Those bodies that were intact were contorted as if posed by the devil himself. The survivors witnessing this visage found the edge of sanity not far away.

Under his breath Sheldon intoned, "It's not my fault.... It's not my fault." Sheldon walked on, in a state of shock. He didn't try and gather the men. He didn't try to take a roll call.

He crossed the twisted railroad which was supposed to be the rails toward the men's salvation. He made his way across the road he helped to build. Sand had gathered on the road and all but obfuscated its presence. It was as if the island was trying to reclaim itself — ridding itself of any man-made evidence.

He looked down the road and cried. The bridge which was the crowning glory of the vet's achievement had been ripped away. The road inclined but a little before it ended against the purple and blue sky. There were no boulders or remains of the vast amount of work along the island's edge. The bridge had been entirely consumed. He turned away, never wanting to look in that direction ever again.

As Ray Sheldon turned away he spotted people emerging from the barge.

"Sheldon!" yelled Sheeran.

Sheldon walked on.

"Hey! Sheldon!" Ed yelled again.

The old man hopped from the vessel and started toward Sheldon.

The barge had made it through the hurricane with little damage. The fact that Sheeran had lashed the barge to multiple locations, both natural and man-made, was the difference. He'd tied some of the lines tight and others loose. Those that gave way weren't the only source of anchor.

As a result of his actions Ed had saved many lives. But there was no sense of pride, no sense of accomplishment, for his job well done. Ed struggled because, had he been more emphatic and had he demanded an earlier exodus from this place, more vets would have survived.

Sheldon stopped. He looked slowly toward the man who was coming in his direction. Sheldon's brain wasn't functioning properly. It took him a while to recognize Ed Sheeran.

Ed looked at the dazed Sheldon.

"Ray, you okay?"

"It's not my fault."

"Hey – Ray... Ray... Are you okay?" asked Ed again, grabbing Ray Sheldon by the shoulders, so he could look him in the eye

Ray finally lifted his gaze and saw the man. This was the man who warned him all along about the devastating storm that was going to hit the island. This was the man who saved the lives of those on board the barge.

It was Ed who decided to keep the water in the tanker car on the sidetrack by the campsite. Had he not done so, the engineer would have taken the car once it was empty. There would have been nothing for Ray Sheldon to hold onto when the tidal wave struck. Ray was alive because of Ed Sheeran.

Sheldon was slowly surfacing to reality — pulled from his guilt induced haze.

Ed spoke slowly, "It's *all* our fault! We didn't do enough and now the dead are *dead!* This is a reality which cannot be changed. We can sulk and stew and spin around in circles, but it all leads us back to the plain and simple fact that they are dead."

Ed sighed, closed his eyes and tried to calm his nerves. "We can destroy ourselves thinking about the past, but, right now, we have men out there who are *alive*."

He pointed in the direction of the now erased campsite.

"They're hungry, thirsty and naked. Ray – I need you to focus on *them*. They're what's important right now. Help is on its way, but our greatest danger is no longer the storm. It's the *heat*. These men have open wounds. If we don't attend to them, they'll fester. We gotta get help, and we gotta get it going fast."

Something roused in Sheldon. Sheeran could've laid blame, but instead he planted seeds of compassion deep in Sheldon's soul.

"The water tank... it's still there. It's still intact," said Sheldon mechanically.

"Good – that's a start," replied Ed.

"I'll gather a team to start looking for viable containers for the water. I've got some medical supplies in the barge. I'll help with water distribution."

"I'll get some men and head to the office," said Sheldon. "Maybe the phone lines are back up. That'll be the first place anyone will go – Hotel Matecumbe."

By the time Sheldon arrived at Hotel Matecumbe, he was wet with sweat. This day was, like so many others, hot and humid. He walked past the littered bodies. Along the northern end of this section of the island there were no survivors.

Sheldon wasn't surprised when he saw that the second floor of the hotel collapsed and was wilting over the first floor like poorly stacked pancakes.

He pushed hard to open the front door because the frame was now bowed from the redistributed weight. The door scraped against the floor and only opened wide enough to let him in. The windows, like all others on the island, had been shattered. Tears of water dripped around the window frames. The wind was so strong that the rain had found its way in along the seams of the frame the structure itself leaving wet lines along the inner walls.

Papers were strewn from the wind and small pools of water were scattered along the floor. As he scanned the room his eyes first stopped on the map. The meandering thumbtacks were still in place ultimately pointing the way to this havoc.

A slight movement caught Ray's eye and he saw a family crouched in the corner. They were huddled and wide-eyed. The locals had lost their own house and had run to the hotel to find refuge.

"Hey, are you guys okay?" Sheldon said in a soft voice.

The father, mother and two little girls were nestled together. The little ones were sleeping. As the man tried to separate himself from the group, one little girl felt him stir and grabbed at his shirt to keep him close.

"We made it okay."

Sheldon knew of the hell that he'd been through last night. He could only imagine how the horror would affect the mind of a child. The girls' hair was disheveled and their faces were dirty, but they looked otherwise unharmed.

The family abandoned their home when it floated off its foundation. They ran to the car to seek escape. The four fled to the car which wouldn't start. When the flooding began, they abandoned the vehicle for the hotel. They were there when the second floor collapsed.

These four were the lucky ones. Sheldon wondered how many parents would have to bury their children. Worse, the parents would only be able to bury their child's memory having lost them to the sea. This storm did not discriminate.

Sheldon checked the phones. They were dead. So, rather than disturb the two little sleeping angels, he backed out of the hotel. He'd walk north as far as he could to get help.

Ghent and Cutler arrived at Snake Creek hoping to head south. The bridge was out. The small creek was now swollen to the size of a river. It churned brown and white. The waters from the island curled and exited along the north side through this channel now turned torrent.

The word spread north about the hurricane. Some of those on the other side of the creek yelled the news across the chasm. Two men were trying to throw a rope to the other side.

Cutler approached the man tossing the rope.

"What are you doing?"

"There's men on the other side who need medical attention. I'm trying to get a line to the other side. Tony's gonna get his canoe."

It made sense to Cutler. The current was too strong to simply paddle from one side to the other. They needed the rope to guide them across.

Ghent yelled to those on the other side. He was worried that a few of the vets might be hurt. He needed to know how much medical supplies he should order.

"How many injured?!"

The man on the other side was a local. He didn't live on upper Matecumbe. He was actually from Key Largo but had been on Islamorada securing his lumber yard when he got caught in the storm. His place was far north of the center of the storm. But he was out in the wee hours of the morning gathering information.

"Injured? Everybody's injured!"

This information was useless to him. "No – I mean the vets! I'm in charge of the vets! How many of them are injured?"

A well dressed man with a pen and pad of paper approached Fred Ghent.

"Mr. Ghent?"

Ghent didn't recognize the man.

"Yes?"

"Steven Wantz – Associated Press."

"It didn't take you long to get down here."

"I was here last night. I wanted to take the train down to the camp, but I was late getting in. I gave up. Had I known the train was also late, I would have been in the heart of the hurricane with the vets. So what have you heard?"

Ghent didn't know what to say. He hadn't heard anything firm but he also didn't want to seem uninformed.

354

"There have been injuries, but there wasn't any great loss of life."

The reporter wrote down the quote. It seemed like an appropriate answer given the circumstances and information. However, only a few minutes later that, just north of the Snake Creek crowd, two bodies washed ashore.

Nikolas, Alexander and Aella didn't waste time. The sun hadn't come up and they were on the road toward Sal's. They knew the roads would be washed away. Aella abandoned her wait at the train station when Timothy didn't arrive. It was a difficult decision but she knew that the rails weren't the only means of travel. Driving a car was also out of the question. She came into the house in the middle of the night to find Alexander, her father and a bottle of Ouzo between them. She passed on the news she'd obtained. The men finished their glass and decided to take a quick nap before securing a boat and returning home after the storm moved on.

They banged on the door and roused Sal from his sleep. The last time Aella had seen the Spanish man was when she first found Timothy and offered him a ride. In this brief period Aella reflected how much had happened.

Now Nikolas and Sal were discussing terms for borrowing Sal's fishing boat. They negotiated in English, but both had trouble understanding the other. Nikolas' strong Greek accent and Sal's Spanish accent were an impediment, but they came to an understanding.

"You will also need these," Said Sal. He went behind the counter. He disappeared as he bent down and returned putting a rifle and handgun on the counter. He reached down and pulled out a box of shells.

"Mucho landrón," said Sal. He couldn't translate this to English, but the three Greeks needed no explanation.

"Muchas gracias," said Aella. It was one phrase she did know in Spanish.

Sal looked at her and smiled. "I hope you find your friend."

She'd hoped that he said, "I hope you find your friend alive and well." But she would take what she could get.

"Aella I want you to stay with your mother," Nikolas patted her hand as Alexander prepared the boat.

"I'm going with you."

Nikolas switched to Greek. When he spoke passionately he couldn't have his translation fail.

"There will be death. Death will be all around. I fear it. I do not want you looking at so much death."

Responding in kind, Aella replied in her father's tongue, "You know that I'm getting on that boat. I'm going to help you. Then I'm going to find Timothy."

He replied, "It would be dangerous to have a woman on the island when the normal rules of society were being tested. If you stray toward the vets' camp you will be in peril."

Her eyes were resolute. "That is why you are going to help me."

Timothy returned to the overturned truck. He'd walked in circles for a few minutes giving Elmer his moment of peace. Timothy had no beer to fulfill the man's dying request. Elmer's eyes were opened and he stared at the rising sun. His chest was still. There was a placid look on his face as the sunrise gave him illuminated him from the outside-in.

Timothy sat down next to his dead friend.

"Have a beer with the other vets for me, will ya?"

He closed the man's eyes.

"We had a hell of a time down here, you and I," said Timothy carrying on the solo conversation. "You know, I don't know where anyone else is. Sheldon is

356

still here. He's too ornery to die. I don't know about the others."

"I told you I fell in love with a conch down here, right?" Timothy seemed nonchalant as he continued. "I think I found out her secret."

Timothy leaned over to his dead friend and whispered in his ear. "I think she's a mermaid."

He leaned back and nodded. "That's right. Of course there are tales where they can grow legs and walk on land for a while. But she is definitely made of the stuff of the ocean. We're getting married. Did I tell you that? She doesn't know it yet, but we are. And we are going to have children and..."

Timothy's voice went tight. Elmer was dead.

"... and I'm going to live down here. There's no taking Aella away from here. You can't take a mermaid from her watery kingdom." He laughed as he cried.

"But I've got bad news for you."

Timothy paused as if the corpse was going to reply with a question.

"There is no way in hell I'm going to name any of my children Elmer."

Timothy sat in silence as a sign of respect for the dead. Without another word, he got up and headed to the one place where he might regain his sanity.

The last of the clouds moved on as the sun beat hard after peeking over the horizon, heralding a hot day. He'd ditched his shirt which was in tatters before he started the trek. He regretted that act now. Along the road there were no flies or mosquitoes. There were no birds. In fact he heard no animal rustling in the mangroves. The only thing he saw was a shark that had somehow gotten caught in a clump of mangroves. It was dead, but looked as though a fisherman had mounted the large creature among the vegetation as a trophy.

Timothy tripped over debris on the road. He caught himself from going face-first. IT felt like he broke his toe. He stood and looked at the obstacle that tripped him up. It was one of the concrete disks propelled from the inlet to the main road. He laughed and looked on. He could see a few more of the round objects, some partially hidden by seaweed, dotting the landscape.

He turned down the dirt road and stopped in his tracks. Along the long drive leading to the Aella's house was *Brizo,*the large sponge vessel, keelhauled on its side but otherwise untouched. It looked placed by intention rather than haphazardly ending up in this precarious location. Timothy squeezed by, making sure he didn't touch the boat. He didn't want it rolling on him as he made his way to the house.

All along the drive and sporadically tossed about the house were the disks they'd submerged in the harbor. The concrete pieces made the area looked like a carelessly tossed checkerboard. The dock and dock house were completely gone. The pilings were all that were left sticking out of the water like cattails on the edge of a pond. One piling had a single disk placed on its top. Timothy wondered how that disk would have ended up there. He knew the force of the water. He felt the wall of wind. Yet there it was – put on the top of the piling like a carefully stacked piece of fine china.

The house suffered damage but wasn't obliterated like so many others he'd seen on his way here. The windows had been blown out. The porch was all but nonexistent. The awning had flapped down over the front door. All that was left of the porch was the framing and steps. He picked his way to the house and tried the front door. It was locked. His midriff was still cut up from the glass on the train and he didn't want to try his luck with the windows on the house. He wondered if the back door was unlocked.

Timothy made his way to the back of the house and stopped. Two large palm trees had fallen and broken through the exterior walls. The kitchen was completely destroyed.

Timothy climbed onto the trunks of the downed trees and, moving on all fours, peered inside the house. He noticed a distinct line where the ocean had intruded and left its high water mark.

He hoisted himself over the downed trees and slid into the house. He hopped down and winced in pain as he landed on some broken glass. He leaned back on the trees.

"Shit!" he yelled more in anger than pain.

He lifted up his right foot and pulled the shards out of his foot. The blood pulsed to the rhythm of his heartbeat. The gash wasn't deep but it was messy. Timothy scanned the room for linens, perhaps a window treatment, or a dish rag — something that would protect him. He found a kitchen towel and tied up his foot.

He hopped back up on the fallen trees and scooted over to the kitchen table still filled the with stuff from the boat. On the table were some large sponges. He grabbed two and ripped out holes big enough to make two natural sponge shoes. He threw down the bloody towel.

He was thirsty. He found a bottle of unopened coke on the floor. He opened the top and guzzled it as fast as he could. It was warm, but satisfying.

He wondered if Nikolas had a shirt and a spare pair of shoes. He'd beg for forgiveness later. The day was going to be scorching hot and he knew he had to cover up his fair skin. He smacked the back of his neck. A fly had landed and bit him.

"It didn't take long for them to return," he thought as he made his way upstairs. He was surprised the winds hadn't done more damage to the second floor. He surmised the thick vegetation surrounding acted as a wind barrier.

He picked his way to the master bedroom. The furniture had been moved by the wind. The covers had been blown off the bed. Timothy paused, feeling guilty that he was invading the privacy of what he hoped would be his future father-in-law. But self-preservation won out over the modesty of relations.

As the boat headed south, the three Greeks hugged the coastline. With each landmark, they knew that the small but intense storm was a destructive powerhouse. At first, they saw buildings without a roof. But only a few feet further along the shore they saw cars half buried in the sand. There was no road. The storm had swallowed it into the sea.

"Oh my God" said Aella as she spied four bodies floating in the water. She spun away in horror. Nikolas had seen them, but didn't know they were human remains. He had to veer to port to avoid hitting them. The figures floated among the flotsam.

"Should we retrieve them?" asked Alexander with his Greek voice trembling. Alexander was a superstitious man and this day didn't bode well. Bringing the dead onboard a ship was bad luck.

"No," replied Nikolas. "I fear there will be more — many more."

Nikolas throttled down. The boat idled past the mangroves. Nikolas was right. There were more bodies — both floating and half-submerged corpses, naked and half clothed, moved with the surf making it difficult to tell if any were still alive. Aella wondered if one of the bodies was Timothy.

Nikolas had a hard time determining their location. Normally Nikolas would see houses he recognized or other man-made landmarks. He would often use the water tower of the vet's camp which was visible for a half mile. None of that was there. Even the lighthouse was gone. On the horizon he saw a large vessel. It was unmoving. He wondered if it had run aground on the coral or if it was simply disabled.

They continued south and Nikolas found the spot where the water cut inland toward his home. He was guided now more by instinct than anything else.

The boat pulled toward the house. Nikolas looked on and didn't say a word. Inside, however, his heart broke. He'd built the dock by hand. His boat was gone. This was his livelihood and part of his identity. It was crushing, but he steeled himself for the others' sake. He saw the house in the distance with the porch in shambles. He saw the disks strewn over the landscape.

Alexander had been right. He'd smelled the coming storm and knew it would be bad. But even Nikolas wondered if Alexander would have known how bad.

Alexander held the line, looking for a decent place to tie off. He chose the last far post which used to be a support for the dock house. He deftly wrapped the line and jumped in the water. The Greek held his arms out for Aella. He lifted her off the boat and set her on dry land. She put her finger to her mouth and bit her knuckle. It was too much for her. The place was in ruins.

Nikolas jumped from the boat and splashed at the water's edge. He had the gun secured behind his belt and held the rifle over his head. He switched the rifle to one hand and handed the gun to Alexander.

"Aella, stay close, don't run off," Nikolas was speaking Greek. Normally he would exercise his English with her, but his instincts were on high alert. There was no time to ponder translating.

Nikolas took two steps and dropped to his knees. The others turned, startled that he'd dropped.

Aella wondered if his father had gone mad. He started laughing. The laugh was a quiet chuckle but soon burst into a full belly roll.

Alexander looked at him quizzically. He couldn't muster a word. He could only point in the direction of the road.

Alexander and Aella turned and saw the boat – *Brizo* – in the road.

Catching his breath, Nikolas finally said, "I'm glad I remembered to put the parking brake on."

Alexander looked and started laughing. Aella joined in as they all found relief in the joke. Nikolas stood up and they started toward the house.

Nikolas tried the front door. It was locked. He pulled out the key and opened.

Timothy, who was upstairs, had found a shirt and belt, but no shoes that would fit. When he heard the front door he froze. He'd not thought about intruders coming to loot. He had no weapon. He scanned the room but couldn't find anything that would be suitable against an armed opponent. He wondered how many thugs had arrived.

The three looked on as they saw the open landscape through the kitchen created by the downed palm trees.

"Oh papa, I'm sorry," said Aella. Tears welled up inside her. She spent hours in the kitchen sharing the family meal, listening to stories as papa and his friends told tales of the sea. This is where she did her homework.

Nikolas walked to the kitchen to assess the damage. He looked at the two trees that lay on top of each other. He glanced at the kitchen table and stopped short. He held up a hand in alarm. Turning to the others, he put his finger to shush the two. He motioned Alexander to come closer.

Holding the gun out, Alexander approached.

Nikolas pointed to the floor. There were blood stains by the glass and a bloody towel flung on the floor.

"Lestes..." said Alexander, suspecting the thief might still be in the house.

Timothy tried to quietly make his way to the window. He wanted to get a sense of his odds. His feet were silent as he padded across the bedroom — the sponges took care of that. But the house still creaked as he made his way. He saw the strange boat tied to the post. He couldn't make out the name but he was sure he'd never seen it before.

Alexander heard the steps upstairs. He pointed the gun toward the stairs.

"Stay here," said Nikolas in a stern voice.

Aella nodded, too afraid to voice her affirmation.

Nikolas made for the stairs but stopped when Alexander started following.

In a whisper Nikolas commanded, "No – you stay here with her."

Timothy heard the steps — slow and even. Not having a weapon, he chose to hide behind the bed. The door opened slowly, creaking as it did so. Timothy peered under the bed. The man's shoes were wet and sodden. He also saw the barrel of a rifle swinging low before being drawn up. Timothy hoped the man would search the area, take what he wanted and then leave. The sodden shoes stopped.

With no other recourse, Timothy did the only thing he could think of. He stood up, raised his hands and said, "Don't shoot!"

Nikolas, startled, pulled the trigger.

The canoe arrived. First to cross was the sheriff and the National Guard. The young men helped pull supplies and medicine across. Cutler found a working phone and gotten a man in Miami with a pontoon plane to come down and assist with emergency medical evacuations. Other locals with boats were beginning to stock their decks with supplies that were beginning to arrive. No one had any idea how much help would be needed.

Fred Ghent and Sam Cutler joined the line to haul supplies to the other side. More boats joined the race to get supplies where they were needed. The makeshift rescue team moved swiftly as cars appeared on the south side to begin the process of aid and recovery.

Cutler and Ghent hopped in a boat and was ferried across Snake Creek. They joined the National Guard on the other side of Snake Creek. The young men commandeered a truck and soon Ghent, Cutler and the boys with rifles were heading south.

The young driver squealed to a stop. A naked body lay across the road covered in seaweed. The heat was taking its toll as the internal gases built up, and the body started to bloat and turn purple and red. Two of the men moved the body to the side. There would be a time to deal with the deceased. Their concern was getting supplies to the living. The men were crammed between the supplies. Many of the men held boxes of cans three deep on their lap.

Cutler looked on in horror. Ghent hoped that it was a local. The storm was much worse than they thought. With each yard, as the truck headed south, the story unfolded in front of Ghent and Cutler.

"Stop the truck! Stop the truck!" yelled Cutler as he stood up and banged on the roof of the cab.

A man was walking south. He looked lost and completely spent. His shirt was a rag draped over his shoulders.

"Sheldon!" yelled Cutler.

Fred Ghent looked at the man and could hardly believe it was Ray Sheldon. He was hunched over with disheveled hair.

"Sheldon!" yelled Cutler again as the truck came to a halt.

Ghent and Cutler jumped out of the back of the truck. Sam Cutler went to the driver. "Stay here for a second."

"We've got to deliver the supplies! We can't stop."

"It won't take long. We're going to get Sheldon in the truck."

"There ain't no room!"

"We'll make room!"

Ghent went over to Sheldon.

"Ray – you okay?"

"Ghent – Fred Ghent... damn. You made it."

Sheldon's voice was soft and hoarse.

"Ray – what happened? How many men are dead?"

"Hundreds..." Sheldon replied.

"No – not injured..."

Ghent thought Ray misunderstood.

"I said 'dead.'"

Ray looked right through Fred Ghent with eyes as intense as silver spears.

"I know what you said. Listen to what I said. *Hundreds* of people died in the storm. You didn't get the god damn train here soon enough. They all died. We got about a hundred or less left. I don't know."

The driver honked the horn.

Cutler approached the two men. "We gotta go."

Aella screamed when the rifle went off. Alexander took off and bounded up the stairs. Aella wondered if she should go. In a split second she was right behind Alexander.

They ran into the master bedroom. There was a hole in the wall. Nikolas had the rifle to his side. Timothy rose up from behind the bed.

"Timothy! Oh my God! Are you shot?"

"Umm – no – I don't think so." He replied as he slowly stood up.

"I didn't know it was Timothy. He stood up. He is a lucky man. I recognized him as I pulled up the rifle and pulled the trigger. Had he stood up quicker he'd be dead."

"I must have..." started Timothy.

"You fainted," Nikolas completed. He translated the last part to Alexander.

Alexander started a deep belly laughed that echoed through the house. The others joined in except for Timothy. He was still reeling from the barrel pointed and the bullet whizzing past his ear. Finally he, too, started to laugh.

Aella ran to Timothy and flung her arms around him. They kissed. Nikolas frowned at the open exhibition of their love. Nikolas' scowl made Alexander laugh all the more.

"Are you okay?" she asked.

"A few cuts and bruises, but I'll be fine. I love you."

"I love you, too,"

The truck arrived at the campsite.

As the young men from the National Guard were unloading, Sheldon could see the looks on their faces. They'd never seen such carnage. Already the flies were covering the bodies. They worked with the survivors of the camp and started distributing the few supplies. A scrap of wood sat beside the mound of bodies the vets recovered. They carved the names of those they recognized.

There would be those they would never identify. In a separate pile were the mangled remnants of human flesh. The stench was growing as the day wore on. The bodies were beginning to disintegrate as sun, seawater and the natural forces of decay took their toll.

Aella joined Timothy in the walk north to the camp. Timothy wanted to find his friends. As they met the point where they joined the new road, Timothy saw two of the young National Guard standing over the body of a man. One man was starting to bend down but stopped when the two approached.

The other man spoke, "What are you two doing here? Go on back home."

"This is my home. I'm heading to the campsite."

"You ain't no vet. Go home."

"No – you don't understand – I volunteered..." Timothy glanced down at the body. "Oh hell..." Timothy dropped to his knees. "Buddy... oh Buddy."

Buddy Brickman lay on his back. His face was greenish with purple hues, but the large frame was unmistakable. Aella couldn't look. She'd seen the death all around. Up until now, they were all unknown people. Though she didn't know Buddy, she felt for Timothy as he crouched over the body.

"Move on... we'll take care of him."

Timothy stood up. Knowing that he would likely encounter more, he took Aella's hand and left the two soldiers who stood over Brickman's body. As Timothy left, one of the National Guard got down on his knees. He was trying to free the gold masonic ring that refused to leave the swollen finger.

Hemingway woke to the news. The word was out that the hurricane traveled north. He made some phone calls, but couldn't get any solid information. There was a rumor that all the vets had been killed. It seemed impossible. Surely, they would have driven out or taken the train.

As a reporter, he knew the best way to get to the heart of the story was to go to the source. Fearing the rumor had an element of truth, he packed up provisions and purchased some medical supplies. He'd been in a war zone before and thought he'd be entering destruction not too dissimilar from that of his past. It took him a few trips to load up *Pilar*. It was getting hot, so he loaded some ice and a few cold beers for the trip.

Ed Sheeran took the giant cutters and snapped the chain on the overturned boxcar. The water level in the quarry had dropped. Half of the large boxcar lay submerged. He was told there were people in the boxcar when it toppled. He knew that it would be a miracle if anyone survived. But there might have been the chance that an air pocket formed. He'd banged on the compartment, but there was no reply.

Cutting the chain, he pulled the door open. A shaft of light protruded into the dark cavern of the car. Floating in the water were two bodies. He recognized them both. The one was Stuart Krebs. He was curled up in a fetal position. Under him was

Harry Burrows. Harry had both arms around Krebs as if consoling him even in death.

Sheeran had lived his life seeing death — in the war and through two hellacious hurricanes. He'd pulled out the remains of tattered soldier corpses from the trenches more times than he could remember. This was too much for him.

He knelt on the boxcar and wept.

The nation had given up on the likes of Harry. Harry had seen hard times. He'd lost everything — land, the farm and his peace. This place was supposed to be a temporary purgatory for all of the 'Harry Burrows' that went back to the nation looking for their bonus, but also looking for what they'd really lost. Lady Liberty was cruel to send them away to fester and burn on a road they'd never finish.

Along the way Ed Sheeran knew that Harry had found redemption. It was no great victory, not the kind found on the battlefield. His victory was finding himself through the bond of friendship with others. This final loss was made more painful because of the loss of a friend, a vet, a coworker and a man who'd regained his soul.

Hemingway sat with a black polydactyl cat he named "Flower" who was purring happily in his lap. One of its paws was white, and it was "kneading the dough" on Hemingway's stomach.

He'd seen devastation in many forms as he traveled the globe. Most of his stories centered on the fragility of human life in the larger scope of human disregard. Whether it was smuggling or warfare, his characters took a beating. But what he saw at Lower Matecumbe rattled the famous war veteran.

He'd poured himself more than his share of rum to forget the pale and bloated bodies that lay strewn along the small shore. It was an alien landscape that, with a small change in meteorological circumstance, might have been his story.

He barely recognized two young ladies that served as waitresses in a small store and restaurant he visited when he drove north. Had he waited a day, nature would have made them impossible to recognize. The heat, flies, and rapid decay of the Keys were rendering any hope of normal burial impossible. As he'd sailed north, many were creating large funeral pyres. Some of the men hadn't been identified.

Yet, Hemingway knew that this should, and could, have been avoided. He knew what would happen next. The political fallout would start with some frenzy of interrogation. Yet, the real power brokers would go unpunished as they had for years and wars past. He'd tried to write stories which pointed fingers.

Now he feared that he was being watched by all sides. He wanted to write about this ordeal but knew they were spying on him. If he did write an article he'd have to be careful.

In this case, he had no doubt who was at fault. Julius Stone had brought the men down here, so he could have his road built. He'd finagled his way through Key West, buying up property without the President's knowledge. He treated the men like slaves. He gave them poor living conditions. And, when the political disfavor started to rise, he chose to forget them altogether.

Beside his typewriter was the Florida City newspaper which described the hurricane. They'd gotten in touch with Julius Stone. His simple, arrogant and defiling response was that, "It was simply an act of God."

Hemingway gently picked up the feline that had finally settled and put it on the chair. He went to the typewriter and rolled in a piece of paper.

Who Killed the Vets?

He paused, took a sip of his rum. After a second of pondering, he ripped the paper from the black machine, crumpled it up and tossed it aside. He grabbed another piece of paper and typed:

Who Murdered the Vets?

That felt better. It implied intent. He would write a story about a man without mentioning his name. Hemingway knew it was about Stone. This was his catharsis. This was his balm of Gilead. He wrote:

… veterans, especially the bonus— marching variety of veterans, are not property. They are only human beings; unsuccessful human beings, and all they have to lose is their lives. They are doing coolie labor for a top wage of $45 a month and they have been put down on the Florida Keys where they can't make trouble…

I'd known a lot of them at Josie Grunt's place and around the town when they would come in for pay day, and some of them were punch drunk and some of them were smart; some had been on the bum since the Argonne almost and some had lost their jobs the year before last Christmas; some had wives

370

and some couldn't remember; some were
good guys and others put their pay
checks in the Postal Savings and then
came over to cadge in on the drinks
when better men were drunk; some liked
to fight and others liked to walk
around the town; and they were all what
you get after a war. But who sent them
there to die?

They're better off. I can hear
whoever sent them say, explaining it to
himself. What good were they? You can't
account for accidents or acts of God.
They were well-fed, well-housed, well-
treated and let us suppose, now they
are well dead.

But I would like to make whoever
sent them there carry just one out
through the mangroves, or turn one over
that lay in the fill, or the five
together so they won't float out, or
smell that smell you thought you'd
never smell again, with luck when rich
bastards make a war. The lack of luck
goes on until all who take part in it
are gone…

He continued writing, drinking and shedding a
few tears for those he'd come to know in the bars
and pubs of Key West. Like others before, the one's
he knew were real men were now gone. The so-
called leadership had failed because of greed.

I hope he reads this—and how does
he feel? He will die too, himself,
perhaps even without a hurricane
warning, but maybe it will be an easy
death, that's the best you get, so that
you do not have to hang onto something
until you can't hang on, until your
fingers won't hold on, and it is dark.

And the wind makes a noise like a
locomotive passing, with a shriek on
top of that...

You're dead now brother, but who
left you there in the hurricane months
on the Keys where a thousand men died
before you when they were building the
road that's washed out now?
Who left you there? And what's the
punishment for manslaughter now?

While he wrote these words he could only think
of Stone and the administration that supported him.
Hemingway knew that no one was going to win. The
road the vets were building would never find the
future.

Epilogue

Little Nikolas loved playing on his father's boat. Timothy grabbed him as he played with the sponge — wringing it out and making himself wet. It was time to leave. Normally Timothy would be taking some of the rich folk out on a fishing excursion. He learned all of the good spots from his father-in-law.

Timothy's marriage to Aella took place in the Methodist church on Islamorada. It seemed right, though the Greeks felt like foreigners when the ceremony spoke of Jesus and the trinity.

Now, years later, the family would be returning to the church. As he picked up the little boy, he recalled the stories from the wedding reception about how his father-in-law almost shot him... twice. The first time was when he thought he was an intruder. The second was when they kissed in front of him in his own bedroom.

Today the family was driving to the unveiling of the monument. He looked forward to seeing Ed Sheeran. Ed had picked up the road project with the Florida State Highway to finish Stone's famed "Highway to the future."

Julius Stone had long since pulled out of Key West and now lived in Cuba, investing heavily there as he continued to try and build his fortune. He was also running from the American government which was looking for its share of taxes on the sale of his real estate.

Timothy never heard from Ray Sheldon again. Some say he'd been broken and never recovered.

Aella met Timothy and little Nikolas on the rebuilt porch. They were living with her parents and the house was cramped. Timothy was still trying to get his business off the ground. Aella purchased a warehouse and converted it to a large shell and knick-knack shop on the south side of Key Largo. The couple was betting on Ed Sheeran finishing the highway. They knew the Keys would become a tourist area. Already people were moving in as the utilities all along the new highway came as part of the package of progress.

"Are you ready?" Timothy asked Aella. "Little Nick got wet. He was playing with sponges."

Timothy handed the little boy to his mother. "I've got just the outfit for you."

She twirled around and little Nikolas giggled. She stopped and looked at Timothy with her wonderful brown eyes. "The question is, are you ready?"

Entombed in the monument were some of the remains of his friends. He'd read the paper and followed the demise of the project, the trial and attempt to lay blame. No one really knew the number of dead — the numbers changed because there was really no way of knowing. Poor records had been kept and some of the vets changed their name to avoid the law. It didn't matter. They headed south to be forgotten — and they were.

Many of the vets and locals still carried the fear that something like the ferocity of that storm would soon return. When the wind rose and a storm blew in at night, Timothy would wake with a start and never fully return to any form of slumber until the trees had quieted their rustling. Aella would roll over and rub his back, aware that he was reliving the nightmare of that night.

But the day would come, like today, and Timothy would remember the good and the bad. He would look both forward and backward along the continuum of his life. The memorial would stand for little Nick and beyond. The child may one day ask about monument with the palm trees blowing and the waves curling with the coming of the angry storm. Timothy would remind his child that the winds will blow and the seas will churn, and it is how you deal with those forces that make you who you are.

Dedicated To The Memory Of The Civilians And The
War Veterans Whose Lives Were Lost In The Hurricane Of
September 2, 1935.

Notes

The truth is I don't know a whole lot about these men. So I've given equal time to those whose names are really in the history books and those that stroll through my imagination. I wasn't there. But I can feel the same Florida breeze at dusk and smell the same ocean. If there are family members who know the men better than me, I apologize if I failed to present the real individual. I leave the reader to explore texts and images that speak more true to the events.

The machines that cut the stone merely resembled those cutting stone in the Panama Canal so I related the two. Where I cannot find history, I invent it. That is part of the tragedy of fiction with tenuous roots to fact. Adhering strictly to the rules of reality is not part of the game.

Sources

Three primary sources cover the events of the Labor Day Hurricane with wonderful detail and insight. The books by Willie Drye, Phil Scott and Thomas Knowles made this novel possible. The following bibliography is not the extent of my research. As I go about life, I take notes here and there. Sometimes my source is a torn out section of newspaper or a memo on a napkin. Other times the source is a fleeting reference on the internet. However, there are many fine sources out there should you choose to investigate on your own.

Bibliography

Boulard, Garry. ""State of Emergency" Key West in the Great Depression." *Florida Historical Quarterly* 67, no. 2 (Oct 1988,): 166-183.

Drye, Willie. *Storm of the Century: The Labor Day Hurricane of 1935*. Washington, DC: National Geographic, 2002.

Knowles, Thomas Neil. *Category 5 : The 1935 Labor Day Hurricane*. Gainesville, Florida: University Press of Florida, 2009.

Scott, Phil. *The Great Florida Keys Storm of 1935*. Camden, Maine: McGraw-Hill, 2006.

Viele, John. "The Florida Keys, A History of the Pioneers." In *The Florida Keys, A History of the Pioneers*, by John Viele. Sarasota, FL: Pineapple Press, 1996.